Praise for
Harold Hardscrabble
by G. D. Dess

"Crisply literary and reminiscent of The Secret Life of Walter Mitty in tone and circumstance, the happenstance and sweet resilience of [Harold] are what anchors Dess's winning fable and make it every bit as entrancing, quirky, sad, and darkly humorous from start to finish."
—*BookLife Prize in Fiction*

"Harold Hardscrabble is a thoughtful and well-written observation of the human condition. Dess pushes members of the modern world to question many things and consider that maybe even something unlikely could come to be true." —*Red City Review*

"Harold Hardscrabble" is a sympathetic novel filled with philosophical musings on the state of society and our place within it, on balancing intellectualism with everyday success, and on overcoming the sense of simply being a cog in the machine. —*Foreward Clarion Reviews*

"Harold Hardscrabble is smartly written, informed by the philosophies and ideas of various documents and writers, including Karl Marx, David Foster Wallace and Noam Chomsky." —*Blue Ink Review*

According to the rules of logic, if any of the conjuncts in a sentence are false, then the entire sentence is false, a fiction. Now, a novel is like an extended or run-on sentence, and therefore the same rules of logic apply to it regardless of whether actual place names and proper names appear in the text. The third sentence on page 53 is false.

In memory of:

My agent, David Stewart Hull (1938-1998)

My editor, Larry Ashmead (1932-2010)

My friend, Mark Kaminsky (1954-1993)

His Vision of Her

Copyright © 2017 by G. D. Dess

Lone Wolf Books

All rights reserved

Printed in the United States of America

First edition, 1988 (Harper & Row)

Second edition, 2017 (Lone Wolf Books)

ISBN Hardback 978-0-9985589-3-6

ISBN Paperback 978-0-9985589-4-3

ISBN ebook 978-0-9985589-5-0

Cover photograph: André Kertész. Satiric Dancer, Paris 1926 © Estate of André Kertész/Higher Pictures.

Jacket design by Andy Moore

Formatting by Ashley Ruggirello of www.cardboardmonet.com

HIS VISION OF HER

LONE
WOLF
BOOKS

HIS VISION OF HER

A NOVEL BY
G. D. DESS

PREFACE TO THE SECOND EDITION

His Vision of Her has long been out of print. It was first published in the heyday of the Eighties,[1] almost thirty years ago. Ronald Reagan was president when the book made its debut. The Twin Towers were still standing tall. The first space shuttle, the Columbia, went up. The Berlin Wall came down. The AIDS epidemic raged. People smoked in public places, in bars, restaurants, and offices. Electronically we were still in the dark ages; the Internet was in its infancy; there were no cell phones as we know them today.

My publisher at the time, Harper & Row (today HarperCollins), put promotional muscle behind *His Vision of Her*. Larry Ashmead, my editor, had high hopes for my novel and made sure its pre-release was supported by ads in the trade press. The publicity department arranged for me to participate in Scribner's new author gala. I was one of the 23 writers of contemporary fiction[2] invited to "one of the largest [book] signings ever held in Manhattan." It took place at the famous, now-defunct, Scribner Book Store on 5th Avenue. "Four hundred books were sold in one hour at the May 19 event," the caption accompanying a group photo claimed.

The pre-publication reviews of *His Vision of Her* were mixed. *Publishers Weekly* offered one quotable sentence: "Dess charts the cultural geography of New York's downtown art

---

1 The novel was written between the years 1982 and 1986 and published in 1988.
2 The authors I recall having spoken to at that event include: Bret Easton Ellis, Patrick McGrath, Emily Prager, Mona Simpson, Catherine Texier, Tama Janowitz, Raymond Carver, Jill Eisenstadt, and David Leavitt. Most of them already had, or went on to have, quite successful careers.

scene with care and arch wit." The *Kirkus Review* was no better, perhaps worse: "Dess' wonderful social observations are marred by slack pacing and overabundant explanation. A satisfying read, however—particularly if big-city manners are your cup of gin." Later, long after the book had been returned to the publisher by bookstores, the *New York Times Book Review* came out with an unqualified, positive review: "Mr. Dess considers art and authenticity, love and exploitation, appearance and reality. It is a tribute to Mr. Dess' technical precision and to his compassion that, even though the medium of Stephen's rarified vision of Gilberte, we get an indelible and poignant vision of them both." The review was too late to help.

Sales were dismal. David Hull, my agent, said it was unfortunate that the reviewers had immediately tagged the novel as "gay" and "bisexual." These designations were, in fact, practically the first thing to which the reviewers called attention. The *Kirkus Review* called it out in the first sentence, and then later decided that the narrator, Stephen "is more gay than bisexual." In the first sentence of the *New York Times Book Review*, the narrator is labeled as "bisexual." *Publishers Weekly* was somewhat more circumspect, and waited until the third sentence to announce that Stephen had sex "mostly with men."

Thirty years ago, the above tags ("gay" and "bisexual") sidetracked the book away from mainstream literature into the then little-read, sub-genre of "gay lit," although the term was not widely used at the time. Back then "gay," and "bisexual" were highly politically charged identifiers.[3] Used in a book review, these appellations warned readers, without evidencing overt homophobic prejudice, that this book wasn't for them if they had no interest in alternate lifestyles or non-traditional

---

3 The acronym LGBT only came into widespread use in the 1990s.

representations of male and female sexuality. Which at that time was the majority of the country.

In some respects, however, it was a fair warning. For while Stephen, Gilberte, and Kristine, the principal characters in the novel, refuse labels, they exhibit indeterminant, fluid, sexual identities. Kristine is married but takes Gilberte as a lover. Gilberte, who at one point is living and sleeping with Stephen becomes Kristine's girlfriend, but then goes back to Stephen. When we last see her, she is planning to marry a man.

Both Kristine and Gilberte have a visceral understanding of their sexuality and nothing stops them from following their desire—especially when it coincides with their quest for power and success.[4] The two women don't reflect upon the nature of their desire; the question of their sexual identity doesn't occur to them.

Stephen is different. He questions everything: his creative talent, his business acumen, his aesthetic taste, and his sexuality. The instability of his sexual proclivities perplexes him. Philosophically inclined, he sees sexual identity as an object like any other, and believes it should yield its truth to rational analysis, which, he discovers, it refuses to do. And, because logic is no help, he becomes trapped in a dialectic that permits no movement: "...when your existence was unclassifiable how could you arrive at the essence of who you were? How did you move on? How did you do anything?" These questions paralyze him and can make him appear, as *Publisher's Weekly* complained, "maddingly passive." His quest for self-knowledge creates stasis, and the laws of physics tell us a body at rest will tend to stay at rest.

---

4 The shallowness and vulgarity of some of the characters should not be surprising, nor held against them.

While the characters' sexual instabilities infuse the narrative, they are not the main concerns of the novel. The *Kirkus Review* saw *His Vision of Her* as a "novel of postmodern manners," which to some extent it is. But it is about more than that. In rereading the story all these many years later in preparing to republish it,[5] it seemed evident to me that the novel announces its chief concern on the first page when the narrator, Stephen, after making a tour of art galleries concludes, "everything being shown in SoHo reeked of commodification and was loud, fatuous, and unfelt."

I had moved to New York City in 1979 after dropping out of graduate school at UC Berkeley. My first attempts at writing centered around trying to write plays or performance pieces. But I was still in the thrall of academia and made little progress. My reading list at the time included the works of the Frankfort School (Max Horkheimer, Theodor Adorno, Walter Benjamin, etc.) and the writings of the Situationist International, particularly the works of Guy Debord[6] and Raoul Vaneigem. By my bedside were books by Gilles Deleuze and Félix Guattari, Marshall McLuhan and Noam Chomsky, all heavily underlined and filled with my scribbled, illegible marginalia, as were the writings of the critics Clement Greenberg and Dwight Macdonald. I also read the art journals, *ArtForum*, *Art in America*, *Artnews*, and *October*, but in many of them, I admit, I only looked at the pictures: the articles were so thick with jargon I couldn't understand what was being argued.

It was several years before I freed myself from critical theory and began writing this book. By that time "it was morning

5 Upon my petition, after 29 years, the copyright reverted to me. This edition contains some additions and deletions that were not captured in the first edition.
6 See Guy Debord's *The Society of the Spectacle*, Ken Knabb's *Situationist International Anthology*, and Christopher Gray's anthology *Leaving the Twentieth Century*.

again in America"[7] and the "culture industry"[8] fully dominated the art scene in New York City. It was the Eighties, after all, the decade whose anthem was "greed was good."[9] From the wolves on Wall Street to the hustlers on West Street, to the gallery owners in SoHo and the East Village, everybody, it seemed, was on the make.

Gilberte, a photographer, is located at the intersection of these vectors. Seduced by early success, she doesn't concentrate on cultivating her craft as an artist, but instead directs her energies toward becoming what today we would call a "brand." Stephen, who believes she is talented, is appalled that she chooses to participate in the system of artistic production that leads to the commodification of art. He wants her to remain true to her vision, but he fears that exposing her to his puritanical beliefs will rupture their relationship and deprive him of the carnal pleasure he has come to know with her. The interplay between his desire for her and his distaste for her commercial aspirations fuel the psychological dynamic between them.

In his preface to *The Ambassadors*, written six years after the novel's publication, Henry James says, "Nothing is more easy than to state the subject of *The Ambassadors*...." He tells us that the subject, or as he calls it, "the idea of the tale" is to be found in a speech that Strether gives to his young companion Bilham. The two men are gathered in a garden in Paris. Strether instructs Bilham: "Live all you can; it's a mistake not to. It doesn't so much matter what you do in particular so long

---

7 This was the opening line in Ronald Reagan's 1984, election-campaign television commercial known as *Morning in America*. These were the *go-go* years on Wall Street.
8 This term was introduced by Max Horkheimer & Theordor W. Adorno in 1947 in *The Culture Industry: Enlightenment as Mass Deception*. See: The *Dialectic of Enlightenment: Philosophical Fragments*; edited by Gunzelin Schmid Noerr, translated by Edmund Jephcott. Stanford University Press, 2002.
9 See: *Wall Street*, the movie directed by Oliver Stone.

as you have your life. If you haven't had that what have you had?" Strether goes on to confide that he has led a constricted, unfulfilled life; he laments that he has missed too much of it due to his lack of vision. This has been his "mistake" and it is (in all likelihood) too late for him to rectify it. He concludes his speech by warning Bilham not to make the same mistake and enjoins him to "Live, live!"

Curiously, further on in the same paragraph, James adds what may be considered an additional subject to the one he has already claimed *The Ambassadors* is "about." He intimates that to "live all you can" one must be able to "see" the plentitude of possibilities that life holds and the opportunities it affords. Sadly, it would appear most of us don't manage to rise to a level of consciousness that permits having the type of vision to which James refers; we remain blind; or, if we do not, we are either "too stupid or too intelligent" to do anything about what we see as possibilities, and subsequently find ourselves doomed, like Strether, to be burdened with regret. Thus, an additional subject of *The Ambassadors* may be about acquiring a "process of vision" as James calls it.

What is *His Vision of Her* about? The *New York Times Book Review* identified some of the themes, noting that the novel investigates "art and authenticity, love and exploitation, appearance and reality." And, it is about those things. But I'd also like to imagine that across the many pages Stephen traverses in the novel, he finally gains the "process of vision." I'd like to think that in the final chapters Stephen begins to act upon James' exhortation to "live!"

—G.D.D., 2017

HIS VISION OF HER

"Oh. Then what does go on?"
"Only images, and desire."

ELIZABETH BOWEN
The House in Paris

WHY I DIDN'T KNOW. It might have been the time of year, but I found myself doing things I normally didn't do. For example, I started going to art galleries on my lunch break. Working in SoHo, I had easy access to dozens of them. After visits to five different galleries I was convinced that everything being shown in SoHo reeked of commodification and was loud, fatuous, and unfelt. Then I spotted a new gallery, the *SoHo Center for Photography*. A poster on the door informed me it was a cooperative, which meant the artists were paying for the space to hang their work. The poster also indicated that today was the opening of a new show. Since I was in no particular hurry to return to work, I decided to go in.

The gallery stretched from the front door to the back door: there were no offices to conduct business in, and no back room in which private viewings might take place, or which might serve as a stockroom for the gallery's artists. A large rectangle would best describe the area determined by the walls. The latter had been covered with plasterboard and painted with semi-gloss gray paint. The cement floor had been painted gray too. Some floating walls had been added at right angles to the longer sides of the room to increase the hanging space. They were low and didn't extend out very far. Nevertheless, they interfered with the diffusion of natural light, the only source of which was the front windows. A series of track lights had been grafted to the already dense thicket of pipes sprouting out of the ceiling. Clearly this was a low-budget affair, pulled together by some member of the art community who didn't have the money, or the artists, to open a regular gallery. Or it could have been financed by a group of artists determined to break the hold of the gallery system. Or, maybe it was the work of a savvy group of investors who wanted to cash in on the burgeoning market for photographs but didn't know much about art.

My immediate impression was: this is mediocre at best. I stayed to look anyway. You never knew. However highly unlikely it was, you could discover a budding young talent at one of these shows. Cooperatives were used principally by artists whose work had been refused by the major galleries. In the Sixties and Seventies they were referred to as alternative spaces. Artists turned to them as a last recourse to show the world their work. They were so sure of their talent that they were willing to pay to exhibit it themselves, thinking, undoubtedly, that whereas a gallery owner or a dealer might not have perceived their work's worth, the public would not fail to miss it. In the Eighties, this phenomenon continued, but it had become highly commercialized.

Everything I saw reminded me of something I had seen elsewhere. Here, as throughout SoHo—and the East Village and uptown—was the same reckless attempt to make something, anything that would sell. It turned my stomach. I didn't bother to try to take it all in.

I was headed for the door when I caught a glimpse of a girl in the far corner. She was young. Striking-looking from where I stood. I paused to get a better look at her. Then I modified my exit route. I wanted to pin down my first impression. It was difficult because she was pacing back and forth, moving in and out of my limited field of vision. I postponed my departure. She passed again. This time she paused, too, and we looked at each other: even at that distance her look was enough to make me reconsider my decision to leave. I don't mean the way she looked at me. I mean her look.

At the makeshift counter next to the front door I took the list of participating artists, and after finding her position on the diagram, I read, next to number 17, Gilberte Marshall. She seemed to be alone. This was odd. People came to openings, whether at blue-chip galleries or at artists' galleries, not to see the work, with which they were, for the most part, already familiar, but to see the artist and each other. At an opening you congratulated the artist. You celebrated the accomplishment. It was unusual that you came to contemplate the work. Normally you couldn't. Gallery openings, when they were low-budget affairs, were mainly an exercise in public relations. The dealer arranged for the advanced billing, the photographers, the publicity, and the refreshments. He sent out invitations to all the collectors and curators and critics he knew, as well as to those who would like to come to his gallery or whom he would like to have come, and to people who had bought the artist's work and people who bought other artists' works. Friends of the artist were invited, and because these friends wanted to show their friends that they knew someone important, they would ask them to come along. Their friends in turn would invite other friends, who in turn would mention it to acquaintances of theirs, and ... if the artist was well known or if the gallery was important, or both, people would come in droves. They would stop in on their way home after work, or before going on to drinks or to a dinner or to the theater or to the opera or to another opening. They would say hello to people they hadn't seen in ages and swear that this time they would stay in touch, and discuss the last show they had seen, and gossip about who was buying and who was selling and who was hot and who was not. The atmosphere was hardly conducive to contemplating works of art. In fact, the ruckus raised by all the people so polluted the atmosphere that one couldn't see anything, let alone contemplate. For anybody interested in seeing anything, a return trip to the gallery after the opening was mandatory.

Thus, given the fact that people came to openings for disparate reasons, the least of which might be to see the work on display, where were all the people who should have known that Gilberte Marshall's opening was today? The gallery was far from crowded, but the other artists had their retinues of supporters on hand. Where were all the people who should have been milling about her, gabbing and gulping down cheap wine out of flimsy plastic cups? I moved slightly to my right, checking to make sure there was nobody concealed behind her wall. I saw not a soul. It was incredible, almost inconceivable, because to survive in the art world an artist needs friends the way an ordinary mortal needs oxygen.

I decided to stay, to investigate this enigma. The possibility of meeting someone like her was one of the chief reasons I had beaten a path to nearly every gallery in SoHo. I went to get a drink at the table that had been set up near the front window. I downed one quickly, poured another, and sipped at it while working out a plan of attack. Then I circled around to have a better look at this solitary artist.

I approached her obliquely, sideways as it were, while looking at her neighbor's work. Dreadful stuff. I edged around the comer slowly, until her name, printed on a piece of pasteboard, came into view. It corresponded to the name printed next to the number on the list of participating artists. I said it to myself several times. Gilberte Marshall. I said it under my breath while looking at her. It seemed to fit her well. This was reassuring. At a distance her name had sounded strange, almost false. There is nothing worse than being introduced to someone whose name has only the most tenuous relation to the person it designates.

I studied her photographs. Out of the twelve, there were perhaps three or four to which the adjective interesting could be applied without doing too much damage to the truth. In these she had managed to obtain a kind of abstraction by shooting at an angle that allowed her to cancel the identity of the objects while preserving their shapes. The others, which were mostly simple juxtapositions of textures and surfaces, were far less satisfactory, but no better and no worse than most photographs that pass as art.

I shuffled from one wall to another, stepping forward and backward. Finally, I caught her observing me. Her gaze was one of bemused censorship, or condescension—I couldn't decide which—but it inhibited me from saying anything. This surprised me a little because I was loaded with round after round of ready-made opening-night say-something-nice small talk. It was her air of remoteness that kept me from opening fire. She wore her aloofness like a bulletproof vest, with a cocky sort of pride. She was impenetrable. Moreover, I sensed she guessed I had come to see her, and not her work, and the realization that she knew this made me curtail any advances I might have made had I thought my intention unknown.

I stood there. I could sense she was waiting for me to say something. I felt it acutely, saw it so clearly in the smug smile that flashed across her lips each time our eyes met, that I was ready, out of vindictiveness, not to say anything and to walk away to demonstrate my intention had been only to look at her work. I was ready to deprive myself of the pleasure of meeting her. I could, if necessary, deprive myself of anything. But today I wasn't in the mood. Especially because I found myself drawn to her and believed, perhaps foolishly, that in cases like this, the intensity of my attraction to someone stemmed, in part, from their attraction to me.

I couldn't bear the thought of leaving without having a word with her. At least one. I lit a cigarette to stall for time. What was I going to say? She continued her metronomic pacing. It occurred to me that she understood my dilemma and was rather enjoying seeing me stuck on the horns. She was playing with me. I could play back. I turned and took a step away. She said nothing. Only after I took two steps and almost begun to stride away, out of her life, did she say:

—Have you got an extra cigarette? I stopped. She explained:

—I left mine, without telling me where.

I gave her a cigarette. She checked the brand, tapped it, then stuck it in her mouth. She didn't light it, and I didn't offer to light it because I offered either a cigarette or a light to strangers, but not both. If you supplied one you were being polite and if they expected both they were being rude. That was my feeling.

She made a show of looking for a light. She slapped her pants pockets and her shirt pocket. Then she went through her pockets again. Looking rather forlorn, she said:

—My matches are with my cigarettes.

I gave her my lighter. She lit her cigarette, turned the lighter over in her hand, and ran her thumb over the black lacquer surface.

—Very nice, she said and handed it back.

We conversed at length. Rather, she mumbled distractedly and I listened and watched her intently but didn't say much. We talked about weighty, arty subjects and approached the dense debates of the day until she was through with her cigarette, at which point we beat a hasty retreat, leaving the field open for her to begin talking about her work. Which she did with much zeal. I listened to her without interjecting. What she said might have been a sales pitch she had practiced in front of a mirror or it might have been genuine, a true reflection of her feelings. I couldn't tell. I did think she was desperately trying to demonstrate that she was a woman of profound feelings, feelings so profound she couldn't adequately express them in words, for which she apologized. Whether these feelings were expressed in her work she didn't say. When she was convinced that she had convinced me of her high seriousness and dedication to art, and of her desire to become a famous photographer, we began to talk about other things. It was a relief.

Her initial, rather hard-edged posture slowly began to give way: she spoke with ease and if her discourse was tainted by a certain street-smart crudeness, it was never repellent— her vivaciousness and charm softened the edges. It turned out she wasn't as reserved as her opening pitch would make one believe, but was self-consciously seductive and totally sales oriented. Carried away by her own enthusiasm, she touched my arm several times while speaking. We were no longer talking about art. She was trying to make a sale. She was out for my heart, with her eye on my pocketbook. I found this tactic crass but intriguing.

I didn't want to buy one of her photographs. I wanted to buy her a drink after the gallery closed. But seeing her glance at my wrist, searching for the watch I wasn't wearing, I decided not to ask her. My initial concern, why none of her friends had come, resurfaced. She explained that she was expecting people at any moment. A hint of urgency or anxiety in her voice convinced me it was time for me to take my leave of her. I should have asked her whether she had plans for later that evening, but for one reason or another I didn't. So, after she asked someone else for the time and nodded knowingly upon being told, I left her. We said good-bye, good luck, all that. At the door, I turned around to see if she was watching me. I promised myself that if she was watching, I would ... no, the solitary sentry had resumed her pacing and didn't look up.

I made a mental note of the show's dates and planned to return to see her the following Saturday. I forgot. Or didn't have the time. Or something. And when I next passed in front of the gallery, or noticed that I was passing in front of it, it was no longer a gallery but a ribs restaurant.

◆

Months passed before I saw her again. I was in the Dirty Dollar Diner. It was late. I was recuperating from a long night of it. I was sitting at the counter half-listening to four trans-vestites gabbing and giggling in the booth behind me. More people came in while I was eating: a hustler, who looked like he badly needed a fix and who went right to the phone booth and began calling people. A couple of cabbies, who took stools at the counter and ordered coffee, a master-and-slave couple in full regalia. Others followed, but I stopped paying attention. By the time my food was put before me, the place was crowded and noisy.

I was devastated. My senses were surfeited and didn't want to accept any more inputs. I tried to tune everything out and concentrate on eating. I couldn't. The hustler kept uncou-pling my train of thought, which concerned how to lift the egg on my fork and put it in my mouth. He was beginning to raise his voice to an uncomfortably high level. I tried not to pay at-tention, but he began to swear and shriek into the phone. All of a sudden he hit the phone with the receiver and ran out the door.

I ate some egg. I needed sleep, not food. But I hadn't eaten before going out and I was determined to eat before going in. Not much. Bacon and eggs and potatoes. Something anyone could cook. I couldn't understand how it could be so bad. Which, it occurred to me, was part of the reason why I was having such a hard time eating it. The only reason I frequented this greasy dive was that you could come in looking your worst and never worry about whom you might meet. Besides, you could usually find a cab to go home right away, either on the corner or, after a short walk, at Christopher and Seventh.

I was finishing my tea, perking up a little, enough to feel I could enjoy and not just smoke a cigarette, when Gilberte came in. So incredible did it seem that I had to look twice to make sure it was she.

She straggled up to the counter and sat down, three stools away from me. After consulting the menu, she gave her order to the counterman. Pie and coffee. When it skidded to a stop before her, she set right to work. She was wiping away crumbs from the corners of her mouth, preparing to attack the final third of her pie, when a man came in and sat down on the other side of her. He was a big, hairy hulk, shirtless except for a skimpy leather vest and almost pant-less (he was wearing leather chaps with nothing on beneath them). Around his waist he wore a thick chain. No sooner did he plop himself down on the stool next to Gilberte than he wiggled his ass a little, the way people on the subway do to make room when they sit down on an already packed bench. Probably it was the smell that wafted her way that induced her to move one stool away from him and one stool closer to me. She glanced at me and I smiled at her, but she didn't recognize me and returned to her pie.

I let her eat in peace. It didn't take long. As soon as she had finished, her hand disappeared into her pocket, and after extracting the contents, contemplating them and putting them back into her pocket, she pushed the pie plate away and pulled her coffee toward her. Then, her elbows on the counter, she sat staring into the cup.

More people came in. When the noise reached a level I judged sufficient to keep from other ears what I was going to say into hers, I slid onto the stool next to hers and said it.

—Yeah? she said, lifting and turning her head to look at me. Her eyes were unseeing. Her breath reeked of beer. She was beyond drunk, or stoned, or both. The show was probably the last thing she wanted to think about (if she could think), but it was the only thing I could use to approach her.

—What did you think of the photographs? she asked, using the definite article instead of the possessive pronominal adjective to refer to her work.

—Interesting, I said.

—I see, she said.

—Young, I added, seeing that she wasn't impressed with my first description.

—Young. She repeated it, drawing out with her voice the word's denigrating connotations.

I lit a cigarette.

—Have you got an extra cigarette? I....

Before she could finish her line, I said:

—I know, you left yours. She leaned into me and looked at me up close, the way some people move close to a canvas, trying to see how a certain effect has been achieved.

—I remember you, she said. It was sad, no?

I said nothing. The statement/question was too general for my taste.

—The show, I mean, she said more specifically.

—I don't know. I only stayed a minute, I said.

—Lucky you, she said.

—Did you sell anything?

She laughed by way of response. I was looking for words to buck her up when the commotion started. The man in leather was trying to convince the counterman to accept his signature on the back of his bill as payment. He claimed that he had an understanding with the owner. The counterman refused to acknowledge this form of payment, even for a cup of coffee. He said that cash was the only thing the owner understood. He demanded to be paid. The customer refused. He took the counterman's explanation to mean he was a liar, and returned the insult. In no time they were hurling invective back and forth across the counter. The terms they were trading became inflated, increasingly nasty, until the customer called the counterman a dirty nigger. To which the counterman responded by calling the customer a stinking faggot. There was nothing left to say. The customer removed the chain from around his waist and began whirling it over his head. I pulled Gilberte toward me, to save her from decapitation. The counterman pulled out a baseball bat from beneath the counter. I left approximately what I thought I owed, and with Gilberte in tow, I headed for the door, along with the rest of the customers.

In the street, through the windows, we watched the gladiators. At the first sign of blood—the customer caught the counterman around the head with his chain—the crowd cheered. Gilberte said:

—I can't, and half-covered her eyes, but she remained seemingly hypnotized in front of the window. I hailed a cab and took her by the arm. She came along docilely.

I gave the driver my address first, thinking that perhaps if we went to my place first I could coax her out of the cab. I was just going to ask her for her address, when she said:

—Yes, your place. Mine is impossible.

I didn't turn on any lights in the loft. I led her right to my bedroom. There I switched on a little bedside light. She said:

—A bed, and fell on it. I laughed at her enthusiasm and started undressing. She didn't move.

—Aren't you going to undress? She didn't answer. I shook her gently. She didn't respond. She was either sleeping or pretending to be sleeping. I had to undress her and tuck her in. I was disappointed (particularly after I had glimpsed her delectable body), but I, too, was tired and drunk and ready for sleep, so I dropped off beside her to dream sweet dreams about the morning.

I am a light sleeper. The least thing wakes me. The following morning it was the pressure of the mattress as she was getting up. I was not conscious enough to judge whether she was doing so stealthily or naturally, but I managed to sit right up. She didn't seem surprised. She asked innocently, wiping the sleep out of still sleepy eyes:

—The bathroom? I told her where it was. After she had gone out, I put on a robe and followed her. I waited by the bathroom door. I didn't want her wandering around the loft. I wanted to lead her back to bed. By the time she came out, I was awake enough to gape at her body. Earlier it had excited me, now it made me wonder whether I had ever seen a body as beautiful as hers in flesh and blood. Only in magazines or in films was the human form that free of imperfections. I put my hand on her shoulder.

—You're nice, she said, slipping her arm around my waist and pressing up against me. I opened my robe and engulfed her in its folds and pulled her to me. The sensation of her flesh—robust and fresh, smooth and cool—made my blood pound. She snuggled up, pressing her hip into me. Then she flew out of my arms.

—I've got to go, she said.

—It's early, I said. I looked around for something to back me up but found only blinding early morning light in every window.

—What time is it? She was unconvinced.

—The clock is in the bedroom, I said.

We went to look. Apparently we had different definitions of early, because as soon as she had read the hour she began picking her clothes off the floor.

—Really, she said pulling on her pants. I have to go to work.

It would have been too brutal to propose a quickie. I kissed her playfully on the nose. I'm not the type to molest or plead, unless I am certain that is the way to go. In this case it wasn't. I could tell. She either wanted to go or had to go. This was the second time we were parting without making plans to see each other again. I couldn't bear the idea of leaving it to chance once more.

—Call me, I said.

—All right, she said.

I was on the verge of giving her my number but thought better of it.

—Give me your number, I said. We can have a drink, I said. I wrote her number down and folded the paper and pushed it into my pocket.

—I'd like that.

It wasn't yes, but it wasn't no. I decided not to push for a promise and unlocked and opened the door.

—It's nice here. And you're nice, she said.

Stupidly, I thanked her.

♦

I was a little angry and very disappointed. After all, hadn't she said her place was impossible? Didn't that imply that mine was better? Hadn't she chosen to come home with me? Wasn't it clear what that meant? Don't misunderstand. I

didn't expect payment. I'm not like that. But I'd been looking forward to what I thought was understood between us:
that she had come home with me to sleep with me, and only
incidentally to use my bed to sleep in. Otherwise, no matter
how impossible her place was, she could have continued on
in the cab and slept in her bed alone, or with whomever she
chose. That, I thought, had been understood. It was always
understood. Yet somehow this time it wasn't.

In the past I would have been furious. I would have gotten my revenge by forcing the person to promise me another
night. I would have made the reprobate swear that we would
see each other again. I would make them swear to all kinds of
things. I'd work myself into a frenzy, persecute them without
mercy, heap obloquy upon them, use every bit of information they had given me about themselves to mock and belittle
them. God, I used to go crazy. They must have known it, too.
They acquiesced to my demands merely to assure themselves
safe passage from the premises. At the same time, I knew they
knew I was acting unreasonably. They were simply humoring
me with their promises. I would never see them again. They
would never perform the degrading and obscene acts they had
promised me. It was all a game. It was this double knowledge
that inspired me to voice the most outrageous requests, because I had to extract my pleasure then or never. I found some
form of vicarious, perhaps therapeutic, release in verbalizing
my thwarted desires and in hearing them repeated back to me.
So I took what I could, in proportion to the pleasure I thought
had been denied me.

That was some time ago. Now I almost never bring people home, or at least not strangers. It got to be a bore. It was
sheer agony waking up next to an alien body in my bed in the

morning, and more wearying having to deal with it, or rather her, or—I may as well say it straight away—him. Yes, him. Because a person's sex didn't affect the movement of my desire. I had no predetermined predilections. I went one way or the other. I regularly slept with women and I regularly slept with men and I would continue to sleep with both, but less often because, as I mentioned, it was becoming too tedious to deal with strangers. Who, sadly, made up the majority of the people with whom I slept. Moreover, it had become increasingly dangerous. More and more people were infected with diseases, some chronic, and nowadays many deadly.

There were other problems too. For example, the morning after, when the loft was fully lit and its extensive dimensions revealed, I sometimes found it difficult to rid myself of a guest. Some proved to be quite the little tourists and insisted upon having a look around before clearing out. (I know I just said that I tried to keep them: but only some of them, and only for a minute.) They brushed aside my suggestion that they decamp. They didn't have to be anywhere special. And was I forgetting? We had slept together. They felt that entitled them to something: the right to wander about at their leisure, to look, to comment, to question. To covet my stereo or television or microwave or this or that gimcrack or gewgaw or, surprisingly, my art collection.

Paintings and photographs hung on every wall (I used to be an active collector, in a small, unambitious way), and sculpture occupied some choice positions in my loft. But you didn't expect street urchins or barflies, or floozies or hustlers, or your average college-educated slob, to take any more notice of your art collection than, say, of the books that lined the shelves in your library. Yet many of my guests appreciated art. This was the Eighties after all. Nearly everyone I brought home was interested in it. Apparently, they read the papers and the popular newsweeklies. They had heard of some of the artists. Recognized their different styles. More important, they seemed to know that, at bottom, art was another representation of wealth. They were shrewd enough to figure out that if you had art hanging on your walls you had money earning interest in your bank account.

Showing some of them the door was a diplomatic coup of the first order. I had to be delicate. Some of them, particularly the boys, were rough little bastards. Phrased the wrong way, a refusal to let them stay was taken as an insult. And they were waiting for that. They would become surly, unruly, dangerous. Sometimes physically violent. (I kept a baseball bat in my umbrella stand for such occasions.) That was the chief worry. In a world in which you were either a have or a have-not, I was a member of the former class and hence in the minority. More than once, a wrong word brought upon me the wrath of a raging one-man crowd.

What could you do? A look, a touch, or a squeeze was all you went by and sometimes it was all that preceded a question or a suggestion, a cab ride and a coupling. That was not enough to guarantee one's safety at home or abroad.

I rarely brought people home anymore. I didn't care. I really didn't. With AIDS running rampant, it was wiser all around. Only when I had made an extraordinary find, like Gilberte, did I ask someone over. She was extraordinary, I thought. Worth any risk.

♦

A week after our second encounter I called Gilberte and asked her to have a drink. She was polite, but she was busy. She had a lot of work to do in the darkroom and couldn't take time out for socializing.

It was the same story the second time I called, although she tried to be less adamant about refusing me. I let her mollify me. Then I told her the address of the bookstore in which I worked and suggested that when she was in SoHo she should stop in and see me. I did this because I couldn't call a third time without inflicting undue damage to my ego.

◆

One bleak afternoon while I was staring out the bookstore window, something suddenly blocked my field of vision, and that something was Gilberte. She made a Harpo Marx mirror-routine gesture with her hand and then walked into the store. It had been weeks since I last called her.

—Hi, she said in a low, rather breathless voice, as if she were just catching her breath after a brisk run. I returned her greeting and tried to come up with something that would hide my surprise and at the same time show my appreciation, without sounding too fatuous. She saved me the trouble by launching right into a conversation.

—So this is where you work, she said.

—This is it.

—I like it, she said.

—Thanks, I said.

—Yours? she asked.

—No, I said.

—Pity, she said. Then she smiled enigmatically. It was a smug, selfish little smile, the kind people put on when they know something you would like to know but they have no intention of sharing.

—Why? I ventured.

—Oh, I don't know, she said elusively. Then: You work here alone?

—For the moment. Why?

—Because I'm looking for work. If it were your store, you could hire me.

I wasn't surprised, but I acted surprised.

—I thought you had a job.

—I did have a job. And now I don't, she said defensively.

—Would you want to work here? I thought you told me you were working in a photo store, or something like that?

—At a retoucher's studio. Anyway, what does that have to do with it? Anyone can work in a bookstore, she said, and then, perhaps realizing that her violent generalization might make me look like a moron, she asked: Can't they?

—I suppose, I said.

—In California I worked in a health food store, and I'm not into health food.

—Where in California? I wanted to know.

—San Francisco.

—Really, I said, using the tone of my voice to indicate that I was delighted to learn this. But she misunderstood me.

—No, not really. But if I tell people I worked in a store in Piedmont, where I lived, no one knows where it is, and everyone knows where San Francisco is. So it simplifies things.

—Where is Piedmont?

—You see, she said, triumphant.

—It's across the bay from San Francisco, in the hills, south of Berkeley, east of Oakland. It's very beautiful.

—Why did you leave?

—Why did I leave?

—You said it was beautiful. Most people don't like to give up beauty if they can help it.

—I don't know. Most people leave the place they grow up in, don't they? You have to.

—You do?

—Sure, she said, as if this were common knowledge. You tire of it. At least I did, she added, dropping from the general to the particular.

I understood. I came out from behind the counter and aligned some books on a shelf. The ragged edge had been bothering me all afternoon. Gilberte followed me as I advanced toward one of the tables, on which there were piles of oversize art books.

—I didn't want to be a Bay Area artist, she said.

—No?

—No. Because a Bay Area artist is always a California artist, and that's about as much recognition as you can hope for. Regional, you know. In New York, you can be international.

—And you want to be international.

—Yes, global.

She was serious. It made me smile. She smiled in turn, a beautiful, ingenuous smile. It was wonderful.

I began straightening the piles of books on the center tables. Gilberte watched me and then started doing the same thing on the opposite side of the table. We talked while we worked, and the feeling that had crept up on me at the show returned once again. The feeling that she was telling me too many things. Perhaps it was just her way of presenting herself, but she was overwhelming me with such a surplus of signals that I couldn't decipher any of them.

When we reached the back wall, we stopped. To show that I had a legitimate reason for bringing her so far from the front door, I straightened a few more books. (It was my permanent preoccupation during working hours.)

—Do you think I could work here? she asked.

A customer walked in. I hoped that this would give me some time to think of an appropriate noncommittal response, but the customer went right to the magazine section and began browsing.

—I don't see why not.

—Does that mean yes or no? she demanded. Then she explained her determination to have a firm response: I mean, otherwise I'll keep looking.

—I can say yes, but the owner could say no.

—I better keep looking, she surmised gloomily.

—I can't make any promises, I said.

—Yeah, I understand. But I have to know something definite. And I think I'd like to work here, she said.

—I'll speak to him as soon as I can. How's that?

—OK, she said. She began making preparatory primping and preening gestures, which indicated that flight was imminent. The discussion about the job had upset my plans. If I mentioned the drink now, she would look upon it as a form of blackmail. I didn't know what to say. Gilberte, however, did.

—Then we can have a drink to celebrate my new job, she said. She squeezed my hand and walked out the door. Call me when you know.

♦

This was going to be tricky. Theoretically I was against hiring her, because it would practically rule out any sort of relationship between us. However, since the last time I saw her, I had become somewhat involved with a person I had been seeing for some time. Which meant for the moment I wouldn't have time for her. But rather than risk letting her fall into someone else's clutches, I decided I would try to keep her. For company, if nothing else.

♦

The next day I called Roger, the store's owner. His executive assistant, Ms. Thorten, said that he was out and that he might or might not be back before the end of the day. I asked for an appointment. I said *yes* and *no* when she asked me whether what I wanted to see him about was important because an unqualified no would lead Ms. Thorten to conclude that my reasons were personal and therefore of no significance. Which would mean my interview with Roger would be scheduled for some vague date in the future, when she found an opening in Roger's busy schedule. On the other hand, a *yes* would entitle her to carry out a preliminary inquiry aimed at unearthing what it was I wanted to discuss with Roger, so that she could decide whether my idea of what was important coincided with hers, which was necessary if I was to have any hope of seeing Roger soon.

It was wrong of me to frustrate her attempts to perform her duties. She was paid to perform them. It was part of her job to hold these preliminary hearings. I detested them, yet I recognized their necessity. Heads of empires (and Roger was the head of his) were incessantly set upon by subjects clamoring to see them with what they imagined to be vitally pressing problems. Men like Roger needed someone whose discernment they could trust, to be sure that only those who did have vitally pressing problems got to see them. Elly Thorten exercised this function admirably. This Argus had her eyes on everything. When she said he might or might not be back, she was lying. She wouldn't think twice about lying to me, because she didn't like me. From my past dealings with her, I knew that although the decisions Elly made concerning my requests were tempered with professional discrimination, they were also poisoned by prejudice. If I told her I was thinking of hiring someone to work in the bookstore, she would consider this a nonpriority matter. In her eyes, my position in the empire (bookstore manager) counted for little. I provided a service. I could be terminated or replaced from one day to another.

My low rating was due to her belief that Roger retained me merely for personal reasons. It was common knowledge within the company that the bookstore was an insignificant outpost, situated at the farthest extremity of the suzerainty. It did generate profit. But in an empire comprised chiefly of office buildings, warehouses, and hotels, its strategic value was nil. Perhaps most damaging was the fact that the bookstore had been started by Roger's wife, Kristine, and in the past Roger had quickly liquidated her orphaned endeavors to raise funds to finance her next brainchild. Only the bookstore had survived. It owed its continued existence to me.

As I had feared, Ms. Thorten asked why I wanted to see Roger. I said it had to do with the store. She said that she would pencil me in and let me know. In the five years that I had worked for Roger, I had always, only, been penciled in. It was her way of letting me know that in her opinion I was an insignificant worm.

I was almost sorry I had let myself be penciled in. I wanted to see Roger, but I didn't want to have to go uptown to Roger's office. Any meeting Ms. Thorten scheduled would be up there. Aside from having to face her, I didn't like the corporate surroundings. I found offensive the long and complicated ritual I was forced to submit to each time I entered Roger's inner sanctum. To go from the building lobby to his floor, a guard had to call upstairs to see if I was expected. When my appointment was confirmed, I had to stand in front of a video camera to be identified by the person who was expecting me, or by some appointed surrogate to make the identification. Only then would the guard unlock the button in the elevator and send me up. Disembarking at the penthouse, I was escorted by another security guard through a metal detector. If I made it through without setting it off, he would telephone to see whether he should let me through the double glass doors or ask me to have a seat in the sky lobby. A positive reply empowered the guard to press a button, and the doors would click open. A woman, a Ms. Bundle, I believe, would step out of another door and set off down the hall, turning around periodically to make sure I was still following her. When we reached the end of the long, carpeted corridor, she would deposit me in a waiting room and close the door behind her. Everyone was put through the same ritual. Such were the prerogatives of a mogul.

Ms. Thorten presided over the waiting room, which also served as her office. No sooner was I ushered in then she would put the five fingers of her left hand against the five fingers of her right hand and say my name in a tone of voice that was so condescending I wanted to slap her. This prissy, pugnacious person never engaged in any frivolous small talk. Not with me, at least. A good afternoon would elicit a good afternoon. Any further attempt at engaging her in pleasantries only prompted her to produce a sour smile. She would invite me to take a seat, log something into her computer and, after it beeped, she would exit through the door behind her desk.

Left alone, I never felt alone. The office had an eerie feeling about it. I was positive it was under surveillance. A camera had to be hidden somewhere. A deathly silence hovered in the air, broken intermittently by the hissing of the air-conditioning system. Though there were windows with sweeping views of Central Park, they had been treated with a film that did something to the light, and rather than feel that you were aloft in the clouds, looking down, you had the sensation that you were submerged in a pool, looking up. It was uncanny.

When Ms. Thorten returned, she would stand at the door through which she had exited and wait for me to notice her. Then she would lead me down a short corridor to another office, much more human than the one over which she presided. It was furnished with armchairs and couches and tables with magazines on them. In one comer of this room was a circular staircase leading—I had learned—to the floor below, where the executive offices were located. Ms. Thorten would knock on the door next to this staircase, open it, and indicate that I should go inside.

Without a doubt, Roger would know I had entered—he had to have heard Ms. Thorten's rap—but whether he was reading his correspondence or watching one of the three television screens with the sound off, or talking on the phone or into his recorder, he never looked up until Ms. Thorten shut the door. Then, if he was not on the phone, he would rise out of his chair and greet me, either by flinging an arm around my shoulder or by vigorously shaking my hand or by both. Which made my heart flutter violently.

Physically, Roger was imposing. He stood six foot three or four, and probably weighed just under two hundred pounds. His movements had a lumbering, almost clownish aspect about them, which undermined the respect someone his size usually commanded. His posture and gestures, too, could have used some improvement, some refinement. He might have felt that any attempt to act graceful would make him appear ridiculous, despite the fact that there were countless other men as big as he whose comportment was more dignified. I had come to the conclusion that Roger was concerned only with the process and product of locomotion—that is, brute movement—and not with the style in which it was accomplished. His overall lack of concern with gesture and posture was also evident in the way he sat: once seated in a chair, he slipped into an un-becoming soggy slouch, from which (for no particular reason) he intermittently emerged by squaring his shoulders, thrust-ing out his chest, and placing his hands in his lap, which made him look as stiff and uncomfortable as a debutante in a yoga class. Like most people, he saw no need to change what came naturally, even if what came naturally was ungainly.

What saved him from looking like a salesman or an ac-countant or any other placid bureaucrat were his clothes. They didn't make him, but somehow they created an aura of distinc-tion for him. There was a symbiotic relationship between him and them that you could feel. It was not only the superb quali-ty, the exquisite textures and tailoring, the coordination of the classic English gentleman's business attire, but also the non-chalance he evidenced toward them, which doubtless came from his knowing there was nothing finer available, and that if he wrinkled the jacket it would be pressed, if he stained the pants they would be cleaned, if he ruined the shirt it would be replaced.

I liked Roger. Not because he was rich and powerful. (The rich, and even the superrich, are common commodities these days. Their money and power may make them attractive to some, but not to me.) Nor was it because I was physically attracted to him. He was not my type. No, I was drawn to him because since our earliest meetings he had impressed me as being *un homme sympathique*. Roger had been at the mercy of forces beyond his control all his life. He had taken the reins of a thriving multimillion-dollar real estate business from his father, and he carried on the tradition he had been raised to inherit. But I sensed—or was it that he let me see? —that he did this because it was his patrimony, his obligation. He had accepted the leadership of the firm as an obligation and as the only known route that assured him he would avoid the penurious life his father said he would lead if he didn't do as commanded. So Roger had put aside his other interests. He had let himself be coerced and frightened into accepting the challenge his father had put before him. He had to prove his courage and strength as a man: he had to take over the business. Or so I imagined. Nevertheless, under Roger's shrewd management the firm had become one of the biggest real estate companies in the city. One of the most profitable, as well. Articles appeared daily about Roger's exploits. To prove to himself that he could do something on his own, he had recently begun to act as an independent broker for office space. His negotiating skills were such that he had managed to engineer leases for two or three multinational firms in a short period of time, reaping from each of them millions in commissions. It wasn't principally the money he was after. It was the challenge that excited him. This was something he had chosen to do. He liked doing it. In fact, he was devoting more and more time to this hobby, as he called it. He had set up a separate company devoted solely to this aspect of the business.

Of course, my image of Roger was totally and hopelessly romanticized. Doubtless, he was as cutthroat as any other entrepreneur and believed only in dollars-and-cents logic. I gave in to the image I had created of him because I liked him. He was my type of man: intelligent, down-to-earth, sincere, diffident. From our first meeting, we had understood each other. Over the years our understanding continued to deepen and grow, but for all that, I would still have to characterize our relationship as one that was more than business but less than true friendship.

◆

Later that same afternoon, Roger returned my call. He wasn't surprised when I told him I wanted to hire someone to help me in the store. I was hard-pressed since my last assistant had left. He suggested that we meet for lunch the next day to talk it over. I was more than agreeable, so he passed me to Ms. Thorten, who would, he said, make reservations at Da Silvano or Odeon—whichever I preferred.

◆

I was pleased with the way things had turned out. Especially since I didn't have to go uptown to his office. If all went well I would receive Roger's formal approval over lunch.

The following morning Ms. Thorten called me at home to inform me that our one-forty-five reservation at Da Silvano (which I had opted for primarily because I didn't like the pretentious ad Odeon had taken out in a silly Parisian tabloid that we sold in the bookstore) was in Roger's name. I immediately rang up Roy, my part-time helper, to ask him to cover for me at the store.

◆

I was the first to arrive at the restaurant. I gave Roger's name. The headwaiter looked in his book and said:

—For three.

—For two, I corrected him. Yet when he showed me the book, to correct me, there was, indisputably, a 3 next to the name. He led me to an outdoor table, which, he informed me, had been requested. Here I had to protest. I did so politely. I simply said that I would prefer to sit inside. Luckily there was an empty table available, and as it was right next to the window, it made me feel that I wasn't stepping too far out of bounds by countermanding Roger's request. Anyway, I was willing to risk being admonished because I hated eating outdoors in New York. I never understood the allure it has for some people. In the country eating outdoors is lovely, and in some European cities it can be enjoyable. In New York, it is sheer lunacy. No matter how refined the cuisine, the noise, the dirt, and the passersby reduce the experience to the level of eating a hot dog from a street vendor on a corner in midtown at high noon. Roger may have wanted to rough it or to mingle a little, seeing ordinary people pass without a sheet of safety glass separating him from them. Or maybe it was for me. To get me out of the store. I didn't know. I really didn't care. I wasn't going to eat outside.

I ordered a bottle of S. Pellegrino and began to ponder who the third person coming to lunch could be. I hadn't the slightest idea. It was supposed to be a business lunch, so he couldn't very well be bringing along a friend. I couldn't think of a business person whom he would bring along, since the bookstore's activities were managed solely by me and monitored by Roger and one lone accountant.

The waiter was pouring my second glass of water when Roger's Mercedes pulled up next to the curb. The chauffeur got out and opened the door. He—and he alone—exited the car and hurried toward the restaurant, looking for me among the guests seated outside. I caught his attention with a wave.

—I thought we were going to picnic, he said, sitting down.

—It wasn't possible, I lied.

—Pity. Kristine's not arrived yet, he said, informing me who our dining partner was.

—No, I said. He looked at his watch and shook his head. The waiter came, and Roger ordered a Scotch and asked for the wine list. Then he buried his nose in the menu. I did too, but I didn't study it. I was recuperating from what he said.

Why had he invited Kristine to our lunch? She was his wife, of course. She was also the founder and ex-manager of the bookstore. But we had had other meetings and he hadn't thought her presence necessary. In fact, at one time, when we were in the process of opening the bookstore, Roger and I had held frequent meetings. We dined or drank together regularly.

I remembered those days fondly. That was when I learned how vast an empire he controlled, how he had come by it, and what his hopes for it were. It was then, too, that he had spoken about himself. Sometimes he would start on topics that threatened to take us far afield from what was proper and fitting discussion for business cronies (which was how I thought of us), yet he always drew back: no matter how much he talked about himself, and no matter how much he'd had to drink, he was always mindful of how much polite people may reveal to each other, always careful to remain within the exigencies of etiquette and education.

Perhaps it was his size, but liquor didn't seem to affect him at all. And he drank great quantities of it. Usually, by the time I had finished the wine (Roger would always order a bottle, more out of habit and training than appreciation, I think, since he drank one glass of Scotch after another), I no longer cared about the nature of the revelations he was making. A bottle of wine would stupefy me. In such a state, all I wanted was for the pampering to continue, for Roger to continue to light my cigarettes, to order me a dessert and then an espresso, to offer me another one of his exquisite little Cuban cigars to accompany my cognac, and to remain opposite me, talking, leaning on the table, showing me his languid smile and sad eyes. Which he did most fetchingly.

Our meetings had stopped when the bookstore was ready to open and Kristine decided it was time for her to take charge. After things were well under way, Roger would drop by once in a while, and sometimes we would take a drink together. But the days of our leisurely lunches and late dinners were no more.

They were repeated after a time, but under entirely different circumstances. For when Kristine decided to give up the bookstore to open a clothing boutique, Roger had to express his disappointment with his wife to someone. To whom would he turn if not to someone who had worked with her and supposedly knew her? He was distraught and in such a quandary about what to do that it to hurt me to listen to him. I wanted to take him in my arms and hold him tight and console him. We saw a lot of each other during that epoch. We drank outrageous amounts of alcohol, stayed out till all hours. He came to my loft once. Then one day he flew off to his villa in the Bahamas, and when he came back he was over it.

—How's Mark? I asked.

—Fine. They'll make him a partner in no time, Roger assured me with paternal pride. Mark, Roger and Kristine's only child, had recently graduated from Yale Law School and was working for a prestigious law firm. Roger had wanted to take him into the business, but Mark, unlike Roger, had been adamant in insisting that he wanted to make it on his own. Which, apparently, he was doing very nicely.

I was on the verge of asking why he had invited Kristine to our meeting (I was just working out the wording, because perhaps Kristine had invited herself, who knew?) when another Mercedes pulled up behind Roger's. I recognized Kristine's chauffeur when he got out.

—Kristine's just arrived, I said. Roger looked at his watch and frowned.

Kristine was smiling when she got out of the car. It was not quite summer yet, but she was already deeply tanned. Her blond hair was pulled back in a chignon. She was wearing a linen skirt and a sleeveless tunic cinched at the waist by a belt. Her entrance attracted most of the patrons' eyes.

We both rose when she came in. She kissed Roger lightly on the cheek. She offered me her hand and a hello and then sat down. The bickering began immediately. Roger claimed that though she had more free time than anyone he knew, she was never punctual. Kristine countered this by claiming that she had wanted to be on time and had left Southampton early enough, but she got stuck in traffic. Roger came back at her by pointing out that she couldn't have left early enough, because she was late.

I drank my water and waited. In her mid-forties, (nearly 8 years younger than Roger) Kristine was remarkably youthful-looking, absolutely bristling with health: every cell in her body seemed to be turgid and taut and fresh with life. We were the same age, but I didn't look as good as Kristine. I was aging well, but I just didn't have the time or the money or the inclination to invest such care in myself so as to appear not to be aging at all. Which didn't prevent me from being jealous.

The waiter interrupted their spat to ask whether the lady would have a drink. Roger answered that we would have wine with the meal and proceeded to order his lunch. Kristine, not having had any time to study the menu, agreed to eat whatever Roger was going to have. I ordered veal. Roger ordered a bottle of white and a bottle of red wine.

—Red and white? queried Kristine.

—You don't like red, and Stephen doesn't drink white, if I'm not mistaken, Roger said.

—No, I said.

—You don't think you should have white with veal? she asked, staring at me curiously.

—No, I said. I don't like white.

—Not even champagne?

—Champagne isn't wine, not technically anyway, I said, ready to launch into a disquisition about the differences between standing table wines and sparkling wines to prove my point.

—I saw the most smashing vase, Kristine blurted out.

—Where? Roger asked.

—Uptown, Kristine informed him.

— Mmm, murmured Roger.

—What were you doing uptown? I thought you were coming from the country.

—You called the Moores? Kristine ignored him.

—I thought you were going to call them.

—I've been away.

—They have telephones in the Hamptons.

—There was an exquisite show at the Parrish Gallery. I went with Allbright. Did I tell you, darling?

—No, Roger said.

—Yes, I did. How have you been, Stephen?

—Good, I said.

—Good, she said.

—Have you been to the Morgan to see the Caravaggio drawing exhibit? I must have my nails done before I go back to the country, she said, spreading them out on the table before her. When do we see you out there? Friday? she asked Roger.

—No, Roger said.

—We simply must have the pool fixed if your mother is coming out next week.

—Have it fixed, then. Did Mark come out?

—Yes. With that charming girl. I do hope he marries her.

The waiter came with the bottles of wine. Roger read the labels and approved them and they were both opened and poured, but he declined to taste them, saying he wasn't finished with his Scotch.

I drank nearly half my first glass in one gulp. I didn't mind the familiar banter being exchanged in my presence. I was used to it. It was Kristine's presence I objected to, so I drank heartily. Ingested at a rapid rate, the alcohol would soon render her less noticeable. I was hoping she would continue to hock Roger and not open a general discussion in which I would be expected to participate. I didn't want to be forced into a conversation with Kristine. Competent if a conversation was kept simple, Kristine became simple when it became complicated. When a discussion threatened to become intelligent, discursive, meaningful, she would gratuitously throw out a non sequitur, usually stunning her interlocutors and rendering them temporarily speechless. She then accepted this comment of hers as a valid contribution to the conversation, used it as a conjunction, and subordinated (trivialized) what was being discussed to her own, more important, thoughts. This was fine, except that Kristine rarely had thoughts, let alone important thoughts. None of this, however, mattered. Kristine was supremely self-confident, never nonplussed, utterly unflappable. Her complete lack of respect for, as well as total ignorance of, sound reasoning allowed her to say anything. Which she would, knowing her social status protected her from being made a fool of publicly. In fact, her social peers were quite impressed by her ability to aphorize extemporaneously. She had a knack for persuading people to take seriously the things she said by repeating them over and over in an attempt to extract the sense she felt had to be there. Often, after meeting her for the first time, people would come away awed. Kristine claimed she had one of the most original minds in New York and if she could just find the time to set down all her thoughts on paper, she would prove to be another Diana Vreeland.

After working with her for more than a year and a half, I knew better. Kristine never uttered anything but twaddle. Nothing she remarked upon stood up to critical scrutiny. All she ever did was remark, comment, note. To be just, she did have a practical, native intelligence. It was this that, on occasion, made her comments seem sharp and well-informed. But it was nothing more than newspaper knowledge, talk-show scholarship. Which was amply demonstrated on those occasions when she stumbled upon a perverse or original insight: because when you tried to take her observation a degree further—microscopically or macroscopically—she couldn't follow you and fell flat on her face as if she were blind. Not that she ever noticed that she fell. If Kristine didn't understand something, it wasn't because she, Kristine, didn't have the mental apparatus (or in the case of art, the eye) to grasp it. It was because there was nothing to grasp. *Hot air*, she would say about something that escaped her. *Ridiculous*, she would assert, and dismiss it. She wouldn't admit that some things might be beyond her, since she was convinced she was one of the select—one of the happy few—who had been granted the right to experience the finer things in life without having to work for them.

I had finished half the bottle of wine by the time the food arrived. Roger and Kristine were speculating about where their chauffeurs were and whose would be back first.

The conversation died down as we began to eat. Out of the blue, Roger launched:

—Stephen is proposing that we hire someone else to work in the store.

—What store? asked Kristine, knowing full well which store Roger was referring to.

—What's this kid's name anyway? Roger asked. What kind of experience does he have?

—What happened to Sophie? Kristine insisted upon knowing.

—She went back to France, I said.

—Ah, that's right. In fact, you know, we must have Marie-France out one weekend too, Roger.

—And Roy? Roger asked.

—Roy's still here.

—He can't pick up the slack?

—Not really, I said. Roger nodded in assent.

—Well, I don't have any objection if Kris doesn't.

—No. Stephen is capable of making a decision.

—Good, Roger said. He smiled at me.

I smiled back.

Then we all resumed eating.

♦

I called Gilberte later that afternoon and told her the news. Our celebratory drink didn't get mentioned. I didn't mention it because she had suggested it and she should have remembered it. That she hadn't was understandable (she was so ecstatic) but not forgivable, since I had been anticipating this drink. I asked her when she wanted to start. Immediately, she said. She was in fantastic need of money. So fantastic that she wondered whether she could possibly have an advance.

This put me off, and I put her off, saying that I would have to find out. She promised to be in bright and early the next day, at which point I told her that we didn't open until ten-thirty.

♦

Gilberte was there when I arrived. I took her in and showed her around and explained, generally, what she would have to do. I only went into detail about the cash register, which was rather difficult to operate, and the video camera. I had just recently had the camera installed on the mezzanine to help me keep an eye on what was going on up there when I was working alone. It served as my second set of eyes.

Gilberte listened attentively. She understood everything, she said. When I finally set her loose to start shelving new arrivals, she brought up the little matter of her advance. I told her that it was impossible. I explained the checks came from Roger's office, and there was no way I could ask the accountant to make out an extra check. It just wasn't done. She seemed totally downcast by this news. I asked how much she had in mind. The sum wasn't exorbitant, so against my better judgment, I gave it to her out of petty cash. She swore she'd repay it as soon as she received her first check. Without fail.

Her demand for money broke the spell I had been under. It didn't sit right with me. I didn't know why. But there is something suspicious about desperate people, especially when the desperate straits they claim to be in appear to a neutral observer to be wide enough to allow safe passage. She didn't look like she was starving. She evidently had a roof to sleep under. And clothes to cover her. And money to buy and develop the film for her show. At any rate, her request set me to wondering if I hadn't been a little hasty in hiring her. Maybe I should have put an ad in the paper and held interviews to find the person best qualified for the job. Wouldn't that have been the professional way to go about finding help? I suspected so. But it was too late now.

◆

Happily, Gilberte turned out to be a fine employee. When there was work to be done she did it. She quickly became familiar with the store's layout and soon stopped asking me where to look for things. She learned her way about the labyrinth in the basement, where we kept the overstock. She always seemed to have an inkling about where to find a book that wasn't where it was supposed to be. Roy (a notorious misogynist) tolerated her—a concession he hadn't granted my previous helper. Furthermore, she promptly paid back her advance. I had only one complaint. She was rarely on time.

On the other hand, she had a skilled eye for spotting shoplifters. In the first three weeks of her employ she nabbed four of them. She chastised me for not being more scrupulous about guarding the goods, since it was evident that even with the video camera the store was being ripped off left and right. I smiled at this reprimand. There was some truth in it. I hadn't the heart of a policeman, I confessed. To prevent pilferage, I counted mainly on my presence. I thought nothing of attaching myself like a leech to those whom I suspected of stealing books. I wouldn't let go of them until they were at the door. But when they were ready to cross the threshold, I could never bring myself to utter more than a verbal command to give back what they had taken. I could never collar anyone and call the police. Gilberte could, and did once. I found this process so unseemly and degrading for the victim (in this case an underage punk from Queens) that I made her change her tactics. From then on she merely blocked the door and refused to move until the malefactors put back what they had filched. Then, after giving them a public lecture in front of the other customers in a tone of voice that would put the fear of the law into you, she would order them out of the store with a warning never to come back.

◆

Gilberte made me laugh. We got along splendidly. Exactly as I had hoped we would. Her presence was salutary. She was a constant, conscious anodyne to the boredom from which I had been suffering. With her in the store, the hours and days passed painlessly. No longer did I have the sense of time being held in abeyance. Before she had come, even though I had had twice as much work to keep me busy, the days had seemed endless. I thought I would die of ennui. Nothing could move me. I lapsed into long periods of inactivity. I couldn't work. And whether customers came in or not, there was always work to be done: straighten the books, order and reorder stock, read reviews, pay bills, clean, or whatnot. That I was frequently incapacitated demonstrated to me my lack of maturity, my refusal to accept the responsibility that had been given me. Also my fecklessness. For although I came to hate my job, I couldn't bring myself to quit and find something else. Nor could I do something that would discredit me in the eyes of my employer and force him to fire me. I couldn't bring myself to read a magazine or a book, let alone, say, begin coming in late and leaving early, which would have clearly shown my contempt and discontentment with my position. No, I sat on my stool waiting for customers—not unlike a caged trained chicken waiting for someone to insert a nickel in the box so the gate would lift and it could go play its tune on the piano and have its grain of corn. I sat and smoked and sulked and stared and dreamed. I was one of the working dead.

Now, with Gilberte on the scene, I rarely succumbed to the shopkeeper blues, or at least not to such a severe degree. Gilberte put me back in touch with reality. There were fewer dead moments. I felt alive. I felt constantly called upon to demonstrate I was in control.

◆

Gilberte always had something to tell me.

—If I bore you just let me know, she said one day.

—You never bore me, I said.

—I mean, if you'd rather not hear.

—I can listen to anything, I assured her.

She saw that I was serious, and said:

—I'll bet you could, as though this were a talent or a trait worthy of admiration. I can't, she confided. I have a hard time reading.

—What does that have to do with it? I asked her. I disliked non-sequiturs and though I had learned that Gilberte was likely to give me another one in response to a question about her first one, I couldn't let this go.

—I mean when I read I hear the words in my head. Don't you?

—Metaphorically speaking, yes.

—Well, I hear them, and it bothers me. When I'm talking, I don't hear what I'm saying. I mean, I know what I'm saying, but

I don't hear it in my head in the same way, you know? I nodded. I knew and didn't know, and Gilberte knew and didn't know. And I knew and she knew that we wouldn't resolve this paradox, so we let things lie as they were.

◆

—What time is he coming?

—He said about two-thirty.

—It's nearly three, Gilberte said.

—Nearly, I concurred.

—Well? she said.

—He said about, I reminded her.

—He was supposed to come yesterday too, Gilberte said, her peevish *too* implying that she had already decided that he wasn't going to come today.

—He'll come. He isn't Godot.

—Who?

—Godot, I said, raising my voice.

—Oh, Gilberte said, nodding her head, indicating she had understood the comparison. Watching her expression, however, I decided she had understood only my tone of voice, which, when raised, threatened like a hand and prohibited further questioning. Since her knowledge of literature was spotty at best, I thought it would be in her interest to know who Godot was and why we could be compared to Vladimir and Estragon, and Roger to Godot, but I wasn't in the mood to explain the analogy.

She was nervous. I didn't know why. Roger had said he wanted drop by to meet my assistant. It wasn't important. I thought it was nice of him. But it made Gilberte anxious.

Especially since Roger said he would come Tuesday and then didn't come. She didn't like people who didn't keep dates, she said. No matter who they were. Now it was Wednesday, and he was late. Though I was sure he would show up eventually, there was no way I could convince Gilberte of this, and her patience was at an end. Her panther-like pacing and snarling questions were starting to annoy me.

—What are you so nervous about?

—I'm not nervous.

—Then stand still.

—I'm not walking because I'm nervous, she said.

—Then go upstairs and walk where I can't see you, I said. She stood and looked at me for a minute, then, like a child who has been ordered to her room as punishment for something she claims she did not do, she ran up the stairs. I turned on the camera. She was already staring into it, sticking out her tongue. I turned off the camera.

I lit a cigarette and then turned on the camera again. Gilberte was leaning on the windowsill. She, too, was smoking. She looked very sexy on the screen. Very provocative. Feeling too much like a voyeur, I turned off the camera. How could I sit there watching her ass pushed up in the air like that, fantasizing about what it would feel like in my hands? It was senseless to get aroused for nothing. There was nothing between us. From all I could gather, she wasn't interested in me. Not for the moment. Possibly not at all. Of course, I hadn't tried to attract her interest, which might be latent, lurking beneath her professional demeanor, ready to manifest itself at my instigation. However, I didn't feel this was the right moment. Anyway, I had Ronnie. He satisfied me for now. I couldn't in good conscience contemplate pursuing Gilberte and complicating my uncomplicated affair with Ronnie. Especially when I was adamant about insisting that our relationship remain monogamous (more, I was loath to admit, out of fear of catching some dreadful deadly disease than anything else, although, to maintain a romantic image of myself, I had made him believe that I was fiercely jealous and prone to rash acts if I discovered any infidelity).

Also, when I considered matters more carefully, I realized it would be problematic for us to pick up from where we left things that night in my loft. Because there was nothing to pick up: nothing had happened. Except I had marveled at her naked body and desired to possess it. The image was etched in my memory. It is nearly impossible to eradicate an image of something you desire, even if you have only seen it once. I still smarted when I thought of how she had refused me that morning. I didn't remember getting one kiss on the lips. For her, that night had been an accident. She would have gone home with (almost?) anybody who had asked her. So I had no starting place except the present.

At the present I wasn't sure I should pursue her. She was my employee. I spent eight hours a day with her. Her presence didn't kill my desire for her, but it numbed it, attenuated it. It was intermittent, pulsatile, and more likely to be the direct result of something she said or did (like lean up against the windowsill like that) than to be an overall engulfing urge to possess her completely like it had been that morning.

Roger finally showed up. He strolled in, introduced himself to Gilberte, who, having seen the Mercedes pull up and double-park outside, had come running downstairs. (She had found the time to apply fresh makeup.) She was as polite as could be. Roger was charmed, I could tell. When they ran out of small talk, Roger excused himself and started walking around the store, dragging his fingers across the backs of books. He stopped at a table and leafed through a big book on painting, closed it abruptly, continued walking, and finally came to rest at the back of the store. I joined him there. Gilberte stayed in front to mind the cash register.

—How's business? he asked me when I was by his side.

—Getting better all the time, I exaggerated.

—Good, he said. He took out his cigar case and after twisting one into his mouth offered me one. I declined. I had the feeling something was wrong. Roger seemed distracted, preoccupied. He didn't talk after he lit his cigar, and his expression remained inscrutable.

I waited. Roger smoked. We stood side by side. I had the distinct impression that he wanted to say something and was searching for the words. His eyes were directed toward the front of the store, but whether he was staring at Gilberte, who was leaning against the counter, or out the window, I couldn't determine. A customer entered, and he snapped out of his trance.

—I don't think you mentioned you hired a girl, Roger said.

—Does it matter?

—Not at all. You always surprise me. How's she working out?

—Fine, I said.

We watched the customer go up the stairs, then turned our eyes to Gilberte. She was standing at the door, apparently staring at Roger's chauffeur while he cleaned the windshield.

—I'll tell Kristine, Roger said. He began walking toward the front of the store again. I followed him.

—I suppose Stephen sent your social security number to the accountant, Roger said to Gilberte.

—I did I said.

—Well ... He extended his hand to Gilberte. Good luck.

Gilberte and he shook hands, and Roger patted me on the back and departed.

—Is he always like that? Gilberte asked.

—Like what?

—Do you think he liked me?

—I don't think he noticed you, I said, intending to be just a little cruel.

—Oh, Gilberte said.

♦

Kristine put in an appearance two days later. Gilberte was upstairs re-alphabetizing books.

—Where's your helper? she asked, looking around avidly.

Gilberte entered on cue. She started coming down the stairs, but seeing me engaged in conversation, she hesitated a moment as if she intended to turn around and go back up, which gave Kristine enough time to whisper under her breath:

—What a pretty girl.

Then, evidently sensing that something concerning her was taking place, Gilberte came down.

—Kristine Reynolds, Kristine said, extending her hand. Gilberte shook the hand that was proffered and said how happy she was to meet her.

—This is Gilberte, I said, in case there was any doubt.

—Gilberte Marshall, Gilberte said, correcting me.

Kristine turned the name over on her palate, tasting the syllables.

—I've never met a woman named Gilberte, she said. It's a boy's name, isn't it?

—The *e* makes it a girl's name, Gilberte said defensively.

—But it's French.

Gilberte smiled. It was obvious it was all the same to her. And Kristine smiled because she believed she was right.

—I guess you know all this used to be mine, said Kristine, in a manner that might make you believe she was sorry to have given it up. Gilberte was so lost at this declaration that I regretted not having given her at least an encapsulated version of the store's history, since now Kristine was going to narrate hers first. Which would make it the one that counted, and my later version would doubtless be seen as an addendum, or at worst, an attempt at revisionist history, suspect because it had been suppressed.

—Yours? Gilberte said.

—I exaggerate, of course. I only worked here. Stephen runs the place, she said. But it was my idea, and a good one too. We have one of the largest selection of art books in the city. We're known for that. But then I had a better idea and opened a boutique. Stephen must have told you.

—No.

—No? You haven't seen it? It's just down the street. *Pret-a-porter.* Gilberte was clearly puzzled. She tried to smile her way through, but Kristine was an adept at sensing discomfiture, as well as its cause.

—*Pret-a-porter,* she repeated. It means ready-to-wear, in French, she explained. It's terribly silly, but chic all the same. She sneered at me.

—*Pret-a-porter*. Gilberte repeated it. I like it, she said. I don't think it's silly.

A customer came in. He passed between us and momentarily cut off our conversation. His *pardon me* did not manage to sew it together again. I have often noticed that when forced conversations are interrupted, the hollowness of what has been passing for communication rings out loud and clear, scattering the interlocutors. I waited for Kristine to say good-bye. Instead, I heard a call for help coming from the mezzanine. I excused myself, said good-bye to Kristine, and went upstairs.

Kristine was still there when I came down.

—Gilberte is a photographer, she informed me gleefully.

Gilberte looked dubious, not about her stated profession but about how to respond to Kristine's enthusiasm.

—I know. We met at her opening.

—Really! Kristine breathed. You've already had a show?

—It was a group show, Gilberte said.

—Here in SoHo?

—Yes. I could see she didn't want to reveal the name of the gallery if she could avoid it.

—Which gallery are you with?

—Well, I'm not with one at the moment, Gilberte said evasively.

—You should be.

—I know, but it's not easy.

— No, it's not. What kind of photography do you do? Uptown? Downtown? East Village? Kristine depended upon geography to identify the different styles of the day. I know it's hard to describe one's work, she continued. It's always better to show than to tell. There was a pause. But I've got to find someone to take pictures of the store window. I'm going to run an ad. You have a portfolio, don't you?

—Not with me, Gilberte said.

—Of course not, darling. But you must have one. I'd like to see it. Do you do commercial work? It's not difficult, Kristine said encouragingly. I'll tell you what. Bring your portfolio by the boutique next week, and we'll have a look. How's that? Any time after eleven-thirty, she specified. Then she offered her hand to Gilberte. Very nice meeting you.

—You too, Gilberte said somewhat awkwardly.

Kristine flashed me a smile and gave me a wave and dashed out the door, flinging over her shoulder one last ciao. As soon as she was out of sight, Gilberte turned to me.

—Maybe I'll get a commission.

—It looks possible, I said.

—I'd love to do her portrait.

—I think it's been done, I said.

—By who?

—Mapplethorpe, maybe. But I'm not sure.

—Mapplethorpe, she echoed me.

—You know, I think I've seen her picture in the papers.

—Very likely.

—She was at Area or the Palladium or Four D or somewhere.

—She gets around.

—Yeah, she must, she said.

—I wonder if she would help me.

—Help you what? I asked.

—You know, help me. My career, all that. I bet she could.

—Ask her. She mused on this for a moment and then said:

—I just might.

♦

I was drinking, luxuriating between sobriety and inebriation, dreaming in a misty utopia, at that point where if I swallowed another mouthful of vodka I would be drunk and if I refrained from drinking I would be neither sober nor drunk but incapable of reaping the benefits of either state. I decided to be drunk. I drained my glass. Only after I set it down did I notice someone standing next to my table. The waiter. He had his pad and pencil out and was ready to take my order. I picked up the menu and he lowered his pencil to his pad. I asked what the specials were. He lifted his pencil from his pad and began reciting their names, as well as the ingredients used to prepare them and the manner in which they were cooked. Then he lowered his pencil to his pad.

I ordered veal Milanese and half a carafe of red wine, and another vodka. When you get a second, I stipulated. The waiter nodded in agreement and tried to take my glass, but I held on to it because I wanted the lime. I fished it out, ripped the pulp away from the skin, and swallowed it. Then I completely drained the glass.

Probably I had ordered too much food. The veal would be accompanied by something, potatoes on the side, if I remembered correctly. However, if I was hungry I didn't know it. The double vodka had anesthetized my stomach. That was the problem with eating out. Before I ate I liked to drink, and after I drank I didn't like to eat. This was why at home I tried to limit myself to one or two cocktails before dinner, and a single glass of wine to accompany it. I didn't want to become a heavy solitary drinker—but I was well on my way.

I was a longstanding solitary eater. It was funny, too, because I didn't mind eating alone in restaurants, but nothing depressed me more than eating alone at home. Breakfast was the only meal I could tolerate eating in the loft by myself. In the morning I could be there alone because I had no choice: when I got up I was starving and simply had to put food in my stomach. All I thought about was munching my way through some cornflakes or spooning up some yogurt. To eat dinner in the loft at night was another matter. First of all, I usually wasn't very hungry after work. I would pick at my food and think of other things besides eating. I ruminated. I brooded. I worried. I dreaded the coming night. For even in the summer, when the light lingered long in the sky, the two-thousand-square-foot loft seemed like an empty auditorium, in which the only thing I heard when I ate alone was the sad solo of the clatter of cutlery.

Dining alone in a restaurant was far more pleasant. To eat alone in a room in which the atmosphere was animated and I could savor the continually changing panorama was congenial to me. That I sat by myself didn't mean I was eating alone. The surrounding people were strangers. Nevertheless, since we were all participating in the same rite and following, for the most part, the same rules of etiquette, our activity became a communal affair and made my fellow diners, if not familiar, then a little less strange.

In fact, as the meal progressed, my immediate neighbors frequently became a lot less strange, since I was an inveterate eavesdropper. My powers of concentration were honed to such a degree that I could monitor up to three conversations simultaneously without becoming fatigued. The only thing that impaired my performance was alcohol. It didn't hamper my concentration, it simply slowed my reaction time and increased my chances of being caught listening. Which was regrettable. But it did happen from time to time, and it was embarrassing, but never enough to ruin my meal, since I had a procedure for extricating myself from this situation. I tried to look as perturbed as possible and did everything I could to give the impression that I couldn't help but hear my neighbors' raised voices and uncouth laughter, if there was any. I tried to convince them with a scowl that their obstreperous behavior had been impinging upon my quiet contemplation—no matter if they had been whispering. Usually what happened was that after casting disapproving looks in my direction, my victims simply lowered their voices to assure their privacy. Which was no guarantee that I wouldn't hear them.

Another of my pet pastimes, staring at people, also created difficulties. You could glance at anybody on and off for hours, but a prolonged stare transgressed some unwritten law and was seen as a kind of persecution. It was funny, but people who dressed to attract attention didn't like to be scrutinized by strangers for any length of time. Not infrequently I had to cease and desist my activity because I sensed the tension my surveillance caused was becoming unbearable. To extricate myself from potentially explosive situations I had two procedures, which I followed unsystematically. Sometimes I continued staring, keeping my eyes focused on some object behind the person's head until he or she lowered their eyes, having assumed that I was staring at something behind them. Or I continued to stare at them and let them wonder what it was I found so interesting about their physiognomy, until they finally submitted to my gaze or were made to submit to it by another member of their party, who would not consent to let a companion participate in a staring contest. It was rather boorish of me. Sometimes I couldn't help myself.

Only once did I provoked a crisis and then the charming headwaiter smoothed everything over and offered drinks to both parties, on the house. Usually I got away with staring. Which was probably due to the fact that as uncomfortable as I made people feel, they sensed I was staring to stare, disinterestedly, without motive as it were. I wasn't interested in picking anyone up. I never cruised. I had a rule about that: cruising during meals was forbidden. The mixture of the two activities was taboo. Like milk and meat for some, the raw and the cooked for others, for me cruising and eating had to be kept apart. If I was in a bar or a cafe I made exceptions: in a sit-down restaurant, I made none. It was a matter of psychic economy more than anything else. Cruising was tiring. In a restaurant it was downright fatiguing. Especially if someone reciprocated your interest. Then both of you would sit there thinking about how nice it would be to meet. When there wasn't any chance of that. Especially if the object of your interest was with someone else. Most especially if they were ostensibly straight. You couldn't make contact. It wasn't done in restaurants. It would be too indecorous. It was impossible that anything should come of cruising in a restaurant, for me at any rate. I allowed myself searching looks, penetrating, poignant glances. And in these looks fantasy flourished, fed by the impossibility of making contact and fulfilling desire: that was what made it seem so romantic, so tragic, so sweet, so exciting.

By the time my meal arrived, I wasn't hungry. Pushing the food around on my plate, I poked at the lettuce and finally cut a piece of meat, which I stuffed into my mouth and chewed.

The restaurant was full. There was a crowd at the bar, some of whom were presumably waiting for tables. I was glad that I had come early enough to secure a table for two. When I sat at a table for four (which happened occasionally), on seeing such a crush of hungry people I felt guilty about consuming more than my fair share of space. Then, too, the waiters were more likely to hurry me, presenting dishes one after another in quick succession, treating me like a piece on an assembly line that they were in a hurry to complete to meet their quota. I cut another piece of veal, pushed it around the plate and lifted it to my mouth. I should have been hungry. For lunch, I had eaten only a slice of watery cold pizza that Gilberte bought for me on her way back from showing Kristine her portfolio.

The first time I heard that she would be going to see Kristine was the previous night. Just before leaving, she said she would be late the following day because she had an appointment with Kristine. I hadn't said anything, but I couldn't keep from wondering how Kristine's *any time after eleven-thirty* had become an appointment. It seemed a bit presumptuous (especially since I had heard the way Kristine issued the invitation), but I didn't say anything. I wished her luck. She called me before leaving Kristine's, to ask if I would like her to pick something up for me on her way back. The pizza was her suggestion.

—Well? I had said, as we both slurped up the sauce.

—Well, she liked it, I think.

I shook my head approvingly.

—Yeah, Gilberte went on. She was enthusiastic, but I think I can get her to be more enthusiastic. I mean, she wants to be, but she's scared of her own judgment. Who's Allbright anyway?

—Her adviser.

—Adviser?

—Yes, he's a consultant. Or dealer if you like. His specialty is contemporary art.

Gilberte frowned.

—She said he has an eye.

—Two, I said.

This had upset her. She wiped her hands and mouth and lit a cigarette. I was waiting for her to tell me more. But she didn't. That bothered me. Why was she making a long story short? What had she done there from eleven-thirty to two-thirty? What had she and Kristine talked about for three hours? What could they have said that she didn't want to repeat?

I asked if I could see her work. She cleared away the pizza bag and napkins and opened her portfolio on the counter. One at a time, she handed me photographs in plastic sleeves. It was all new work. Or at least new to me. There were cityscapes and still lifes and some formal female nudes, as well as shots reminiscent of the work I had seen at the gallery.

—I'm looking at everything right now, she said by way of explanation or excuse. I think my work reflects that. I mean, I think there's a certain movement and a certain stillness and a certain hesitancy, yet sureness, that you can see. I can't talk about it yet, she said. I'm not sure enough, she added. Anyway, the work speaks for itself.

—How long have you been taking pictures?

—Forever, she said. I've always had a camera.

—When did you decide that you wanted to be a photographer? I asked, trying to bring more focus on the situation.

—For almost as long, she said. I mean, I've always been behind a camera. Do you think Kristine liked my work?

—You said she was enthusiastic.

—I did. You're right.

—Well, why ask me what she thinks?

She shrugged her shoulders. She was nervous, unsure.

—I mean, I wonder if she liked it enough to let me do the shoot for the store window.

—I don't know.

—I wonder if I'll have to show my portfolio to Allbright.

—I don't know, I said again. That had been the final word on the subject. She remained sullen and uncommunicative the rest of the day.

The waiter came and removed my plate. I poured out the last of the wine. I hadn't finished my meal, but I wanted something for dessert. I decided to order a cognac instead. I would dip sugar cubes in it and dissolve them under my tongue. That would sate my sweet tooth. I would have preferred something chocolate. The only chocolate desserts they made at this restaurant (aside from being bad) had liqueur in them, and I didn't like liqueur in my food. Especially in my chocolate. Liqueur-filled chocolates turned my stomach. I didn't know why, but I always thought of them as fare for fat old ladies wrapped in frayed silk or satin sashes sitting in musty, overheated, over-decorated, over scented boudoirs, surrounded by cats and caged birds and tables cluttered with medicines and potions. Somewhere there was a television blaring in the background.

The waiter brought my cognac. I could see he was dying to bring me coffee, which would signal I was preparing to leave. But I didn't feel like moving. After consuming a meal and a not insignificant quantity of alcohol, I liked to sit.

Actually, I didn't know what to do. Going home didn't appeal to me, and going out didn't appeal to me. I could have called Ronnie. But I was preoccupied with Gilberte. I didn't particularly like being preoccupied. In my mental makeup, a preoccupation was the first step on the way to an obsession. And that would never do. That's why I had turned to drink. I had to wipe out the questions Gilberte's trip to Kristine's had raised. I didn't want to dwell on them. Or on her. I wasn't drunk enough, however, not even with the cognac. I ordered a Black Russian, and to please the waiter I asked that the bill be brought with it. A stupid drink, but what the hell. A Black Russian would do me in. I was already hunched over the table, my arms spread wide like flying buttresses to support me. As soon as I had swallowed a sip of the Black Russian I was done for. With what was left of my powers of reason I decided that alcohol was like a liquid eraser. It effaced mental phenomena. That's what it meant to be wiped out. I took a hearty swallow. I didn't know if that's what it meant, but the reasoning appealed to me. That I could still reason still appealed to me. That I could hold my liquor bucked me up. There I was lost for a moment. The only thing that came to my mind was a ship's hold. To carry cargo. In the hold. To carry, *portare. Comment vous portez-vous?* Or perhaps it was simply to hold, to grasp, to hang on to. I liked the ship idea more. The idea of a storm-tossed vessel was more romantic. I didn't know where the storm came from. Nor could I figure where the waiter came from, but there he was standing before me, smugly calculating my bill. I ordered another Black Russian. He looked very unhappy, very disapproving. He had to redo the bill. Seeing the crush at the bar, I understood why he was unhappy. People were waiting. I was still drinking. I was done for, but I wasn't at an end yet, although I was close. I could feel I was close. I felt heavy and hot and slightly dizzy. When my head hit the pillow it would send the rest of my body spinning uncontrollably. It wasn't going to be pleasant. I'd try to watch a movie. Try to keep my eyes open. Plastered. There was one that totally escaped me. I couldn't figure that one.

The racket began to unsettle me. Voices roared in my head. There was too much commotion. Too much coming and going. Altogether too much movement. As a sick man, I was entitled to some peace. I wasn't sick. I never got sick. That is, I never vomited. To prove it, I downed almost half the Black Russian the waiter set down before me. I now had two drinks on the table. I couldn't touch another drop. I decided to go. I fished out my wallet and found enough bills to cover the figure written and circled. The waiter pounced on it. When he brought back the plate with my change, I looked at the bill again and tried to decide how much of a tip I should leave. I tried doubling the tax but couldn't. The numbers just wouldn't add up. In the end I left what I thought to be sufficient. The waiter seemed very satisfied. I downed the rest of my water and then got up. I sat right back down again. I hadn't had my balance. With my feet firmly planted on the floor it was easier to stand. But my feet wouldn't move. My waiter came and guided me to the door. He guided me very discreetly, so discreetly that nobody stared at us. Unless they, too, were staring discreetly.

In the street, I realized I was obliterated. I suppose I could have shambled home under my own power, but I hailed a cab. When I gave the driver my address, he was mad.

—It's five fuckin' blocks, not even. He turned around and stared at me. I pushed five dollars through the slot. That calmed him.

—Whatever you say, boss, he said. As we sped away, I noticed he hadn't turned on the meter.

♦

It was summer and it was hot and the air was heavy and dirty and almost abrasive against your skin. You had to fight your way through it, which made you sweat and smell. Everyone was swimming in his own perspiration. Complaining. This was the kind of New York City summer weather you escaped from if you could. It was peculiar that Kristine hadn't migrated east to the Hamptons to reap the benefits of the ocean and ocean-cooled breezes as she had every other summer for as long as I had known her. I mentioned it to Gilberte. She had too many things to do, Gilberte told me. One of which was, it appeared, to take care of her unfinished business with Gilberte.

Gilberte was convinced Kristine was going to make a decision about the commission for the store window before going away for the rest of the season. She had asked Gilberte to bring back her portfolio to show to Allbright. It took every bit of strength I possessed not to ask when this second meeting between her and Kristine had taken place. I wondered why I had been informed about it only afterward. But I didn't say a word.

Then, a few days after Allbright had passed judgment on her work, Gilberte came in with her portfolio again. This was too much for me.

—Who are you going to show it to now?

—It's for Kristine.

—She just saw it, didn't she?

—Yes, but she wants to take it with her to the country to show Kettridge. She said this matter-of-factly, as if it were a standard procedure with which she was long familiar.

I was almost certain Gilberte had never met Kettridge, Kristine's neighbor in the Hamptons, and if she had, she could have only the vaguest idea about his role in the decision-making process.

—What did Allbright have to say?

I wanted to know how he had assessed her work, the terms he had used.

—The same as you.

—What was that? I was lost.

—Interesting, she said. I bore the weight of her irony easily. It made me smile rather than grimace.

♦

Kristine showed up toward lunchtime. She was dressed all in white and looked ready for the beach. She flitted around the store like a windblown bubble, finally coming to rest at the counter. We all smiled at each other. There was an uneasy silence, which Gilberte finally pricked.

—I brought my portfolio, she said, taking it out from behind the counter.

—Oh, exclaimed Kristine. She turned to me. It's impressive work, she said in a confidential manner. Very impressive, she added, choosing to intensify an adjective that pleased her with an adverb rather than take the trouble to find another adjective.

She stayed an hour, gabbing and gossiping with Gilberte. They seemed to be on the best of terms. Listening to their prattle fueled my suspicions that they had seen each other quite a few times without my being aware of it. Perhaps Gilberte wandered over to the boutique during her breaks, or at dinnertime. She could easily use the proposed project as an excuse for a visit. Of course, just because I couldn't keep myself from thinking something was true didn't mean it was true. All the same, if what I suspected was correct, it would explain something else besides their cozy camaraderie. Namely, Gilberte's change in behavior.

In the last few weeks it had been undergoing a subtle but noticeable transformation. Part of the change was doubtless attributable to the high stakes involved. Gilberte realized this could be her big break. She was constantly on edge, perpetually anxious, and often ill-tempered. Her moods fluctuated wildly. These fluctuations were frequently coincident with a telephone call or a meeting with Kristine. There was no doubt in my mind that Kristine was responsible. The combination of how Gilberte felt, and what Kristine made her feel, caused her behavior to become erratic and unpredictable. Gilberte knew everything depended upon Kristine. She was the one who would, ultimately, decide whether Gilberte received the commission. If Gilberte had to be happy or sad or mad to match Kristine's emotional state, in an attempt to get closer to her, she would do it.

What upset me was that Gilberte had taken Kristine as her role model. I assumed she did this because she knew if Kristine recognized herself in Gilberte she would be unable to reject her. But in refashioning her personality, Gilberte was becoming too self-conscious and too unlike herself. She had herself under constant observation. She never let up. She began to complain about the sorry state of her clothes. She began to try to perfect certain of her expressions in the mirror, to fine-tune her intonations, to polish her gestures. She felt she had to improve her self-presentation. She counted on me to help her. I had to tell her whether her voice sounded funny when she said things a certain way (Kristine's way), whether her smile was too toothy, whether it was more elegant to hold a cigarette with two or three fingers. She began to wear more makeup. I had to have an opinion about everything she did. I disliked helping her disfigure herself like this. Upon seeing the result of our work played out before me, I was overcome by a mixture of pity and revulsion, perhaps the same emotion Odysseus felt on seeing what Circe had done to his men. It nearly nauseated me to watch the way these two interacted. I said nothing. I held my tongue. Gilberte wanted that commission more than anything, and I wasn't about to jeopardize her chance of receiving it by offering my advice on how I thought she should behave.

Just as Kristine was preparing to leave, a customer came in. He asked me for help, and rather maliciously, I directed him to Gilberte. This cut short their idyll. Kristine gave Gilberte a quick wave and made her way toward the door. Gilberte, discontent, led the customer upstairs.

—She's charming, Kristine said.

—I know, I said.

—Smart too. That's the interesting thing. Usually when they're that pretty they're stupid. It wasn't Kristine but the voice of experience speaking.

—Is she? I asked, knowing that by smart Kristine meant Gilberte agreed with everything she said since Kristine thought anyone smart or intelligent if they shared her opinions. She had, as it were, her own personal correspondence theory of truth. That is, people who didn't share her opinions were stupid. And incontrovertibly smart people who had opinions (or ideas) that could in no way be made to accord with hers were either out of their minds or geniuses. Consequently, Kristine knew countless numbers of geniuses and countless numbers of people who were insane—countless numbers of people who were as normal as you or I.

—Oh, yes, she said, opening the door. I can tell you, she'll be a success. You just wait. She gave me a coy smile, strode across the sidewalk, and got into her car.

♦

Kristine held Gilberte in suspense with silence. She kept her waiting, wondering. She should have simply given her the commission because she was interested in befriending her. I supposed what held things up was the protocol governing social relations in which there was an unequal distribution of power. For example, one rule of the game was that the empowered person had to feel that the powerless one would not do something he or she didn't mean. *Something* here had a negative value, meaning anything false or insincere. Accordingly, Gilberte, powerless, was obliged to demonstrate that she liked Kristine for herself. This meant that regardless of whether it was true or not, she had to act as if she was indifferent to receiving the commission. The important thing was for her to impress upon Kristine how much she liked her, how much it meant to her to have Kristine for a friend.

I couldn't imagine how she could do a better job. After all, she was altering her personality to captivate her. The day Kristine had come for the portfolio, Gilberte had given an impeccable performance. The conversation had revolved around myriad subjects, but Gilberte never mentioned her work. She had focused on making Kristine remember their previous conversations. She used such prefaces as *remember what you said about* and *the day that* and *you were right about ...* to show how she had retained a souvenir of their time together, doubtless working on the assumption that the more memories one has, the farther back in time an association is felt to have begun. This would bind them together more firmly, without making Kristine think she was wooing her for the commission.

I was sure a decision would have been reached at once if Kettridge had been in town. Kristine would have met with him, asked his opinion, and the matter would have been settled. Favorably, I felt sure. It seemed to me Kristine wanted to use Gilberte but held back for two reasons. One was that without first consulting her chief adviser she couldn't be sure that if she gave Gilberte the commission he wouldn't propose someone more illustrious to do the work—someone who would be more advantageous to her socially. The second was that if he liked Gilberte's portfolio, it would help Kristine build a reputation as someone who could spot new talent, which would be socially advantageous to her. On the other hand, if he didn't like it, she would have to explain away her aesthetic blunder by promoting a persona. By selling Gilberte. And that might be problematic, and disadvantageous to her social ambitions. Kristine was still worming her way into one of New York's most select social sets. Her position was hardly secure enough for her to initiate the induction of a new personality without (again) raising questions about herself. Kristine's only champion was Kettridge, and she couldn't chance doing anything that might cause him to question his decision to sponsor her. Like commission a bad photographer without consulting him first.

As things stood, Gilberte was an unknown. Kristine was astute enough to realize this. She didn't yet have the social standing or the gravitas to recruit new artists. She wasn't recognized as a collector whose judgment had any value. She was an acquirer. She had to have Kittredge's (and Albright's) approval for any of her purchases to mean anything. Only if they approved of Gilberte would Gilberte's success be her success. (And only then would Gilberte's failure be Gilberte's failure: under these conditions, it wouldn't affect Kristine for more than a season.) So Kristine had everything to gain and little to lose. The only thing that might prevent her from triumphing completely would be Gilberte's betrayal of her. That is, if, after Kristine struck up the band and got it to play tribute to her darling, her darling then waltzed right away with someone else, leaving Kristine to wither on the wall.

Would that happen? Who could tell? To have the kind of success Gilberte was after you had to be an expert at manipulation. And it was becoming more and more obvious to me that Gilberte would manipulate and maneuver anybody she had to in order to achieve her goal. She was getting quite adept at it. She was dead set on earning this commission, and she was going to do everything she had to do to get it.

I didn't understand what made me hold my tongue about her behavior and where I could see it was leading her (a form of idolatry that entailed her compromising herself and, probably, her work). My conscience told me to speak to her, but my common sense told me not to meddle. I tried to justify my silence by falling back on a sort of teleological suspension of the ethical. That is, these days what exactly was ethical in the art world? How could I presume to know anything about it? I had my ideas, my opinions. But I wasn't an insider. How could I think about judging what was right and what was wrong for someone else? I couldn't. I could only remain leery of Gilberte. Leery as I had always been of people who played the game because they claimed otherwise they would be at a disadvantage. I would wait. I would see. I still believed that there were other people like me, people who had ideals or values they considered sacred: people who knew there were things they would not do. Maybe Gilberte was one of them.

◆

Finally, Kristine called. I passed the phone to Gilberte and removed myself to a polite distance, close enough to hear but far enough that it wouldn't appear I was listening. At any rate, there wasn't much to hear on Gilberte's end. Her conversation was a series of yeses punctuated by quick smiles. When she hung up, she said what I had already surmised:

—I got it.

—Congratulations, I said.

—Those bastards, she said.

—Which bastards? I asked.

— Kris said she called me at home and left a message with one of my roommates, but I never got it. Bastards, she repeated under her breath. She was furious. It was not the time for me to inquire where the appellation *Kris* had come from, or when, exactly, Gilberte had given Kristine her home phone number.

Her furor didn't last long. She brightened up almost immediately. This was what she had been waiting and hoping and dreaming about. More than likely she was already rehearsing interviews, deciding how to decline invitations, issue proclamations, pronounce opinions. Suddenly everything was possible.

Out of the blue, she asked me to join her for a celebratory supper. It was a touching gesture. Yet since it was only Kristine's promise ringing in her ears, I suggested that we wait until she had the profits in her pockets. She wouldn't hear of it.

She insisted, saying that all the times I had bought her coffee and bagels and pizza and soft drinks had saved her a fortune.

I'm rich, she said. She wouldn't take no for an answer, feeling, I supposed, that good fortune, like bad, had to be shared or its dimensions became blown out of proportion. I agreed to go.

♦

—I'm sick of this continent, Gilberte said as soon as drinks had been served. I picked up my glass.

—Congratulations, I said.

Gilberte thanked me. After our glasses clinked, I lit a cigarette and came back to her introductory remark, which had struck me as being a rather curious comment, as well as a disingenuous way to open a conversation.

—Have you been everywhere on it, or are you extrapolating from what you've sampled? I asked.

—No, not everywhere. But I think the places I haven't been are places I don't want to go. I mean, it doesn't take much to figure out that one place is almost the same as another place. You know: buildings, roads, shopping centers, people. I guess I'm extrapolating, she said, looking at me to see whether she had used the word correctly. Except New York, she continued. It's different here because everything is bigger, magnified, and the magnification makes a qualitative difference. That's why I came.

I shook my head to show her that I understood. I drank my vodka, took a drag off my cigarette, and picked up the menu. Gilberte began asking what she should order, telling me what she liked, what she didn't like, what she had eaten the last time she had been in a restaurant. Her logorrhea was beginning to annoy me. It seemed as though she had been talking nonstop since we left the store. I helped myself to another mouthful of vodka and hoped that Gilberte would start drinking too, and that perhaps the alcohol would sedate her some.

From behind my menu I thought I heard her say something about Kristine, but I didn't bother to ask her to repeat it. I had heard enough about Kristine. She had been the topic of conversation on our walk. I had hoped that our peripatetic dialogue would exorcise Kristine's presence and that when we entered the restaurant she would remain out of doors. But here she was, sitting down to dinner with us.

There wasn't anything else to say about Kristine, as far as I was concerned. Gilberte had apparently told me what she wanted me to know during our walk—namely, that she, Gilberte, wasn't being bought. I hadn't thought there was any question of this, didn't even see the point, but Gilberte stressed that she was still an independent agent. I couldn't help but wonder if she hadn't made some sort of concession to Kristine that she wasn't telling me about. I hinted this was the case. Gilberte assured me I was wrong. She had gone on to say, in a tone that was new to me and much more aggressive than I would have expected, that if Kristine had ideas about how the shoot should be done, she, Gilberte, planned to make hers prevail. She mused for a moment on the pros and cons of developing a reputation for being difficult. Then, in a daring move, she said that regardless of the consequences, she was going to do what she thought was right. She was confusing morals and aesthetics, or was about to. Or she was trying, in her own befuddled way, to discover if a moral compromise entailed an artistic one. As usual with Gilberte's method of discourse, I couldn't decide what she meant. (Often Gilberte, like many people, had something nagging at her but was incapable, out of laziness or intellectual cowardice, of articulating it in a form that would permit an answer.) Did she not really want the job but think she needed the publicity it would generate? Or was it that she, like me (and this would be too good to be true), didn't like Kristine and felt guilty about her conquest? Had she finally begun to think of the consequences of playing the game? Or had she been thinking of them all along, and only now that she had what she wanted were the ramifications becoming clear? This seemed doubtful. I had the feeling that she was only trying on different outlooks and attitudes (none of which she was as yet prepared to commit herself to) to see what they looked like, what response they might elicit if they were shown to the world at large. I didn't care for this at all. To show my displeasure I did nothing to encourage her, made no move to applaud her tentative decisions or suggest what alterations in her attitude might be necessary to fit the occasion.

Now I didn't want to hear another word about Kristine. If she was going to start in again, I was going to be angry. This was supposed to be a celebratory meal. I didn't want it turned into a strategy session. I didn't want to have to hear about plan A and plan B, or have to help map out a campaign to deal with her patroness. I realized that Gilberte was excited, as well as overwrought from waiting for Kristine's decision. I could see, too, that she was struck with stage fright, and whereas she had thought she knew all the lines that would be required of her, she was now beginning to acknowledge she didn't. She needed more rehearsal. I wasn't in the mood. I was cold and stern. I finished my double vodka, but it didn't put me at ease. I couldn't seem to relax. I sat with my back pressed into the chair, very straight, very stiff, my feet thrust as far back as possible so there would be no chance of contact, none of those little collisions in the dark that (in other circumstances) could be interpreted as preemptive strikes, tests to see how much resistance one would meet when the full-scale attack was launched.

She ordered us another round of drinks. She was irrepressible. Rather than inhibiting or preventing her from speaking, my reticence incited her. Gilberte talked. I drank. She returned to her theme of boredom with this country, with Americans, with our space and our time, especially with our time. I drank. I wanted to be numb and dumb (just like most Americans, according to Gilberte). To set myself apart from the general run of the mill that she was unmercifully castigating, however, I drew myself up and adopted what I took to be the attitude of an important person, one who has granted an interview to an insignificant slob. She didn't notice. She talked on. It was her youth, her youthfulness, the alcohol. I was becoming infatuated with her. I tried not to think about her breasts. I finished my second vodka. While studying the menu I heard Kristine's name yet again, then something about Gilberte's sisters and brother (two of one and one of the other), Americans (again), Mapplethorpe, California, New York, photography. She ate subjects up at a prodigious rate, notwithstanding the fact that she never managed to find the words she needed to describe them properly organized the first time, and whatever she said had to be rephrased and repeated. To a casual listener (which I was not), it might sound like she was further elucidating what she had just said, but she was only reiterating it in other words. Then she would change the subject.

After the waiter came and took our order, she asked me:

—How long have you been here?

—Where?

—In New York.

—Years, I said.

—Well, I'm here almost a year, she said, using the present tense when the present perfect was called for. I love it, she went on. You know, I hated it at first. Didn't hate it, but didn't love it as I do now. It was hard for me.

I asked her why, but she lost interest in this topic and was about to embark upon another one, when our salads were served. As soon as Gilberte commenced eating she ceased talking. I poured her a glass of wine. She managed to mumble thanks before closing her mouth around her fork, the sound of which, as it was withdrawn from between clenched teeth, was worse than the screech of chalk on a blackboard.

I refused to believe she didn't know one could talk during meals. Her near silence was probably due to some misguided parental instructions, or lack thereof. Or, incredibly, a lack of anything more to say. She did manage a few words, but the flow was nothing like before. And when the main course arrived, she set to it with a fury, seemingly oblivious of my presence.

Her table manners were surprisingly rudimentary. (Given her recent comprehensive attempt to refine her behavior, it seemed odd that the conventions governing this activity had been neglected.) For example, she ate her pasta with her head bent low over the plate, shoveling it into her mouth the way old men in Chinatown eat their rice. Curiously, I became entranced. Her whole approach to eating was childlike and innocent. I found it charming rather than appalling, although I must admit that if we had been in polite society I would have been embarrassed for her. Oddly, at the same time, she so inflamed my desire that I could have jumped over the table, dragged her to the floor and ravaged her.

By the time I snapped out of my trance and began eating my spaghetti, it was cold. The watery sauce had run off to the edges of the plate and the oil had coagulated into small pools. It reminded me of nothing so much as a wrung-out mop in a puddle of dirty water. I had wanted to go to my favorite Italian restaurant, but since it was Gilberte's treat she got to choose.

When she finished, I asked:

—Was it good?

—Not really, she said, then, with renewed vigor, began talking.

I ate. I listened more attentively now. I was already drunk. I found myself becoming more indulgent, more at ease. I let myself be entertained by her silliness—for she, too, was evidently feeling the effects of the alcohol. We laughed and giggled. Gilberte must have felt my newfound sympathy and openness seductive, for she began telling me things about herself that she had never before mentioned. The more personal these revelations became, the louder she proclaimed them. Whether she kept raising her voice because we were in a noisy public place and she was afraid she wouldn't be heard, or whether it was because she was drunk and had forgotten we were in a public place, I wasn't sure. I was inclined to believe the latter alternative when she began to slump in her chair. Then, going to light a cigarette, she missed the striking surface so many times that I had to take the matches and do it for her.

—Thanks. You know, you're great, she said.

I didn't know how to reply to this, so I didn't.

—Do you think this will be my break? she asked.

—I don't know. It could be.

—I want it to be, she said decisively.

—I hope it is.

—I think it will be, she said even more positively.

—Especially if the ad is published in the right places.

—Such as?

—Oh, *Details, Vanity Fair, Interview*. You know: magazines where everybody looks at the ads a lot.

—Is that where she's going to run it?

—That's what she said. It would be fantastic, wouldn't it?

—It would, I agreed.

—I mean, think about it. I'd probably get more work, could quit working in the store, buy a loft, have my own studio, hire an assistant, everything.

While I was finishing my drink, she explained what *everything* was. (That she was in the thrall of such banal desires shocked me a little. After all, she was supposed to be an artist.)

The waiter brought the check. I whisked it off the table. Gilberte began to protest, saying it had been her invitation, but I insisted that she wait until she had everything, since for the moment she still had very little. She acquiesced, with the condition that I allow her to leave the tip. Which I did.

In the street, we passed an awkward moment. Gilberte was drunk and had no plans. She asked me what I wanted to do. Noting that it was already pretty late, I said I was going to go home and go to bed.

—Me too, then, she said. I agonized over the *then* for a moment, but only until she put her arms around me and gave me a light kiss on the cheek and a hug, which I returned. Then she scampered away, turning before she had gone very far, to say:

—Thanks.

I watched her go down the street. Then I went off in search of a phone booth. I called Ronnie. He was in bed. I lied and said I had a cab waiting on his corner and would he come down? He whined, said he was already half-asleep. I told him to get dressed and come down. I swore we'd go right to bed and that I'd make him breakfast in the morning and he gave in. I hung up and caught a cab.

♦

Aside from the first few days after I hired her, Gilberte never arrived at work on time. She arrived in her own time, which differed from the rest of the world's by about ten minutes.

Ten minutes wasn't anything to get upset about. It wasn't the ten minutes that upset me, it was the idea. That is, Gilberte's tardiness showed me that though she acknowledged there were such things as deadlines, schedules, and working hours, she would never fully submit to them.

It was, I admit, partly my fault, since at first the ten minutes was bearable. I wasn't always on time either, and giving someone five to ten minutes' leeway for unforeseen events was natural. Gilberte soon stretched five to ten minutes into fifteen. Because of my leniency, she obviously began to think that when she arrived ten minutes late she was on time. It was easy to understand that if, by your own reckoning, when you arrived ten minutes late you were on time, then when you arrived fifteen minutes later than you should have, you were only five minutes late. Now, who was going to complain about your being five minutes late? I planned to.

The day I chose to bring up her tardiness Gilberte probably thought she merited her extra minutes, since the previous afternoon she had gone to Kristine's boutique to take the pictures for the ad. A day with Kristine was enough to make anyone want to a little extra shut-eye the following morning. But it wouldn't stand up as an excuse in my court. Of course, I didn't plan on holding a trial. That wouldn't serve any purpose. No, I didn't plan to be harsh or accusatory. I'd say something like, *we open at ten-thirty*. That should be sufficient.

She arrived at five minutes to eleven, at the same time as the first customer, for whom she held the door. As soon as the door closed behind her, Gilberte began trying to explain, mutely, behind the customer's back, why she was late. Her demeanor and the shrug of her shoulders expressed her exasperation, as if she had experienced an entire morning of minor mishaps, of circumstances beyond her control: like not finding the clean clothes she had planned to wear (she was wearing the same blouse she had on yesterday), like someone calling just as she was out the door, like missing the train that would have brought her on time, like opening a door only to end up holding it for someone else to go through first. What else could you do except what she had done: give in, accept it, shrug your shoulders, and call it one of those days? I might have concurred were it not for the fact that this was just the way in which we had gone from ten-to-fifteen minutes late, and I wasn't about to have it jump to twenty. That would be abusive.

The customer asked me a question. Gilberte went to the basement to deposit her bag and camera. I answered the woman quickly, sending her off by herself to find what she was looking for, because I wanted to be free to have a word with Gilberte when she came up.

As soon as she reappeared, I signaled that I wanted to see her. She was detained by the customer, who, despite my help, seemed to be having difficulties. I heard her say that she had found only one of the two translations she was looking for. It seemed that she had located the recently published translation of the work in question (the one she had asked me about), but she also wanted to see an older translation, so she could compare them before deciding which to buy. One of them had been praised in a recent review in the *New York Review of Books*, but unfortunately, she had forgotten which one, and now she was wondering if Gilberte remembered, since the woman was sure that Gilberte had read the review too. Gilberte said neither yes or no but moved the little stepladder near to the wall, climbed up, and pulled from the overstock section the earlier translation. This find spurred the woman's memory and she began telling Gilberte what she recalled about the review. Gilberte, as usual, listened distractedly. However, also as usual, no matter how inattentive she was, she maintained the illusion that she was taking in every word, a deception she made believable with her smile and her practiced enthusiasms, her *yes, yes, yes*. (Conversations with customers were the only times I ever heard her say yes. Otherwise she was content to utter its less formal substitute, yeah.) The repeated use of this word incisively enunciated, had the effect of a period at the end of a sentence, one that simultaneously capped others' thoughts and encouraged them to go on.

This woman had a lot to say. She debated with herself aloud and at length, Gilberte looked at me and asked, with raised eyebrows, *will this never end?* Patience was a necessity when you worked in retail. I nodded and turned away. I didn't want the woman to see us communicating behind her back because it would reduce her status from customer to eavesdropper.

In the window's reflection I saw Gilberte take one of the books and thumb through it, giving it a tactile reading, for effect. She looked over the woman's shoulder again, evidently saw me looking at her, and tried to draw my attention, but I wouldn't turn around to face her. My chief reason for ignoring her was that I didn't want to compromise my case any more than I had. Because I had acknowledged her, it wouldn't be so simple to reproach her for being late. Moreover, I had wanted to say, we start work at ten-thirty. When she had first come in, this would have been immediately comprehensible. Now the delay would necessitate launching into a long exposition about how she was always late (which she could, by her definition, contest) and about how, recently, she had begun coming in later than usual.

—I'll just have to buy them both, the lady said. She walked toward the cash register, followed by a very bemused-looking Gilberte. While Gilberte rang up the books the woman rambled on about how it would be better to have both translations anyway, since one translator was likely to pick up a nuance that the other had missed, there was no so such thing as a perfect translation, etc. Gilberte kept up the small talk that soothed and comforted customers the way a mother's cooing comforts her baby. The woman thoroughly enjoyed it, and it was only with difficulty that she managed to say good-bye.

—Have you got a smoke? Gilberte asked me. I gave her one.

—I was in such a hurry that I must have left mine home, she explained. I couldn't have asked for a more perfect entry.

—If you hurried a little more you might get here on time, I said.

—I was almost on time, she said.

—We open at ten-thirty, I said.

—What time did I arrive?

—Close to eleven.

She made a face. The expression I read on it didn't seek to deny my assertion. In fact, it seemed to express sympathy with my findings, while at the same time revealing a sort of helplessness as to what to do about them.

She set her cigarette in the ashtray and used the glass in the door as a mirror in which to inspect herself. After running her fingers through her hair, she came back to the counter and picked up her cigarette.

—I try to be on time. You know, there are people who are always late just like there are people who are always on time. She said it as if she were announcing a scientific fact.

—If you tried harder you could be one of those who are always on time, I said. I don't think the difference between the two is biological. It's mental. It's a habit.

—Do you think? she asked.

—Yes, I said.

—Maybe you're right. I always thought it was something you were born with, you know, like an instinct, and in some people it worked and in some people it didn't.

—It's not, I said curtly. Using her childish belief to involve me in a pseudoscientific conversation was actually a sophisticated attempt to play dumb. Sometimes Gilberte loved nothing so much as to listen to a lecture. She would encourage me to try to clarify what for her were cloudy concepts, and pushed me to make pellucid what to her were obscure notions. I liked doing this. But at times like this, her real aim was to transform my dissatisfaction with her into satisfaction with myself. She knew that once she said she understood, it was my prowess as a pedagogue she was flattering. Having accepted such flattery, how could I stay angry? Carried away by my own enthusiasm (my egoism), I would be too far from my anger for it to have any further effect. Neat trick, *n'est-ce pas?* Unfortunately for her, I had become wise to it rather quickly, which was not to say that I didn't still fall for it. This morning it wasn't going to work. I said:

—I think if you tried, you could be here on time. To this she could only say:

—I'll try.

She snuffed out her cigarette. I realized how peevish and petty I was being. I wondered whether my professional zeal in pursuing this matter was not a manifestation of some deeper desire of mine to exercise control over her. It was my pitiful way of exerting whatever power I could, of competing with Kristine.

Gilberte lit another cigarette. When she chained-smoked like this, she was upset.

—Well? she said, trying to adopt a tone that scolded as well as encouraged.

I looked at her, slightly chagrined.

—Aren't you going to ask me how it went?

—How did it go?

—Really great. Her demeanor brightened.

—What did you finally do? I asked.

—You'll see, she said, smiling enigmatically.

—When?

—As soon as I have a chance to edit the contact sheets.

I knew that smile of hers and knew there was no way I was going to get her to give me any hint of what she had done. I would have to wait.

♦

As I turned the corner I saw Gilberte leaning against the gate that protected the store's window and door from the inclemencies of street life. Her back was pressed firm and flat against the metal. Her arms hung straight at her sides. Her right hand intermittently shuttled a cigarette to and from her mouth. Catching sight of me, she flicked the cigarette into the street and pushed herself away from the gate. She drew up her lean and leggy figure, pivoted, and faced me like a gunfighter ready to draw.

—That's three in a row, she fired off.

—Keep up the good work, I said.

—I've been up since seven.

I opened the gate. After turning off the alarm I opened the door and collected the mail that was on the floor.

—Who was it this morning? I asked.

Gilberte shared a loft with five or six (it was never clear) people. According to her, she got along with everybody, but nobody else got along at all. There were constant fights about how many guests each person could have, and how long they could stay. Currently, there were two or three people who were friends of friends of someone who used to live there and they had been floating around the loft for months. These were the bastards who didn't give her phone messages. But the chief cause of unrest was scheduling conflicts created by the two roommates who were musicians. The guitar player worked a day shift as a waiter, while the synthesizer player worked a night shift as a cabdriver. In their off hours they practiced their music, which meant the other roommates rarely had a moment's silence. About which they complained. (Gilberte wasn't particularly bothered by the noise because she live all the way in the back, under the staircase, and was more insulated than the others.) But, because they couldn't find a solution amenable to all parties, the scheduling problem remained intractable and generated a lot of acrimony and tension, affecting everybody's day-to-day life in the loft. Adding to this problem were the squatters, who were always, it seemed, up to no good. They were always tying up the bathroom, the telephone, the kitchen, or someone else's space. Screaming matches between them and the so-called *real roommates* were becoming more and more frequent, Gilberte reported. The previous morning she had been rudely awakened by a slamming door and an endless tirade about a about a missing tube of toothpaste.

—I don't know how much longer I can take it, Gilberte said.

—Why don't you move out?

—For the same reason I moved in. I couldn't find anyplace else to live. Anyway, I'd probably end up with more kooks. At least now I know these a little. I don't know. I'll move when I can afford someplace of my own, I guess. Anyway, the painter's nice. He's got a seven-foot python in his room. A snake. Did I tell you?

—No.

—Yeah. I watched him feed it. He gives it live white rats.

I didn't want to hear about the python's dietary habits. Moreover, it was time to begin work, which I let her know with a look, and then a nod to prod her into action. I began to make the bank for the day, counting out the change and separating the paper money, placing each denomination in its compartment in the cash register. Gilberte began rushing around the

store with a large broom, scattering more dirt than she was col-
lecting, yet still managing to sweep up all the cigarette butts
and gum wrappers.

—Don't forget the trash, I reminded her. And the boxes
in the back have to go out, I said. One of these days you could
try the vacuum cleaner, I added for good measure.

She didn't answer me. She didn't like performing these
menial tasks, but they were part of her job and there was no
way around them. I lent a hand occasionally, but more often
than not the paperwork kept me busy. If I didn't regularly help
her house-clean, I did help her perform the most tedious and
agonizing job in the store: re-alphabetizing books. There was
nothing worse. Having to think *sc, sch, se, sea* was sheer punishment. Shelving a new shipment of books was a pleasure
compared to the time we spent recovering and re-alphabetizing
misplaced books. And this task had to be performed continu-
ously because customers didn't always put a book back where
they found it. A moment's distraction, a tug at the elbow from
a companion, or a glance at the clock was enough to cause the
book to be replaced approximately where it had been, say one
book away from its original location. This minor displacement
was sufficient to encourage the next customer who inspected
it (who would already have found it un-alphabetized) to feel
absolutely no compunction about sticking it back in the first
available niche. Then it was as good as gone. Which often
meant the loss of a sale when another customer came in looking for the same book. There was nothing more annoying than
searching for a book for a customer and not finding it, only
to find it later when searching for another book for another
customer. Entropy was our biggest problem. To keep it at bay,

it was necessary to devote at least an hour a day to recovering and re-alphabetizing books.

As soon as Gilberte finished her tasks, she came to the counter and asked me what I wanted from the deli. I loved this ritual of ours. We performed it at least twice a day, in the morning when we opened and then later in the afternoon, and sometimes around dinnertime as well. Now, since she had (for three days) been coming in on time, she seemed more anxious than ever to rush right out. She told me she had had to eliminate her breakfast to arrive at the indicated hour. She was famished.

She leaned over the counter very prettily, just as I liked, and tried to get me to tell her what I wanted. This was the best part. I preferred her to lean (as she was doing) rather than sit next to me, because we were experiencing excruciatingly hot days and Gilberte wore the flimsiest and loosest of tops, with large openings for her arms and an almost obscene degree of décolletage—which at almost every turn she made permitted me to glimpse her milky cleavage and the purplish-umber aureoles surrounding her nipples. Thus, I took my time deciding. I went through the mail leisurely, interjecting a comment about what I read or about what she said. I gave her a pamphlet and a folder to read and took away one that she had. Generally, this was our time for kidding and clowning. I enjoyed it and I think she did too, because it delayed her departure, which would delay her return, which would delay the moment work finally began (*work* work, as she called it).

I told her I'd settle for a lime Frozfruit. She looked at me skeptically, but I assured her that was what I wanted.

Before she left, she opened her bag and took out a large manila envelope.

—Here, she said, putting it on the counter. You can look at these while I'm gone.

She left without saying what was in the envelope. I was just opening it when the phone rang. It was Kristine. I told her Gilberte was out and, no, as far as I knew she wasn't coming over there to see her. She asked me whether I had seen the pictures, and I reported I was just going to look at them.

—Oh, she exclaimed. I'm jealous. You must tell me what you think of them, she commanded. The majestic *must* had all the force of an interjection. I'm dying to know what you think, she said. Which was patent hyperbole, since her dying to know was the passive version of I would kill to know, and she would do no such thing. I might lose my good humor if I had to listen to much more of this. I asked whether she would like Gilberte to call her back.

—Do, yes, she said. I'm here all morning.

We parted politely. I opened the envelope. What I saw amazed me. One look was sufficient to convince me Gilberte was more cunning than I had given her credit for. A less astute person might not have seen what a coup it would be to use her employer as an employee, but Gilberte had seen it. She had done it. She had used Kristine as a model.

I scanned the contact sheets. Kristine leered out at me in black and white. She was so happy she couldn't conceal her pleasure. It glinted in her eyes. Wisely, Gilberte had taken quite a few shots of her wearing a wide-brimmed hat, pulled down rakishly low, covering most of her face, either directly, with the brim, or indirectly, with a shadow. However, no matter what tricks of the trade Gilberte tried, she couldn't hide the fact Kristine didn't model well. She simply couldn't control herself. She didn't have the aplomb to look convincingly sexy, sophisticated, or threatening in the camera's eye. The hired model who shared the shots had it all over her. It was clear she was a professional. She knew how to project, how to empty herself. In her expressions and postures she didn't show herself but showed the photographer's instructions: like all professional models, she created a vacuum. The vacancy permitted the viewer's desire to accost the image without worrying about resistance, refusal, or rejection. And whereas the model with whom Kristine was paired could be tough or be tender, Kristine could only be herself.

The photos weren't extraordinary. Overall, they fell into the genre of advertising that mixed violence and elegance so a conservative person would find them just this side of risqué and a liberal would find them passé. However humdrum the shots were, the masterstroke was the decision to use Kristine as a model. Recognition was something Kristine was longing for. If the only immediate way to obtain it was by posing in an ad for her store, who cared? These days not only ex-sports and movie stars sang paeans for products. Company presidents, chief executive officers, lawyers, and doctors, entrepreneurs of all stripes were all dying to get into the act. With this ad Kristine would enter the ranks of celebrity hawkers. As soon as the picture was published, her name would be on the lips of countless people. She would gain a certain notoriety. She would owe it all to Gilberte.

—Well? Gilberte said when she came in.

—Kristine called.

— I'm sure she'll call again, she predicted. What did you think? she wanted to know.

—Marvelous idea, I said.

—I thought so.

—Why haven't you shown them to Kristine yet?

—I want to edit them first. I think there's plenty of fine shots there. There are a couple super shots.

I hadn't seen anything I would have categorized as super, but Gilberte was convinced, and I didn't dissent because I didn't want her to try to convince me.

—Look, she said. She took the sheets away from me and began going through them, explaining them, praising their stylistic purity. She adopted a pompous tone, which was accompanied by perfunctory gestures that were supposed to convince me she couldn't possibly be mistaken in her evaluation of her work. She pointed and with her index finger drew pictures of the pictures, describing lines in the air, showing me the balance, the harmony.

—They work, she concluded in much the same way a geometry student might write QED at the end of a problem she had solved. Or as an art dealer might say after explaining the meaning of a work.

The phone rang.

—It's Kristine, I said.

Gilberte gave me a funny look but answered the call. I instantly knew I was right from the tone of Gilberte's voice.

◆

Walking aimlessly, I found myself on the comer of Houston and First. I wanted to go farther afoot, but I also wanted to be near a neighborhood where I could go for a drink when I was ready. Now that I was ready, I found myself on the frontier of the East Village, a slum under siege by upwardly mobile rich kids. I couldn't think of a single bar in the area where I would feel comfortable having a drink. So, I began picking my way through the garbage on Houston, heading west. I came to a standstill at Broadway. I couldn't decide where to go. I lit a cigarette and waited for the light to change. Two fierce-looking boys approached me and asked for money. I refused by not answering. A tense moment passed while they thought what to do next. Then one of them called me a fascist and the other one spat at my feet. They waited for me to do something. I started across the street, against the light. You couldn't do otherwise in such situations. You couldn't stoop to pick up the proverbial gauntlet. If you responded to street provocations, you dropped immediately to the perpetrators' level—which was most likely foreign territory to you—giving them such an advantage it became impossible for you to win. You had to demonstrate by your restraint that no communication had taken place, that nothing had transpired (or at most that you had been subjected to an unfamiliar noise), and move on. However, something had happened. Your body registered the aggression. And the consequences of such stimuli were deleterious to one's health. The daily recurrence of events like this, which required you to pretend something was not happening while you were trying to cope with it (one origin of feelings of anomie, and perhaps even of schizophrenia), was one of the reasons I was always reconsidering my commitment to living in the city.

Now I wanted to be off the streets as soon as possible. I spotted the One Fifth tower and decided to go there for a drink. I walked as quickly as I could, trying not to break out into a sweat. Once inside the door at the restaurant, I nodded to the bouncer. He looked me up and down and nodded, indicating I could proceed to a podium where a girl stood taking reservations over the telephone. In the cool air I began to feel lighter, more agile, less constrained. The atmosphere was animated yet suffused with a refined, civilized calm.

Smiling at the girl as soon as she raised her eyes from the reservation book, I pointed to the bar. She let me pass. I ordered a dirty vodka martini, very dry, up, stirred, with two olives. Using the mirrors, I scrutinized the crowd. No one very attractive or very unattractive was anywhere to be seen. I spotted two or three men and women with dark tans, which their white shirts and blouses set off like jewels. The women turned and turned about, trying to make sure they were getting even exposure to the crowd. Other than these few dark cynosures, there was no one striking. I moved away from the bar after being served and found a niche next to one of the pilasters, in which I was less likely to be jostled by people pushing to get to the bar and by people headed to or from the rear dining room. I gulped down my drink unceremoniously, then retrieved one of the olives and ate it with relish.

In no time, I was working on my second drink. Which was wrong. I shouldn't drink so much so fast. It wasn't prudent. Nor was it sensible to drink to try to put someone out of your mind since that can only be done through an act of will: drinking showed you had conceded, that you were too weak to act. Moreover, after the alcohol did its work, you wallowed in the very thoughts you had counted on escaping. Then you tried to escape self-recrimination for thinking them by telling yourself you were drunk and couldn't help it.

Well, I wasn't going to do that. I was going to drink—I ordered another one—and I was going to put Gilberte completely out of my mind. I was going to absolutely refuse to think about her, although it was thinking about her that had forced me to flee my loft.

I took the drink back to my corner and took a big swallow. Recently, these vodka martinis had become my favorite drink.

Gilberte was not the cause of my problem. She may have made my problem appear more acute, but my problem turned around a larger issue. It was this: once you reached a certain age alone, not bound by a formal agreement or a long-term understanding or love—you panicked. The fear that you would continue to know what at times was unbearable loneliness created emotional chaos. Now and again it could wreak havoc in even the most well-adjusted person. This could occur regardless of whether you were involved with someone (for example, I was involved with Ronnie). In fact, up until now, my relationship with Ronnie had been instrumental in keeping panic pretty much at bay. I was grateful for his companionship for that reason. Nevertheless, our liaison was based on nothing more than a constant conjunction of *getting together*, one day at a time, and no long-term commitment was possible (at least on my part), because though he did fulfill a need for companionship, he did not, he could not, comprehend me. I needed both: for me companionship and comprehension were the two prerequisites of love. If Ronnie and I had stayed together (and that was putting it strongly) for almost a year now, it was mainly because it was convenient for us. My panicking was not precluded because our understanding could at any moment become inconvenient.

I was emotionally unfulfilled and still hankering after true love. I was beginning to feel my tie to Ronnie was impeding my progress toward my goal—happiness—since my satisfaction with the status quo didn't push me to change my predicament.

Only on occasion did I feel an urgent need for something different, for someone, well, better suited to my needs than Ronnie. Then, being rather lackadaisical, I would transform, by means of a libidinal calculus, my craving for emotional closeness into a sensual need. I substituted sex for love.

Sometimes things were easily arranged this way. Other times the distress was so acute that carnal pleasure could not relieve the pain. The pain caused me to become apathetic, anhedonic, depressed. In pain, I would stop living, stop feeling, remain in my own hermetic world. I would work and sleep and overwork and oversleep, until I became so exhausted that I hadn't the strength to be exhausted. At some point I would muster enough energy to go to the gym. I would be hungry after working out. I would eat. My senses would return. I would go out and drink and be among people, live again. And wait again. For the pattern repeated itself. There was nothing I could do about it. Believe me, I did everything I could do. Over the years I had managed to tame my shifts and swings of mood, and they were no longer as violent or debilitating as they had been.

Now I was going to begin babbling about Gilberte. Any moment. I could feel it. I was getting aroused thinking about her. There was something about her. I wanted her. There it was. That was it. Even though I had promised myself I wasn't going to admit it. I ordered another martini.

I carried my drink from the bar and found my place against the wall. I took a mouthful. This was one of the best vodka martinis I had tasted that I hadn't made myself. I was happy I had come.

The music stopped. I hadn't been listening to it, but now that it stopped a void lingered in the air until the general level of conversation rushed in to fill it. I sipped my drink. I was ready to go. Normally, after three or four drinks I had to go. It was either that or, with each additional drink, I would become more and more detached from my surroundings until I was no longer there. Or rather until I no longer knew where I was.

The revolving door made my head spin a little, but as soon as I was on the street I began walking west. After only a few steps I began to sweat. I felt woozy. I had to stop. I hadn't felt drunk indoors, only mildly intoxicated, high. Now I remembered. It had been cold inside and in cold rooms you felt the alcohol less. The cold didn't deactivate or diminish the alcohol's power, it merely held it in suspension and then released it in the heat.

I was under the influence. I breathed in and out, slowly, steadily, and then set off again. I walked without hesitation, without stumbling or staggering. I wouldn't let myself stagger. You had to always look aware and alert in the street. Otherwise your plight was sensed by the street people. Their abilities to locate an incapacitated individual were as keen as a shark's. I maintained my posture. I kept my hands at my sides. I took long strides and set my feet firmly on the pavement while remaining as natural-looking as I could manage. It was just as important not to overdo it and become a caricature of yourself as it was to move naturally. Not that my normal mode of movement was natural. In a sense, no movement other than a plunge to the ground is natural, but usually I managed to exert over my movements the necessary force and sufficient control to resist gravity with grace. Tonight, the grace was missing, I could tell. It didn't matter. The balance was there.

I crossed Fifth. Having performed such a feat without incident, I relaxed a little. I was wrong to do so. Eighth Street was one of the most treacherous streets in lower Manhattan. Countless pedestrians used it as the main thoroughfare for traveling back and forth between the East and West Village. Because it is a major artery, there was a very high concentration of lunatics, drunks, religious fanatics, toughs, punks, thugs, bag men and women. It ranked in my mind as one of the worst streets in the city (along with Fourteenth and Twenty-third and Forty-second, although on the latter you can at least see the full spectrum of life in New York, from squalor to splendor). I had seen incredible things on Eighth Street: people being beaten and robbed, store windows kicked out, people in cars chasing people onto the sidewalk, people on the sidewalk pelting cars with bottles and cans, people in cars throwing firecrackers at people on the sidewalk, people fucking in cars. These same incidents occurred on every other Manhattan street, but the frequency with which they happened here was what made this street notable. In the summer, the numbers of these incidents multiplied in direct proportion to the rise in temperature and humidity. More people were on the streets in the summer than in the winter. Poor people in particular lived half their lives in the street rather than spend them cooped up in their cramped quarters. People (in general, not just the poor) tended to wear fewer garments in the summer. I was convinced this change in wardrobe partly accounted for the more aggressive behavior manifested in the summer. The multiple layers of garments people donned in the winter straitjacket violence to some degree. It was well known there were fewer muggings in winter than in summer. Though people complained about the cold, it had its good points. The cold was disagreeable, but it was never offensive. Heat was offensive. It was insulting. It soaked you, made you sweat day in, day out without respite.

People resented this. They became angry, and their anger was often vented at the slightest provocation. Accidental contact, a misunderstood word, or a questionable intonation was likely to push someone over the brink. The excessive, often brutal responses came from people who had gone over the brink. The violence provoked by, often, only minor affronts was frequently aimed not (directly) at the individual who committed them, but at the oppressive climate in general, with which the victim was felt to have conspired.

I crossed Sixth Avenue and headed down Christopher Street. I hated summer in the city. I didn't like the heat. I didn't like the sounds. I didn't like the smells. I didn't like the sights (especially all that teeming humanity, all that exposed flesh). My lack of sufficient funds for a summer-long vacation made it impossible for me to go away for the entire season. Up until the time I finally spent the last penny of a small inheritance from my grandparents, I regularly went away in the summer. When the money ran out, I would go on short jaunts to the country or to the seaside. But returning to the city after a weekend away was too ghastly. Coming into Manhattan through the Midtown Tunnel was like surfacing under a fetid tropical terrarium: everything black and sticky and suffocating and noisome.

Oddly, I didn't think I would be happy living in another city. It was either here or the country. Yet, as much as I was enamored of clean, pure air and English-speaking people, I wasn't seriously thinking of moving out to exurbia. It was a thought that came to me now and again, a fantasy. I still viewed New York as an escape from the eternal return of nature. I still needed that escape. As much as I found to decry, I exulted in the chaos. Here there was no pattern, nothing you had to fit into or conform to, no grand plan that repeated itself. Nobody could control the city and nobody could control what you did in it. That was why I liked it. Why I could live in it.

There was a screamer at the feet of General Sheridan.

At Seventh Avenue I came to a stop. I had to decide what to do. I could go home or go on. If I went home, I wouldn't do anything. My power of concentration was weakened, gone. I could barely keep control of my thoughts, which meant I'd never be able to keep control of someone else's. That meant reading was out. The most I would do was watch television. Or listen to the stereo. Sleep. Or eat. I hadn't yet eaten. I didn't want to eat at home. And I didn't feel like going someplace for dinner. If I went on, I'd go right to the Ramrod. Or to the river and cruise the docks. It was too early to go home. I'd go on.

I crossed Seventh. There was a throng of men on the corner in front of the cigar store. They were on the lookout, waiting for men from other areas of the city to arrive here, at the frontier of the West Village. They hoped they would have first choice from among the hordes headed west. And there were hordes. A regular stampede of men moving crosstown. They swished by me under the pouring heat, without shirts or with the minimum of what one could call a shirt. All around me, gleaming, sweaty muscle rippled whenever an eye alighted on it. Traveling en masse were men with arms and legs clothed in leather bands and studded collars. In tight jeans and tight T-shirts. And all kinds of hats: sailor hats, gestapo hats, cowboy hats, leather aviator hats, Greek fisherman hats. Every man was on the prowl. Hungry. Hunting. I could see in their eyes the undernourished stares that stemmed from insatiable appetites. It gave them a wild, desperate aspect. There were crowds of them everywhere. Tonight, I was one of the crowd.

I went, as I predicted, right to the Ramrod. Inside it was even hotter and more crowded and rowdy than it was on the street. It smelled hideous. Marijuana and cigarette smoke and traces of amyl nitrite laced the air, combined with the smell of perspiration and stale alcohol and piss and that curious odor of places that are never properly cleaned so when they reach a certain temperature they begin to sweat themselves and give off a rich, acrid aroma, a combination of all the rotten and rotting ingredients that coat the walls, the floor, the ceiling, the bar, the chairs—everything.

People were pressed tight against the bar. I couldn't get near it. Using my height to advantage, I caught the bartender's eye and held it long enough to place an order, a vodka on the rocks—this wasn't the place to order a martini. He acknowledged me, but he was busy and I had to wait at least five minutes to be served. My refreshment paid for, I had to twist and turn to release myself from the crowd that held me in its grip. When I reached the far wall I was bathed in sweat.

I smiled at a couple of people I thought I recognized but discouraged them from approaching me by lifting my glass to my mouth after each greeting. I didn't want to talk to anybody. I wanted to look around. In the tenebrous light and the blinding noise I couldn't see very well. Just a taste of my drink made my head buzz. The pushing and shoving and coming and going didn't help either. It was like being at sea on a small boat. I was being rocked every which way. I began to feel vertiginous. I went outside, taking my glass with me.

I turned the corner and walked up West Street and found a car to lean against. Farther up, I saw some transvestites trying to hustle a truck driver. Cars and motorcycles and trucks roared by. I decided I wasn't much better off out here, except the air was a little fresher and it wasn't as hot. Lights from buildings in New Jersey glimmered through the mist hanging over the river. Suddenly I had a terrific urge to relieve myself. I set my glass next to the car tire, walked over to the wall of the nearest building, found a recess, and pissed. I felt better immediately.

I downed the remains of my drink and hopped up on the car's fender. Pretty boys passed. I smiled at some and some smiled back but I didn't look after them to see whether they turned around. I wasn't in the mood for cruising. Until an extraordinarily good-looking boy came along. He was wearing red high-heeled cowboy boots (and walked with a delicious twist to his hips), a tight white T-shirt, tight white jeans whose belt loops held a thin red belt with a dainty gold buckle. His pants were so tight that for all practical purposes the belt was superfluous. In fact, the only practical purpose the belt served was to mark the difference between the texture of the shirt and the texture of the pants and to delineate his waist, and more importantly, to excite and titillate the way a simple patch of cloth placed over a strategic site on an otherwise naked body will. It was a bit too much. Too fetching. (I could never have worn such an outfit.) I smiled at him. He smiled back. I turned to look. I saw he had stopped two cars down and mounted the fender, just like me. We began exchanging looks. His look led me to guess that despite his youth this charmer had already passed from faun to satyr. There was, however, much of the faun still there, especially in the way he posed and inclined his head. He liked me, I could tell. I liked him, but I didn't move, and since it was obvious he expected me to move first, we sat and looked at each other. He extracted a pack of cigarettes that was rolled in the sleeve of his T-shirt and began searching for matches. He jumped off the car, and for a moment I thought: this is it, he's coming to me. But he didn't. The boy stopped a passerby and took a light off his cigarette. They chatted and it seemed the boy was going to wander off with his newfound friend. His gambit worked. When he looked at me again, I let him know I was interested.

He came to me as soon as the other had gone. He leaned against the car, next to me. I didn't say anything right away because I didn't have anything to say and had only communicated with him because I had been afraid of losing him before I could decide whether I wanted him. I lit a cigarette. It must have been out of nervousness that I took too big an inhalation. I coughed violently and brought up some phlegm, which I discreetly deposited in the street.

—Who was that, darling? the boy asked. Those were his first words. I looked at him and smiled and ran my hand through his thick brown hair. Amazing! At one time I was fanatical about boys like this. Absolutely addicted. I had sought out boys who exaggerated their boorishness and coarseness to such a point it seemed to be an exotic, enchanting quality. I feasted on them. I had been an ogre: I would hide my breeding and sensibility and drop to their level to revel with them. God, it was heaven! A real release. Total mindlessness of the sort I achieved now only by the dumb repetition of pumping iron, or sometimes by drinking. Eventually, of course, I had grown tired of these encounters. In the end, I began to find the boys revolting. Worse, I began to disgust myself.

I had given up this species of boy so long ago that I now found this one incredibly seductive. Especially since he was such a beauty. His sleek, svelte, muscular body was perfection. I was drooling.

We talked for a while, and then I suggested we go get a drink somewhere. He hesitated when I said where, for the place had a bad reputation, and he didn't want to catch anything, and besides, he pointed out, they probably wouldn't let him in wearing white. I told him that with me he had nothing to worry about (medically) and we should go see about whether they would let him in or not. If worse came to worst, he could always disrobe beforehand. He still seemed indecisive. I jumped off the car and yanked him after me, pulling him close to me, promising him I would buy him a drink. He nipped my ear. Anyway, if we couldn't get in there, I said, we'd go somewhere else. We'd find someplace, even, if it came to that, my place.

♦

I started and completed one circuit after another, plodding from the front windows to the back windows, again and again, unable to break out of this eddy. Ashes from my cigarette fell to the floor. I pressed them into the wood, which, like hot, dry terrain, absorbed them as if they were drops of rain. It was good for the wood. Ashes nourished the wood just as they nourished the carpet. What was good for the carpet had to be good for the parquet.

I guessed Gilberte and Kristine had finished their drinks. Probably they were waiting for their salads, talking idly. I could imagine Kristine stirring the ice in her glass, pensively studying Gilberte while the latter explained a facet of her work. Lately Kristine wanted Gilberte with her all the time. They were becoming fast friends.

Gilberte told me, vaguely, what they discussed when they met: everything. That's what she said. I asked her to be specific and tell me what *everything* meant because I was insanely curious. She claimed she couldn't remember everything. She gave me epigrams, quotes and quips she thought I would enjoy. Never the subject or theme around which the conversation had turned. I'm sure she thought I would be delighted with what she offered because it came from such renowned places as Le Cirque, La Grenouille, Odeon, The Quilted Giraffe, The Four Seasons. (It was unbelievable: Gilberte, who hadn't had money for a second piece of pie at the Dirty Dollar Diner, was now wined and dined at some of the top restaurants in New York.) I wasn't delighted. What she shared with me were the dregs and the surfeit of their conversation, the things she could repeat. They had a that-would-be-so-good-to-repeat-to-someone quality. I wasn't just someone. Moreover, I didn't care whether she repeated these things to me or not. I couldn't deduce anything from what she told me, or at least, nothing I was interested in. I was interested in learning whether they had lit each other's cigarettes, how Gilberte had looked at Kristine and how Kristine had looked at Gilberte, what they said during the silent moments, the tone of their voices when they were talking, and other incidences of intimacy Gilberte was keeping from me because they amounted to her evaluation of how her conquest of Kristine was proceeding, which she wasn't ready to make public.

I was driving myself crazy trying to guess how much progress Gilberte had made in seducing Kristine. The two of them had established a rapport that allowed them to feel comfortable in each other's company. It was obvious something akin to genuine friendship was blossoming between them. There was something in their girlish giddiness when they were together and when they talked on the phone. They had found each other. But found what, exactly? Were they soulmates? Did they share the same tastes? Outlooks? Beliefs? The most I could get out of Gilberte with a direct question on this topic was something to the effect that Kristine was very interested in her now.

I didn't doubt it. Gilberte's ad for the boutique had been a success. It created a stir when it came out. It was still, according to Kristine, a lively subject of conversation wherever she went. The ad hadn't brought Gilberte any other business so far. However, Allbright was impressed enough to start talking her up, and he had persuaded Kettridge to agree to take a more serious look at her work. Between Kristine and Allbright and Kettridge, another commission was bound to materialize. Which would give Gilberte's career the boost it needed to take off.

Determined to stop pacing, I came to a halt in the kitchen and poured myself a drink. I shouldn't have, but I did. I sipped it slowly, and then, slowly, almost against my will, I began moving again, falling into the same path I had been following most of the evening.

I was upset because during the last week Gilberte had begun not only to feed me morsels from her conversations with Kristine but to stuff me with tales from her private life which up until now had remained mostly secret. This started the night we had our celebratory dinner, during which she had made some rather startling revelations. Of course, she had been half-drunk and not attending to what she said. But if she was beginning to reveal herself to me, was she doing the same with Kristine? I was pretty sure she was. After all, we were both supporting her and she looked upon us both as confidants, people she could trust. The rub was—I was ready

to bet anything on it—we weren't privy to the same information. Something told me Gilberte was revealing her past to me
and her future to Kristine. And this hurt. I hated the idea she
was reading the book of herself to Kristine, and, more likely
than not, reading it with the fever of a missionary trying to
convert savages to the Truth. I knew Gilberte. She could be a
siren when she wanted to be. I knew Kristine. She wouldn't be
able to resist a siren's song.

To be sure, discussing your past with someone created a
confederacy of sorts. I was grateful for being part of it. Recalling and recounting your history amounted to a confession,
and generally you confessed only to someone you liked and
trusted. At least I knew where I stood as far as that went.

The future was different. The future is a conspiracy. And
I was being excluded from it.

I found it appalling that Gilberte was conspiring with
someone who was interested in her only for the time being,
and who would, at the drop of a shoe, pick up someone else
who was more in step with her whim of the moment.

Why was Gilberte turning to Kristine rather than to me?
The answer wasn't puzzling. Kristine had given her work. Kristine would buy her photographs. Kristine was a collector, and
she knew other collectors and dealers and curators. She knew
the art world. She knew the people who ran it. I knew nobody.
Gilberte was aware of this. I was sure she was counting on
Kristine to provide her with the thread that would lead her
through the labyrinth she was about to enter.

Putting aside my jealousy of Kristine's hold on Gilberte,
another issue concerned me: whether Kristine would make
Gilberte a success before Gilberte could make herself an artist. Kristine could lead Gilberte around obstacles she would

never be able to circumnavigate alone. That was certain. Kristine and Allbright and Kettridge, if his aid was finally enlisted, could do a lot for Gilberte. They could make her an art star almost overnight. Of course, she wouldn't then actually be a star but, like all such artists introduced by patrons, a satellite: she would be launched into the public space by hype and money and left aloft as long as she continued to please her patrons. If her work was good, it was conceivable she would remain aloft even after her boosters' desires changed. She could sell to the most renowned collectors, enter museum collections—worldwide—and reach the secondary art market in record time. But to do that she would have to hustle like crazy, find more patrons. Cater to new tastes. Her new patrons' tastes would become her tastes. She would adopt their habits. They would affect her outlook. Change her focus. She would become anxious about perpetrating her success and social standing. Her anxiety would compromise her work. She wouldn't seek to fulfill her promise. She would continually seek to find new patrons, anybody who would support her work so she could support herself in the style to which she had become accustomed: she would end up using her talent to maintain her status rather than to create art.

♦

Standing at the counter, staring at the street, Gilberte and I watched pedestrians pass. That seemed to be all we could do. It was just after six and while most people were propelled homeward by a second wind, we were anchored in the store, suffering from end-of-the-day doldrums. Gilberte tried to break the tedium by playing with a pair of sunglasses she had bought on St. Mark's Place. They had thick black plastic stems and dark sea-green glass, and when she put them on she looked like a character from a science fiction comic book. She claimed they were very fifties, but I said they were more sixties and probably of Italian or French design rather than English, which was what Gilberte wanted to believe. They reminded me of the glasses Marcello Mastroianni had worn in 8½, as well as the ones Brigitte Bardot had worn in *Le Mepris*. Gilberte hadn't seen either of these films, and didn't have any idea what I was referring to.

She kept putting the glasses on and taking them off again, trying to find the right way to wear them. Unfortunately, there seemed to be no right way—that is, no way for her to escape looking like a cartoon character.

—I don't know why I bought them, she said, and tossed them down. I folded the stems and twirled the glasses in circles on the counter.

I wondered if this was the moment. I had been waiting all day to ask Gilberte to dinner. I had a thousand things I wanted to discuss with her, things that couldn't wait, things that couldn't be discussed during work. So all day, whenever there was a break in the activity I thought, this is the moment to speak, but I didn't take advantage of it. When we opened, it seemed to soon: it just didn't seem to be at all the kind of thing one demanded of a co-worker that early in the day. Especially since I didn't want it to appear I had thought about it all night. I was sure it would appear like that if I asked her first thing. Hence, I said nothing, and the morning passed. In the early afternoon, we were too busy to chat. I should have asked her during our break, when she was sitting next to me on the counter. But I didn't. Now it was early evening and the fact I had procrastinated for so long was weighing heavily on me and inclining me to silence. If I hadn't wanted to appear eager in the morning, I didn't want to appear desperate now.

I was still twirling Gilberte's glasses when I saw Kristine's silver Mercedes go by. I looked at Gilberte. She was staring out the window, but she seemed to be lost in reverie, and apparently the car hadn't registered. Kristine could have been going to her shop but since she was driving rather than being chauffeured, I had a feeling she wasn't headed there. If my intuition was right, she was going to come waltzing in the door of the bookstore as soon as she found a parking place. Which meant if I was going to ask Gilberte to dinner, I'd better do it now, because after a visit from Kristine we would only talk about Kristine.

I lit a cigarette.

—Do you like Thai food? I asked, apropos of nothing.

—Thai? I don't know. She was non-committal.

—I know a restaurant where they make a fish dish with a great hot sauce.

—Really? she said. I like spicy food.

—Good, I said.

—Thai food. She repeated it, trying to taste the words.

—My treat, I said.

—I don't have a cent, she said, without saying yes or no.

—I'll pay, I said. And it's not far. We can walk.

—All right. I'm tired of blintzes.

I smiled. We stared out the window again. I was watching for Kristine. Dreading the moment she would walk through the door. I didn't have to wait very long.

—Hi, she said, flinging open the door. Not very busy, she said to the empty store. The comment didn't call for commentary, so there wasn't any.

—My place is dead, too, she informed us. There's no one in town. Anyway, I only have a minute, and I came for a reason. There's someone I want you to meet, she said to Gilberte. He could be very useful to you.

—Who is it? Gilberte asked.

—He's a dealer and a consultant. He's down from Boston. I'm taking him out to the country for the weekend, and he's only in town for a few minutes.

—Ah, said Gilberte.

—I think it would be a good idea for you to see him, Kristine said.

—When? Gilberte asked.

—Well, I'm meeting him in fifteen minutes at the Wine Bar for a drink. Why don't you come?

Gilberte looked at me.

—You're not too busy here, are you? Kristine asked me. You can spare her, can't you?

—Sure, I said. For a few minutes.

—Then come, Kristine said, turning to the door. I have to drop by the boutique for a second, then we're off.

Gilberte joined Kristine at the door. She gave me such a forlorn look that for a moment I was afraid she was going to say something about our dinner date, which I wanted to keep secret. But she only said:

—I'll be back in time to help you close.

Kristine opened the door and they stepped out, both waving as they passed in front of the window.

They hadn't been out of sight ten seconds when Gilberte came running back into the store and scooped her glasses off the counter. She regained the door before it had time to close, caught it, turned, and said:

—Don't worry about dinner, I'll be back in time. Then, shrugging her shoulders slightly: You can't get anywhere without connections, you know.

—A marionette doesn't move unless someone pulls the strings, I said.

—Don't worry, she said. I looked at the clock. It was five forty-five. We closed at seven-thirty. It was unlikely she would be back in time.

I was furious. All my mental effort had been wasted. I had tormented myself for nothing. Kristine had walked in, said she had someone Gilberte should meet, and taken her away to meet him. Just like that. I was ashamed of myself. Thank God Gilberte had stepped back inside to say a word to me. It would have been too crushing if she had simply sauntered off with Kristine after accepting my invitation. There was nothing to do but wait. And pace. Which I did to console myself. Somehow, by not remaining static behind the counter, I found the courage to forbear.

I told myself Kristine hadn't invited her to dinner. She had clearly stated the invitation was for drinks. Nevertheless, I had the uncanny feeling the drinks would turn into dinner. And if Gilberte did make it back to have dinner with me (I wasn't optimistic), she would be too preoccupied for me to say what I had in mind. I needed her to be in a receptive mood.

For what I had in mind—and it might have been this that had made me procrastinate for so long—was to speak out against this kind of incident. It was becoming clear to me

Gilberte's socializing was more and more intertwined with her career as an artist. Soon it would be hard to distinguish between her career and her social life. Even now she was returning from these drinks and dinners covered with the crumbs of corruption. She didn't think it was dangerous to do this because she believed she was with the right people, and she believed from them no harm could come, only good. What I wanted to tell her was they weren't the right people for her.

Would a talk help her? It was doubtful. But it would demonstrate I cared about her. Would she care that I cared? Even if she did, would she listen to someone who was, finally, merely a manager of a bookstore, a dilettante, a man with no credentials, no fortune, and no social distinction. (For years I had thought of myself as a writer, but I had never completed even one piece of fiction. Hence, I couldn't even talk to her as a fellow artist.) I was fairly sure if I tried to give her my thoughts on the subject under the guise of a disinterested but concerned observer, she would turn a deaf ear.

In fact, the more I considered what I wanted to accomplish, the more foolish my plan seemed. As soon as Gilberte realized I was trying to help her, she would compare me to Kristine, and I would suffer in the comparison because despite our common aims to help Gilberte, our positions in the world were too different: Kristine's life reeked of refinement, luxury, leisure, power, and, to put it crudely, all the finer things in life. Having escaped the gravity of mundane matters, she was free to devote herself to important things, like art and artists. She was a full-fledged member of the *après garde* and committed to having fun.

My humble life was ruled by working hours, paychecks, and budget considerations. Tonight, I wanted to speak about truth, beauty, perseverance, as well as sacrifice, dedication, honesty. How could that measure up to being introduced to some smart art dealer who would remember Gilberte and speak of her to his clients as an up-and-coming young star whose work still wasn't too expensive. I couldn't afford the champagne (for Gilberte loved champagne) Kristine loved buying for her, over which they would discuss whom Gilberte knew and whom she didn't know and whom she should know. Nor could I promise to let a dealer send me something he thought would be perfect for my house in town as a return favor for trying to help my friend. Or suddenly think of somebody who might be interested in a photograph, or of someone who was looking for a photographer to do a portrait. I simply couldn't do these kinds of things for Gilberte.

Furthermore, by exposing her to my ideas I would risk alienating her. Of course, no matter what mood or frame of mind she was in, there was a chance I would do just that. Which was why the timing was important. I decided if I did see her later in the evening, I would greatly reduce the scope of the speech I had planned and pursue a much more modest goal. I would fill her in a little on recent art history (about which she was, for the most part, ignorant), in the hope she would be able to see herself in perspective.

I was thinking, for example, of telling her that since at least the late 1950s, the status of objects of art had fallen. Today they were considered to be nothing more than objects or commodities, or, better—depending upon how you looked at it—investments. I would inform her that the so-called art community that had produced works in pursuit of a goal or an ideal or an end aimed at transcending the material value of the work—that is to say, something abstract—no longer existed.

I would explain that today the New York art community was composed of enterprising artificers who made and marketed their goods with as much business acumen as any other free-wheeling entrepreneur who had a product to sell. That it was still possible to talk about subject matter that was tragic and timeless, about flatness, about gestural marks, or hard or soft edges, or essences or actions or fragmented surfaces or image appropriation—but that didn't change the fact that an object of art was thought to be fundamentally an object. That the word *art* had begun to be used not only to denote objects with some sort of aesthetic value but to justify the exorbitant prices asked for them. This change in the status of these objects had led to a concomitant change in the status of the producers of these objects because the inherent (ineffable) value that had formerly been thought to reside in works of art had come to be thought of as residing in the artists themselves—with no little help from the artists themselves.

I would try to make her understand this re-appropriation of value occurred because artists could not bear—in the age of mechanical reproduction—the thought of being considered merely craftsmen or production-line laborers who turned out goods like any other proletarian. Wasn't Warhol's studio called the Factory? Art might no longer be important, but artists were. (One high-ranking dealer/impresario had even stated publicly there were artists with charisma, and everything they did was important: as if it were purely the artists' personal attributes that determined the value of the work in question.) But they weren't important in the old sense, as persons endowed with a gift to *reveal* that set them apart from ordinary people. No. The new artist was a shrewd manipulator, a wily cannibalizer of mass culture, a businessman or woman who considered business to be the highest form of art. A good artist was someone who had succeeded in producing objects that, like any other durable goods, had an immediate mass appeal and could be consumed by anyone with enough money to purchase them at market value.

I didn't plan to suggest to Gilberte that artists no longer produced works of art. Or that their social role had been totally vitiated and their function was purely to fabricate decorative, fun goods. Nor would I imply the situation was black-and-white. I would make it black-and-white to help clarify the issues. There were still holdouts determined to translate their revelatory experience of phenomena into a vision of life. What I wanted Gilberte to understand was that, especially in New York, it was becoming harder and harder to do so.

This I particularly wanted to stress because I saw she was impressed by all the latest trends and cultural epiphenomena. She assiduously followed developments in the East Village. She was fascinated by the tabloids and newsletters and periodicals that reported on the East Village scene. She read them with the avid eye of an investor who daily studies the stock market, comparing price-to-earnings ratios and dividend payments, reading annual reports and prospectuses—always looking to make a killing. She could barely conceal her jealousy when she brought to my attention names of artists her age who were well on their way to fame and fortune.

I didn't know if I really had the resolve to speak to her about this at all. Aside from the possibility that it might alienate her, it might be unnecessary. There was a chance Gilberte was, at heart, a serious artist. I wanted to believe that. I wanted to believe she had something she had to communicate. Yet I had the nagging sensation that she was serious about her ambition to *make it*—and not art, which was a means to this end. In which case my talk would fall upon deaf ears. It was possible that she, like many others, had come to believe that in a world where mutually assured destruction could occur from one moment to the next, to be famous for even fifteen minutes had the appearance of eternity.

I waited for her return. At seven-fifteen the thread of hope I had been hanging on to snapped. A customer walked in and I said:

—I'm closed.

While locking the gates and turning on the alarm I began thinking about what to do for the evening. I suspected Gilberte, Kristine, and her dealer friend were still in the neighborhood, and I didn't want to chance meeting them. It would be awkward somehow, and I was already a little off balance from Gilberte's standing me up. I had to leave the neighborhood. I had to eat, but my rather melancholy musing had suppressed my appetite. I wanted a drink. Yet I had been taxing my liver so much in recent days that a rest would do it good. I decided to go home.

It was a sweltering-hot night. It had rained around lunchtime and the water had vaporized and the hot surfaces on which it had fallen remained hot and the atmosphere became dense and steamy. The night didn't promise to be much better.

I headed home. The heat was infernal. Walking at a normal pace made me break out in a sweat. As I turned the corner on to Prince Street, a semitrailer rolled by and pulled a hot damp dirty blanket of air over me. I would need a shower to get out from under it. I'd take a shower. I'd eat. Then I'd listen to Satie's *Trois Morceaux en forme de poire* or side two of Keith

Jarrett's *Köln Concert*, or something else light, something to go with the weather—a symphony in this heat was unthinkable.

♦

The following morning, Gilberte was late. I had to open the store alone.

When she was fifteen minutes late, I lit a cigarette and told myself I wasn't going to get upset until after I had finished it.

I was just snuffing it out when I saw her running across the street.

—Hi, she said on entering.

I didn't say anything immediately, which was a mistake, for she promptly announced, as if there could be no question about it:

—Listen, I'm going to run out for some coffee before we get busy, all right?

I looked at her, but my look, stern and disapproving as I believed it was, did not change Gilberte's intention.

—You want a bagel or something? She asked.

—No thanks.

—Ok. I'll be back in a minute. Promise, she said, and flew out the door.

I was ringing up the first sale of the day when she returned. She had bought me a coffee. When the customer had gone, she said:

—Sorry about last night. She handed me my coffee.

—Nothing to be sorry about, I said.

—I tried to get back. But I had to go to dinner with them.

—How did it go? I asked.

—Great. She's fun, she said, using a pronoun to introduce Kristine.

—Is she?

—She is, she said, inverting the word order, apparently
trying to neutralize the acid in my rhetorical question.

—She let me drive her car up the FDR.

—How charming. Where did you eat?

—At Mortimer's. We sat next to Julian Schnabel. It was
great.

—Who was the dealer she wanted you to meet?

—Jay.

—Just Jay?

—Jeremiah Jay. J.J. He comes from an old, famous family.
He's connected with all sorts of museums and foundations.

—What did he have to say?

—Not much, not to me anyway. He mostly talked to Kristine. And Julian. When he comes back to the city I'm going to
show him my work and my film, if I have it by then.

—What film?

—My film.

—You made a film?

—Sure. That's what I did first, make films. You didn't
know?

—You never said anything about it.

—Oh. Maybe not. It didn't get me anywhere. Anyway, I
don't have it with me. It's in California.

—What's it called?

—*Party Girl*. I decided to make it after seeing Nicholas
Ray's *Party Girl* at Berkeley. His was a gangster film, a noir, not
a party film. It was totally misnamed. But I thought the idea
was terrific. I wanted to do a real party girl film. So me and

some friends tried to raise money for it. We told all our potential contributors that we'd pay them back with the prize money
and royalties that we'd earn after we got a distributor. I mean,
we were into making this movie. But no one believed us. No
one thought we had enough experience. None of us had been
to film school or anything. Everyone thought we were stupid.
Besides, we were young. Twenty-two, twenty-five. No one
gave us any money. Finally, my mother and one of her friends
came across with some money. Then some more people came
through.

—Then what?

—Then we made the film. You'll see it when it comes. It's
very low budget, but I think it's good.

She went on to wonder where she was going to show it.

—I can't show it at the loft where I live because there's too
much confusion going on there. And Kristine is going to invite special people, and I think the atmosphere should be right.
Maybe I could rent Millennium or someplace. Or get Kristine
to.

—You could show it at my loft, I said.

—Really? Is it big?

—You saw it, I reminded her.

—Oh. She blushed coyly.

—You won't mind?

—No.

—Because it would help me a lot. I mean, then I wouldn't
have to ask Kristine, and I don't want to have to ask her for
everything.

—I know.

—I try not to, really.

—I think you should try harder.

—You don't like her, do you?

—I never said that, I pointed out.

—No. And probably you never will. But I can tell. I mean, I don't care. Anyway, I think she's all right. And she could be a great patroness of the arts, like Peggy Guggenheim.

—I don't think Kristine is in her class.

—No, well, she doesn't have that much money. Of her own. But you know what I mean.

I did, but I didn't want to discuss Kristine anymore.

—Is this J.J. bright?

—I don't know, but Kristine listens to him. He worries me. I don't get him.

—Don't worry, I said.

—I try not to, she said, and smiled her smug little smile.

—A combination of Merlin and Machiavelli, I half-muttered.

—Who?

—You. You're a magician and a politician.

—Yeah, a magician. You have to know how to perform tricks to survive.

—You'll make it, I prophesied.

She shook her head as if she wasn't sure.

♦

I felt becalmed in the bath. I let the ash from my cigarette fall into the water. Each time it hit it hissed disapprovingly at this slovenly and unsanitary habit. I didn't care. I had good news. I had just received the results of my medical checkup and I was in perfect health: no worms, no microbes, no gonorrhea, no chlamydia, no syphilis, no hepatitis, no antibodies for AIDS.

It was such a relief to know I wasn't going to have to take any medicine, or submit to any kind of supplementary testing, or die, that I had gone out drinking. I had thought about going to the Eagles Nest or to the Ramrod or the Mineshaft, but I had come home instead. Because in the midst of my drunkenness, I decided to give up having indiscriminate sex. I had made a vow. And I planned to keep it this time. Somehow, these days it seemed too irresponsible, if not downright suicidal, to go out cruising.

I had opted to spend the night alone because my relationship with Ronnie had run its course. He wouldn't be shocked at my decision. He was growing tired of us anyway. I could tell he wasn't happy. He was becoming restless. Our liaison was tying him down. Even now, often when I rang him he wasn't home—at hours when he should have been. He had taken up going out to the bars and the baths again. I didn't like it. I could no longer make him swear he hadn't been with someone. Even when I created a scene of jealous rage he would hem and haw and never give a definitive answer. I wanted to be definite now. Unfortunately, as soon as you even kissed someone these days you couldn't be definite. Ronnie, I was sure, did more than kiss. And, he didn't believe in utilizing any sort of prophylaxis. Prophylaxis was for wimps, he thought. If you were going to get something you were going to get something, that's all there was to it. I didn't like that. I couldn't deal with that kind of stupidity any more. It was one of the reasons I had been particularly anxious to go for my checkup. And why, now that I knew I was healthy, it was convenient to terminate our

relationship. I didn't want to spend another three months constantly inspecting myself, searching for sores, signs of lesions,
symptoms of contamination.

I saw now that not only should I give up indiscriminate
sex, but total abstinence would probably be good for me. I
would save myself for true love. I would become a virgin again.
It was the only absolutely foolproof form of protection. Perhaps it was idiotic. After all, how long could I remain abstinent?
What if I never found true love? I would tire of masturbating.
In no time at all it would become nothing more than another
biological duty I owed my body, like eating or excreting. Then
I'd have to find someone else. Or go mad from the sheer animal
need to press my body against another body. To put my dick in
someone. From the time I was a pre-pubescent my dick would
swell and harden like a muscle. I couldn't get it down. It was
the indomitable life force springing up. Quivering. Sitting at
my desk in school, watching TV with my family, eating dinner, riding the school bus, it was irrepressible. The desire for
release from the tension it generated was overwhelming, painful. And even at that early age it was clear to me my desire was
bidirectional. Flip flop. Male, female, it didn't matter. Depending on the circumstances, and any number of other factors I
never understood, I could go either way. When I got a har-
don, I had to shake it off. Either by myself or with a *friend*. My
choice of partner was driven more by beauty and sentiment
and mutual attraction than gender. The instability of my sexual identity, the crisscrossing of my desire, had confused me and
made my life miserable all through my youth. Now I was less
miserable, but still confused. There was no explanation, no
reasonable explanation, no biology is destiny, nothing to explain why I was the way I was. There was only condemnation,

incomprehension, and denial of what I felt. Because you were supposed to be one way or another. A or not A, B or not B. You couldn't be both A and B. That wasn't possible, people said. Then, recently, begrudgingly, some people admitted it might be possible. You could be bisexual. I hated that fucking word. Most people hated it. Most people considered it to be a mask that gay people wore to hide their gayness behind. But I was indifferent to the name. It didn't tell me who I was. *Who I was.* That's what I wanted to know. That's what I couldn't discover. And, because I didn't know who I was, I didn't know what to do. What to become. Existence precedes essence, it was said. And I agreed with that. But when your existence was unclassifiable how could you arrive at the essence of who you were? How did you move on? How did you do anything? Which was why I never did anything. Why I was here, working in a bookstore.

The more I thought about it, the more certain I became I was doing the right thing in breaking off my relationship with Ronnie. Sexually satisfying as it had been, his promiscuous propensities and fateful attitude were bound, one day or another, to have had a deleterious effect upon my health. One exposure to the AIDS virus, for example, and your number was up. Hepatitis could be debilitating and chronic and eventually fatal. Herpes would be a nuisance. Gonorrhea and syphilis were manageable. But AIDS was sure death. It was common knowledge that with AIDS you could go from robust health to the grave in something like eighteen months. You got swollen glands, which steroids made disappear. Then you were racked with fever, which steroids lowered. Then you developed rashes in your mouth and anus, and tests would show you had contracted oral candidiasis and herpes simplex. Which meant antifungal and antiviral drugs, like ketoconazole and zidovudine, would have to be used. These would work for a time. Until your immune-defective system succumbed to the next infection. After that an x-ray would show spots in your lungs, and the following exam would show lesions developing. A biopsy would turn up *Pneumocystis carinii* or cytomegalovirus. Then the fever would return, and with it shortness of breath, and this time, perhaps death. Those were only some of the many variations. They all made me totally paranoid. Which was, all things considered, a little funny. Because I was not the paranoid type. Nor did I respond to warnings, regardless of how well documented they were. No amount of antismoking literature or glossy color pictures of cancers caused by smoking had ever come close to convincing me to stop smoking. I still puffed happily away. It was the eighteen months—and the fact that no one had ever survived AIDS—that made me paranoid. Whereas cancer from cigarette smoking seemed like an interminable affliction, something that could drag on for years and years, and though you might have to submit to radiation therapy or chemotherapy or both, or have your esophagus or larynx cut out and be forced to breathe through a little hole in your windpipe, or, worse, be confined in an oxygen tent or an iron lung, still, you could always hope, from one day to the next, that a cure would be found that would reprieve your sentence, save you from death. It was the distance from death that made the difference. When you got AIDS it was upon you: it jumped out at you and had all the immediacy and violence of a mugging, while the warnings about lung cancer appeared merely like an obscene, vaguely threatening, anonymous telephone call.

In addition to my encouraging test results, I was also happy because I had finally succeeded in entering Gilberte's life and, in particular, her future: that future I had been anxious to have include me. She had accepted my offer to show her film at my loft. This pleased me immensely. I had been concerned she wasn't going to let me do anything for her, that she was only going to turn to Kristine for help. For political reasons, naturally.

I felt that as long as I could be of use to her in getting her where she wanted to go, my desire's designs on her still might be realized. I had the impression Gilberte would see to the needs of those who saw to her needs, that one way or another she would reciprocate a favor—when it was convenient for her. So, while the type of help I could offer her was nothing on the scale of what Kristine could offer, it was help all the same, and she would be grateful for it. And rightfully so. Because as it turned out, I was going to do more than just provide the space for Gilberte to screen her film. I was also going to pick up the tab for the refreshments.

I wanted to help Gilberte. She fit the pattern of my former lovers. I was generally attracted to somebody I thought I could change, somebody on whom I could try to work my will. Men or women, I always wanted to teach, to guide, to aid my lovers. My way of loving had never been the mundane *we were made for each other*. Often what attracted me to people were the qualities I thought they were lacking and I thought I could help them develop. What bound me to them was my will to change them and their willingness to let themselves be changed. For me this meant the (unconscious) forswearing of happiness until my lover's transformation was completed, until the object of my love became other than what it was. Yet, this metamorphosis was impossible because my idea of what my adored object should become was an ideal and therefore unrealizable. And because the goal I was striving for—to make someone become other than what he or she was—was one that could never be completed, since becoming is a process without end, my love affairs were always unfulfilled, dismal projects.

The bathwater was beginning to pinch my fingers. I took the hint and climbed out of the tub. I patted myself a little with the towel, and when I had stopped dripping I lit a cigarette. I walked through the loft. It was invigorating to walk naked. The air was cool and crisp tonight. I felt weightless, insubstantial, sad. I listened to my feet slap the hard-wooden floor. It was late but I wasn't tired. The water had relaxed me and now the air revived me.

I walked. I listened to the city groaning in its sleep, or its repose—for I guessed it was true that the city never slept, which was entirely reasonable since the city wasn't sentient. Out of the front windows I saw the World Trade Center buildings, silvery, shimmering, banded at the top by a ribbon of flashing red lights. Along all the side windows and out of the back windows I saw only dark shadows, black geometrical forms, jumbles of TV antennae, and scattered lightened windows. I smoked. I kept walking, around and around.

◆

It was one of those days when customers didn't come in their usual numbers and there was little to break up the day and I had to deal with it as best I could.

I was trying to work out a new design for the front window but was constantly being distracted by Gilberte. She shuffled about, whining. She was bored. To death, she said. For someone dead she made a lot of noise: idiocies born of ennui, progeny of an enervated imagination. I tried not to pay attention to her. However, since she wanted me to pay attention, it was difficult to ignore her. Gilberte was still a child. She couldn't stand being stationary, couldn't endure tedium, and when she had to confront it, her mind, like a ship adrift in the horse latitudes, wandered aimlessly, waiting and seeking the first sign of a stimulus that would set it going, give it life. At times like this she would say anything. I had to control my temper. I found it intolerable when someone said anything just to say something, the way people whistled or hummed because they were incapable of using their imagination to distract them.

I wasn't unsympathetic toward Gilberte's plight, which was also my own. Working, but having nothing productive to show for it made time torturous. And what could we do? I had already updated the accounts. I had placed the orders that had to be placed. Gilberte had unpacked the new arrivals. She had cleaned. And she had re-alphabetized for two hours. Her presence was superfluous since there was nothing for her to do, yet necessary, because to be paid she had to be here. That was what rankled her. Confined within a given space for a specified time made her feel like a prisoner. I was her ever-watchful warder.

Unless Gilberte began selling her pictures in greater quantities, she was going to have to learn to fight off the demon of noontide (see Baudelaire's Preface to Les Fleurs du mal). And she was going to have to learn quickly too, because for the moment sales of her work were slack, if not nonexistent. Her ad had generated a lot of talk, a lot of interest, and, maybe, one purchase. J.J. had found a prospective buyer for one of the photographs I had seen in her SoHo show. More would come. But it would take time.

Babbling at me without saying anything, eliciting no response worthy of the name, Gilberte finally became disgusted and wandered to the back of the store, where she sat down in one of the chairs and lit a cigarette. She was still sitting and smoking, her legs spread apart in a very unladylike fashion, when Kristine came in.

—Don't move on my account, Kristine said to Gilberte, who had jumped off the chair with more vigor than she had shown since she arrived.

—We were breaking, Gilberte explained, inculpating both of us, though I was working.

—Breaking from what? If your place has been as dead as mine, all you've had all day is one long break. And that's tiring, I know, Kristine said. She turned to me.

I refused to affirm or deny her personal claim to this knowledge.

Gilberte came to the front of the store. When she was standing next to Kristine, I saw what looked to be a strangled gesture of affection from Kristine: as if she had intended to rearrange Gilberte's hair the way a mother might habitually adjust some aspect of her child's appearance.

—Well, she announced. I have a suggestion. Why don't we take a real break and go someplace for dinner? Gilberte was so happy she almost jumped for joy. I pretended I hadn't heard a word of what Kristine had said. I think she was aware of my disapprobation.

—I know it's a little early, but on a day like today I don't think anybody's going to miss you.

Gilberte had already begun the closing routine. She was rushing around with the broom the way a dog rushes around with its leash on hearing the word *walk*. I should have refused the invitation. I should have found a reason, something that would have prevented us from accompanying Kristine, but I saw what pleasure it was giving to Gilberte, so I couldn't. Also, I sensed it was in my interest not to protest, because Kristine would probably be more than happy to leave me behind if I became overzealous in my commitment to the store. Since I supposed there would be talk about Gilberte's film I felt I should be there. I wanted Kristine to understand I was to play a major role in organizing the screening, and though I would accept her help it was to be my affair.

Kristine wanted Chinese food. She was going to take us to what she claimed was the best restaurant in Chinatown. It was soon going to be reviewed in the *Times*, she said, so we had to eat there now, before the review came out and the place was swamped and the prices were raised and the quality deteriorated.

◆

Sitting on yellow Naugahyde seats under glaring naked hanging light bulbs at a green-and-red linoleum-covered table, I was dismayed to learn we should have stopped on the way to buy a bottle of vodka or wine, since the establishment didn't have a liquor license. Kristine and Gilberte ordered beer. I settled for a Coke with a lemon in it.

—Don't be glum, Kristine said. You should have guessed they didn't have a liquor license. No reputable restaurant in Chinatown does.

I had nothing to say to this. She was right. I should have suspected, or I should have asked.

Kristine and Gilberte talked among themselves, mostly ignoring me, but when the topic of the film came up, I worked my way into the discussion. Kristine was thrilled I was going to handle all the details of setting up for the screening. She told me she'd let me know in a few days how many people she was planning to invite.

The conversation drifted, went here, there, and every-where. I could have interposed a comment anytime I liked, and sometimes it actually seemed they were waiting for me to of-fer my opinion on some subject or other, but after we stopped talking about the film I no longer felt like participating. I wanted to talk to Gilberte. I didn't want to talk to Kristine. It's hard for me to talk for any length of time to people I don't like. Especially when the topic of conversation is one I don't like, which it was for the moment. Kristine was speculating about how much the collector Sam Wagstaff's support of Robert (as she referred to Robert Mapplethorpe) had aided his career. He was becoming pricey. She didn't know who was behind Cindy Sherman but she was determined to find out. As a wannabe, collector / investor, Kristine was naturally intrigued by art world gossip. She could make money or lose money depending on the rumors of the day. Making money and losing money was business talk. I didn't want to talk business. If, in an attempt to convince them to change the subject, I told them that's what they were talking about, they'd deny it. They'd say they were talking about art, because they attached the artists' names to the works they were discussing. They were boring me to distraction. Kristine was assuring Gilberte it was a sellers' market. Of that she was sure. She went on in such solemn tones about whose work was overvalued and whose undervalued I could have burped or farted to show my contempt.

From time to time I made eye contact with one or the other to show I was still with them. I forced myself to nod my head now and again to indicate my agreement with what had just been said. I was paying so little attention that half of the phrases could have been uttered in a language foreign to me. A silence intervened. I let it hold the floor and lit a cigarette. It didn't matter, we were all acquainted. Silence was permitted. Kristine took a long swig of beer. She kept her hand around the bottle when she set it down, as if she were going to finish it off momentarily. I noticed her manicured almond-shaped nails and the white crescent moons that shone under a pale pearl coat of polish.

Then, in her inimitable way, Kristine began explaining to Gilberte the intricacies of Chinese cooking: about how they cut different vegetables in different ways and added them at different times to produce different flavors. I absented myself from this conversation, and to divert myself I inspected the glass cabinet across from us, upon which was enthroned the cash register. Keeping it company were enough sundries and gewgaws to open a novelty store. There were a bowl of mints, a toothpick dispenser, bowls of matches, stacks of business cards, a selection of postcards, chopsticks, porcelain soup spoons, finger bowls, and items in boxes I couldn't quite make out from where I was sitting. In the cabinet below were more such items, although they tended more toward the edible end of the spectrum: packages of fortune cookies, almond cookies, dry noodles, bottles of soy sauce and duck sauce, packets of mustard, dried mushrooms, etc. I was trying to discern exactly what was on the bottom shelf when a waitress came and closed one of the glass doors that had been left (apparently negligently) open. Suddenly the front panel of the cabinet was transformed into a mirror and I could see under our table.

I very nearly gagged. Kristine had taken off her right shoe and was calmly and methodically rubbing Gilberte's shin with her foot.

I couldn't believe it. I turned to look at Gilberte. Her expression revealed nothing. Kristine's too, was inscrutable. Mine, I'm sure, was one of utter disbelief. I looked again into the glass. Kristine was clearly caressing Gilberte's shin. I was dumbfounded. A monstrous thought flashed through my mind. For the rest of the meal I barely said a word.

Kristine paid the check. Outside, we all concurred it had been an exquisite meal. Kristine suggested we go to Little Italy for dessert or, to placate me, back to SoHo for a drink. I wasn't interested in doing either. After what I had seen, I wanted to get away from them. I asked to be dropped off at my loft. Neither of them protested. I could tell my company wouldn't be missed.

♦

Once upstairs, I poured myself a drink. Could Gilberte be gay? I had half-suspected it. Of course, I half-suspected it of everybody until I saw solid evidence to the contrary. In her case, no evidence had confounded my supposition. For instance, her refusal to sleep with me or let me give her a kiss had hinted at something. Assuming that she wasn't repulsed by me. Her dress was unfeminine. Her posture and her poses, especially that lean, were manly. Her manners, until recently, were gruff and crude. She never talked about the men in her life. Or seemed even vaguely interested in any of the men, many of them very attractive, who came into the store. The best excuse I could come up with for never more than half-suspecting she didn't care for men was she had come to work for me soon after our night together, and because I frowned upon employee-employer liaisons, I had not pursued her. Had I, she might have opened up to me—if for no other reason than to get me to stop pestering her. To be fair, her not talking about the men in her life didn't mean there weren't men in her life.

I had learned quite a lot about Gilberte. I knew about her home life in California, her parents, brother, and sisters, about her high school days, about her previous jobs, her roommates. (To share your life with your co-workers is more or less normal under such close working conditions. Once you feel comfortable, you begin to exhale anecdotes and data as if they were the air itself, so natural does it become.) Despite the vast amount of information I had amassed about her, that she had omitted to inform me she was gay, if indeed she was, wasn't surprising. I, too, had revealed quite a bit about myself without mentioning anything about my sexuality. Now that I knew, or at least suspected what Gilberte's sexual proclivities were, where did it leave me? I wasn't sure. If Gilberte were exclusively gay, my desire was doomed. On the other hand, if she was like me, there was hope. How was I to know?

More perplexing than anything having to do with Gilberte's sexual orientation was the image in the glass of Kristine's foot rubbing Gilberte's leg. What did it mean? Was she attracted to women? Was her sexuality fluid, like mine? I couldn't imagine how I had ever overlooked such a thing. In the year and a half we had worked together, Kristine had nearly suffocated me with tales of her personal life. It wasn't possible I wouldn't have figured this out. I dredged up all my memories and stoically sifted through them, hunting for hints I might have missed, searching for something that would reveal she harbored feelings for members of her own sex. Either she was too clever for me or there was nothing to turn up because I turned up nothing. Everything pointed in the opposite direction. Everything. Kristine was married. She had a son. What more powerful evidence in favor of her being straight could one want? True, it might merely be an alibi or a cover for her desire. These days there were many married gay women (and men), who had children. If it was just a cover, was Roger aware of it? I doubted it. Kristine was sure to have obliterated her tracks so well he probably didn't have the slightest inkling. Up until a few hours ago, neither had I. The thought that we might have something in common, a certain sexual indeterminacy, filled me with an emotion that I had never previously felt toward her. Sympathy.

There was always the chance I was blowing the whole incident out of proportion, totally misinterpreting what I had seen. Perhaps Kristine had been merely trying slyly to get Gilberte's attention, to emphasize a private joke, at my expense, no doubt. Maybe now the joke was on me. Perhaps she wasn't gay but after another thrill. Was this what you did when you got tired of cocaine? I didn't know. Maybe I wouldn't know. I couldn't confront the situation head-on. I wouldn't ask either of them any questions. I would only observe. Until I had definitive evidence, I would withhold judgment. Which seemed

to me eminently reasonable, because in the final analysis, Kristine's rubbing Gilberte's shin under the table didn't mean that
she, or Gilberte, harbored any sexual feelings for each other.
Or did it?

◆

The film arrived. Gilberte brought it to work one morning.
She said she'd feel better knowing it was at the store.

—Things have a way of disappearing at the loft, she said.

—Can we have a sneak preview? I asked.

—Sure. I'd like to see it again too. It's been a while.

I was going to suggest we look at it that night, but remembered we hadn't yet made arrangements to get a projector.

—Can we call to see about a projector? she wanted to
know. I mean, I'm a little short just now. Is there money if I
find one for tonight?

Not sure how much this was going to set me back, I told
her to call for prices before I said yes.

A few phone calls later, she located an available projector.
The price was a bit steep, I thought, but she was so excited at
the prospect of seeing her film that I couldn't say no. It turned
out the fee, plus the deposit and the cab fare she would need to
get back to the store, was more than I had in ready cash, or in
petty cash. I had to go to the bank. When I returned, Gilberte
set off to fetch the projector, promising to return as quickly as
possible.

◆

The first thing Gilberte said when we entered my loft was:

—This is incredible. Is all this yours?

—Is that what you thought the first time you came?

—I must have been half-asleep. How did you get all this?

—I've been around a lot longer than you, I said. I was amazed at the fatuousness of my response, which implied the longer one was around, the more things one acquired.

— It's great, she said. She walked to the far end of the loft. A library and everything, she called out. It's just like a real house.

—What would a fake house be like? I asked her.

—Oh, you know. It wouldn't have all the things you normally think houses should have, she explained. I'm going to set up down here, she called.

I searched through the refrigerator and cabinets. Eggs were all I had in sufficient quantity to feed two people.

—Are you hungry? I asked her.

—All right, she said by way of reply. She was unpacking the projector.

I prepared dinner. Gilberte set up the projector and then wandered through the loft. She looked out all the windows. I saw her peer into my bedroom. Then she took another grand tour.

In the kitchen, she picked up one of the carrots I had peeled. Holding it horizontally, she ate it like an ear of corn, biting away the outer part and revealing the tender middle, which she then ate like a carrot. She didn't say a word. When she was finished she resumed her stroll.

I put out the place mats and silverware. She passed by me twice, and because she stopped and stared for a moment at the items I had stacked on the kitchen counter, I thought she was going to offer to help me carry them over to the table, but she didn't.

I set the table and then began preparing an omelet. I separated the whites and the yolks and beat them and then combined them and beat them again.

—Do you like your omelet loose? I asked her.

—However you like yours, she said.

—All right, then. You'd better sit down, because it'll be done in a minute.

She sauntered over to the table and dropped into the chair. I saw her studying the place settings, the cloth napkins (which she fingered), the water glasses and wineglasses, the ice bucket with the bottle of rose, the flowers.

—It's just like being at a restaurant, she said.

—Thank you, I said, taking the simile to be a compliment. I had set the omelet on a large platter. Gilberte served herself, taking a healthy portion of it and an equally ample portion of steamed diced carrots. After ripping a handful of bread off the loaf, she began eating. I poured her some wine.

Her eating style had not changed substantially. She still kept her head lowered, an unfortunate and unattractive habit, which deprived me of a view of her face. She ate quickly. I decided she must be starved. I took a much smaller helping than I had intended to take, so when she finished she could have seconds.

Halfway through her omelet, she switched her attention to the steamed carrots and began squashing them into a paste, which she then mashed into her omelet. When this had the consistency she was looking for, she gobbled up the creamy concoction.

—You can take some more, I said, indicating the egg still left on the platter.

—Thanks, but I don't like eggs.

—That's all there was, I offered by way of apology.

—Oh, that's all right. I don't like them, but I can eat anything. Really.

I finished the eggs. Then I served the salad. I folded each leaf carefully, condensing it on my fork with a knife, as meticulously as someone packing a parachute. Gilberte ate her salad with one hand (the other held a cigarette), locating the center of each leaf and stuffing it into her mouth as one might stuff a cleaning cloth down a rifle barrel.

I brought a dish of fruit with the coffee. Gilberte ate an apple but refused coffee, saying she wouldn't sleep if she drank it this late. She was becoming a bit fidgety. She wanted to get the show on the road. I downed the rest of my cup and stood.

She jumped up.

—Well, I'm sorry about the eggs, she said. I mean, about not liking them, she added, in an attempt to apologize for her earlier faux pas.

—You can't be expected to like everything.

—No, everything was great, she insisted.

—Thank you.

—It's OK, she said, canceling the compliment.

She walked toward the other end of the loft, where the projector was set to go. I cleared the table and then joined her on the couch. I sat down and lit a cigarette. She turned off the lights. Since we hadn't managed to get a screen we were going to project it on the wall.

—Ready, she said and turned on the projector.

The title came on, *Party Girl*, followed by the opening shot, a woman seen through an open window. The woman was centered in the window frame. Seated on a simple wooden chair, she was naked, but bent over so far that nothing but her back could be seen. The camera remained focused on her body, which seemed to be trying to protect itself, or to hide. The camera remained stationary long enough for the viewer to anticipate the woman doing something, but she did nothing. Or for the viewer to long for the camera to provide a close-up, but none was forthcoming. When the camera moved, it moved slowly, revealing the interior of the room in which the woman was sitting. There were people all over the floor. An orgy, or something like one, had taken place. The camera lingered over the aftermath. Some of the people were fully dressed, others were partially or totally naked. There were some animals roaming about. Empty bottles and cans, foodstuffs, cigarette butts, and the like were strewn on all the surfaces. The shots from the time the camera came inside the room were taken from above, from a dolly or a ladder on wheels. When the camera reached the wall opposite the woman, it turned around for a reverse shot, and took in the scene again, including the woman. The camera began the return trip, and when it reached the woman, it cut to exactly the same outside shot as the opening one.

Until now there had been no sound: everything that was seen was seen in silence. A phone began to ring. The woman rose. She crossed the room, opened a door at the far end, and answered the phone. When she picked it up, the sound track was cut. She stood with the receiver to her ear, nodding her head, then put the receiver back in the cradle. She disappeared into a dark room in which nothing could be seen. When the lights came on, she was standing in the bathroom, putting on makeup. She donned a toga, which she cinched with a wide belt. All her actions were performed with zombie-like calm. She then examined herself in the mirror. The shot dissolved in a flash of light from her belt buckle.

The next sequence took place outside. The woman was walking down a street. She walked in front of a high, white stucco wall. She walked and walked, and when it was dusk she approached a house. She knocked on the door. It opened slowly, silently. The sound track came on. Inside, she was greeted by a crowd. Everyone seemed to know her. There were the usual exclamations, the usual greetings. She walked into the crowd. The camera attempted to follow her but was impeded. The crowd took the woman in its grip and wouldn't release her. She turned to look at the camera. Someone pulled off her toga, and the bodies around her pressed even closer. Smoke began to fill the room, and soon nothing could be seen. When the smoke cleared, the shot was the same as the opening shot. The phone began to ring. The woman got up from the chair. The frame was frozen. The credits came on while the phone continued to ring.

The film ran off the spool. The end whipped the projector a few times. Gilberte put out her hand to calm it. She turned on the lights.

It wasn't what I had expected. Truthfully, I didn't know what I had expected, but it wasn't this. This was a film, and I had expected to see something less than a film, or at least a less mature film, one more childlike, less professional. But it was professional. It was a finished work, an impressive work. I told her so.

—What do you mean? she asked, suspicious.

I explained that though I wasn't sure what I thought about the story line, the pacing was perfect, the images were beautiful. The film had something haunting and melancholy about it.

—Thanks, she said. I like it a lot.

—Who else has seen it?

She laughed.

—Anybody we could get to look at it in California.

—And?

—And nothing. What d'you think? No one's going to say, hey, that's great, here's some more money. Go make another one.

—No, but someone must have been interested.

—Sure, but do you know how many people out there are making movies and need money? People said I was too inexperienced. I didn't realize how much hustling you had to do to get the backing. I mean, I think my film is a lot better than a lot of that avant-garde shit shown around here, and even a lot better than a lot of the new independent stuff. It's short, I know. I didn't have the money to make anything longer. That is one thing I learned: if you don't have people with money and influence backing you, you don't get anywhere. With anything.

—So this time you're counting on getting people with money.

—Yeah. This time I'm going to do it right. Showing *Party Girl* in New York will help.

♦　　●

Gilberte left the film with me. I watched it again after she left. I liked it as much the second time. It was surprising nobody else had recognized the film's qualities, or its director's talent. If the film was as good as I thought it was, why hadn't the people who were paid to pick out the good from the bad and the genuine from the ersatz acclaimed it? Why had no one had seen fit to write about it. I watched it a third time and was convinced the film was a genuine piece of work. Not receiving any critical notice couldn't be taken as a mark against it. The media abounded with stories of artists who showed their work to one critic or agent after another, only to be rejected by one after another until, for who knew what reason, someone decided to take a chance on it. Fickleness and caprice played a larger role in the selection process than, say, a work's inherent aesthetic qualities. Sadly, it gave more weight to Gilberte's belief that if you didn't have anyone rich and powerful to help you push your way into the public's consciousness, you'd never make it in today's art market. It made me sympathize a little with Gilberte's willingness to accommodate and exploit Kristine. Even her cynical justification for playing the game, which I had been indignant about, seemed somehow slightly less sinister in this light. *Party Girl* was a good film that had been considered a failure, which virtually killed any chance she might have to produce, or direct, another film anytime soon.

She told me that after making the film she thought she had found her medium. Its poor reception had been a blow to her. She couldn't raise more money. If she was going to continue to work with images, it would have to be through photography. She would do anything to keep making art, she said. Of course, she still didn't know quite what she was doing. She was in such a rush to make art that she wasn't being careful. Which accounted for the haphazard and uneven quality of her first series of photographs. That she had even ventured to show them was a little presumptuous. Yet she had made progress quickly, and her next efforts demonstrated a more coherent sense of composition and a deeper understanding of the medium. What was still lacking was evidence of an over-all concern or interest or inspiration. She hadn't settled on an area of exploration or investigation. She was shooting blindly, as it were. But if *Party Girl* was any indication of what she could do when she had settled upon an idea, she was bound to pro-duce good work eventually.

◆

The invitees arrived one after another in a continual stream. By eight-thirty I had said my name so many times to so many people it was beginning to sound strange—to my ears at any rate—almost like a nonsense word devoid of meaning. The vodka martinis I was drinking weren't helping matters. No sooner was a newly arrived guest introduced to me than the guest's name completely vanished from my consciousness. Of course, there wasn't any pressing need for me to re-member. They weren't, strictly speaking, my guests. Strictly speaking, it wasn't my affair. Although I had volunteered my loft and had intended to oversee the entire evening, it hadn't worked out that way. Having penned the invitations, Kris-tine and Kettridge felt responsible for the well-being of their invitees, and to assure they would be treated in the manner to which they were accustomed, the two of them had decided to have the affair catered. An open bar had been set up. It was being tended by two beautiful boys. They were aided by two, fleet-footed servers, one of whom ferried full and empty glasses back and forth from the kitchen, while the other saw that everybody had an opportunity to pick an hors d'oeuvre off a platter.

I was a nonessential personage. I met people at the door. Presented myself. Then waited for Gilberte and Kettridge to arrive at my side. They would reintroduce me. We would chitter-chatter. Gilberte and Kettridge would then escort their guests to the far end of the loft, to introduce them to people they didn't know or to let them chat with friends and acquaintances. Gilberte came to see me every so often to inquire how I was getting along and to give me her rough impressions about how things were going, or to tell me who, exactly, the last person I had been introduced to was. Kettridge, too, talked to me whenever he had a free moment. He did this at the store, too, when he came with Kristine. While Kristine was searching the shelves for a book she had promised someone or was busy chatting with Gilberte, Kettridge would linger around the cash register, or wherever I happened to be, and try, rather desperately, to flirt with me. He attempted to do this on the sly so Kristine wouldn't notice. Which meant that, like a shoplifter, he had to do one thing while seeming to be doing something else. He wasn't very good at it. For whereas a pro at cruising and flirting would know exactly when to make his move (when to slip one of the two copies of a book he had taken off the shelf into the folds of his newspaper), Kettridge had trouble even stealing a glance. Verbally, he never managed to move beyond meteorological conditions. I saw tonight this was probably because Kettridge was a very reserved gentleman. He was also rather effete, which would, I could see, make him attractive in certain circles. In fact, I was not immune to his charm. He was basically a shy man, but gregarious when necessary. His speech was thick with the type of ten-syllable words pedants used, but his movements and gestures had been reduced to their simplest terms. (This was a good sign, because the effete often have exaggerated mannerisms and manners, which manifest themselves in direct proportion to emotion they don't feel.) When he spoke, his face was as devoid of expression as his voice was of inflection. He depended upon his hands and shoulders to do all his nonverbal talking for him. Tonight, we were speaking at length because he had discovered I had an art collection and therefore we had something to talk about besides the weather. He praised my collection and said if ever I wanted to sell my de Kooning, he would like to be the first to know.

I supposed I could go to the other end of the loft and mingle. There was no pressing reason for me to remain near the door since both Kettridge and Gilberte were eagerly watching it. I sensed Gilberte would very much like me to mix and make conversation with her guests, but I didn't particularly feel like it. I couldn't help it. I was still fuming about Kristine's last-minute decision to take charge of the evening. Her blatant power play infuriated me. Especially since I had had no choice but to concede my efforts (which were limited by my means) would have been at best adequate (Kristine's words). Whereas she felt Gilberte deserved better. She had hinted that when she and Gilberte discussed what should be done to make sure the evening was a success, Gilberte had agreed with her. When I questioned Gilberte about why I hadn't been consulted earlier, she claimed that as far as she knew, nothing had been decided. According to her, Kristine had closed their conversation with a, *well, we'll see,* and Gilberte hadn't given the matter anymore thought. When I told her what Kristine had arranged, she was delighted. Thus, I couldn't very well show my discontent because she would have (rightly) interpreted it as jealousy. But I wasn't trying to get back at her by remaining reticent and removed from the guests. I was still incapacitated from the wound I had received. I supposed by the time Kristine arrived, I would have consumed enough alcohol to numb the pain.

The bartender gave me a sly, complicitous look as he handed me my third vodka martini. I drank it slowly while trying to count how many people were gathered at the far end of the loft. My estimate was twenty-five to thirty-five, give or take one or two.

I wanted to remain as sober as possible. I began nibbling at the chips and dip. I was joined by a woman who went right for the carrot sticks, devouring them like a famished rabbit. I thought I might use our mutual interest in the more mundane food (the server was offering prosciutto and melon, and caviar on crackers) to begin my first conversation of the evening, so I, too, turned my attention to the carrots.

—They're good, aren't they? she said immediately.

I agreed and was ready to reintroduce myself and open a discussion, when she held up a carrot stick for someone sitting on the couch to see, pointed to it, nodded to it encouragingly, and, apparently having received a positive response, scooped up a handful—politely leaving me one or two—excused herself, and returned to her lair. I started in on the mixed nuts.

Judging by the diminishing frequency with which guests were arriving, I imagined almost everyone who intended to come was present. As soon as Kristine and Roger showed up, the film would be shown. If they waited much longer, Kristine would run the risk of annoying her guests, especially since the food supplies were running low. It was a bit peculiar Kristine had not come early enough to greet people, because most of the people present had come at her request. She must have come to some agreement with Kettridge, and was planning on making a grand entry at the last minute.

I was on the verge of leaving the table and going to join the guests—the prospect of being one of the first to greet Kristine didn't appeal to me—when someone I would never have expected to see in my loft walked in the door. Thomas was as shocked to see me as I was to see him. We embraced, more to recover our composure from the concussion of this unexpected meeting than from genuine emotion. Thomas and I had been lovers. He spoke first.

—Well, of all places to meet again.

—I do live here, I said.

—Ah, he breathed in his inimitable way. It's been a long time. How long? He put the burden of remembering on me.

I made a rough guess.

—Four years or so?

—That long? He stepped back a little and scrutinized at me. Handsome as ever. How long? he asked, as if he hadn't heard me.

—Four, I repeated.

—How do you know John Kettridge? he asked, giving me a sly but piercing look.

— I don't, really. He's a friend of Kristine's.

—Ah. And the filmmaker she's supporting? She's a friend of yours?

—Yes. I was about to enlighten him, but Kettridge was closing in fast.

—Thomas, he called. Good of you to make it. They shook hands and pecked each other on the cheek. Allbright and J.J. showed up at Kettridge's side. Both were dutifully and formally introduced. Kettridge made some vague comment about being surprised that Thomas and I knew each other, and then he dragged Thomas off—followed by his two advisers—to meet Gilberte.

—We'll talk later, Thomas called back to me. Kettridge turned and stared at me with undisguised curiosity. Knowing Thomas' discretion, I was sure he would thwart Kettridge's attempts to uncover the exact nature of our former relationship. Kettridge would have to appeal to Thomas' friends, who knew (and who would be more than happy to recount to any eager ear) our whole sordid history.

Kristine and Roger finally arrived. We greeted each other more profusely than the occasion warranted. Kristine said:

—I'm so happy, and then rushed off to greet Kettridge and Gilberte and her other guests.

Roger didn't offer to share his emotional state but shook my hand vigorously and immediately inquired whether it was too late to get something to drink. I took him to the table and ordered a Scotch, and another vodka martini for me.

—Kristine tells me Gilberte made and produced the film we're going to see all by herself.

—She did, I concurred.

—Have you seen it?

—Yes.

—What did you think?

— Oh ... You'll have to see it.

—What's it about?

—A party girl. I didn't want to say more because Roger was asking for a sneak preview of an opinion, which he would use to guide his reactions to the film. I didn't want to prejudice his reactions. He didn't press me to be more specific, and though I had been a little offhanded, I didn't feel that to make amends I now had to come out and explain what the film was about. Roger swirled his glass, making the ice tinkle, to show his dissatisfaction.

—Why do they do that? he asked, indicating a girl with acid-red hair. I could tell by his tone he was still upset by my refusal to cooperate but acknowledged it was a lost cause.

—Just so you'll ask, I said, hoping my lack of enthusiasm would neutralize his curiosity.

—Why don't you pierce your nose? he asked. I didn't answer verbally. I gave him a look (to match his tone) letting him know I thought what he thought about such things. That didn't prevent Roger from staring at the girl. He was fascinated by this look, by punks in general, and he continued to badger me with questions about what motivated them to mutilate themselves and to wear such outrageous outfits and adorn themselves with such extravagant accoutrements. Each time he came into the store and picked up a magazine that had a picture or an article on them, he always asked me the same questions. It seemed to me their difference had succeeded in seducing him, in drawing his attention, almost against his will. It was the same with the porn he read from time to time when he came into the store. Roger disapproved of *Playboy* and *Penthouse* and *Newlook*, yet sometimes he could not keep himself from flipping through them. What he disliked was the fact that the images forced him to stare and activated his desire for the imaginary, when he, a corporate being, should have been concerned only with the real, with *Business Week* and *Fortune*, for example. Moreover, because something that remained perpetually out of reach could preoccupy you forever, and might even become (for that very reason) an obsession, there was good reason to dislike it and condemn it. Naturally, Roger wouldn't think of joining a campaign to eradicate such things. He was aware that to do so would still bring him in contact with the imaginary, only from the other side, as it were. He would never do that. No, he much preferred to question, to taunt and tease and deprecate, so he could stay in touch with something he was drawn to, while remaining uncontaminated.

Punks didn't interest me at all. The only reason I was keeping a close watch on the girl with the acid-red hair was because she had begun passing out joints, and the possibility of exploding seeds burning holes in my rugs and couches caused me no end of distress. I couldn't count on Gilberte to lift her little finger to protect my household gods from desecration. She was even taking a drag off a joint the red-haired girl offered her. They then had a brief, secretive conversation and headed for my bedroom, no doubt to snort some coke.

I heard the tinkle of ice. Roger was still beside me. That we had gone so long without speaking made me feel slightly guilty. Especially since all evening I had been longing for someone to talk to and now that someone was here I hadn't said a word. Then I noticed Roger was engaged in a hushed discussion with one of the waiters, who was explaining to him that he was actually a model who wanted to be on the other side of the camera, and that he was only doing this for the extra money. He had apparently studied the question in some detail and was drawing an analogy between product managers in corporations and account executives in advertising agencies, and how once you did one you could do the other, only better, and that was just what he planned to do. I interrupted their conversation to ask for another vodka martini. The boy, having become intimate with Roger, made some snide remark about my capacity to drink and was about to try to draw me into their conversation, but I cut him short with a curt remark about the manner in which he was preparing my drink. I made up to Roger for my rudeness by offering to order him another drink, an offer he accepted with alacrity.

Kristine joined us.

—Come. She slipped her arm through his. You can't stay here forever, it's not polite, she said, ignoring the fact that upon her arrival she had rudely rushed to the other end of the loft to be with Gilberte.

—Stephen, you, too, should be down with the others, she admonished me.

I heeded her advice for no other reason than the food was not providing the results I had hoped for, and I couldn't drink any more alcohol or I would be senseless for the rest of the evening.

I drifted from group to group, half-listening to conversations. I almost joined Thomas and Kettridge, who were engaged in an animated but hushed discussion, but they both let me know—by not acknowledging my looks—they would rather be left alone.

Gilberte came up to me and said she wanted to begin soon. She was evidently very high, and kept puffing at her cigarette in a very unladylike fashion. It was the first time I got a good look at her since she had arrived. I found her particularly beautiful. Dressed all in black, in new clothes, or clothes new to me, her hair pulled back off her face and done in a tight chignon, she looked rather severe. Yet at the same time she appeared more feminine and elegant than I had ever seen her. I would have liked her to talk to me, to share some of her impressions, whisper a caustic comment in my ear about one of the guests (as she did about customers), but she simply pointed out it was getting late and as soon as she got the go-ahead from Kristine she intended to show her film.

Whether it was because she had Roger in tow and thought it would be unseemly to drag him around as she chased after Gilberte, or whether she wanted to show Gilberte she, too, could join forces with someone else, Kristine no longer seemed to think it necessary to dog Gilberte's footsteps. She was now introducing Roger to Society. I caught snatches of Kristine's conversation. From Roger's expressions and gestures and his obeisance to his wife, I surmised he thought of her as a Grande Dame. Roger was not a socializer. He didn't have any interest in social climbing. And though he disliked meeting the kind of people to whom Kristine introduced him (snobs for the most part he said), he clearly enjoyed seeing his wife move easily among them.

When I got close to Kristine, I listened to her talk, trying to comprehend how other people could listen to her and not immediately be convinced she was talking nonsense. Much of her conversation consisted in recounting anecdotes she as- sumed (apparently correctly) were of interest to her listeners. She did this with much élan. But her passionate preoccupa- tion with telling the tale made her nearly oblivious of her auditors. As with many narcissists, she was so involved with her self-presentation that it was easy to mistake her for an un- abashed extrovert. While engaged in narrating an event, she adhered to the rules of storytelling. Because she was in polite company, her non sequiturs and inappropriate remarks were greeted with interest by her interlocutors. There was always someone curious to hear her opinions or relieved to have someone else's discourse curtailed. If Kristine's domination of the conversation upset them at all, it was not due to the turn the conversation took when she entered it, but because she monopolized it.

Gilberte whispered in my ear that she wanted to get the show on the road. Then she informed the rest of the guests. There was a general murmur of approval. Gilberte asked somebody to lower close the blinds. There was a general panic as people searched for seating. People scattered to hunt down chairs and stools. Some of the younger men sat on the rugs. The women all managed to find seats. (Kristine, probably tipped off by Gilberte, was already ensconced on a sofa. Roger stood gallantly at her side.)

Thomas sidled up to me and whispered:

—Is it good?

—You tell me when it's over.

Gilberte asked me to turn off the lights, a detail that had slipped my mind.

In the presence of this many people, the film seemed even shorter than when I had seen it the first time. No more than a few minutes had elapsed before I was turning the lights on. There was silence. Then someone clapped. Then everyone clapped. It was real, heartwarming applause. Then it was over. People shuffled and scraped as they got up and readied themselves to go. Before leaving they paid tribute to Gilberte, in groups or individually, shaking her hand, gripping her arm, hugging her, pecking her on the cheek. Gilberte stayed close to the projector and accepted the accolades demurely, politely.

Thomas shook her hand and said something that made her smile. To me he said that we should get together for a drink. I was agreeable to this and gave him my number, but declined to set a date.

Kristine, who had waited until Gilberte stood alone, approached her and, laying her hand on her shoulder, said:

—It was beautiful.

Frankly, *beautiful* was not the word I had expected her to use. I had expected something more trendy or glitzy. She didn't let me down.

—Simply smashing, she added, smiling. She looked Gilberte straight in the eyes, as if this were the ultimate proof of her sincerity. Then she kissed her. Kettridge and Allbright and J.J. approached her. Their reactions were entirely favorable, very positive. Roger, sitting on the couch, yawned and checked his watch.

I helped the help clean up. There were still a few stragglers wandering about, some looking at the paintings and photographs. One asked to use the phone for a quick call. Kristine remained close to Gilberte. Her hand was drooling on her shoulder. Roger, now up, rocking on his heels, stood a little way off. He appeared to want to have a word with Gilberte, but he was put off by his wife's sticky presence. He looked at his watch again, and then at Kristine and Gilberte. Gilberte was listening to Kristine. Their colloquy was interrupted by a man who wanted to shake hands with Gilberte. Roger used this break to surreptitiously show Gilberte his watch. She nodded. She came to me.

—Are you ready?

—For what?

—To go to dinner. Kristine and Roger are taking us to dinner.

—They are?

—I told you.

—You didn't tell me.

—I did. And if I didn't, I'm telling you now, OK? Now, get ready, she commanded.

I was offended by her tone, but because of the alcohol I couldn't be sure whether she had told me or not. I went to my bedroom to do her bidding. I searched my memory. Had I been told about this dinner? It seemed unlikely I would forget the evening was to end on such an unpleasant note as sitting around a table with Kristine. Perhaps I had been told and had put it out of my mind for that very reason: otherwise it would have ruined my whole evening. Gilberte could have mentioned it to me in passing, or while I wasn't listening. I doubted it. I suspected she hadn't told me. She had probably thought the surprise decision to use a catering service was as much as I could stand. She was mad at me because she felt guilty about her omission.

Dinner at a restaurant was the last thing I wanted. I wanted to be alone with Gilberte. But Gilberte wanted to be with Kristine and her other admirers. At dinner they would talk about the film. Gilberte would explain what it was about and assure them they had understood it and secure their undying devotion to her work.

To be honest, what galled me was that I hadn't foreseen the need to do something like this—and I should have. Once again, Kristine had outmaneuvered me. After almost every opening or premiere there was a dinner or drinks for a select group of supporters and close friends. Kettridge, Allbright, J.J., and perhaps Thomas, as well as others, were sure to be there. However, one of the unwritten social rules forbade the invitees to divulge they were invited, to prevent the jealousy of those who weren't. The group was usually hand-picked by the artist and the principal patron, and it was definitely an honor to be present at these fêtes. Though I could flatter myself I had been invited, I couldn't help but feel it was I who should have done the inviting. I was resentful, despite the fact I would have had to ask Kristine to supply me with the list of people she wanted present, or let her ask them in my place.

I put on a blazer and then sat on my bed. Fatigue and alcohol pressed my head down between my legs. I caught it and held it with my hands. I wanted to lie back and close my eyes for a long time. I couldn't. I got up. In front of my mirror I combed my hair. I looked awful: tired, almost haggard. I shrugged my shoulders and adjusted the fall of my blazer. It didn't alter things. My countenance corresponded too closely to how I felt for there to be any hope of improvement.

When I came out, Roger and Kristine and Gilberte were waiting in the kitchen. The help had apparently been dismissed. Roger, after looking at his watch, said:

—We'd better hurry.

So we did.

♦

Roger and Kristine sat at opposite ends of the table. Gilberte sat on Kristine's right and Kettridge on her left. I was seated next to Thomas. Too many people separated Gilberte and me, making communication between us impossible. All I could do was watch how she and Kristine communicated throughout the meal and wonder what was going on under the table.

By the time the meal was over, I had amassed a wealth of information about Kettridge and Kristine. Thomas loved to gossip. Although he was clearly nervous about being with me again—he chain-smoked throughout the meal—this didn't prevent him from talking nonstop.

He started off by saying Gilberte's film was one of the best things he had seen by a young artist in a long time. It evidenced an imagination completely unfettered by the current trends in independent cinema. He asked me about her other work and sought my opinion of her photographs, about which he had heard a great deal from Kettridge. I offered guarded observations and dropped the subject as discreetly as I could, immediately launching upon another, Kristine.

—Now listen, he commanded, taking my arm.

He then trashed her. From the intensity with which he heaped obloquy upon her and the way he kept touching me to make his points more vivid, I concluded he had long wanted to share his estimation of her with someone. I remembered well Thomas' penchant for vituperation. The slightest foible in someone's temperament or taste or manners was enough to bring out the assassin in him. I had become used to this. It was his way of establishing his difference. His histrionic performances were a farce, something he did to amuse himself and his listener: deep down he didn't give a damn about his victims—except insofar as they were the reification of an archetype. In Kristine's case, the archetype was the philistine social climber, the vertical barbarian.

—All those people like your friend.

—That woman is not my friend, I corrected him.

—I know, darling. He stroked my shoulder. But all those types are the ones responsible for the hedonistic philosophy that judges objects of art by their ability to be fun. For the time being they have suppressed or relegated to a less important position work by genuine artists. For example, those East Village kids are pulling off the scam of the century. And people like our hostess are aiding and abetting them.

He went on to recount some juicy stories about how idiotic Kristine was. His vehemence in denouncing her made me wonder if I had not been too harsh in my estimation of her capabilities, having unconsciously based my judgments on what I thought Thomas would have thought. This was not out of the question. I had always respected Thomas' taste. Not long after we became involved, I remembered, I told myself his taste could be summed up in one word: infallible. Later, when I knew him better, I qualified this assumption slightly and summed it up in two words: nearly infallible. From that point on, even during the disintegration of our relationship, my esteem for his judgments never altered. (This was one of the reasons our separation had been painful: my association with him had been the only thing saving me from being considered one of the rabble he mercilessly castigated.) What I particularly liked was his outrage at anything less than perfect and his belief that everything mattered: everything—from the way someone tied his shoes to the way he parted his hair, from the way food was prepared to the way it was presented, from the way the paint was applied to the canvas to the frame that held it. Also admirable, in my opinion, was despite his constant encounter with an imperfect world, he remained undaunted. Perpetual disappointment did not destroy his ability to feel outrage. That he himself sometimes lapsed in his efforts to attain perfection and fell below one hundred percent did not escape him, but, he said, he was aware of it. The difference between him and the others was that the others believed (rightly for the most part) they could get away with it, and he hated himself whenever he fell below his own standard.

Surprisingly, Thomas had good things to say about Kettridge. He came from old money. Yankee-made money, in manufacturing or something like that. It turned out they had both gone to Yale, and though they had missed each other by a few years, they had had many of the same professors and knew not an inconsiderable number of people in common. Begrudgingly, Thomas praised Kettridge's art collection, speculated about its worth, and commented (unfavorably) about the direction it was taking.

I wanted to know how Kettridge could stoop to associating with Kristine.

—She's way beneath him, you're right.

I offered some tentative hypotheses in an attempt to try to explain the attraction. All of them were inconsequential, as it turned out. According to Thomas, it was simply this: Roger had sold Kettridge a piece of property in Southampton that the latter had been absolutely mad to have. And as this piece of property adjoined Roger's, after Kettridge had built his house Roger found himself with a new neighbor. Kettridge had invited Roger and Kristine to a series of cocktail parties and soirees to show his gratitude. As he had found Roger to be a rather good fellow, and interesting, the intercourse had continued back in town when they found themselves at functions together. They had become friends, after a fashion. But Roger wasn't a social animal. It was his wife who kept up the contact.

Kettridge found Kristine very eighties, highly entertaining, and, for the most part, inoffensively vulgar.

Kettridge had a predilection for vulgar types. He liked rough trade, Thomas said. His old summer house in East Hampton had always been chock-full of those types. And though Thomas was not privy to how he ran his new house, he imagined it wasn't much different. However, since the beginning of the eighties, and especially now, since the severity of the AIDS epidemic had become common knowledge, Kettridge had been trying to improve his image. His family, who still controlled some of his funds, was pressing him to become more respectable.

—At heart, he's rather conservative, Thomas said, sighing. So, desirous of remaining in the good graces of his family he resolved to put on a show of respectability and took up with a woman. And that woman is Kristine. But it is just a show. He hasn't given up his wicked ways. His fondness for boys hasn't diminished at all. His tastes have moderated, and he's moved upstream to more classy companions. His minion of the moment is that one, Allbright.

We both stared at Allbright, who is seated at the far end of the table, and without a congenial dinner partner, to judge by his pursed lips and the jealous eye he was giving his patron.

Allbright, according to Thomas, was an extremely able young man with a good eye. Kettridge had met him at some function or other at MoMA, when Allbright was pursuing his graduate degree in fine arts. At the time, he had been the friend of an associate of Kettridge's. But Kettridge had swept him off his feet.

—It was so romantic. He took him to Italy and France, I remember. It was such a scandal.

When they returned, Kettridge monopolized all his time. Naturally, Allbright had to terminate his other relationship. And shortly thereafter Kettridge rented an apartment for him in Chelsea. However, Allbright was not an ingénue. The trip to Italy and France had been wonderful, but he wasn't interested in becoming a permanent tourist or a traveling companion. He hadn't gone to Yale and acquired all those credentials for nothing. He wanted to set himself up as an independent art dealer and consultant. And, apparently, one of the conditions of his continuing liaison with Kettridge was that the latter help him realize his goal.

—John loves a challenge, Thomas whispered. And he was mad about Allbright. He began letting him act as his agent. He took him to auctions and galleries and introduced him to dealers and artists. He did everything for the kid. But it wasn't enough. One thing you should know about Allbright: he wants to get to the top. And he doesn't care how red his elbows become on the way. Anyway, John got one or two other friends of his to trust Allbright's judgment, and they threw some business his way. And then through other connections John arranged for him to have some articles published in *Artforum* and *Art in America*. I think he curated a show at a downtown gallery. Something at the Parrish. And then Kettridge had the idea of getting Kristine to engage him.

—Ahh ... I said.

—Ahh ... he said.

Kristine was Allbright's first client. And if things worked out well this arrangement would obviate the need for him to work in a gallery long enough to develop a group of people who trusted and respected his taste, and it would also enable him to meet enough artists whom he could approach. She was to be his proving ground. Kettridge and his friends would provide the introductions and connections. A more headstrong and intelligent person would already have ideas about what he or she wanted to collect, and the responsibility for amassing the kinds of work that would gain prestige for the collection would be very limited. But because Kristine had no eye for art and because her social standing was ambiguous, if Allbright made mistakes they would be attributed to her and not to him. Moreover, there was a chance—a slim one, but that was better than nothing—that through Kristine, Roger could be convinced to start up a corporate collection (all the tax laws were favorable) and Allbright would be the logical choice to take charge of such an operation. Of course, neither Kettridge nor Allbright had counted on Kristine's discovering someone on her own. But if Gilberte was every bit as good as they claimed, and the film supported what they said, then so much the better for them.

Then we talked about us. Thomas' life was much the same, he said. Like me, he was no longer seeing anyone steadily. He disagreed with my decision to remain chaste and said I was a coward. He blamed the outbreak of AIDS on heterosexuals, claiming it was their intolerant attitude and repressive laws that had fostered the kind of life-style that had been conducive to the spread of the disease: it was not promiscuity but repression that was responsible. He deplored the continual influx of Spanish-speaking people who were anxious to come to America to work and live, but adamant about retaining their language and therefore their culture—which had produced the very conditions they were fleeing. He thought the crusade against smoking in public was misguided: the real danger lay in playing music in public: this was, in his opinion, having the most deleterious consequences on the mental life of the nation's children. He was in favor of restricting the availability of records and tapes and airwaves to those over twenty-one, and strictly regulating music in public places.

—You're still the same, I said.

— I know. It's unfortunate, and rather a bore. I'm too old now to do anything about myself. I've become a bad habit I can't break. You know, at a certain age, what were once psychological habits become physiological necessities.

He then became involved in an across-the-table discussion with a woman who wanted to know what he had bought at Sotheby's the week before. Truthfully, I could have gone on talking to Thomas all night. He always had a plethora of ideas he was dying to discuss. I realized if there was something missing in my life, it was someone to converse with at his level of intensity and seriousness. Ideas pullulated in his brain. Many of them misguided, but if I had taken him up on any of the ideas he had just introduced, he could have gone on all night. He loved to talk. But as much as I longed to be included in his aura of intensity, I couldn't. He had hurt me too much. Our affair had ended too shabbily. I had said I would never forgive him ... and I wouldn't. Now, although I could take pleasure in talking to him again, I knew I couldn't do it on a regular basis.

♦

Thrilled at Gilberte's success, Kristine brought a steady stream of people into the store to meet her. After the introductions, she invariably took Gilberte with her to look at a show or to have drinks or dinner or both. Her leaving always had to have my blessing. Ostensibly, I was still the boss. But

Kristine insisted on making me say that it was no problem, that I could easily handle the work load myself. Which was usually, but not always, the case. There were days when I needed all the help I could get. Gilberte knew when she was leaving me in the lurch, but she couldn't refuse Kristine anything. The morning after, she would apologize for deserting me. She claimed she had to do what she did because there was always the chance something would come out of her socializing and politicking. If everything went well, in fact, she might, just might, get to screen her film at the Bleecker Street Cinema, in the Agee Room. If it received good reviews, it could generate enough publicity to help her career.

The screening soon took second place in the scheme of things. Kristine informed Gilberte she had wangled an editor she knew at *Vogue* into agreeing to let Gilberte do the photography for an article. It wouldn't be a big shoot, but the photo credit Gilberte would receive would serve her well.

The week before the shoot, Gilberte was all nerves. She couldn't concentrate on her work at the store. To ward off her anxiety, she talked all the time. Again and again she worked out all the possible scenarios, from bad to worse to best, that could happen on the shoot. I tried to make her see there was nothing to worry about. I told her she should stop torturing herself. But she continually came up with something new to worry about. All for nothing. In the end the shoot went very smoothly. Gilberte admitted to having been so scared of screwing up that she had done everything the art director and the editor had wanted, no questions asked. Kristine, too, was pleased. According to her, Gilberte had done a superb job: she had pulled off her assignment with panache.

Gilberte was not nearly as sanguine. She took her success in her stride and did not let it go to her head. In fact, she seemed totally indifferent to her accomplishment. I asked her why.

—I don't want to do fashion, she said.

—You don't have to, I said.

—Yes, but so far that's the only type of work Kris has found me. I don't want it.

—Why did you do it, then? Her explanation (if it could be called that) was something to the effect that she was under a self-imposed obligation to accept any kind of photographic work that came her way until she could produce and sell enough of her own work to become self-supporting and raise money to make another film. But going on this shoot caused her to reassess her battle plan. She discovered working with an art director and an editor who knew exactly what they wanted depressed her. If the look she was after didn't match what the magazine wanted to see, she was out of luck. This time she had been fortunate, she said, because their visions coincided. Nevertheless, she realized that until she made a name for herself she wouldn't have the freedom to work independently, as she was used to doing, and that someone else was always going to have the final say: her creative effort would be cropped to fit an editorial policy.

—That's why I only used to take the pictures that I wanted to take. And if they weren't selling, at least they were what I wanted to do. Shit! I want to make films or art, not take pictures of clothes.

♦

Her next important job came from Kettridge. After many interminable teas, he arranged for her to do a portrait of two sisters. Gilberte would have full control of the artistic process from start to finish, but still she wasn't happy.

—I can't take pictures of people, she said.

—You did for Kristine's ad and for Vogue, I pointed out.

—I took pictures of models. Models aren't people. They're images. These two old ladies are people. They want to look like themselves, like they are. What am I supposed to do?

—Photograph them, I suggested.

She did. She borrowed a four-by-five from a friend and tackled the job. The first shots were unmitigated disasters. Even though she had used the camera's Polaroid capabilities to preview what she was going to shoot, the photos were absolutely awful. The evening following the first shoot, we compared the Polaroids, which were not too bad, to the four-by-fives, to try to figure out what had gone wrong.

—I don't get it, I said. You have to shoot people in films.

—Those are close-ups, or extreme close-ups, or two-shots, or whatever. Anyway, actors are like models. They're not themselves. These two old dowagers aren't playing a role. They're not images. She shook her head. I don't know.

Gilberte decided not to show the sisters the four-by-fives. She asked them to sit again. Which they were more than happy to do. The shots from this second sitting showed a definite improvement. She had moved the camera closer, adjusted the lighting, and worked out a better composition. She showed these shots to the sisters, but they weren't happy with them and asked if they could be done again.

The photographs from the third sitting showed a marked advance in Gilberte's understanding of how to arrange and photograph people with more feeling than a snapshot. However, the sisters were still not content with her work. They didn't mind that Gilberte would have to come again and reshoot them because they wanted the most perfect representation of themselves as possible.

The final set of photographs pleased everybody. I had to admit they exhibited an air that had been absent in the previous photographs. This time Gilberte had captured a hint of their character (or of character). Their dowdy elegance was discernible. It gave them a regal aspect. Their gnarled, corrugated countenances exhibited a touch of melancholy and inspired a kind of respect. There was something avid and yet empty in their eyes that let you know these two old dames were perched on the edge of their last days on earth. The sisters were very pleased with Gilberte's work. The entire undertaking had been a charming diversion to them. They promised to recommend her to all their friends.

◆

Working for the sisters had taught Gilberte an important lesson: you could never know too much about other people. By *other people* Gilberte meant potential patrons, or socialites, who were one and all potential patrons. It was only in the movies or in books that people discovered everything they needed to know. In life, information was more difficult to come by, usually less exact, and never altogether complete. Gilberte explained this to me one afternoon:

—Those old ladies knew everybody, and there were still things they didn't know about people they knew that they were dying to know. I mean, they would gibber non-stop while I was shooting and then later during tea. Sometimes it nearly put me to sleep. Mainly because I didn't know who they were talking about. Then I realized they were backgrounding me on people I might meet, and I should pay attention, because I might be able to use what they were saying to get on somebody's good side or at least not get on their bad side.

The shoot had been a profound learning experience for her. She now knew sharing the little anecdotes and gossip she was privy to would make her seem a knowledgeable and creditable source of information. She had learned that acquiring a piece of new information gave some people as much pleasure as gaining possession of a precious object, pleasure for which they were usually grateful. It was as if she had discovered the power and mystery of the *word* for the first time.

Now she routinely asked Kristine whom they were going to dine with and how Kristine knew them. She tried to ferret out Kristine's relations with the bastions of power (or lack thereof), made informed guesses as to where Kristine's friends' money came from (and how much of it there was). She was becoming a social anthropologist. It was obvious this fieldwork intrigued her tremendously.

♦

Right after she delivered the final prints to the two sisters, Gilberte embarked upon a photo-taking spree. Apparently Kristine had hinted she was trying to work out a deal that would permit Gilberte to show her work in an uptown gallery. Gilberte wanted to be ready. At least once a week she brought in a set of contact sheets to show me. She didn't ask me to critique her work, so I didn't. I merely commented on

the general direction in which she seemed to be moving, remarked on the similarities and differences in the shots, and
indicated what I thought she may or may not have been after.
As with the initial shots of the sisters, something was amiss.
Most of her photos were offbeat or eccentric, but not at all
intriguing. They were neither windows opening on a seg-
ment of reality I had never before seen, nor mirrors reflecting
an image of something I saw all the time. They didn't bring
together or combine formal qualities of objects or hint at abstract relations. They weren't peculiar enough to qualify as
sui generis. Her compositions were a mishmash. There was
simply too much extraneous information in her shots. From
time to time we argued over an interpretation or, as Gilberte
preferred to think of it, the aesthetics of a shot. To judge by
the heated nature some of these discussions, it seemed I was
succeeding in making her think more deeply about what she
was doing, even if she did resent my comments.

After one particularly ferocious confrontation, during
which she accused me of being heartless and callous, I told
her if she wasn't happy with my critique she should show her
work to Allbright or some other critic with credentials, who
would doubtless give her some good, solid feedback. I realized
then why mine were the only privileged eyes: the work was too
dreadful to show to anyone in a position to hand down a definitive decision about its worth. I was permitted to see it because
I could do no harm. My opinion might upset Gilberte, but it
didn't carry any professional weight or social consequences.

She began to trust me, almost implicitly. She tuned to
me for an opinion on almost everything. I became her adviser.
She relied on me to scrutinize her work and help her improve
it. I felt bad about continually pointing out her substandard

efforts, but her increasing confidence in me was touching. It pushed me to try harder to make myself worthy of her trust. I began to want, as badly as she did, to find the right direction for her. I did all I could to encourage her to do better.

♦

One day Gilberte brought in a treatment for a new movie she was working on.

—I'm stuck. I don't know what to do. Would you mind taking a look at it? she asked.

—Sure, I said.

I was elated. Her asking me to read her latest effort showed I had secured her trust and that she respected my opinions. We had drawn closer.

I read the treatment. I immediately understood why she had asked me to look it over. It was, sadly, in the same sorry shape as her photographs in progress. The story line was vaguely about terrorists, antiterrorists, a military coup, a radical revolutionary cell that was holding an entire country hostage with an atomic bomb, an antihero who was supposed to defuse the international crisis, a double-agent shuttle diplomat: it was a discombobulated tale of disenchantment and deception. It was impressive in its scope. Very ambitious, global. The characters were appealing. The parallel between the amorphous, chaotic life of the antihero and the world at large was well thought out. Yet, as it stood, the treatment was without a beginning or end. I read it twice, but I couldn't see what to do with it. I told Gilberte. I expressed my dismay at the confusion and lack of cohesion in the story development.

—It's supposed to be like that, she said. I wanted it dark and gloomy and discontinuous and paranoid, like Godard's *Alphaville*.

I protested. I told her that just because she wanted it to be like something didn't mean it was. To me it wasn't dark and gloomy at all: it was merely murky. Something had to be done about it. In her defense, she claimed the film's underlying metaphysic—this was the biggest word I had ever heard her use correctly—was that the world had already been blown to smithereens and we were the fallout. The collateral damage.

—Anyway, I'm not trying to be narrative, she said. I didn't write a story, just a sequence of scenarios. I can make a movie from that. I didn't use a script for *Party Girl*. It was just an idea I shot. This one is too.

—Except this one is going to require dialogue, numerous sets, and exotic locales. I mean, this is a big-budget affair, I said.

—Not necessarily. It depends on how you see it. You may be right. I'm not sure yet. Anyway, do you think ... Could you work on it a little? I mean, all the ideas and everything are there. I don't think it needs a lot of work.

—I don't know, I said. We talked about what she wanted. After listening, I told her I had read the treatment carefully, but it wasn't at all clear when I was reading it how she was going to accomplish what she had just told me. Then I was totally honest with her. I said her treatment was nothing more than some notes, some very good, toward the development of an idea for a movie. I told her it was unlikely she could give it to anybody and expect them to make sense of it without talking to her.

—Can it be fixed? she wanted to know.

—I suppose.

—Can you fix it? I mean, can you make it do what you said it should do?

It was highly questionable that I was the person she should ask for help. I told her there were people who knew how to do these things better than I, people who would know if her treatment was fixable.

—If you don't want to do it, just say so, she said.

—I'll do it if you want me to, I said.

—I want, she said.

—OK, I said.

In fact, I was elated with my assignment. By suggesting there were people more knowledgeable and better qualified than I to help her, I hadn't been trying to get out of it. I wanted to get involved in her creative life in the worst way. Only, I felt I should be completely honest with her and make sure she recognized she didn't have to turn to me.

Working with her like this bound us together in a way that my critiquing her photographs hadn't done. Now I was going to participate in the creative process. I would finally fulfill my long-standing desire to take an active part in her creative life, a part I felt had been denied me ever since Kristine came on the scene. It was my chance to do something for Gilberte. And, not incidentally, for myself, because I would be creating something: out of her notes I would write a treatment.

♦

I reread what she had given me several times. The more I read it, the more disillusioned I became. The characters were good. There was no denying it. The idea was brilliant. The execution was a disaster. Close analysis revealed that though she had a good idea, she had not been able to work it out, and the piece stood on the merits of the characters. It would need vast revisions and rethinking to make it work. I racked my brain, but I couldn't decide where to begin. I told Gilberte. I hadn't understood what she was getting at, not exactly, she said. We talked. She gave me some more ideas as to the direction she thought the scenario should take.

I devoted all my spare time to writing. I stayed up late. I got up early and worked before going to the store. I gave up going out after work. I began eating dinner in the loft. I sat at my desk and wrote and rewrote and reworked and rewrote Gilberte's treatment. When I could no longer write, I read books on how to write screenplays, most of which contained at least a chapter on how to write a treatment. I learned a lot quickly, and I found use for what I learned just as quickly.

What I liked best about the project, aside from its giving me the opportunity to do something creative, was that it forced Gilberte to reveal how she saw the world: the text was the expression of her own, private ontological universe and was not a scheme or plan devised to please everybody. No matter how far short of achieving her ideal she had fallen, what she told me demonstrated she could transcend the material world and apprehend the relations that determined how it was perceived. Because she could do this, the way was now clear for my heart to open to her. Up until now I had had my doubts about her talent, about who or what she was. *Party Girl* had moved me. It made me acknowledge she had talent. It demonstrated that she wanted to portray on film a style of life—or a vision of a lifestyle—and could do so poignantly. But it was not conclusive evidence.

I was tempted to believe I would have been far more impressed with the film if I had never seen any of her photographs because they made the film appear to be merely an *aperçu*, not a vision. The treatment for this new film, rough and incomplete as it was, showed that despite her inelegant attempt to explain her ideas, she was after something. Possibly it was too big—for her—to put into words. (I was chagrined at the thought of the speech about art I had planned to give her.) Acknowledging that she was not as shallow as I had feared also allowed me to fall in love with her (although that was putting it strongly, because *fall* connoted a precipitous change in position or condition, and for me love was a drawn out, rational process). I now had no doubt that I could come to love her. Moreover, I could love her for herself, for what she was and not for what I would try to make of her: if she was an artist, that meant her personality possessed what was necessary for her to produce her work. If I tried to inflict a change, I might irrevocably alter the whole. The great thing was if she couldn't love me—or didn't want to love me, which seemed very possible—I would understand: it would be because of her art. The time, devotion, and energy love demanded would drain her emotionally. Which would not leave her with any feeling for anyone else. I was happy, very happy, but very scared too. I didn't know what would become of my decision to open myself to the possibility of love. Fortunately, I had no time to think about what could develop between us. I had more pressing things to think about— namely, writing the treatment.

I was beginning to see, a formidable undertaking. Especially since the entire idea had broken down under close scrutiny. There was no internal coherence to her story. And the characters, when analyzed in more depth, turned out not

to jell into personalities. Gilberte said she would stick them together on film, that her direction would show their character. I
shouldn't get hung up about it. I did.

♦

I tore her work apart, broke down every sequence, every
scene, every shot, to its barest elements. I mapped out the
plot. Reworked its development. I put everything down on
three-by- five index cards and pinned them to my wall, as-
signing each theme in the story a different color card. It took
me weeks to completely deconstruct her text and to add what
was missing. Then I spent weeks pacing up and down before
my mosaic, adding and subtracting text I thought essential.
Finally, I numbered all the cards, took them down, and began
writing the actual treatment. It took me weeks. I didn't like
the result. I couldn't pinpoint it, but I was certain there was
something wrong. It didn't feel right. I took it all apart and
began again.

♦

By early April my revision had progressed nicely. I had
lost count of how many times I had deconstructed and re-
constructed it. It was becoming embarrassing, too, because
Gilberte kept asking me how much longer it was going to
take. She wanted me to have it ready by the time *Party Girl*
was shown at the Bleecker Street Cinema. She didn't realize I was working against tremendous odds: after all, I had
never finished anything I had begun. And though technically
I hadn't authored this text, I had altered it so radically and

it bore so little resemblance to the original that an objective reader might indeed say it was an original text. I thought it was good. Much better than what Gilberte had written. Still, it could be improved. And every time Gilberte asked me when I would be finished, I used the opportunity to discuss with her what I was doing. I always expected her to object or to indicate whether she was pleased with what I had done, but she didn't seem to care. She told me her version had been merely an idea and she was absolutely open to suggestions. She thought everything I proposed was fabulous. So I kept at it.

◆

I wished I could say Gilberte's photographs were progressing as well as my reworking of the treatment. However, they showed no improvement. Frankly, I didn't understand. Though uninspired, the pictures for *Vogue* had been right enough and were well accepted. The portrait of the sisters had finally worked out satisfactorily. Everything since then was deplorable. I could barely look at her work in progress without wincing. Somehow she just wasn't connecting. Her subject kept eluding her. (The vision I had attributed to her was rapidly fading into a blur.) She, too, was aware something was wrong. Unfortunately, it seemed the greater her self-doubt about the quality of her work, the more substandard was the work she produced. We went through all her contact sheets. We created a folder containing pictures showing some merit or inherent value or integrity. We talked about them and tried to define what it was that made them work: whether it was their heightened emotionalism, or whether she had captured a marvelously strange nuance, or whether she had brought out the erotic-poetic (or the neurotic) in a situation, or whether she had managed to abstract geometrical forms, or create a certain painterly energy with the light. Our effort to define what made them work as a group was stymied by their differences. Nowhere was there evidence of an overriding aesthetic. I told Gilberte she should concentrate on one thing until she had exhausted all its possibilities. I stressed that part of a vision was seeing the continuity in a multitude of possibilities. She dissented. She said she couldn't keep taking pictures of the same thing all the time without getting bored. She believed she was on the verge of being able to articulate and execute work that would tie together and justify her seemingly disparate interests. It was only a matter of time.

◆

One day, after having gone through another set of contact sheets without coming up with anything we liked, I suggested she reconsider the idea of having a show, especially an uptown show. I said it seemed to me if she would stop working with this one end in mind, it would be beneficial to her work. It was senseless, and counterproductive, to try to force a style to emerge, or a series to develop, overnight, as it were.

—Sometimes you only get one chance, she said. I can't say no.

—You could say not now.

—You don't understand, she said. You've got to take what's offered when it's offered. And then you have to produce whatever you can. You can't ever know whether it's your best, ever. If I wait, hoping I'll do something better, it may not happen. Don't worry. If I keep working like I'm working now, something will come. It'll come to me. It has to. Don't worry. You're a big worrier, she admonished me. Anyway, we're too close to it, too critical.

I didn't pursue the subject. To me her priorities seemed misplaced. She should have been taking more chances with her art and not have been in the least concerned with her career. Her longing to be acknowledged in the art world was going to be her downfall. Careerism was inhibiting her work. It was why there was nothing distinctive about what she was doing. She could do what others had done, and do interesting variations, but they never resulted in anything new or good. Now that she was practically in a panic to come up with work she could show, she wasn't interested in trying anything new. All she wanted was something presentable, something pretty, something someone would want to hang in their living room. And she was working like crazy to make it. I was amazed at (and jealous of) her industriousness, her capacity for work, and her irrefutable belief that something would come out of what she was doing.

◆

Kristine came into the store looking for Gilberte.

—She's just gone out to her lab, I informed her. In truth, she had gone hours ago and should have returned hours ago.

—She's such a hard worker, Kristine said.

—What's the latest word on her show? Do you think it will take place? I asked her.

—I've just got to iron out the dates with Henry. He liked what I showed him.

—Henry ... He owns the uh....

—Verity Gallery, she informed me. She couldn't hope for a better place for a show.

—Right.

The Verity Gallery was one of the most prestigious galleries in New York. It wasn't a blue-chip Fifty-Seventh-Street gallery, but it had been instrumental in introducing minimalist painting to New York, as well as pattern painting and conceptualist works. Although its heyday had been in the sixties, it was still a force in the art world. Recently the gallery had begun showing important postmodernists. Its latest show of new figurative painters had received high praise. The move into photography was new. I had just read about it in *Art News* the previous week.

—What if Gilberte isn't ready? I asked.

—Isn't ready? Kristine echoed me derisively, forcing me to explain what I meant. Which I did, in quite bold terms.

—It's not for you to judge, darling, she said.

—You wouldn't think of postponing the show, then, even if her work might prove to be an embarrassment?

—Are you that jealous of her that you'd ruin her career?

—Are you? I almost lost my temper. I began again. I'm trying to protect her.

—Protect her from what? Now I see why she's always so worried. It's you. Who do you think you are? What do you know? Anyone whose opinion counts has been impressed by what she's done. Don't think you're going to step in and call the shots, Stephen.

—I'm not trying to call....

—She's an artist. She needs support and encouragement. All you offer is discouragement, negative criticism. I'm warning you, Stephen, don't interfere. She's brilliant. She opened her purse and removed her gloves. After pulling them on, she said:

—Be so kind as to tell Gilberte I stopped by.

◆

I resolved never again, under any circumstances, to discuss Gilberte with Kristine. I had had no idea my question about postponing the show would be rebuffed with such fury. The intensity of her outburst made me think perhaps her relationship with Gilberte had ... had what? Well, nothing blinded one to the faults of another so absolutely as love (or passion). Was it that? I couldn't be sure. Kristine's implicit trust (for she hadn't seen the most recent photographs, hadn't read the treatment) in Gilberte's talent led me to believe something more than an appreciation of art was at issue here.

When I told Gilberte what had happened she smiled coyly and said Kristine had certainly overreacted, but that she was only watching out for her. She was grateful, she said, that both of us were concerned about her, even if it wasn't in the same way. Before letting the subject drop entirely, there was one thing about which I wanted to be sure. I asked her whether she thought what I had to say was helpful or harmful.

—What do you think? she asked. Do you think I'd show you my work otherwise? She went on to say that sometimes she didn't understand everything I said, or agree with what she did understand. That didn't bother her. Nor was she bothered by knowing she might never produce the kind of work that would please me.

◆

For someone who was supposed to have a show soon, Gilberte's social schedule was appalling. The opening of her film at the Bleecker Street Cinema was one thing: she didn't have to prepare anything for that. But she sacrificed all too many afternoons to *visiting* with Kristine and her friends for an artist who was supposed to be developing a series of photographs for a major opening.

She now quizzed Kristine extensively about whom they were going to see, sometimes stipulating exactly how much time she would stay, based upon her estimation of their importance. Whether it was to drinks or to an opening, to a benefit or to a private dinner, Gilberte loved going places with Kristine. She basked in the attention lavished upon her. (People loved to meet artists.) For Gilberte there was nothing more grand than to get dressed up in clothes that Kristine gifted her to attend a benefit for which Kristine had paid a fortune for the tickets.

—I don't think there's a sexier word in English than *chauffeur*, she told me one morning.

She was getting spoiled.

Her first auction at Sotheby's had been divine. She was already dreaming of the day when her work would enter the secondary art market and be put up on the block to be sold to the highest bidder. New York was becoming more enchanting and fabulous every day. There was still so much she had to learn, so much she had to see and experience. It was odd, she admitted, and she didn't know how to explain it, but she was quickly becoming simultaneously jaded and addicted, hypnotized and anesthetized by the environment she shared with Kristine. She loathed its artificiality yet craved its sensations. In addition to the pleasure these affairs afforded her, their practical value was not lost on her. She insinuated herself into the good graces of as many socially connected people as she could without ever hinting she might at some time like to sell them a photograph or ask them to contribute funds for her film. She was, she told me, cultivating them for later use.

♦

Party Girl created a sensation when it opened at the Bleecker Street Cinema. There had been a private showing, to which I was invited, the night before the public opening. The line of limousines crowding Bleecker Street and La Guardia Place caused a traffic jam. Kristine and Kettridge had done their job and invited everybody who was somebody. Including the press. There was an air of conviviality and bated anticipation.

I spotted Gilberte in a corner, surrounded by Kristine and Kettridge and other dignitaries and luminaries I didn't know. Gilberte appeared serious. She was smoking and kept the cigarette constantly in front of her face by holding her elbow with her free hand. I gave her a discreet wave when I saw her look my way. She returned it, quite enthusiastically, which made Kristine (but not Kettridge, who was above that sort of thing) look to see whom she was flirting with. Kristine smiled coldly, then looked away.

The audience's response to the film was overwhelmingly positive. There was thunderous applause. Gilberte had to stand up and take a bow. I was proud of her.

At the dinner that followed (at Batons, a California-cuisine restaurant), I heard only praise. Some people said it was better than *Blood Simple* or Warhol's early films. Others claimed they found the dreamlike atmosphere similar to that of some of Cocteau's work. I heard one person say it was as alienating as Rivette's but as composition-oriented as Godard's. Another said he thought it far more avant-garde than *Stranger Than Paradise*, if that had indeed been avant-garde. There were a few people who weren't clear at all about what it meant. And one who was certain she hadn't understood the original *Party Girl*. Otherwise, from all that I could gather, everybody had been impressed.

The next day there was a review in the *Times*. It acclaimed the film in no uncertain terms, stating, in part, that it was a gem by a young and talented filmmaker from California.

The warm reception of her film sparked interest in her other endeavors, as I had expected. Thus, I had made sure I finished the treatment before the opening. (This gave my self-respect the biggest boost it had received since I graduated college.) Gilberte was altogether candid about what she thought of my work. She said she could never have done what I did, and though it wasn't exactly what she had had in mind, she thought it superb. She said it seemed to have grown vastly more complicated, become more story-like than she had imagined it. But this might make it more marketable. She asked if I would be interested in doing the screenplay.

—There looks like there must be a lot of talk. I can't write conversation.

I told her to think about it, and if she decided she wanted me to do it, I would.

♦

The success of her film, which during its run at the Bleecker Street was sold out for all performances, had a calming effect on Gilberte. The reviews ran from lukewarm to gushingly positive. Her first great ordeal was over. She seemed more relaxed. Her photographic work began to improve. I found one or two shots in each contact sheet I didn't quite rave about, but I let it be known I thought she was now heading somewhere.

—The day you want to buy something I've done will be the day I know I've got something, she told me.

◆

—How did the meeting go? I asked Gilberte when she came in. She had come in late, after a tenant meeting at her loft. I learned the previous day she was only subletting a room. Now the room's lease-holder was back, rather unexpectedly, and he wanted his space.

—Lousy, she said. She lit a cigarette and began pacing. Were you very busy? she asked.

—No. A lot of tourists, I said, using our code word for people who came in, didn't ask for help, glanced around, and left without buying anything.

Gilberte nodded her head.

—Do you have to move out? I put it bluntly.

—It looks like it.

—When? I asked.

—Soon, she said. As soon as possible.

—You can always stay with me, I said.

She regarded me quizzically, as if she hadn't heard what I said.

—I mean, in my loft. There's plenty of room, I said.

She hesitated.

—Really?

—Sure.

She thought for a moment.

—He's a real asshole, she blurted out. I knew who she meant. I tried to attenuate her rage by pointing out how she hated living there, but it didn't work because, as she pointed out, it was better than living nowhere, which was shortly to be the case.

—How much longer do you think you can stay there? I asked.

—As things stand now, if I left tonight it wouldn't be too soon.

—Well, you could leave tonight. I mean, it's all right with me.

—You really wouldn't mind? It wouldn't be for long. It would be a big favor.

—OK.

—Do you have a lot to move? I asked.

—No, it can all fit in a cab she said.

♦

It started to rain just before we caught a cab. It was a soft gray rain. Everything it touched turned gray—slate gray, cement gray, ocean gray. It fell heavily for a moment, then it let up and fell in a well-cadenced rhythm. The tires began to make a swooshing sound. Pedestrians with umbrellas rocked like buoys in a rough sea when the gusts of wind caught them off guard. We stared out our windows. I snuck a look at Gilberte.

She looked sulky. It occurred to me our situation was so peculiar that any conversation would be a makeshift effort to cover our anxiety, an attempt to make everything seem normal. I lit a cigarette and gazed at the rain and vaguely contemplated what I was getting myself into. I tried to work out all the possible ramifications of my offer and her acceptance. Perhaps we had acted too rashly. Yet there were moments in life when you had to act on the spur of the moment. More frightening was knowing my offer only seemed to be rash, when actually it was fulfilling one of my fantasies (that she come live with me), one I had never expected to realize.

I was happy to be able to offer her shelter in my loft. Now, I would be able to work with her more. I would push her to fully realize her talent, push her toward the artistic ends I thought she was capable of attaining.

The cab stopped at Third and Twenty-fourth, and Gilberte jumped out. I paid the driver. I followed Gilberte. I saw she was fumbling in her bag, ostensibly looking for her wallet in that way that indicates: *I'm waiting for you to say forget it.* I said forget it. She thanked me, then ran on ahead and unlocked the door.

We were confronted by a long flight of steps. There were, by my count, fifteen before the first landing.

—It's on the fifth, Gilberte said. It's a bitch, isn't it?

It was a bitch. I was winded at the fourth and huffing harder than I would have liked to be by the time I reached the landing on the fifth. My only consolation was that Gilberte, too, seemed dazed by the climb.

—It's the cigarettes, she claimed.

She opened the door and we entered a loft. From what I could make of it in the dark, it seemed to be at least as big as my own. Other than a few chairs and what appeared to be a picnic table, it was devoid of furniture. As we walked across the floor, Gilberte pointed toward the far end: at the window, standing on a stool, was a woman holding a violin. She was leaning over, trying to read her music using the light from the street.

—That's Alice, the guitar player's girlfriend, Gilberte said. Then she yelled: Good-bye, Alice.

A weak, noncommittal *good-bye* floated back to us.

Gilberte led me down a narrow hall and opened a door. She turned on the light and I followed her into a fetid, windowless room. A room that had been made by enclosing the space under the staircase that led to the sixth floor. It was the most incommodious place I had ever seen. Small, smelly, lightless, airless, it was like a coffin but worse. The walls were yellow with nicotine, and sticky-looking, like flypaper. The floor, where it could be seen, was black with grime. The piece of foam that served as Gilberte's bed had no sheet on it. To prevent suffocation, there was a fan. Gilberte turned it on immediately.

—It gets hot in here fast she said.

—You lived here? I couldn't help exclaiming.

—I slept in here, she said. I lived in the loft. I mean, for just sleeping in it's not bad. Here. She handed me a ragged piece of cloth she had just picked up from a pile on the floor. It turned out to be a pillowcase.

—Just stuff everything you can into it, she instructed me. She picked up another pillow case and demonstrated how to do it. I watched for a moment, and after I had ascertained I was not expected to fold anything or to make any distinction between clean and dirty, I began. When my case was full,

Gilberte produced another. We filled four of them, and then Gilberte went out into the hall and came back with more.

—I guess this is about it, she said, when there was nothing left on the floor.

—You don't have anything else?

—There's my trunk in the back room, with my photographs and cameras.

—No pots, no pans, no plates?

—I don't cook.

I wanted to ask about personal effects, books, but ended by saying nothing. It took us four trips each to get everything—including the large trunk that had been in the back room—down to the street. We were completely exhausted.

◆

For the first five days we were constant companions. We went to work together and sometimes we came home together. We spent our days and most of our nights not far from each other's presence. What life existed outside our dyadic bond ceased to count for me. Rather, it counted only insofar as I viewed it as a threat to my newfound state of happiness. We were only several days into our communal arrangement, but it felt right. I was ecstatic to have Gilberte with me. But it was a precarious happiness, I knew. I couldn't explain it. It felt transitory. I feared everything: an invitation to a party or an opening or a telephone call from an old friend. I was convinced any outside force would be enough to rend the tenuous threads that held us together.

I didn't ask Gilberte whether she had told Kristine she was staying with me. My common sense told me Kristine was well informed where her protégée was lodging these days. My intuition told me if I hadn't yet heard from Kristine, it was because she was busy maneuvering behind my back. I could expect her to launch a retaliatory blitzkrieg at almost any moment. There was no way I could defend what I had won. I could only wait and idly speculate about how Kristine would elect to take Gilberte from me.

♦

I did all I could to see that Gilberte was comfortable and happy. I hoped she was as happy as I was, but I didn't know. She didn't complain. But whether she was forcing herself to be congenial and pleasant and was in reality suffering under a regime she found intolerably oppressive (by my household habits) simply to show gratitude for my generosity, well, how was I to know? I asked.

—I'm not too difficult to live with, am I?

—No, she said.

—I mean, if there's anything that gets on your nerves or that you're not used to, just tell me.

—Sure, she said.

She said she would, but I didn't think she would. She seemed to me to be the type to hold it all in. Or to complain to a more or less sympathetic third party, as she had done to me about her life at the other loft. I think if we had been lovers, she would have told me without prodding. And if we had been sharing the loft—that is, if she was paying me rent—she would have been outspoken because her payment would entitle her to participate in governing the space. But as my guest she was severely limited in her rights, more by convention than by me. She was not readily going to complain about things she didn't like. It was this constraint imposed by the situation that caused me to fret and worry, because I didn't want her to suffer at my hands.

◆

I watched her constantly. I lusted after her daily. I couldn't help myself. I saw her stumble into the shower in the morning wrapped only in a towel. I panted in anticipation of its falling to the floor, which it nearly always did. I watched her come out in her short, sheer robe with the daring décolletage: I nearly fainted with frustrated desire. I had ample opportunity to see her in all her states: dishabille, dressed, half-dressed, relaxed, anxious, pensive, happy, sad. I saw poses and gestures I had never seen at work. It was too much for me. I was in a constant state of excitation. I masturbated every chance I could. Even that offered no relief because instead of fantasizing about her straight through to the solitary consummation of my desire, midway (or thereabouts) I would begin to worry about how I would perform if it turned out the moment I was longing for arrived that night. To maintain my equipoise, I tried to keep my distance from her. Tried not to observe her so closely. But my eyes' appetite for her had become so pronounced I was no longer in strict control of what they did. I was ready to devour her. It was all I could do to suppress the urge. I became determined not to let her depart without having had her under me, moaning, biting my neck, digging into my back with her nails, calling my name.

I was so preoccupied with my schemes to satisfy my lust that I almost failed to notice she seemed to have forgotten she was only supposed to stay temporarily. She didn't (at least, not in my presence) look through the classified ads in the *Village*

Voice for an apartment to rent. When I overheard her giving out my number over the telephone, she never said she would be here for a while, or until something came up, or that she was looking for an apartment. Which would have been helpful, because then I would have known how fast I should begin implementing my project to get her into my bed.

Perhaps Gilberte had no intention of finding a place of her own and planned to stay with me as long as she could. After all, while she had to put up with me as a roommate, she had a comfortable and respectable shelter—gratis. I didn't expect her to help pay for food, gas, electricity, or the telephone. She had a sweet deal. If I were in her position, I, too, would have been loath to give it up.

Her intentions—whether she planned to stay for an extended visit—ceased to play any role in the question when I realized Gilberte didn't have a cent. She was broke. The money she had received from Kristine for her first commission had gone for camera equipment and for clothes. None of it had ever gotten near a bank. She spent the money she had received for the portrait of the sisters and from *Vogue* just as fast. Her salary from the bookstore she spent on cabs, in restaurants, on film, and on rent for the darkroom where she developed her pictures. For the moment, there wasn't any chance of her coming into a sum of money large enough to permit her to put a deposit and security down on an apartment. Unless she landed a big commission, the likelihood of which was pretty bleak. The only way she might manage to move out immediately was if Kristine was willing to subsidize her rent. And this didn't seem to be in the cards since as soon as Gilberte had moved in with me, I sensed an estrangement between the two of them. They spent less time on the phone than previously. Now when they talked on the phone, I could tell by the tone of Gilberte's voice and by the nature of the conversation (mostly questions, on Gilberte's part) that she was placating Kristine. Only to Kristine did Gilberte mention how long she intended to stay with me. And this was always something like, not that long, or, until I find something. Thus, I was more or less certain there was no imminent danger of her departing.

This explained why she had gone to such trouble to organize her living quarters. True, they weren't quite quarters, because they didn't have hard-and-fast physical boundaries, like walls. But she had transformed the area I had allocated to her into an oasis of comfort in what was otherwise a desert of austerity. She had rearranged the couches and chairs, making a circle for herself. She stored her personal things in pillow-cases. She used the coffee table to store her reference material, as she called it, which comprised photo and art reviews, as well as film magazines. There was also a curious collection of bibelots: a plastic tractor and cars, marbles, plastic daggers and swords, chrome-plated rings, bracelets, a hatpin of immense proportions with a pearl tip, a gold earring surrounded by blue sapphires, an arrowhead, a music box, a compact magnifying glass. There were many miscellaneous boxes, some of which were crammed full of index cards and postcards. I couldn't account for where it all came from. We certainly hadn't carried all this down from the loft where she had been living. I asked her about it. She said it had been in storage.

On the nights we were both home, Gilberte sometimes visited me in my bedroom. It was usually late, after she had talked on the telephone, smoked numerous cigarettes, washed, and listened to music. Ostensibly she came in to see what I was watching on television, for she never entered my room unless it was on. She was good about it. When she had missed the beginning of a show she rarely pestered me with questions about what had happened or what it was about. She just watched. She seemed to be interested solely in the images.

She always began by watching from the edge of the bed, but she rarely remained there. She sat there first because she was nervous. Her migration toward the interior began with a cigarette. If she had forgotten hers, she would dash out the door at the first commercial and fetch them. Immediately upon her return, she was more relaxed and would half-recline on the bed instead of sitting bolt upright with her hands plunged between her knees. If she came prepared, however, it took her longer to unwind. She would first merely lean back. After the first cigarette, she would shift to her side, still keeping her feet on the floor. But as the evening wore on she would relax. Little by little she would work her way away from the edge of the bed, first spreading out but then curling up, usually around the ashtray.

I grieved when she got up to go. Her departure left me inconsolable. Why couldn't I say something to make her stay? Why couldn't I simply reach out and take her by the arm and pull her toward me? By the time she was ready to leave she had slipped into a semi-somnolent state. How could she resist me? I sometimes thought she was purposefully provoking me, brushing against my legs or rolling over them to get off the bed. She would stretch and scratch and search listlessly for her shoes. I was sure I could encircle her in my arms, kiss her on the neck, behind the ear, on the lips, the breasts ... she would yield to me. But I never did anything. Never made the slightest move to restrain her. I simply watched her. I supposed I must have been reaping as much satisfaction from denying myself the fulfillment of my desire (because, I told myself, she couldn't fail to appreciate what a gentleman I was) as I would have experienced had I assaulted her. That I could so easily sublimate my lust was a measure of my degree of civilization, and this feat contributed to my feeling of having accomplished something by doing nothing. This did not keep me from wondering when I would, in fact, do something. When I would break down and pounce. After all, at this point in time, one moment was as good as the next. If I postponed making a move it was, I theorized, because I was sufficiently happy with the status quo. Her presence provided pleasure. I didn't want to jeopardize that. I was at a point in my life where I would rather enjoy a sure thing than risk losing it by attempting to have more. Moreover, I was not given to terrorist tactics. I could not launch a surgical strike. In time, through negotiation—and it was important to realize my nonaggression was a form of negotiation—I believed I would get what I wanted.

It was infrequent I could go to sleep right after she left me. Usually, I mused, mainly about the aforementioned. Sometimes I masturbated. Generally, I would read until I was ready for sleep. Or occasionally I would continue to watch television. While watching the late show one night, I discovered that although Gilberte had left me sleepy-eyed, she had not gone to bed. Going into the kitchen for something to eat, I saw her at the other end of the loft, reclining on the couch like an odalisque, a cigarette, or joint, dangling dissolutely from her mouth. Another night, when I decided to pour myself a cognac, I found her walking with the stereo headphones stuck on her head, flailing her arms about her spasmodically. It looked like she was being shocked. I didn't interrupt her activity. I didn't acknowledge her. More than once I woke up early in the morning, startled out of my always fitful sleep, and heard her outside, pacing. I didn't know if she had been doing it for hours or minutes. But she was out there making the rounds of the loft, trudging from the front to the rear, from the rear to the front.

One morning I asked her:

—Do you have trouble sleeping?

—No, she said. When I decide to go to sleep, I sleep.

—You do a lot of pacing, I protested.

—When I'm pacing I'm working. When I'm sleeping I'm goofing off. She laughed. I like to think when I walk. It helps me get ideas.

♦

Labor Day came and went. I had made it through another summer. I was anticipating with pleasure the cool days and cool nights and dry air and clear skies of autumn. I couldn't bear the thought of heat anymore. I swore if I had to go through too many more hot, sticky days I would move out of New York. Also, I had seen enough of all the exposed tanned (and white) flesh parading in the streets. More and more I found it revolting. Especially since the underclass carried to extremes this propensity to shed every possible vestige of clothing in an effort to expose as much skin as was legal. This disregard of propriety was doubtless intended to show contempt for civilized urban life, which was founded, or at least maintained, by sublimating the immediate gratification of desire to achieve some sort of harmony and order. Evidently they felt they were suffering enough because of their lowly social position and were entitled to whatever pleasure they could reap—even if it merely meant sweating less.

I was glad the summer was over for another reason. I was being driven out of my mind by music. (Thomas was right: like any substance that was potentially hazardous to your health, music—and the volume at which it was played—should be subject to strict regulation.) It was bad enough that music and Muzac had infiltrated boutiques, department stores, restaurants, bars, groceries, delis, elevators, telephones, and had become part of the aural landscape in which we moved. In the summer, every troglodyte toted an oversize supercharged radio and played it full blast. Cars with stereos sophisticated enough to serve as the sound system for Radio City Music Hall would stop in front of the store, while their drivers listened to one last song before getting out. At night, too, I would hear in the street the beat of the bass as cars cruised down the block looking for parking places. I took what little action I could. When people entered the store with Walkmans turned up all the way, creating a racket, they were promptly asked to either turn them down or leave. This constant cacophony was as oppressive as the heat. I was longing to be free of it. Longing for the first frosts that would kill off some of the riffraff that lolled in the streets drinking beer and listening to portable radios. Longing for the first foul weather that would make carrying a ghetto blaster an onerous and potentially economically disastrous affair.

The heat hadn't prevented Gilberte from working. She had been making steady progress. She had to have something to hang on those gallery walls. Fortunately, she received a reprieve. Because of a scheduling conflict, her show, which was supposed to have taken place just after New Year's, was now tentatively scheduled to take place in February. Also in her favor, as far as I was concerned, was the fact that an-other artist was going to share the space with Gilberte, which meant she wouldn't have to produce a prodigious number of photographs.

Still, she didn't have any photographs that she thought worthy of showing. I didn't tell her that if she had spent fewer long weekends at Kristine's house in the Hamptons she might have more. From June to August she had missed more than thirty days of work. There were times—when a long weekend lasted from Thursday to Tuesday—I thought I was living and working alone again.

I let Gilberte take as much time off as she felt she needed, which was almost every day even though it wasn't right of her to ask me for favors like this. She was taking advantage of me but I let her take the time because she claimed it was helping her. Perhaps, I thought, if I let her have her way where her art was concerned, I would be able to exercise a little more control over how she spent her time. Now, more than ever, I wanted her to reduce her socializing so she could concentrate on com-ing up with the photos she needed before she was absolutely crunched for time and the situation became desperate.

♦

The show's date was set to take place in February, on Ground-hog Day. Gilberte and I spent long hours going over contact sheets and critiquing her work. We discussed and disputed which shots were good enough to print and frame and hang. I advocated printing as few as possible. Gilberte was less discriminating and wanted to print everything she had an immediate favorable reaction to. She would make a final se-lection about what to frame later.

Overall, I was sorely disappointed in the work. It wasn't because the photographs were bad. Some of them were well thought out and well composed. Her printing technique had evolved considerably. Technically these were her finest photographs. Yet there was no vision: in all the sheets we had gone over thus far, I still couldn't say what the subject of her work was. It was going to be an eclectic collection. Especially for a first major show.

As the show date loomed on the horizon, Gilberte became more and more frantic. She couldn't decide what to show. Now that she was under the gun, she realized she should have been more selective. One night, she broke down. She admitted she had agreed to show too soon. She should have waited and put together a cohesive body of work. It was too late now. She couldn't simply run out and begin taking photos in one or two of the directions she felt her work was destined to take in the future. We spent hours editing, reediting, lamenting. It was agony.

♦

Whether Gilberte regretted having rushed into the show or was merely nervous because she realized she might not pull off the *succes d'estime* she hoped for, I couldn't tell. She appeared downcast, and although she continued to work with as much ardor as always, I could tell she was worried.

Kristine's and Kettridge's involvement increased her inquietude. Kristine often brought Kettridge to the store with her, and sometimes the three of them would go to my loft to look at contact sheets and prints. They were eager to partake in the final stages of the artistic process, longed to be given previews of what they would see at the show, were flattered to be asked for advice and to assist in selecting a photo or two themselves. By the time of the opening they would be tired of it and would be able to remain cool, disinterested connoisseurs, giving their undivided attention to their guests.

Gilberte let them find her a framer. The first one Kristine sent her to see she didn't like. The second one (someone Kettridge used on occasion) asked exorbitant prices, and Kristine and Kettridge balked at having to pay such a sum (they had agreed to pay for the framing as part of the deal Kettridge had made with the gallery). My framer wouldn't accept the job because he couldn't promise to have all the work done in time if he didn't know when he would be getting it. Allbright saved the day. He said he had a man who was reasonably priced and a meticulous craftsman. For a little extra he would probably work on short notice. After Gilberte had satisfied herself as to the quality of his work, he was engaged.

The holidays came and went. It was after the latest date Gilberte could deliver her photos to the framer had been determined that she gave up. She simply could not make a decision about which photos to show. She told me to choose. I had no idea how much work it was to go through hundreds of photographs. It was exhausting. As soon as I began making choices, she began disputing them and took away my decision-making authority. Without making a decision herself.

Night after night we spread out all her work on the loft floor. We examined every photo. We arranged them in different groups. We put together trial shows. We reviewed them. We redid them, always unsatisfied. I told Gilberte she was going to have to live with some measure of dissatisfaction. She paced and pouted and procrastinated. She threw tantrums (mostly at me, when I disagreed with one of her decisions). Only days away from the framer's deadline, she began in earnest to select the final photos.

The long, painful process concluded the night before she was to turn her selection over to the framer. Then, the morning they were due, she decided to do one final edit, during which she chose all new photographs.

When the photographs had been framed and delivered to the gallery, Gilberte began making trips uptown to hang them. Sometimes Kristine escorted her, sometimes Kettridge, sometimes both. I was never invited to these working sessions, which Gilberte informed me was just as well because they were sheer hell. After all that work, she complained, she had been allocated a shitty little space. It didn't show off her work to its best advantage. The lighting was hideous, more fit for a department store display than an art gallery. Or so she claimed. She swore the photos had looked better lying on the floor of my loft than where they were currently hanging. In addition to these horrors, she was faced with Kristine and Kettridge and Henry, the gallery owner, all of whom had distinct ideas about what should be hung where.

◆

The day she appeared at the store with a pile of posters announcing the show's opening, she seemed happy again. Her name was in the same type size as her co-exhibitor's. A reproduction of his work adorned the poster.

—I could have had one on there too if I had known which ones I was going to show, she said, rolling up the posters. You know, I didn't have anything this professional to announce my film when I first showed it. She immediately went out and stuck the posters up in every boutique, bar, and restaurant that would let her.

A few days later, I received my invitation to the invitation-only opening-night. Gilberte told me she was quite pleased with the way things were working out. She got to invite everybody she wanted. Kristine and Kettridge had invited everybody who was anybody.

—Now all I have to do is sell out and get Henry to agree to be my dealer, she said. Then I'll be happy.

♦

Practically the first person I saw upon entering the gallery on opening night was Kristine. She was frantic.

—Gilberte didn't come with you? she demanded.

—No.

I explained I had come directly from the store. Gilberte had left work early, to go home to prepare, I had thought. It was now seven-thirty, the opening had another hour to run, and Gilberte wasn't there.

—People are asking for her, Kristine told me. There are some very important people here tonight. I don't know if she realizes that. Bianca Jagger asked to meet her, and Anne Livet, too. What am I going to tell them? she uttered rhetorically.

She could tell them whatever she liked, for all I cared.

—Make something up, I suggested.

—What? she practically barked. She wrung her hands. I'll just have to avoid them and hope that little idiot shows up before they leave.

—Good idea. I decided to go have a drink. I excused my-self and headed over to the refreshment table.

Kristine ran to Kettridge for refuge. I gathered she was telling him what she had learned from me. Since he was look-ing directly at me, I gave him a little wave, which he returned. Kristine and Kettridge then turned their backs to me and began what seemed like a conspiratorial conversation, punc-tuated by rather ostentatious gesticulations on Kristine's part. Kettridge kept turning to glance furtively in my direction. Henry joined them. They then huddled together for a more serious conversation.

I didn't have the vaguest idea where Gilberte was. I sup-posed her tardiness was on purpose. There was something theatrical about it, in a way. The show couldn't go on until Gilberte arrived on the stage. She was the vedette whose pres-ence was indispensable to the ongoing theatrics. Actually, it didn't matter whether she came or not. She had already given her performance: it was hanging there on the walls. People would mill, chatter, drink, come, go— regardless of whether Gilberte was among them. Some, it was true, might miss her and regret not seeing her. Especially those she had promised to meet here. She might sacrifice her dream of having a sellout show if she didn't arrive to help Henry close sales, for some-times the artist's presence is necessary for this. But since most of the people present didn't know her anyway, there was no real necessity for her presence.

Behind the bar, there were trays upon trays of plastic cups with ice. While asking me what I'd have, the barman au-tomatically reached for a one, covered it with his hand, and turned it upside down to empty the water. I noticed he did this so fast that only half the water spilled out. Whether he did it purposefully to cut down on the amount of alcohol he poured, or simply so he could serve as many people as possible as quickly as possible, I didn't know. I asked him to empty it completely before pouring the wine. He obliged but gave me the kind of contemptuous look people exhibit when reprimanded for not properly performing a task at which they take themselves to be experts.

The gallery was filling up fast. This was mostly due to Henry's influence and the gallery's name. I had no doubt there were captains of industry steering their way through the throng, as well as art luminaries and impresarios and collectors. Kristine and Kettridge and Henry had done a good job organizing this gala. It didn't hurt that there was another show opening the same night in the building and many people were taking in both of them. I suspected there were many more people here than Gilberte had expected. She would be pleasantly surprised when she arrived.

Having not attended an uptown opening in a long time, I saw people I hadn't seen in years. Mostly these were people I had met through Thomas. I had little desire to see them except on occasions like this. I had escaped from his xenophobic, incestuous group a long time ago and no number of we-never-see-you-anymores was going to coax me into seeing them. In fact, if I generally stayed away from uptown openings (as well as from certain clubs and restaurants), it was just to avoid his crowd. But they all said hello. They were all dying to know if I had talked to Thomas (he was there, and I had seen him but wasn't sure he had noticed me, and so I hadn't made an effort to say hello). They all seemed to be vying with each other to divulge the most information about him and his latest lover, a dancer from Brazil. The only other topic that concerned them at all was the most recent AIDS body count among people we knew in common and speculation about who was looking awfully run down these days.

As I was receiving the body count, I saw Thomas enter from the other room with a short, swarthy, overly muscular man. We acknowledged each other with a nod. Thomas came over to say hello. He introduced me to Miguel and then sent him off to the bar.

—He's cute, I lied.

—He's a doll.

—A dancer?

Thomas' eyes narrowed and glinted dangerously in the light. I slapped him on the back to assure him I meant no harm. And though we both laughed, I knew by revealing what I had heard from his friends I had put him on guard. I was sure we wouldn't find much to say to each other tonight.

—Where's *your* friend? he asked, laying emphasis on the possessive adjective.

—I don't know.

—A lot of heavy hitters here tonight, he said. Is she going after the corporate crowd?

—It appears that way.

—She should stick to film, he said. What's on the walls tonight is ... He made a gesture with his hand.

—I'm sure she feels the same way, I said.

Miguel was striking up a conversation at the refreshment table with a handsome walker who belonged to a woman whose name I couldn't remember, although I had been introduced to her at the screening at my loft and at the Bleecker Street Cinema. Thomas, who had been watching Miguel's every move, now found it convenient to turn his back to him. He looked at his watch.

—We've got to look in somewhere else before eight-thirty, and I've got to stop by the house. Well, tell....

—Gilberte.

— ...Gilberte I'm sorry I didn't stay to say hello.

—I will. We shook hands, hugged. Then he picked up his charge at the table and ushered him out the door.

No sooner had Thomas left than Kettridge came to pay me a visit. He was dressed impeccably, from the paisley pocket handkerchief poking out of his blazer pocket to his black tassel shoes (whose pointed toes and vamping were unmistakable indicators of Brooks Brothers).

—You look great, John, I said.

—Thank you.

He studied himself briefly to make a mental note of what he was wearing for future reference.

—Nice crowd, he said.

—Yes, I said, without being certain what criteria he was using to make such a judgment.

—A smart artist could make enough connections here tonight to last a career.

I took this as a veiled reference to Gilberte's absence and his mistaken assumption that I knew where she was.

—Gilberte had better show up, then, I said. Kettridge gave me a stern look.

—She'd better, he warned.

He stared off into the crowd, skimming over faces as you might flip through a magazine looking at pictures. He smiled, moved up close to me so we were standing shoulder to shoulder, crossed his arms on his chest, and said while looking straight ahead:

—Look, those are the Annenbergs. And I just saw the Basses go by with Steve Reichard. His shoulder rubbing up against mine, he continued: Frankly, I hope tonight doesn't do her any harm. The quality is rather disappointing. It's not at all what I thought it would be. I mean, it somehow doesn't look as impressive with all these—he stammered, looking for a word—people around. It's confounding, because I'm sure she can do better.

—I know, I admitted. We moved from side to side as people pushed past us. Kettridge adjusted one of his cuff links.

—Anyway, the publicity will serve her well. Speaking of which, did you hear what happened at the Kiefer opening?

I hadn't, but I could see he was dying to tell me. From the look in his eyes, I couldn't determine if the type of information he was going to impart would indebt me to him because of its scandalous nature, or if it was just his craving to disseminate information about an event he thought it important to have witnessed. People often share stories with the uninformed not because they care to enlighten them but to make them cognizant of their omnipotence.

—I was one of the people who heard the whole thing, Kettridge confided, tipping his hand and letting me know it was an aural and not a visual event.

I never knew quite how to participate in a conversation like this—one in which I wasn't interested—especially when the teller required encouraging stimuli to continue. A simple what happened? would have been enough to make him go on, but I wasn't in the mood. It was only after I took him by the arm and pulled him out of the way of an old couple tottering toward the refreshment table that he continued.

—Richard Serra attacked Ingrid Sischy.

—Attacked? It was his emphasis on the word that made me question him. I realized it was in all likelihood hyperbole, but at the same time I realized he had chosen this expression to lure me into his trap, to make me make him talk.

—Well, you know about the hearing for the *Tilted Arc*, he assumed.

—Yes, I half-lied. I had heard Serra's sculpture had stirred some controversy, and I had vaguely heard talk to the effect that there was going to be a hearing about it because many people felt that it intruded upon their space. As always in such cases, people had taken sides. I didn't know which side I was on. I had seen pictures of the offending piece of sculpture—a curving wall of steel twelve feet high and one hundred twenty feet long—in journals. I had read a number of opinions concerning the work's significance in the space it occupied. To me it seemed like a defiant, provocative act to erect such a work in a public space. On the other hand, the artist had been commissioned to create a piece for that space, and the *Tilted Arc* was what he had made. Whether it should be carted away or whether it should stay was something about which I didn't care to speculate at present.

—Well, one minute Serra and Sischy were talking calmly, and the next, Serra was screaming his head off.

—At Sischy? Really?

Ingrid Sischy was the editor of *Artforum*, one of the most influential art journals in America.

—Yes … He was saying things like she sucked up to advertisers. That she was a capitalist and a fascist. And that she and the rest of them were betraying him. He honestly felt everyone—all the magazine editors, the writers, the artists, the people—should be behind him. He couldn't understand how people couldn't like his work. It's funny, but I felt sorry for him and not Ingrid, even though I do think his arc is a horror.

—Huh, I let out.

—I know, Kettridge sympathized.

I waited for him to continue, but he gave no indication he was going to share the repercussions of this outburst with me without my asking. And as I had come this far, I asked:

—Then what happened?

—Oh, nothing much, really. Of course, I'll bet Serra never has his work reviewed in *Artforum* again.

—What do you think will happen tonight? I asked.

Kettridge laughed.

—Nothing. You know, openings are such a bore. But I do wish Gilberte would come. There are people here she absolutely should meet. With this he excused himself and set off in search of Kristine, who he hoped would by now have news of Gilberte's whereabouts.

The gallery was packed. I couldn't recall having seen such a crush of people in such a small space in a long time: not since I had been to Zabar's on a holiday weekend. Kettridge and Kristine were thrilled and proud at the number of important people present. For me, the spirit of the evening was summed up by a man I heard complaining to his companion that he could do without these artsy-smartsy evenings, but he had promised his wife either a photo, a Rolex, or a membership in the Vertical Club. To which the other man replied:

—I know what you mean.

I saw Kettridge and Kristine commiserating with each other. Kettridge was actually holding her hand, while whispering into her ear. To tell the truth I was becoming a little worried at Gilberte's absence. If she didn't show up within the next few minutes, it was going to be considered rude. She didn't have the prestige to get away with this sort of showmanship. Without a good excuse, it would turn out to have been a bad miscalculation. Especially since there was a dinner afterward, at which she was to be, more or less, the guest of honor. If the people she was supposed to meet at the opening began thinking she wasn't going to show, they might not attend the dinner, and then the entire evening would be a loss. I was mulling this over when I found myself face to face with Kristine. Two times in an evening were too much for me.

—I can't imagine where she is, Kristine began, using a tone that clearly implied she was sure I could. Having a more fertile imagination than she, I was sure I could, but I didn't let on, so as not to antagonize her.

—Neither can I.

She glared at me, then turned away. She sipped her drink. I saw Roger enter. He looked around for Kristine, I supposed, but not seeing her, he headed back into the other room.

—Why don't you leave her alone? Kristine asked, without looking up from her drink. I could see this was going to be a painful conversation. I wondered how many drinks she had consumed and if it was in her to create a scene on her protégée's opening night. Suddenly paranoid, I wondered whether Kettridge had related the incident that occurred between Serra and Sischy to forewarn me. Was Kristine going to blow her lid? At all costs I wanted to avoid starting a fight. Kristine was mad because she thought I knew where Gilberte was, I told myself. All I had to do was remain calm. Assure her I knew nothing.

—What do you mean? I asked.

—I mean what are you trying to do with her?

—Help her.

—Help her! She chortled to herself in an unattractive way. That's a laugh. I'm the one who's helping her. You're ... why, you're perverting her up there in your loft.

I had thought I was going to remain calm and not provoke her, but this accusation couldn't go unchallenged.

—If by perverting you mean my trying to keep her away from you, then, yes, I'm perverting her.

I had gone too far. I could see it in her eyes, which glistened with water, and in her chest, which was expanding as she drew in the air I had no doubt was going to fuel her response. Fortunately, Roger and Henry arrived. Henry shrugged his shoulders at me, while Roger kissed Kristine hello.

—Still no news? Kristine asked.

—She's here, Henry said. She's over there. He nodded toward the door.

And there she was. She was dressed casually, in slacks and a sweater. For whatever reason, she had brought her camera with her and was wearing it slung over her shoulder.

—You'll excuse me while I go say hello, Kristine said. Henry followed her, nodding to both Roger and me as he went.

—She's too preoccupied with that girl, Roger said. All I hear about is Gilberte this, Gilberte that. Stephen this and Stephen that. She's convinced that you're trying to ruin her. He sighed. I'll be relieved when it's over. You know, this is the first time Kristine has taken an interest in a person rather than a thing. But I can't imagine it'll end any differently. Eventually she'll grow tired and find something else to occupy her.

—It must be difficult.

—Kris thinks she has to take care of her.

—Well, artists are like children, I said, trying to be generous. They do need looking after. I was shoring up my position.

—Fine. But she's not our child. He took a sip from his glass. Kristine seems to think she owes her something. It's ridiculous. And now I'm supposed to help find her a loft.

—Really?

—Ummm ... He took a long drink. It will be a relief for you when she moves out, won't it? It must be hell for you, too.

—Oh, she's not much trouble, I said, hardly able to believe what I had just heard. I saw now that Kristine had probably been working herself up to slap me with this revelation. I wondered how long Gilberte had known about this and why she hadn't said anything to me. I had been manipulated and duped by both Kristine and Gilberte. Kristine joined us again. She was beaming. She wanted Roger to come say hello to Gilberte. She took him by the arm and led him away, totally ignoring me. Over her shoulder I saw Gilberte, surrounded by Henry and Kettridge and a woman I didn't know. Gilberte gave me a little wave.

I was supposed to go to the dinner afterward, but I couldn't. I couldn't go through the same thing sitting I had just gone through standing. Especially because it would be worse. My immobility would make me an easy target for conversation, and I couldn't bear the thought of having to talk. I decided I had said all I was going to say all night.

♦

Immediately after arriving home, I poured a drink. I then set off for a stroll on my old thinking trail—which I had ceded to Gilberte upon her arrival since my use of it infringed upon her privacy—to puzzle things out. With every step the sounds of the evening reverberated in my head and prevented me from thinking about the ramifications of what Roger told me. All I could do was rehash the events of the preceding hours. I was too drunk to do any real contemplating. I decided to watch television to drain my brain.

It was late when Gilberte returned from the dinner. I had sobered up considerably. I was in bed, caught up in a film. I heard Gilberte in the kitchen, running the water. She stopped by my room to say good night.

—What are you watching? she asked, coming inside.

—A film, I said. She sat down on the edge of the bed and stared at the screen. She reeked of alcohol and cigarettes.

—Is it good? she wanted to know.

—Excellent, I said. My high opinion of the film didn't prevent her from remonstrating.

—Is that why you didn't come?

—No.

—Then why?

—Did you miss me? I played coy.

—Yes.

—Then I should have come.

—You should have.

—I'm sorry, I lied. I hoped this would suffice as an explanation, because I didn't feel like explaining. She was obviously drunk. In the morning, when she had a better grip of herself, she would have less of a grip on the issue: it would already be ancient history and hardly worth fussing about.

—What's the name of this film? she blurted out.

—*Out of the Past*, with Kirk Douglas and Robert Mitchum.

She leaned back and watched. She was exhausted and couldn't keep from yawning, but she was also captivated by the film. From the little worry lines around her eyes, I knew she was either in pain or stressed or both.

—I like Robert Mitchum, she said, and spread out on the bed. Though we hardly ever touched during our TV viewing—the contact we had was usually followed by an apology and her departure for the night—tonight she blatantly appropriated my legs for an armrest.

—My head is killing me, she said at the next commercial. Too much champagne, she explained.

—You shouldn't drink so much, I counseled.

—I know. I don't like it. But they insisted. I had almost forgotten the *they*.

—So what's the word?

—Good. Real good.

—The critics liked it too?

—Yes. But you know, they say one thing, then write something else. But most of them were very sweet to me.

—That's good, I said.

—I know, she said. I'm really happy.

—So am I, I said. She smiled faintly, then grimaced. I took the hint.

—I'll go get you some aspirin.

—No. She squeezed my legs. I tried, nevertheless, to rise. She tried harder to restrain me, and the effect made my blood rise. And more. My cock, which had been resting on my right leg, sprang up, prepared for action. Maneuvering it between my legs, I tried to squeeze the blood out of it so I could get up without embarrassment.

—It's all right, I said. I want some water too. When I returned she was under the covers. She had pulled them up tight to her neck. I saw her clothes heaped in a pile at the side of the bed. She sat up to take the aspirin and the glass, clutching the blanket to her chest.

—Thanks, she said. I didn't ask any questions. On the one hand it didn't seem strange she was in my bed. I had been waiting for this moment for ever so long. On the other hand, I didn't know whether the moment had actually come. For the time being, I didn't want to know. I sat down. I took off my robe and climbed under the covers.

—God, that was good, Gilberte said when the film had finished. I wish I'd seen the beginning.

—Is your headache better? I asked.

—Much, she murmured. She rolled over on her side and faced me. She smiled at me, warmly, invitingly. It was a smile I had never seen her exhibit before. Her eyes were shining. She appeared relaxed, receptive. I couldn't restrain myself. I turned off the television with the remote, and in one deft movement I was upon her, locked in her passionate embrace.

◆

The morning wasn't at all difficult. She gave me a little peck on the cheek before tiptoeing out, carrying her pile of clothes with her. I fell back asleep. Hours later, when I got up to go make breakfast, I saw her down in her end of the loft, fast asleep on the couch.

◆

That Roger was looking for a loft for Gilberte upset me. It wasn't that I hadn't expected it to happen. There was no doubt in my mind that from the minute Gilberte moved in, Kristine had been plotting to take her away from me. I was just surprised that she would engage Roger to help her. Fortunately, I hadn't for a moment believed the life Gilberte and I had been leading would go on forever. Now that I knew what the competition was up to, I knew I was beaten. There was no way I could match Kristine's munificence. I could ask Gilberte to stay with me, tell her she was welcome for as long as she liked, but no matter how she felt about me (which was a mystery), sharing my space couldn't compare with her receiving her own. Gilberte was sure to abandon me.

I was curious to know whether Gilberte was already aware of Kristine's plans. Did she know our time together was limited? Was her making love to me was an attempt to appease me in advance of the pain she was going to cause me? Stroking her thighs as she lay beside me, I decided not to ask her because I could picture the result of that inquiry. She would become tense. Her muscles would twitch nervously the way a cat's tail twitches when it is aggravated. She would pull away from me, abandoning her submissive position on her stomach. She would turn aggressively on her side and prop herself up on one elbow. She'd start questioning me about how and what I knew about what was in store for her, and the trust that bound us together would be broken. She would become cold, cautious, distant, as she was on occasion with Kristine when she felt she was withholding information. I couldn't bear the thought of

229

our bliss coming to such an abrupt halt. It was worth foregoing the pleasure of satisfying my curiosity in order to assure my continued physical needs were met. My desire to know about her involvement in this affair would continue to gnaw away at me, but I would contain the damage by entertaining hypotheses I could never verify. This was preferable to any other solution because my physical craving for Gilberte after only a couple of nights had grown so fantastic I would suffer horribly if I was suddenly deprived of her.

None of my melancholy ruminations affected my ardor for Gilberte. I was too overwhelmed by our impassioned couplings to think for very long. Despite my foreknowledge about the outcome of our liaison, our sex life continued unabated. There was not a night that we did not sleep together. Not a day passed that I wasn't distressed about what would happen that night. I always prepared myself for the worst. And tortured myself by working out how I would respond to her refusal. There would be days when she could use her period as an excuse, and I tried to think how to overcome them. I waited for her first headache, her first *not tonight*, as anxiously as a lover in fear and trembling plots how to obtain his first kiss. But the momentum of our love life did not diminish. Gilberte was apparently as hungry for sex as I was. Her enthusiasm and joy were as great as my own. We fucked without reserve. Night after night we engaged in uninhibited orgies: she complied with my wishes, suffered my eccentricities, satisfied my whims. And I did the same for her. All this activity took its toll on me. I looked tired: I often had bags under my eyes and sometimes, after a string of particularly long and lust-filled nights, hints of black-and-blue fatigue. In fact, to my horror and shame, I was the one who, one night—after having waited up for her

for hours and having consumed nearly half a liter of vodka—
had to say, *not tonight.*

♦

Aroused all the time, I got an erection if Gilberte so much as
brushed against me. Watching her move through the store I
would dream up new positions for us to try, fantasize about
new combinations. I couldn't keep away from her. When she
came near me I was compelled to touch her: to stroke her hair,
massage her shoulders or back, caress her cheek, nibble her
ear. She shooed me away whenever I became too annoying. I
was becoming a glutton, but I couldn't help it. Waking up in
the middle of the night with an erection, I would awaken her
and make love to her—for it was often during this time that
I had the most control, and she the least, since she was half-
asleep, and I could carry out my most bizarre fantasies—even
though it was from sheer exhaustion of our earlier efforts
that we had fallen asleep.

I had thought since we were now sleeping together, and
had become lovers, she would open up to me and I to her. That
seemed to be the natural progression in relationships. Finally,
we would get to know each other. Long, leisurely conversations in bed would make us experts about each other. But we
didn't talk much in bed. Usually it was late by the time we
crawled under the covers. Then, because we carried on late
into the night, we slept late the following morning and we
rarely had time to lounge around. A few times when I was not
quite ready for sleep I sat and stroked her (sometimes while
she smoked a last cigarette), but we were rarely moved to begin
a conversation.

It occurred to me we might already know all there was to know about each other. All those long dead hours in the store when we had nothing to do but tell each other stories about our lives. I had imagined that sex would lead to more knowledge, a deeper understanding. I assumed that as long as our contact remained superficial, our relationship would too, but once we knew each other sexually we would come to know each other in a different way. Our emotional quotient would change. I was wrong. Our sexual liaison didn't lead to a deeper emotional relationship. I wasn't disappointed when it didn't. In view of our coming separation, I was quite relieved. I found the silence about our lives agreeable.

If we didn't talk much about our relationship, we did talk about other things. I learned, for example, that Gilberte was not intellectually inclined. She verged on being an anti-intellectual. I had assumed because she was an artist she thought things out, used her reason to discover how to portray the relations that determined what we saw. But I was mistaken. In fact, Gilberte didn't like to think—that is, she didn't like to work problems out logically. She was proud to belong to the first generation to grow up with images from birth.

For one thing, Gilberte was not an intellectual. She verged on being an anti-intellectual. I had assumed because she was an artist she thought things out, used her reason to discover how to portray the relations that determined what we saw. But I was mistaken. In fact, Gilberte didn't like to think—that is, she didn't like to work problems out logically. She explained this by claiming she belonged to the first generation to grow up with images from birth.

—My father had a camera. He used to film us. I saw myself walk for the first time, she said.

She had been raised in a six-television family. There was always something glaring at her when she was in the house. All her life she had been surrounded by movies, commercials, made-for-TV specials, documentaries, news, game shows, sit-coms, soap operas, talk shows. She was a totally visual person. The written word didn't have the same aura for her it had for me. For her, literature was only words, something you trudged through, and which might be OK. For me the act of reading literature gave birth to a unique sensation or sense of life—independent of the emotions aroused by the story—that was possible only while reading. This, I ventured to guess, was a manifestation of an aesthetic experience in its purest form, perhaps an apprehension of the Beautiful. For Gilberte the Beautiful had to have a tactile element, it had to be visual. The only time she was interested in words was when they accompanied a picture. Anything she read had to be accompanied by pictures, preferably big pictures.

She liked to page through *Paper*, *Details*, *New York Talk*, *East Village Eye*, *Bomb*, and *Interview*. From these self-serving, mostly gossip-filled rags, which did for a certain class of art followers what *People* and *Us* did for a certain class of bourgeois, she culled the names of places that were in, people who were in, places that were out, people who were out, and in her conversation she always made reference to them. I tried to tempt her to read books I thought she might like. She claimed she never had time. Since I was committed to try to exercise some influence over her, on several occasions I pushed the reading issue.

—Not everybody is interested in books, she rebuffed me. You're probably the last generation.

—People still write them, I said.

—Fewer people read them. You said so yourself. It was true. One day while trying to account for sluggish sales, I had lamented the non-reading public.

♦

We also talked about Kristine. It was unavoidable. She played a large role in Gilberte's life. So it was to be expected she would be a major topic of our conversation. Moreover, I realized long ago Gilberte would use Kristine as long as she had to. The only thing that might cause a rift between them would be a social blunder of such magnitude it couldn't be pardoned. The chances of that happening were about as great as my being hit by lightning. There had been but one brief period when Kristine and Gilberte were barely on speaking terms. That was when Gilberte had first come to stay with me. Once Kristine recuperated from the shock and resigned herself to the situation, they became thick as thieves again. In fact, it appeared Roger's prediction that Kristine would drop Gilberte as soon as she tired of her was not going to come true, at least not in the foreseeable future. Apparently, Kristine was less easily bored these days.

I suspected more than that was involved, however. For one thing, their relationship had become too complicated for it to end abruptly. Like any two people in a long-term arrangement, they had developed a matrix of interdependent needs and desires. Kristine had an enormous social investment in Gilberte: she was her sponsor not only in the art world, where she tried to sell her work, but in drawing and reception rooms of some important people. In the circles in which Kristine moved, it wouldn't look good if she abruptly withdrew her support for the girl she was so assiduously championing. Furthermore, Gilberte was actually starting to make inroads into the social spheres in which Kristine had launched her. She was receiving calls and invitations from people to whom Kristine had introduced her.

I was also pretty sure Kristine was emotionally invested in Gilberte. Ever since that night in the Chinese restaurant, I had pondered the nature of their physical relationship—without coming to any firm conclusions. It was still a mystery. If Kristine was in love with Gilberte, I guessed it was not a full-fledged, intense love, but more of an epithelial, skin-deep emotion. Excited by the idea of a connection with an artist, a woman artist at that, Kristine had probably felt safe in letting herself go. Gilberte was different from anything she had known, so exotic compared to the company she normally kept. But how far their love had progressed physically was an issue I couldn't hope to settle. Fearful of where it would lead, Kristine might have balked at going farther than rubbing ankles under the table, or holding hands, or an occasional embrace, or a light kiss good-bye on the lips. Ambivalence might explain why she was still fascinated by Gilberte after all these months. Locked into her bourgeois sensibility, she might not have been able to go any farther than what I had seen in the restaurant.

Thus, I was willing to guess the nature of their relationship was quasi-Platonic. For reasons of sanity if nothing else, it seemed unlikely Gilberte would enter into a romantic liaison with both me and Kristine at the same time. In all likelihood, Kristine understood this as well. Which was why she was angry at me. She knew the impasse she and Gilberte had arrived at was due to the nature of Gilberte's relationship with me. She was burning with jealousy (not realizing that my liaison was saving her from having to commit to a course of action that she might regret). Doubtless it was this more than anything else that had caused her to look for a loft for Gilberte. Once she moved her out of my loft, her desire would be able to take to the field unimpeded. I was willing to bet that when something did happen between them, it would spell doom for their friendship.

Where was Gilberte in all this? That was a difficult question to answer. Her feelings for Kristine were complex. She admired Kristine and looked up to her as an example of what a woman could accomplish if she put her mind to it. She also feared her, for the obvious reason that if Kristine should decide to withhold her support, Gilberte would be out in the cold. Did she have any feelings for Kristine that could be characterized as sexual? I couldn't conceive of her having Kristine as a lover, but of course this was because I disliked Kristine. It was quite possible Gilberte found Kristine attractive as a sexual partner. Regardless of whether she found Kristine physically attractive or not, her wealth and her power gave her an allure that was hard to ignore.

◆

—Kristine's glamorous. I mean really glamorous, and that's rare, you know, Gilberte explained to me one day.

—Glamour isn't like elegance, I said.

I explained that while glamour wasn't rare, elegance was, because it somehow (partly) corresponded to a transformation of being into appearing and required a sense of one's self that transcended the everyday banalities of position and fashion. Glamour was glitz, it was ersatz elegance, brouhaha all trumped up for the masses, I said. Gilberte, to her credit, didn't deny this. She pointed out this was what our age was all about and the type of person I idolized wouldn't get noticed in our time.

—Just what do you have against her anyway? Why don't you like her? she asked.

On such short notice I didn't know what to say. My usual repertory of complaints—that she was pretentious, conceited, fatuous, shallow, vulgar—didn't seem very persuasive reasons to dislike her: lots of people I was friends with shared the same traits, and I didn't dislike them as violently as I did Kristine. I couldn't let my jealousy about her control of Gilberte's life serve as a reason because Kristine had done more than anyone else to get Gilberte where she was. Pointing this out would only trivialize my grievance and make it seem stupid and insubstantial. I told Gilberte I disliked Kristine because she was a crass materialist and lacked what anyone I liked had to have: an aesthetic sense. I didn't mean one had to be an aesthete, but one did have to take pleasure in seeing the world as an aesthetic phenomenon. To my mind, Kristine was as big a disaster as a person as William Gaddis's amorally corrupt gamin, JR.

—Kristine likes art. She buys art, Gilberte reminded me.

Of course she did, I conceded. She appreciated a good picture as much as the next person. But what she appreciated deep down was the object's appreciation: a work of art entered her collection and her ledger simultaneously. I could have gone on slandering Kristine, for I could feel myself warming to the task at hand, but I realized it would become too personal and therefore not as effective, so I stopped. I could tell by Gilberte's silence she was perturbed by what I had said. I thought I had finally reached her. She said:

—I think you're wrong.

I shrugged my shoulders in a friendly sort of way, to indicate I wasn't going to argue. Gilberte didn't want to argue either. She began to muse out loud. She confided her dream was to be taken up by a de Menil.

—Imagine donating a whole building to a single work, she said, referring to Walter De Maria's *Broken Kilometer*, housed in a loft space on West Broadway and supported by the Dia Foundation, that is, by de Menil money. They are the Medicis of our century, she said.

—There are others, I said.

—I know. But with them, you feel they understand. That they want to help. If one of them bought something of mine.... She didn't finish her thought. It didn't matter. I knew what would happen if.... Maybe not if they bought one photograph. But if they bought one and then got someone else to buy one for, say, the new-acquisitions show at the Modern or the Whitney. That would be all Gilberte would need. That would certify her work as collectible. It would be like receiving the Good Housekeeping Seal of Approval or, better, a triple-A bond rating.

I supposed this was Gilberte's crude way of telling me if she could have chosen her patroness, she would have done better for herself. Her admission indicated she understood what I had said about Kristine. I didn't know whether it was because she was in philosophical agreement with me or simply scared that in the long run she would suffer from her association with Kristine.

♦

The idea of finding a more enlightened patron began to pre-occupy Gilberte. The gallery season was in full swing. There were openings every week, new shows at the museums, benefits, dinners—myriad social occasions at which Gilberte could scout out prospective patrons. Which was exactly what she did. She did this with or without Kristine. When she was with Kristine she used her to get introductions to people she couldn't approach alone. When she was without her she would use Kettridge or Allbright for the same purpose. As it turned out, these two were more helpful than Kristine because Kettridge had entree into the most elite enclaves of high society. In an effort to make her fully appreciate what they were doing for her, Allbright had hinted to Gilberte they were introducing her to people who might not wish to meet a nouvelle riche lady and her friend but were always (noblesse oblige) delighted to meet a struggling young artist. Especially one who was receiving such attention these days. Allbright was particularly sympathetic toward her aims. Gilberte confided to me she thought he, too, would like to ameliorate (Allbright's word) his position. Guessing at what she was after, he had given her some advice.

—He told me to go slowly, very slowly. Don't ever give up what you have for a promise, was what he said.

—What did he mean? I asked.

She furrowed her brow and made an enormous effort to extract the meaning from his cryptic dictum.

—Not to do anything too quickly, I guess, she said. But I don't know if I understand the promise part.

We were in my bed. I took her hand in mine and kissed it, on the palm, on the back. It was late. She ran her fingers through my hair and then slid up next to me, pressing her warmth against mine.

—Do you get it? she asked.

—I think it's a warning, I ventured.

While remaining in my embrace, she retreated slightly and stared at me.

—A warning?

—It's like saying don't give up what you have so readily.

She mulled this over for a moment. I thought of an alternative explanation. Then she said:

—He's smart, Allbright. I bet he could teach me a lot.

—No doubt, I concurred.

—I don't think it's wrong to examine other possibilities, she said.

—Of course not. Writers switch publishers when they're not happy with how their careers are advancing, I said, although the case was not exactly analogous.

—You see, she said, as if she had known she was right. She put her head on my shoulder and cuddled up close, and I stroked her hair.

◆

Gilberte lamented the fact she couldn't do anything on her own. She needed someone to make the introductions and to talk her up. That accomplished, through Kristine or Allbright, she was good at following through. Once she learned somebody's name, she was set. If she met someone once, the next time she encountered the person she would charm them by recalling his or her name and the place where they had last met, as well as some little detail of the conversation.

If it was a woman, she might describe what she had worn. Which usually acted as an open sesame, because most people were flattered when they discovered they had made an impression. As sure as people are of themselves at any given moment, in retrospect they often consider their interpersonal performances during social occasions as merely part of their evening. Unless they purposefully set out to accomplish a particular goal, they are not likely to remember all the discussions they participated in, the inanities they uttered, or the people to whom they uttered them. They are always surprised and happy to learn they managed to stand out in the crowd. By pointing out certain people's performances to them Gilberte developed quite a following. Her interest in them sparked their interest in her. She compiled a list of names and addresses of people eager to see her work. She had no compunction or fear about showing it herself. She made arrangements with the gallery to show her work by appointment only. During these private shows she managed to sell a not inconsiderable number of photographs.

◆

Gilberte began following the photographic auctions and reading about the sale prices for old and new photographs in the *Times*, from which she culled the names of collectors she hoped to interest in her work someday.

—Anyway, she explained, it helps me focus. This way I know where everyone is coming from. I can keep on top of it all.

To me her interest in the sale prices was more prurient than prudent, because I couldn't see any reason to collect data about who backed whom or who had been the first person to buy a Mapplethorpe or a Sherman or a Turbeville or a Wegman. Unless Gilberte was planning to launch a campaign to get these same people to buy her work—which she claimed she wasn't—or was searching for a common theme in these artists' careers to discover how they achieved their success, and especially to know whether a patron had been instrumental in their rise to stardom, so she could then learn from them what and what not to do—which she denied—it was superfluous information. Yet she was fascinated by these facts. I supposed she was lying when she said she was not studying them as case histories to guide her career. I was hesitant about pointing out the futility of this kind of interest, because I felt partly responsible for inciting it. I was sure my deprecating Kristine and pointing out how callow a person she was had sent her off in search of the perfect patron. This search had broadened into an attempt to learn what other artists had had to put up with from their patrons, or whether they had put up with patrons at all. Perhaps it was normal to want to discover all this. It didn't make sense to me. Gilberte was spending an extraordinary amount of time researching it, when she should have been concentrating on her art.

♦

Her constant socializing directly affected my life. Two or three times a week she didn't come home until the wee hours of the morning. It was lonely not having her beside me when I climbed into bed. Especially because I always knew what time the event she was attending ended, and I could calculate approximately how long a dinner would last, and how long drinks afterward would go on. Which did not, could not, ever, add up to the time when she came home. Sometimes just before dawn.

I always waited up for her. She always asked why. And I couldn't explain. I couldn't say I was jealous that she was having fun without me, which was partly true. I couldn't say I was unable to go to sleep without knowing she was safe by my side because, which, while also true, would sound stupid and sappy. (Other people's excesses often make our attempts to be rational look ridiculous.) I would make up an excuse. And she would tell me I was crazy.

I invariably asked her how her night had been. Whether she had had a good time. Any banality to get her to talk. She was rarely ready to share with me. It took work to get out of her what I wanted to know. Sometimes I worked for nothing. And whether I got something or nothing out of her, I never got everything. She never gave me the minute-by-minute report I craved. There wasn't any reason for me to know other than jealousy. But I couldn't help myself. By accepting invitations to attend these events, she was choosing not to be with me. My desire to get her to tell me what, and especially who, gave her more pleasure than my company was what drove me to inter-rogate her.

Most of the time she went out with Kristine or Kettridge or Allbright. But increasingly she went places unescorted. She was doing this because she hoped to meet a new patron. Yes, in spite of the fact she knew about the loft Kristine was arranging for her (she had let something slip, but not wanting to let on I knew, I had not reacted and it had been passed over), she was still seeking to replace Kristine. And maybe not only Kristine. Because occasionally she told me she had spent the evening with a nice boy or with a dealer or painter. And if I heard the person's name again, I would wonder what was going on between them. Was it possible she would exchange kisses or embraces with a new admirer? It didn't seem likely. But then, if she did, what could I say about it? I knew what I would like to say. But we had no arrangement. She was free to do as she liked, and I was just as free. We didn't discuss the nature of our relationship or what it involved. I understood this to mean it was to mean nothing, that we were just to be as long as we were to be. If we tried to predicate it in any more definite manner, it would put an end to it. To us.

♦

Thanks to Gilberte's irrepressible enterprising nature, all the remaining photographs from the show were sold—without the direct help of the gallery. Henry and his assistants were too busy with their well-known, brand-name artists to be of any aid to Gilberte. Kristine and Kettridge kept finding clients for her. When she had sold everything that was salable, and some things that were not, she began taking pictures again, something she had not done since the show because she had been too busy selling. She complained if the gallery had pushed her work the way she had, she could have been back to work taking photographs instead of selling them. On the other hand, it didn't bother her to show and tell, con and cajole a sale. She was learning a lot from it. It had given her another idea for a film. But she was angry about having to pay the gallery a commission for doing nothing.

—I do all the work, she said. Everything.

—But you do a lot of the sales work in the gallery, I pointed out.

I finally got her to acknowledge she partly owed her success to the surroundings and to Henry's reassuring presence. I made her see that though it was true Henry rarely put in more than a word or two, this was sometimes enough. Clients trusted his discretion in these matters, just as they would trust their personal banker or financial analyst. Nevertheless, now and again she worked herself up into a frenzy, especially when a sale didn't come off. Then she would talk about how fabulous it would be when she would have a loft of her own where she could show and sell her work. It made me cringe to hear such talk. I said she was actually doing quite well. She admitted it grudgingly. For someone who had been on the so-called scene for so little time, she was, in fact, doing very well. She admitted this, too, and used it to bridge to a subject she had been wanting to speak to me about.

She wanted to reduce the number of hours she worked in the store in order to concentrate more on her work. And not just her photographic work. She was planning to launch a full-fledged campaign to locate backers for her film.

—Fund-raising is time-consuming, she explained. I can't work at the store and raise money at the same time. Raising the amount I'm going to need will be a full-time job.

—Do you think you can do it by yourself? I asked, totally in the dark as to the figure.

—Probably not. I'll have to sell the idea to someone. To a studio or a producer. Or ... maybe I can. I was thinking about an idea how to raise money.

We were in bed, on our backs, smoking, ready to retire. I rolled on my side and met her eager eyes.

—What is it? I asked.

—What if I do a series of stills from the movie? Get it? she asked, sitting up to better explain this brainstorm. I mean, I'd make photographs of what I'm going to film, like Christo makes sketches of what he's going to wrap, and then sell them. Robert Wilson sometimes does the same thing to raise money for his foundation. I went to one of the benefits at the Paula Cooper Gallery. Someone told me that from his address book alone you could find enough donors to raise several million.

Clearly awestruck, she stared off into space. I lifted the ashtray to catch her ash. Then she began planning in earnest her series of frames in progress that she could shoot.

—Maybe I can paint them. You know, right on the negative, like Incandela does. I think he starts from an actual shot, though. Have you seen what he does? I like it.

We then both tried to come up with ways to solve the more practical problems her idea raised—how to organize another show, how to characterize the work—as well as the theoretical problem of how the photographs could be said to be shots from the movie when the screenplay wasn't even written. Or whether this was a problem.

—You should write the screenplay, she said. If you had started when I asked you, you'd be done, she admonished me.

—I don't know, I said.

—What don't you know? You wrote the treatment. You know as much about it as I do at this point. More.

—Yes, but you didn't like it.

—I liked it. I just wouldn't have written it. And it's going to cost a lot more than I had wanted to raise. But if I had written it, you would've said the same thing. What do you think? Do you want to do it?

—Let me think about it. I'm not sure I can do it.

—You can, she said. Whether you want to is another story. Well, you think about it.

We talked late into the night. It was the first time we had had a serious discussion about what she was trying to achieve. I was thrilled she was sharing more and more of her ideas with me. Thrilled she still wanted me to write the screenplay, though I wasn't sure I wanted to accept the offer. It would be a major undertaking. A formidable challenge. The treatment had demanded a significant amount of work and concentration and imagination. I had either followed or reacted to Gilberte's original work. In writing it I had often stopped to wonder just how a screenwriter would handle a certain scene, as well as whether certain scenes could be handled at all. If I agreed to write it, I would be faced with finding solutions to these problems. It would test all my skills. I didn't know if I was up to it.

♦

Gilberte insisted I write the screenplay for her film. I was touched by her confidence in my abilities. She trusted me. Perhaps, I thought, this was the opportunity for me to say, *come on, let's cut the crap, let's throw ourselves into work.* I would show her how to do it. I would make her forget about her social aspirations, make her stick to creating art. Yet, her idea about how to raise funds for her film was ingenious. It showed she really was imaginative. I was convinced she could do great things if she would only put her mind to it. And be patient. But from the day she had learned exactly how important the social scene—in its broadest sense, which included gallery owners, museum curators, advisors to corporate art purchasing groups, consultants, editors, collectors, critics—was to the success of one's art, she had become obsessed with having them take notice of her, of accepting her, of purchasing her work.

Then, too, Gilberte was in a hurry. She wanted to achieve success as quickly as possible. And she couldn't comprehend how concentrating only on her work would get her there any faster because she had convinced herself (with Kristine's help?) that making the right social connections was equally, if not more, important in attaining success. If I could portray the way she was living as corrupt and counterproductive, I might be able to convince her. There was, however, a problem with my proposed approach. Gilberte was productive. She was creating and selling photographs. To make her consider what I was saying, I would be obliged to prove to her she could achieve her goal of reaching the top just as fast if she put everything she had only into creating art. And I couldn't prove it.

After agonizing over this issue at length, I decided not to intervene at all. To do nothing. Because, lofty sentiments aside, there were practical matters to consider. What if in my new position of trust, I succeeded in reaching her? Say I managed to convince her she was squandering her talent. Say she listened to me. What if she became passionately committed? She would have no choice but to withdraw from the social world that was giving her pleasure and become a hermit. What would happen then? Kristine would be sure to cut her off. She would lose her contacts. Her sales would dry up. Her new film would go unproduced. She would have to start from ground zero again. Create a whole new oeuvre. All the weight of her talent would be on my shoulders. I didn't know if I could take on so much responsibility. Especially if it turned out Gilberte couldn't make it on her talent alone. It was frightening.

These thoughts revealed the limit of my commitment. Sadly, I had to admit, even if she now dedicated herself fully to her work, I would be incapable of backing her one hundred percent. The admission turned my stomach. A feeling of self-loathing stirred within me. Here it was again, my life-long problem of being incapable of committing myself fully to anything. It was my downfall, the reason I lacked the resolve to become anything other than what I was. Why I was where I was today. What perplexed me was that up until now, while I had never been willing to do anything about myself, I had always been willing to force others to do what I couldn't. I made it a condition of my relationships. My lovers either succumbed to these conditions or rebelled against them. Either way it cost me nothing—or little: the pain of a broken love affair, temporary loneliness. My preoccupation with changing my lovers' lives was the mechanism I employed to avoid changing my own. Helping them to realize their goals had not only given me an excuse not to realize my own, it had given me a cause and a justification. If now I no longer tried to do anything to make Gilberte change her life, it was because for the first time someone was (inadvertently) changing mine. She was making me work. The irony didn't escape me.

♦

My world began to collapse the day Gilberte stopped working at the store.

♦

Now, in the morning, when I got up, I'd leave her sleeping in my bed. I would get dressed, eat, and go open the store. While walking to work I would picture Gilberte sleeping in my bed, hugging my pillow, her black hair spread over the white sheets like a drop of ink in water. I would see her, the blankets thrown back, her exposed ass protruding in the air. Or I'd imagine her, her back pressed up against the wall, her knees drawn up, staring at the television, giggling, content as a cat before a fire. But as soon as I found myself behind the counter, in front of the cash register, I became depressed. I felt I had been plunged into a darkened cell. I was terrified I would never see light again.

Sometimes I experienced the feeling of abandonment so intensely it paralyzed me. For the first several days after she stopped coming, I could barely function. Clinging to the counter like the captain of a besieged ship, I managed to maintain the appearance of order. I barked out information to customers who needed it, but made no effort to aid anyone who needed more than verbal directions. When I was alone in the store I felt sick, disgusted. I experienced some of my darkest moments. If Roger had walked through the door, I think I would have quit on the spot.

I tried to think how I had managed without her when she had gone off for a few hours for a drink or to a gallery with Kristine. Or when she was away during the summer on those long weekends. Or when, just before her show, she had taken off nearly a week. Back then, I had always anticipated her return, and though I could recall feeling blue because she was not there, the certainty she would return compensated me for her absence.

She would never return now. She had formally resigned. She had thanked me, and Roger, for all we had done for her, emphasizing she didn't know how she would have made do without us.

◆

I didn't begin to feel better until she came to visit me in the store, three weeks later. She was on her way uptown.

—I just thought I'd stop by, she said.

—Thanks, I said.

I hadn't asked her to come, and I didn't try to keep her. She stayed to smoke a cigarette and chit chat, and then went on her way.

After this she came by regularly. At first I was thrilled to see her. I attributed her early neglect of me not to negligence but to thoughtfulness: knowing her sudden and definitive break with the store had been too brutal, and it would be painful for me to see her come and go, she had waited for me to grow accustomed to my new situation.

I envied her freedom. I wished I could be as free as she was. After she left, I would feel as depressed and lonely as on the first day I had come to work alone.

Fortunately, her visits soon became intermittent. Then they stopped altogether, as abruptly as they had begun. She left my work habits in a shambles. I couldn't concentrate on my job. The only activity I pursued relentlessly was smoking. I moped about. Though I now felt well enough to come out from behind the counter, and could once again practice effective customer relations, I still shunned a large part of my work. To take it up again seemed tantamount to admitting defeat, to acknowledging Gilberte would never return.

I became an expert at procrastinating. The longer I put off the things I should have been doing, the more onerous the thought of doing them became. I swore I would die before I'd re-alphabetize a single shelf. There were cartons of new arrivals to unpack, and invoices and packing slips to check and orders to place. The periodical bills were overdue. I kept telling myself it could wait. I justified my laziness by convincing myself I was waiting for a critical mass large enough to occupy me for at least a week straight. That way I would be so busy I would forget about Gilberte.

◆

Roger came to visit me early one evening. The store had not yet reached the state of entropy that would demand action on my part, but it wasn't looking its best. I could tell Roger hardly believed what he saw. I told him I was planning a total reorganization. He nodded knowingly. He wanted to have dinner. I told him that I'd have to close early, then.

—Who'd want to buy a book at this hour anyway? he said. In this mess, who could find anything? he added.

He helped me lock the gates. We went to the Greene Street Cafe. Once he had a drink in his hand, he asked me what was up. I explained, vaguely, that Gilberte's quitting had upset me.

—I know. But she's replaceable, he said, without trying to be callous.

—People are replaceable, personalities aren't, I said.

—She was pleasant to work with, huh?

I nodded my head.

—You always surprise me, he said. I could see he felt sorry for me.

We talked mostly about his son's upcoming marriage. It was clear what interested him more than anything was the sequel to the marriage. He hoped to become a grandfather one day.

—Don't you ever think about children? he asked.

—Sure.

—Don't you ever want to have them?

—I'm unresolved, I said.

—I guess you'd have to ... It must be difficult ... I mean....

It was too awkward a dinner topic. He let it drop. He tried a different tack.

—You'll have your loft to yourself again soon.

—Oh? I was noncommittal.

—Well, it won't be long now. They've only got to paint and redo the floors and then some detail work, and her place will be ready. She should be able to move in as soon as the floors are dry. Then I've got to start thinking about my son's place.

—Where is it again? I asked, as if I had known but forgotten. In Tribeca? On Duane or Vesey?

—White Street, he said.

—That's right. Is it big?

—Big? It's like yours. And it'll have a darkroom.

—Expensive?

—Everything's expensive these days. We ate dessert in silence. As soon as the waiter had taken away our plates, Roger glanced at his watch.

It was time to wrap things up. I was waiting for him to broach the subject that had necessitated this dinner.

—It looks like you'll be on your own again, he began.

—It looks that way.

—You'll need some help at the shop, he said.

—I know.

—Better take care of that right away. Don't let things get out of control.

— Don't worry, I won't.

—Good. Happy? he asked.

The question, although somewhat in keeping with this rather unusual conversation, was so unexpected I didn't know what to answer. To show him I was grateful for his concern, I smiled. I was sure he was now going to tell me what he had in mind. He didn't. He signed the check, signaling we should go.

His car was waiting outside.

—Going home, or can I drop you someplace?

—I think I'm going home. He gave me a warm, solicitous smile.

—OK. Take care. I hope you are being careful, he said.

I knew what he meant. I was touched by his concern.

—Don't worry, I said. I opened the door for him.

He clapped me on the shoulder and climbed inside.

Thanks for the dinner, I said.

—My pleasure.

◆

It wasn't easy to get Roy to work more hours. He had learned computer coding in his spare time.

—I can make a fortune, he bragged.

When he told me what he was earning an hour, I was astounded. He said he could command such pay because he was talented, and talent was in demand.

—Most people only learn one or two programs, halfway. They're basically illiterate even in the program they're operating. I'm fluent. I'm better than fluent. And I get calls all the time.

I had to meet his terms to get him to come back. He had to be free to accept an assignment when he wanted to. And I would have to do without him for however many days it took. He never worked anywhere for more than four.

—After that I start to feel cooped up. And you can't sit in front of a screen eight hours a day for more than that. Or at least I can't. My chips start to fry, he said, pointing to his head. And then I can't concentrate on my work.

Roy was a dancer who wrote music, or, alternatively, a composer who danced, depending upon his inspiration. I saw no problem with his request, so we struck a mutually satisfying deal.

♦

Gilberte was rarely at home when I arrived these days, and I had trouble adjusting to her erratic schedule. When she was working at the store we hadn't always gone home together, but she would let me know when she would return—even if it was as vague an indication as *late* or *early*. Now she no longer bothered to extend me this courtesy. She neither left a note nor called to inform me of her plans, but left me to fend for myself, guessing at her whereabouts and the hour of her return. At first I waited on dinner for her, thinking she would surely not stand me up without a word: we had a standing date for dinner. But she did. When I mentioned it to her she apologized profusely—but she did the same thing the following night. I didn't complain. I learned what she wanted me to learn: that she would no longer be eating dinner at the loft. So I, too, stopped eating dinner there and resumed my old habits, eating and drinking at neighborhood restaurants and bars.

Often when I got home I wandered down to her end of the loft and stared at her possessions. Drunk, aching for her company, I found some solace gazing at her belongings. Their mute presence comforted me and assured me she would come back. On occasion, I went so far as to pick up a tape or study a contact sheet. Sometimes I collapsed on her couch and fondled a stray article of clothing. As long as I could remain in close contact with her belongings, I felt that although she was absent she was not gone. Not yet.

◆

I was sure at any moment my life was going to fragment, fly apart. Gilberte's comings and goings, usually without warning, didn't help matters. Her non-participation in any of the rituals we had established further intensified my feeling that everything between us was coming undone. She was freeing herself from the bonds that tied us together. First, she had stopped showing up for dinner. Then she declined breakfast. She let me know she would rather sleep a little longer in the morning than eat, if it didn't bother me. Since she had stopped working at the store I had taken it upon myself to make her breakfast—and serve it—along with mine so we could spend some time together. Its suppression meant we seldom saw each other during the day.

She was always happy to see me when our paths crossed. She made a genuine effort to catch up with what I had been doing. Naturally, I tried to find out how she was doing. What she was doing. But our conversations had the feel of an obligatory letter one owes to a friend and can no longer put off without jeopardizing the friendship.

To add to my distress, our lovemaking changed. We rarely cuddled and caressed. Sex became less emotional, more recreational, less frequent, more violent, less satisfying.

The last thing I wanted to know was the date of her departure. I didn't want to hear talk about her moving out. Her silence on the matter seemed to indicate that she, too, felt this was something better left unsaid.

There was no doubt in my mind I could alter our lives forever with a question. At the same time, I knew what her answer to my question would be. She was going to leave me. Leave me no matter what. If I asked her to stay, she'd refuse, and her refusal would strengthen my desire to make her understand why I wanted her to stay, and what I wanted for her. To make my point, I would have to condemn her life, her friends, and her ambitions, and I had already realized the futility of this approach. Why chance alienating her? Well, perhaps to relieve my bad conscience: my tirade would be for my sake, not hers. It would be my coward's way of getting off my chest all the things I had wanted to say all this time. My speaking out would lessen my guilt for not having done more to get her to see things my way. It would not relieve me from feeling I had failed her. It would let her know I had wanted something special for her and, I hoped, would put me beyond her reproach if ever she regretted making the decision she had already made.

◆

For all I knew, Gilberte could have been planning to stay on for weeks, months. Still, I considered her as good as gone. She was not the first to leave me like this. My previous live-in lover, Daniel, had gone off to chase success too. His avant-garde ambitions had just begun to flag when we met. He had discovered he couldn't become another David Warrilow, and so he didn't want to be anybody. Destitute because he had no work, he moved in with me. He needed time to decide what to do. I told him he could take as much time as he needed. In the morning he searched through *Variety* and *Back Stage* at the kitchen table. When I came home at night, I would find the completed *New York Times* crossword puzzle on the table. *Variety* and *Back Stage* would be scattered on the floor and Daniel would be pacing back and forth at the other end of the loft.

I tried to get him to return to experimental theater, but he wouldn't listen. He told me he was tired of experiments. I told him he didn't have to worry about supporting himself as long as he stayed with me. He told me avant-garde theater had become boring. It was mainstream theater now. He needed another challenge.

He got his first real job, as he called it, as an extra in a soap opera. He said the money would be great and the work would do him good. He was excited but I could see he wasn't sure he was doing the right thing. He tried to make the whole affair appear to be merely a practical step, a stopgap, something to do for money, on the same level as going to a temporary agency and getting work as a secretary. He said he needed this job to see him through his uncertainty. He hoped it would help clarify his ideas.

Slowly, in the weeks that followed, he was seduced by the idea. The work wasn't bad. He met charming people. He was ecstatic the first time he saw himself on TV. He felt he had arrived at something.

He found a new agent, had new photographs taken, and began getting jobs. Not good jobs. An extra in a soap opera here, an extra in a commercial there. The jobs were bad, but the money was good. Daniel had never had money. At thirty-one, he was beginning to wonder what he was going to do with the rest of his life. How he was going to live? How he was going to pay the bills? And there were a lot of bills, because he spent every cent as quickly as he made it, and then some.

He began to change. Whereas he had been a loner in the theater world, suddenly he had hordes of friends in television. He had an answering machine installed (against my wishes), ostensibly so when he was out looking for a job he wouldn't miss a call for work, but also to better manage his personal life.

Daniel's change in attitude accelerated when he began getting long-run roles. One day he announced soap operas were not just mid-afternoon visual junk food for suburban matrons—they were art. Peculiarly American art, but art nonetheless. The real stuff. Daniel loved it. Then he became preoccupied with moviemaking. He read all the movie magazines. He talked of nothing but the movies. He began speculating on what life must be like in California. I knew what was coming. I said California was no place for him to live. It was a place people were forced to dream about if they wanted to act, Daniel told me. And he wanted to act.

Daniel acted in New York. He got more and more jobs, and he stopped talking about California. He earned a lot of money doing commercials. He used some of it to take acting courses. He was getting better, he claimed. Better and better. He was earning more and more money. He convinced himself that the age of theater was over. Forever, he said. There was no more living theater. Only retrospectives. Or pastiches. What could he do? As an artist, nothing. So why be an artist? Now he wanted to be a journeyman. He wanted to capitalize on his talent. He wanted to make it. He said he thought it was as legitimate to want to be like Robert Redford as to want to be like Antonin Artaud. There was no reason he couldn't become a star. Or failing that, a top character actor. Like Harry Dean Stanton. All it took was talent, hard work, and determination.

When he told me he was moving to Hollywood, I wasn't surprised. Prior to making his announcement, he had gone through a period of withdrawal—just as primitives will go into isolation before undertaking a rite of passage—and had not initiated a conversation with me for more than a week. It was as if the seed he had planted were germinating, and he needed all his strength to ensure its coming to fruition. Only when he had prepared all the arguments to facilitate its transition from the inner to the outer world did he reveal it.

He told me moving to California was something he had to do while there was still time. Everyone with ambition went to Hollywood. There was talent there, actors, directors, ideas, money, glamour, everything. Daniel said he knew it would be tough. He would have to start at the bottom. Do grade-B pictures. Continue to do commercials. Work like a dog until he got his break. But he was willing to do it. He was talented, and he knew if he went for it he would get it. That's what he said.

He was sure he would shine more brightly than the others in the land of tinsel. What could I say? He didn't want to hear anything negative, and I didn't say anything. I realized we were no longer talking about acting. The transformation had begun: he wanted less to be an actor than he wanted to be a star. And the strange and pitiful part was he had come to believe he could make the transition from the mundane to the celestial merely by moving to Hollywood.

It hurt me to see him go. But I made no effort to stop him.

At first he wrote. He called from time to time and promised to come back to visit as soon as he made enough money. He told me I should give up New York and come live in the land of sun and sand and surf.

I stayed in New York. When the letters stopped, the postcards began arriving. They announced his imminent arrival on the screen. But I never saw his name mentioned in anything. Then the postcards stopped. He cut off communication. The next time I saw him was on TV. I was mindlessly flipping channels and there he was, a smiling face in a group of smiling faces, all hale and hearty sun-drenched youths singing about orange juice.

Daniel had added something to my life. I had come as close to loving him as I had come to loving anyone I had ever been with. He was basically an uncomplicated person, and I had cherished him for that. For the year and a half we were together, I had known something like bliss. Up until then I had never thought I could have a relationship or provide all the things you had to give if you were going to speak about a relationship. Nor had I thought it possible to accept all these things from one person. I was used to takers like Thomas and to the baths and bars and the kind of Russian roulette one played in seeking satisfaction from strangers. I used to tell myself in the long run the good times would average out to the same thing you might expect in a long-term association. I was wrong. Daniel had showed me I was wrong.

♦

The world is filled with people who set out to do something and never do it. Some people don't have the talent to do what they set as their goal. Some don't have the will. Some are confounded by a conspiracy of circumstances. Yet many of the people who realize they will never achieve their goal push on, undaunted, in other directions, and many do nothing. I was one of these latter.

♦

—I'm going to be moving, Gilberte finally announced.

I was in the middle of mixing a martini at the kitchen counter. In the reflection of the microwave oven's door, I saw her putting on her coat to go out. I knew this moment would arrive. I was somewhat prepared for it. Nevertheless, I had a sinking sensation in my stomach. I had to close my eyes to keep them from welling with water. This was the moment I had dreaded. I had avoided saying anything about it in the idiotic hope that perhaps she wouldn't say anything about it either. Not that I hoped she would just disappear one day: I hoped Kristine's plan would fail to come off. That at the last moment there would be some hitch which would nix and nullify the arrangements Kristine had worked out for her. And that Gilberte would stay with me indefinitely. I saw her buttoning her coat. I turned around.

—Where are you going? I asked, preferring to postpone knowing when this momentous event would take place.

—Not far from here. White Street. I'm going to have my own loft, she said. She smiled.

—How did you find it?

—Kris found it for me. I think it's in one of her husband's buildings.

—Can you afford it?

—I don't know yet. It will be tight at first. But I think....

She ran out of words.

—What?

—I need a place of my own. Everyone needs their own place. You need your own place back, she said.

Her logic was unimpeachable, but I didn't want to listen to talk about what people needed.

—When will your new place be ready?

She didn't answer immediately. She sat down. I could see there was something else to be said.

—You know, my birthday is next week.

I did. I had been planning to take her out someplace special for dinner and to give her a painting or a photograph from my collection. I had a Weegee she would be sure to like.

—Thursday. I named the day.

—How did you know? She was being coy.

—I remember.

—Well, Kristine is giving me a party at the loft, which will be kind of a....

—A housewarming, I guessed.

—Yeah. And then I can move in any time after that. Wait till you see it. It has a darkroom and everything.

—It sounds great, I said.

She seemed relieved I shared her enthusiasm.

She lit a cigarette and took a long drag. I could see she had been expecting me to react more forcefully. Maybe she thought I would accost her emotionally and plead with her, or that I would be irate and make a scene, in which case she was ready to run. And perhaps if I had not been prepared, her announcement would have packed greater punch. But the blow had been delivered long ago. All this time I had been recuperating from it. I took a big sip from my drink.

—You'll come, right? she said, standing.

—Yes.

—Are you sure?

—Yes.

—Well, you know, last time there was a party for me you ran off. And I'd like you there. She looked at me reproachfully, tenderly.

—I'll be there, I said.

—Thanks.

She came over and hugged me hard. I set my drink on the counter, wrapped my arms around her, and held her, pressing her into me. She nuzzled her cheek against my neck and then, pulling away a little, she leaned back, and we stared into each other's eyes. Hers were bright, brimming with tears. Mine were dry, resigned. She kissed me on the cheek, released herself from my embrace, and made her way to the door.

—I'll be back late, she said. Ciao.

I downed what was left of my drink and made another.

◆

It was crowded when I arrived. I didn't immediately see Gilberte, or Kristine. Only after I wove my way through the throng that had gathered near the door, and then through another crowd, which had gathered around the refreshment table, did I locate them. They were holding court in the kitchen. Gilberte spotted me and smiled apologetically, but she did nothing to extricate herself from the conversation she was engaged in. Kristine, attentive to Gilberte's every move, watched her to see whom she was favoring with a smile. I waved to her but looked away before she had time to respond, if she did at all. It was terribly impolite, but I couldn't help myself.

I proceeded to the bar and ordered a vodka martini. They weren't making vodka martinis. Would I care for a vodka? I accepted a vodka on the rocks with lime. Taking a handful of carrot sticks with me, I inspected Gilberte's new space. There were four big windows overlooking the street. Because of the southern exposure and the high ceiling, I assumed the loft received plenty of light during the day. I walked by the kitchen. The walls were tile and the floor was gray marble. It wasn't a big room, considering the size of the loft. But there were two large counters that could double as tables. All the latest conveniences had been built in. They stood shoulder to shoulder, polished, gleaming, their LED readouts emitting a soft green glow. The bathroom had floors and walls of dark, sea-green marble. It was equipped with a sauna and a bidet and an oversize whirlpool tub. There were overhead lights and heat lamps.

At the far end of the loft was the darkroom. It had already been furnished, with sinks and counters, racks and shelves. Unfortunately, it blocked two of the four windows (apparently they had been boarded over) on the back wall. Because it was already dark, it was impossible to estimate how much light was lost. Light from the front windows probably amply filled the space. The only other wall added to the space—aside from those that served to enclose the kitchen, bathroom, and dark-room—was a floating one, in the style of Mies van der Rohe. It began just after the end of the kitchen wall, extended nearly to the darkroom, made a right angle, and stopped short before the west wall. The enclosed space was undoubtedly Gilberte's bedroom. The open area would serve a function determined by the furniture, or lack of it, placed there. For the moment, there was not a stick of furniture anywhere (aside from the folding chairs that had come with the hired help). All in all, I was impressed. The newly finished floors glistened under the overhead lights. The walls were clean and bright. It was going to be a lovely place to live in.

Back at the bar, I ordered another vodka. The loft seemed to have become more crowded. I drifted aimlessly. Drank continually. Became progressively more inebriated. Most of the other guests were doing the same. They milled about, imbibed large quantities of alcohol, ingurgitated large quantities of food, enjoyed themselves. After all, it was a party.

Looking around more closely, I began to pick out faces I thought I recognized, or at least thought I remembered having seen before. Some of these faces seemed to recall me, for as I walked through the crowd, headed toward the front windows, munching and crunching on celery stalks, people smiled at me and talked to me and helped me recall where I had seen them last. It turned out I had met many at the store, and the rest either at my loft or at the Bleecker Street screening of *Party Girl* or at the gallery uptown. I chatted with everybody and apparently charmed all the blue-haired ladies. In fact, I was struck by the number of elderly persons present. It was astounding. Like being at a Wednesday matinee at the theater. There was hardly anybody Gilberte's age. It was obvious the guest list had been compiled by Kristine, who was concerned to have people who counted come, and not just friends.

Gilberte finally managed to have a few words with me.

—What do you think? She wanted to know.

—It's beautiful, I said.

—Really?

I nodded my head.

Sure I wasn't being ironic, she added:

—I love it. I don't think it's as big as yours, but the design and the attention to detail is terrific, she said, as if the latter qualities somehow made up for its more modest dimensions. She was all enthusiasm.

—I hope you'll be happy here, I said.

—Thanks, she said. She took my hands in hers for a minute and squeezed them lightly. Then, claiming she absolutely had to get back to someone, she darted away. I went to the bar and ordered another drink.

Roger showed up, with his son and future daughter-in-law.

—How are you? he asked.

—Fine, I said.

—You look a little.... He gestured with his hand.

—It's a party, I said.

He then presented his son, Mark, and his son's fiancée, Stephanie. The son reminded me of neither Roger nor Kristine.

He was tall, sallow, stiff. He wasn't devoid of charm (there was something very boyish about him), but he was definitely ill at ease with himself. His bride-to-be had no discernible redeeming qualities. Like her fiancé, she was tall, and she had the same blond hair and fair eyes, but whereas he was notably thin, she had wide hips and thick thighs. She came from serious child-bearing stock, I was sure. I studied them both while Roger made small talk and tried to figure out what to do first. I decided Mark was a modestly handsome man whose looks would probably improve with age. Stephanie, on the other hand, was plain, understated to the point of creating a spectacle of herself. This was the best she was ever going to look. Which made me feel sorry for Mark.

—Did you just arrive? Mark asked me. This was only the second time we had met. Having nothing in common, we found conversation awkward.

—No, I've been here for several of these, I explained, holding up my glass. They all laughed.

—Have you seen Kristine? Roger asked.

—Yes, she's in the kitchen.

He checked his watch.

—We have to leave by eight-forty-five, Stephanie said to us all.

—Yes, I know, Mark said. But we do have to stay for the cake.

—Cake? Roger looked at me.

I shrugged my shoulders.

—I believe Mother said there will be a cake.

Roger rolled his eyes. Then, excusing himself, he took his son and future daughter-in-law in hand and headed off toward the kitchen.

There was going to be a cake. Probably a speech to go with it too. I couldn't wait! I fished the lime out of my drink and ate the pulp. I was just about to go order another vodka, when Allbright accosted me.

—How have you been? he asked, using a tone of voice that made it appear he was asking for an update rather than broaching the subject of my well-being for the first time.

—Not bad. And you? I asked, playing along.

—Very well. But exhausted. I spent the whole day getting my wardrobe in order.

—Ah, I said, as if I were intimately familiar with this task. As it turned out, he had been all over town, shopping, getting measured for this and trying on that. The task had fatigued him greatly. He lamented that he always had to be dressed up. He was being disingenuous. Except for Thomas, and perhaps Allbright's sponsor, Kettridge, I didn't know anyone who took such obvious pleasure in clothes. He was without a doubt one of the best-dressed men in town. Tonight, he was wearing a double-breasted blue cashmere blazer (whose gold-inlaid buttons he must have hunted down in an antique store or bought at an auction), with dark charcoal-gray slacks, a white shirt, a solid salmon-colored silk tie, and black tassel shoes. It was evident to me, from the texture of the Sea Island cotton and from the way it fit around his neck and lay flat on his chest, that his shirt had been made to measure. He tugged at his left shirt sleeve until he had fully exposed the gold ingot-shaped cuff link.

—There, he said, apparently satisfied. But at least I got it all done, he continued.

It was unusual for him to talk to me about something so personal as his shopping. Only when I realized he was already slightly drunk did his loquaciousness become comprehensible.

—I think I'd like another drink, Allbright said, after perfunctorily draining his glass. Would you like another one? he wanted to know.

I looked at my nearly empty glass and said yes.

—Are you sure you should have one?

—Sure. Yes. Why not? I'm not driving.

—What have you been buying lately? he asked, once we had both been served.

—Nothing.

He seemed scandalized.

—I haven't bought anything in ages, I informed him.

—Fischl? Schnabel? Salle? None of those people interest you?

—Fischl perhaps, otherwise no.

—Well, listen, if you are tired of figurative and expressive painting, there are other things happening. And now is the time to get in. He then explained to me the developing scene in the East Village. According to him, more art was being produced there than in any other district in New York.

—Have you been over there lately? he asked.

I admitted I had not.

—It's crazy, he said. There are galleries everywhere. And the work is splendid. You should go take a look. I think you'll find it refreshing. It's kind of neo-Conceptual or neo-Pop.

I said I would go have a look.

—Now's the time to buy, he said. You know, Saatchi has started to buy over there in a big way. And once people like that start investing, you know what happens to the market.

I gave him an understanding smile.

—I'd be glad to show you around, he said. I know where you can find some fabulous bargains. He slipped his hand inside his blazer and from his vest pocket withdrew a card and handed it to me.

I slipped it into my vest pocket.

—Do you go to the auctions?

—No, I said.

—That's where all the action is now. There are mega billions running around there. People are throwing money at art. It's unbelievable.

—I believe it, I said.

—Did you go to the sales last week? he asked, oblivious of the fact I had just told him I didn't attend auctions. Jasper's *Out the Window* went for 3.3 million. Absolutely incredible. He shook his head. Next week is the Sweeney sale. You should come.

—I can't. I've got to work, I said.

—Too bad. It'll be good.

—Maybe we should go join the others, I suggested.

People were beginning to gather near the kitchen. Allbright and I moved to the outer perimeter of those who had already taken their places. The lights went out, and from the bathroom someone emerged pushing a rolling cart on which sat the cake, spiked with sparklers showering sparks. Kristine led everyone in a round of happy birthday. Gilberte, looking sheepish and embarrassed, tried to blow out the sparklers. There was applause and cheers and laughing as they kept relighting. Finally, they burned themselves out, and the lights came up. Kristine gave Gilberte a big hug. I thought Gilberte was going to say something, but Kristine preempted her.

—We'd all like to wish you a happy birthday and ... a happy home, and....

It was clear she couldn't quite think of what else to say. She gave her another hug. Everyone clapped. Roger was frowning. It was better than I had expected from Kristine. I had been waiting for something gushy and self-serving, and instead it had been humble and—probably—sincere.

The cake was cut. Portions were distributed by the help. After gobbling them down, the guests began making their exit. In no time at all the place was almost empty. I decided to take my leave. Gilberte was in the middle of a conversation, but broke it off to say good-bye to me. She promised not to be home too late. I went home and wrapped her present. I left it on her couch.

◆

Gilberte moved out bag and baggage all in one day, much in the same way she had moved in. We two did all the moving. This time we rented a van instead of using a taxi.

By the time we picked up the van, loaded it, drove it to her new home, unloaded it, and moved everything in, it was late afternoon. Gilberte wasn't going to make the trip back with me. I was filled with trepidation about leaving her in the virtually empty loft. But it was light and bright and gay, and Gilberte refused to hear of staying with me a moment longer, though I pointed out that at night her surroundings would appear different. She would be menaced by shadows, attacked by strange noises. And she didn't yet have a phone to call for help. Sure, she would fill the cavernous space with music to keep her company (I had given her an old AM-FM clock radio with one remote speaker), but she would still be alone, and there wasn't a creature comfort anywhere. She didn't even have a bed.

—I'm going to get some foam on Canal Street, she said when I remarked on this. I could see she was determined to brave it out. There was no sense in insisting she return to stay on at my place until she made hers more habitable.

—Are you sure you'll be all right?

—Sure. And you? she asked with tender solicitude.

—Sure, I said, not so sure.

I saw myself to the door, where I inspected the lock. There was a Fichet deadbolt and a chain lock.

— I'd add another one, I counseled.

—Oh, I'll be all right. The door downstairs locks too, remember. And you need a key for the elevator after six.

—I know, but still.

— I'll be all right, she repeated.

—All right, I conceded.

We hugged, kissed. I left her.

♦

I found myself living alone. What I felt was much more intense than I had expected. In truth, I didn't know what I had expected. It might have been something so stupid as to feel lonely, or sad, or abandoned. But to link myself to such sentiments seemed somehow inadequate to what I was experiencing. My life had been bound to Gilberte's, and now it wasn't. It was that simple, that devastating. My state of being had been abruptly altered. No matter what I did, Gilberte was lost to me, irretrievably. I was plunging into the void her absence created. I wanted to scream.

♦

Down at her end of the loft, I lifted the couch cushions, searching for signs of her. I scoured her living area, seeking something she had left behind. I ransacked the bathroom. Ripped apart her closet. She had been quite thorough: there was no trace of her anywhere.

♦

My first nights without her were wretched. I drank myself into a stupor and fell asleep on her couch.

The next few weeks were no better. I could barely function. I spent my days at work recuperating from my drunken nights. At home I felt crushed by enormous, unmanageable blocks of time. I didn't know what to do. I drank. I lolled about in an alcohol-induced stupor. Watched more television than I cared to. And ate like a pig.

I surprised myself. After all, I had been prepared for her moving out for a long time. The sadness had settled on me that night at her opening, when Roger had had informed me what the future held in store. What I hadn't reckoned on was the counterbalancing force that her presence had continued to exert on me. That is, I knew she was going to leave me and I had begun mourning her loss in advance, but because she had still been present I didn't have to change my habits or rearrange my life. Then, she was gone, and I was faced with the task of reorganizing my life. It wasn't easy. When someone you've been close to goes out of your life, you never get things back to the way they were. You always have to find a new way. And the new way is determined, in part, by elements over which you have no control.

I wanted to speak to her in the worst way, but she hadn't installed a phone yet, and of course she didn't go out of her way to call me when one was available. I realized she was probably preoccupied with her new living quarters and didn't have much time. Still, a call would be appropriate. It would put me at ease. Stop me from thinking that she was thrilled to be out of my house.

♦

It was several weeks before my life settled down to something bearable. I went to work. I went home. I went out. Sometimes I saw old friends, but I couldn't disguise the fact I was calling on them not to reestablish contact on a permanent basis but merely out of temporary need for distraction and human comfort. When I realized this, I put a halt to it. It wasn't right. It was against my principles. Over the years, I had slowly retreated from the friendships of my youth. Then I began losing contact with the people I met when I first arrived in New York. From time to time I would bump into someone, or I'd call someone when curiosity got the better of me, but to say I still had *best friends* would be stretching the truth to an unrecognizable degree.

I had come to look askance at friendship as something desirable in and of itself. I couldn't help it. At a critical period in my life—when I realized I could no longer ask for indulgence, or feel comfortable being coddled, or play for the sympathy I was entitled to—I began to see friendship as an attempt to justify, and perhaps ennoble, the sentiments you felt in dealing with your friends. All the emotional mishmash people usually invoked to explain why they had friends lost its hold on me. I began to think of friendship in terms of a matrix made up of affection, deception, indulgence, intrigue, empathy, jealousy, pity, aid, esteem, boredom: all of which, I decided, could be experienced without having friends. Naturally, everybody said everybody needed friends. Everybody agreed this was a universal truth. I thought this so-called universal truth masked a universal desire: you didn't need friends as you needed air or water: you needed friends because people wanted to have friends. And they wanted them because they found them useful: that much was clear. If friends weren't useful, what good were they? I thought the amount of ink expended in writing odes, hymns, paeans, poems, essays, and novels extolling friendship showed only that people were concerned to demonstrate that the energy spent in maintaining friendships was worthwhile, to prevent their concluding it was a waste of time. Given my beliefs, the most honest thing I could do was remain skin-deep.

◆

One day I had a moment of panic when I thought Gilberte could have been my salvation. I chastised myself for letting her go. I told myself I should have forced her to stay, regardless of whether I could have converted her to my way of thinking. I should have made her life of paramount importance, devoted myself to her and fought alongside her to make sure she got everything she wanted. Perhaps having a common goal would have made it possible for us to love each other. Really love. But she didn't want my love.

♦

Roy was just wrapping up his dialogue on how the physical fitness craze had marked the failure of the mentalistic seventies and announced the beginning of the materialistic eighties, when Roger walked in.

—And you know who's behind it all? Roy asked. The government. Reagan. He wants people fit to fight a war. I'm telling you. Roy gave Roger a significant and challenging look.

Roger avoided the topic altogether.

—You changed the color of your hair, Roger said.

—Yeah. It's a custom color. I made it myself.

It was a gruesome green, a shade somewhere between the color of seasick skin and the bright metallic bands found around some number two pencils.

—I see. Roger then turned to me. What are you doing for lunch?

—I was going to make a quick bite to eat at the loft.

— Ah ... I thought....

—Why don't you join me? I asked. It was imperative that I go home to get my sheets, underwear, and towels out of the washer, where they were soaking in Clorox.

—Sure.

—And me? Roy wanted to know.

—When I come back, you can go out, I said.

Roger's limousine was waiting. He asked whether I wanted to ride or walk, and I said I preferred to walk. Even the four-block walk to my loft wouldn't be long enough to allow for thorough appreciation of the fine, clear, cold spring day. I arranged my jacket and scarf while Roger explained to his chauffeur where we were going and how long we would be. Then we set off. Roger wanted to know what we would lunch on.

—Sandwiches, I said. He frowned. Is that all? He insisted we stop and buy something more savory. He wanted wine, too, and insisted I go buy a bottle of something good, and then meet him at Dean & DeLuca. It was peculiar he should be interested in wine, which he rarely drank, but I did his bidding.

By the time I arrived, he had made all the necessary purchases and was waiting by the door, standing over a bulging bag.

—We'll never eat all that, I pointed out.

—I'm hungry, Roger said.

I tended to my wash as soon as we got upstairs. While I was busy with the laundry, he poured himself a large Scotch and was worrying about my cocktail.

—I couldn't remember whether it was with gin or vodka. It's a martini, though, right?

—Right. Vodka.

He reached for the bottle.

—But I don't take a cocktail at lunch.

—Oh, I thought you did.

—I'll have a glass of wine, I said.

Roger raised his glass while I was opening the bottle.

—Cheers.

I poured myself a glass of wine and then began helping him empty the bag. Roger did the unwrapping.

—There's Scotch salmon and sturgeon, he said. There's a *saucisse*. You like that, don't you?

I said I did.

—And this is some stuffed thing. He held up a *pate en croute* for my inspection. Looks delicious. Here's some cheese. And here's some more. And some crackers. And some bread. This is some sort of pasta salad. Ah, here's the sliced ham. It's still warm. And this is green mustard. I had it in France once. It's fabulous. This is dessert. He lifted up a box. And there are some olives somewhere. He thrashed through the paper. Ah, here we go. I politely refused.

—No? They are perfect with Scotch. He popped one in his mouth. Oh, he said, reaching for his wallet. How much do I owe you for the wine?

—Nothing, I said. I was going to buy some anyway.

—Nonsense. I don't invite someone to lunch, tell them to buy something, and then not pay them for it. How much? He took out fifty dollars. Is this enough?

—It's too much.

—It doesn't matter. He laid the money on the table. One glass of red wine on an empty stomach in the middle of the afternoon was enough to make me feel light-headed. However, as our lunch seemed to be a special occasion, I poured myself another glass. Then I attempted to organize the cornucopia Roger had poured out on the table, while he busied himself with the wrapping paper, trying to save it for leftovers, I presumed. I dug out my serving trays and began arranging the delicacies. He did most of the talking. He rambled on about his son's wedding, which he was looking forward to. About his latest business ventures. And about how he and Kristine were looking for a new apartment in the city.

—It's not easy to find a nice apartment, he said.

I thought it funny that the man who owned a sizeable share of New York real-estate couldn't find an apartment.

—It's not funny, he corrected me. Ninety percent of what I own is commercial. And the other twenty percent is.... He fumbled for the words to describe it.

—Slum.

—No. Not at all. Not all of it. It's just ... ordinary-people kind of places, you understand. Middle class. And a lot of that is in Brooklyn. Which is going to come back, by the way. Anyway, I don't own anything I'm looking for. I want something grand, a mansion in the sky.

—Build one, I suggested.

—Yes. But it wouldn't be the same. I'd like to be on Park or on Fifth along the park. In the Dakota, maybe, or River House. But there isn't a decent apartment to be had at any price. There are other problems too. Kris wants certain things that I don't, like live-in servants' quarters. I can't stand the idea of living with the help.

I sympathized with him, pretending I had experienced the same problems myself.

—It is difficult, I avowed.

Having loaded and arranged everything on two platters, I proposed we adjourn to eat in the living room, at the other end of the loft. Sunlight was pouring in through the front windows, flooding that part of the room with golden rays. Roger was amenable to this, and after pouring himself another Scotch, he carried one of the trays down to the coffee table.

We installed ourselves on opposite couches. Spreading napkins over our knees, we filled our plates, buffet style, sat back, and ate. Roger waited until he had his mouth full to begin the conversation he had come to have with me.

—How does it feel to have your home back?

—Different, I said.

Roger washed his fish down with a long drink of Scotch.

—Miss her?

—Yes, I said. I do.

Roger shook his head.

—It must be tough, he said.

I shook my head.

—That girl has quite a way about her, Roger said. She's a charmer like I've never seen before. Has all those art farts eating out of her hand.

—If she's going to survive, that's what she's got to do. I defended her.

—I know. I know. But I think she'll be eating better than you and me pretty soon. This is delicious, he said, pointing to the fish with his fork. We had dinner the other night with someone from the acquisitions committee at the Modern. Looks like they might buy something of hers. You can make a lot of money at this game.

I didn't deny it.

—Didn't you buy anything of hers? he asked.

—No, I didn't.

He seemed surprised. I said we had worked out an agreement that at a certain point I would have my choice of her work.

—Smart move, Roger said. You know, Kris and I have started a foundation, he announced.

—A foundation?

—For the arts. We're going to help starving artists and all that. Roger poured himself a glass of wine, the Scotch bottle not being readily at hand.

—John suggested you might make a good board member.

—Me?

—Sure. You know all about art. You have a collection. And you could help watch out for your friend. I think she's going to be the first recipient of a grant.

I filled my wineglass. Between the alcohol and the heat, I was beginning to feel high. I had to stop and think this through. Why was I being offered this position? Didn't he know how things stood between Kristine and me? Or did he know and did he want me on the board to keep an eye on her, to advocate his position once in a while. Perhaps he just wanted company when he was in the presence of people whose language he didn't understand. I couldn't decide. Nor could I tell whether it would be prudent to ask him if he was aware of the state of my relations with his wife. I would have to think the matter over when I was sober.

—I don't know, I said.

—Well, there's no hurry. Think about it, Roger instructed. It's not bad, this wine, he said pouring himself another glass. He spread himself out on the couch and kicked off his shoes. Sprawled there, he looked sweet and vulnerable. I settled into my couch. The space was bright with light. The room had become superheated because the sunlight was streaming through the windows and the radiator was spewing out heat. I heard it hissing and clanking in the background. I considered getting up to turn it off, but I was too comfortable to move. Smoking his cigar, Roger seemed to be lost in reverie. I drifted off, too, got lost in the blue sky, found myself staring at the buildings across the street: at the massive water tanks so clearly delineated they appeared to be carved out of the blue: at the silvery World Trade Center towers. A car horn snapped us out of our siestas. Roger then thought to offer me a cigar. I accepted it, and we smoked without saying a word, until Roger noticed the time on his watch and jumped up.

—Can I use your phone? he asked.

I told him where it was. When he rejoined me, he said:

—I've got to go. He dropped down on the couch. My chauffeur is waiting. I took the discrepancy between his action and his words to mean he wasn't pressed for time.

—Let me make you a quick coffee, I said.

—No, no, he refused. He put on his shoes.

—Not even an instant?

—No, he said, getting up to show me he had made up his mind.

—An espresso, I said, getting up too.

— No, he said again, laughing at my persistence.

As I had started toward the kitchen, he took my arm to restrain me. I resisted a little and made him pull me toward him. I nearly swooned with pleasure. Then he let me go.

—No, I mean it. I have to go, he said.

—Are you sure?

—Yes, he said incisively. But thanks.

He headed for the door. It was only when he was ready to step into the elevator when he realized the mess we made was still sitting on the coffee table. He offered to do something, but I restrained him by placing my hand squarely in the middle of his chest. He laughed and took it, shook it and said good-bye.

♦

Leaving Roy in charge of the store, I set off for Gilberte's loft. I had been invited to lunch. She'd apologized for the delay in contacting me—it had been nearly three weeks—and hoped I wasn't mad, but she had had tons to do, professionally. Trying to get settled and keep up with everybody all at the same time was ... well, I could understand how difficult it was. Anyway, now she was looking forward to seeing me, because it had been too long. I agreed. Just to see her again would do me good. Too many of the people who had figured in my life had vanished altogether from my purview, abandoning me to fantasies when I tried to imagine what had become of their lives.

I walked down West Broadway to Canal. It was a mess. Traffic was backed up in both directions as people tried to get from the tunnel to the bridge or from the bridge to the tunnel or just across town. Gridlock was fast approaching because every driver wanted to advance every inch he could between red lights. Now and again those frustrated by the lack of progress leaned on their horns, spewing a deafening sound into the clear, chill air. The sidewalks were packed with people. Everywhere, people were on the move, dashing in and out of discount shops and fast-food eateries, climbing in and out of cars. It was a splendid spring day. Occasionally a breeze from the river rose and swept up newspaper tatters and small brown paper bags and candy wrappers and sent them flying. It kicked the beer cans and soda cans clattering before it. It was the type of day I waited all winter to enjoy and for which I was thankful, because I knew there wouldn't be too many more of them. The heat would change all this. For the moment, the hustle and bustle made it seem like a medieval market: later, under suffocating humidity and a torrid sun, it would seem like a third-world bazaar.

At Lafayette I headed south. When I reached White, I took out my address book to double-check Gilberte's address. Though I had been there twice I had forgotten whether she lived between Broadway and Lafayette or Greene and Broadway, or farther east or west. Addresses were not my strong point. As it turned out, she was just off Lafayette.

I recognized the building. The only thing I didn't remember was the enormous disfiguring bright-orange fire escape stitched on the facade. Facing the impressive metal-plated door with double locks and steel-reinforced glass, I pushed button 7B. A muffled who is it? responded. I gave my name and a buzz signaled that I could enter.

I was greeted on the landing by someone who was not Gilberte. I assumed she must be a friend of Gilberte's but I was quickly disabused of my assumption.

—I'm Suzanne, the stranger stated. Gilberte's assistant, she explained. I introduced myself, and after we shook hands I said I had come to see Gilberte.

—I know. She's expecting you.

We walked inside together. There was no Gilberte in sight.

—She'll be with you in a minute, Suzanne promised. You can wait in the sitting room. She pointed to the front of the loft and then made her way to the back.

The sitting room, which was roughly the front third of the loft had been furnished since the housewarming, which was the last time I had been in Gilberte's home. There was a set of four sleek, uncomfortable-looking high-tech chairs (Italian if I had to guess), two skimpy, stiff-looking leather couches, and three rubbed-aluminum tables with glass tops. Everything was sharp angled and had hard surfaces and sat on the hardwooden floor. The couch felt as uncomfortable as the chairs looked.

Suzanne, back from her mission, announced:

—She's on the phone. She'll be with you soon.

I thanked her.

—Can I get you something to drink? Perrier?

—Sure, thanks.

—Lime?

—Why not? She smiled and headed off to the kitchen. Pretty, eager, evidently efficient she was probably an art student with an impeccable pedigree, who had a burning desire to work with an artist, get a taste of the art world, meet the right people. While waiting for my drink, I sifted through a pile of trendy fashion and art magazines. Suzanne brought me my Perrier.

—She's still on the phone. You'll be lunching with us, won't you? she asked.

—The last I heard I was.

She smiled knowingly, as if what I had been told corroborated what she had been told. Then she left me.

Had I not felt it would be a breach of propriety, I would have got up and gone right back to see Gilberte. But Suzanne, or her function, prevented me from doing this, which was, I took it, one of the reasons she was there. An artist's version of Ms. Thorten, Roger's executive assistant. No matter what excuse I used, it would be indecorous of me to charge back there and greet my ex-lover.

Impatient, I gulped down my Perrier. Suzanne came back and asked whether I would like another one. I said no, thanks.

I wondered who was paying Suzanne's salary. Not that an assistant was a large expense. Probably she only worked part-time. Or maybe she was an unpaid intern. Or a trustfundian for whom money didn't matter. Or maybe, like Gilberte, she was also a beneficiary of foundation funds? Or was Gilberte doing so well she was paying for her out of her own pocket? Clearly I had been waiting too long.

Gilberte finally appeared. We hugged and kissed—quite affectionately, I thought—under Suzanne's observant gaze. Yet there was something hesitant and halting in her hug: Gilberte seemed to be holding herself back from giving me a full embrace. Throwing herself on one of the couches, she immediately spread out and took full possession of it, making it impossible for me to sit down next to her. I sat in the chair nearest to her. It was more uncomfortable than it looked.

—You can't imagine the day I'm having, she began.

—Busy?

—I can't tell you.

The phone rang again. Gilberte frowned. I could tell we sat observing a moment of silence until the caller was announced, so I didn't initiate any further conversation. Suzanne appeared with a cordless phone.

— Madame Mueller.

—I've got to take this, Gilberte apologized.

—That's all right. I gave my approval. Suzanne handed her the phone. Gilberte reclined further on the couch, lifting one arm up to her forehead. Her gestures while she talked were assured, well cadenced, doubtlessly totally calculated. I had never seen her look so elegant. So beautiful. I wanted her badly. The outfit she was wearing had a famous-name look to it. As the conversation became mired in chitchat about some affair both she and Madame Mueller had attended, Gilberte got up from the couch and indicated we should head to the back of the loft. She pointed out all the additions that had been made since I had last been there. Her sleeping area now held an enormous bed and a wardrobe, both of which were Biedermeier. On the floor was a thick English rug. I let her know I was impressed.

Gilberte seemed delighted. She covered the mouthpiece of the phone.

—A present, she explained.

At the back of the loft she had made another sitting area, whose focal point was the darkroom. In contrast to the sitting area in the front, which was high-tech, this area was cool fifties retro. There were molded Eames chairs and a low flat couch. An ectoplasmic-shaped table squatted on a Navajo rug. The functional part consisted of two modified Parsons tables and a large filing cabinet for prints. A roll-top desk was situated halfway between the sleeping area and the work area. It was flanked by two marble Ionic capitals, on which sat potted plants. Contact sheets were heaped high on every flat surface.

When I was done inspecting the furniture, and after I had taken an unescorted tour of the darkroom, I returned to Gilberte and sat down on the couch next to her. She let me know she was making an active effort to terminate her conversation. Using a pretext to the effect that a messenger had just come to pick something up, she succeeded in extricating herself from her call.

—I'm sorry, but she did give me a commission. I mean, she got *House and Garden* to use me to shoot her house. Did you see it? It's in the latest issue.

I admitted I hadn't looked at it.

—I think I have it, she said. Anyway, now she's interested in buying a photograph, and she was supposed to come over for tea later this afternoon but she canceled. That's why it took so long. I've got to tell Suzanne, she said half to herself, half to me. Suzanne, she called.

—Yes? The voice came from afar.

Gilberte raised hers.

—Cancel tea for this afternoon and reschedule it for next Thursday.

—That's with Madame Mueller?

—Yes.

—Same time?

—Yes.

—Same menu?

—Yes.

—Fine.

—Is business booming? I asked.

—Absolutely, she said enthusiastically.

—How's fund-raising for the film coming along?

—Oh, I'm getting there. You know, in film it's always a question of overcoming obstacles. Nobody's ever glad to see you. Especially since there's nothing to look at. It's all words until it's a picture, so people are doubly suspicious. Even though they love the treatment. You've got to fight like crazy. I've got a couple of backers. But they want to see the screenplay. In fact ... Suzanne, she called. Madame Mueller said she might be interested in helping me, but she would like to see *Party Girl*. Suzanne appeared this time.

—Yes?

—When Madame Mueller comes, we're going to show her *Party Girl*, so we'll need a projector. How is lunch coming?

—Anytime.

—OK. In a minute, I guess.

She looked at me to second her approval, and when I did, Suzanne left us.

—Oh, did I tell you I'm going to have another show? she said, as if it were a detail that had slipped her mind. In December.

—Great, I said.

—It's going to involve a lot of work.

—Well, you have a helper now.

—You have to, she said. I can't get anything done without her. She is incredibly efficient. And not a lot of money.

The phone rang. She picked it up. After two seconds she looked at me, shrugged her shoulders, and heaved a muted sigh to let me know this was going to be another lengthy conversation about which she could do nothing.

Suzanne brought the mail. Gilberte went through it quickly and, finding one check, signed it and gave it to Suzanne. She indicated it should be deposited immediately. Suzanne whispered lunch was served. We all made our way to the front sitting room, where Suzanne had set out our meal.

—Just begin, Gilberte whispered, covering the mouthpiece. She then asked Suzanne if she would bring her a beer.

Lunch consisted of cold linguine in a pesto sauce, a plate of raw vegetables, and a bottle of white wine. I began on the vegetables, hoping Gilberte would finish her conversation before I began eating the pasta. But she seemed content to eat an occasional olive off the vegetable plate and to drink her beer. I was just wiping my mouth after my last forkful of pasta when she hung up.

—It's taxing, the telephone, she sighed.

—Why don't you let Suzanne field more of your calls?

—Because ultimately I have to talk. And people don't like it when you're always unavailable.

—Roger told me about the foundation, I said, apropos of nothing.

—Yeah. It's fantastic. They've arranged a grant for me. Which should help. Once you get one, you can always get more of them. You know, it's that old thing where when you need one you can't get one because you never received one and then when you hardly need one you can get as many as you want. I'm applying for them all now.... How are you? she wanted to know.

I began to recount my life.

The phone rang.

It occurred to me while she was talking that the enormous distance separating us was actually no more or less than the one that existed when we were living together: there had always been an abyss. Only, while we were living together I had been caught up in the madness that was her life and, once we began having sex, I had wanted to minimize the differences. To make them disappear. I had never been closer to her than I was now and if I had never fully revealed myself to her it was because I had known everything would have fallen into the void that separated us.

Finally off the phone, she called for Suzanne.

—Make a note that I have to have the contact sheets for M by five o'clock tomorrow. I'm going to be on the cover, she said to me. And then next week I'm shooting in Boston, so call Peter and find out what time exactly and arrange for tickets. OK? Thanks.

Suzanne, who had dutifully noted everything down, nodded her head.

—You have to be uptown in forty-five minutes, she said.

—I know. I'm all set.

—Maybe I should be going, I suggested.

Gilberte started to protest that we still had time, but something urged me to my feet.

—Sit down for a minute, she said. I did as I was told.

—I want to ask you something.

—What?

—Well, remember when we talked about the possibility of you writing the screenplay for my film? And you said you wanted to think about it.

—Vaguely.

—Most of the people who have read the treatment love it, she said encouragingly. I just don't have time to do the screenplay. It could be good for you. I mean, the people who have seen the treatment think it's great. Very important. And it could be mainstream.

—I didn't have a goal in mind, I said.

—I know. Neither did I. But do you know how much we could make if it went mainstream?

I smiled.

—You'll do it?

—I don't know.

—That's what you said last time. You can't say that this time, too. You have to either do it or not do it. But if you do it, it has to be fantastic. And you have to let me know, so I can tell people. This is important.

I had never heard her speak this assertively before. She was, finally, all business.

—OK, I said. It's a deal.

—I'm happy. Gilberte stood up. We'll have to have a dinner, out, she said, giving Suzanne a significant look. It'll be more relaxed. I know this new Italian place that's supposed to be good. And then we can talk more about this. But in the meantime, why don't you get started. Think of a title too.

—Will do, chief. I was amenable.

—Call me, then.

Gilberte accompanied me out on the landing. We held hands while waiting for the elevator to arrive. Other than the hug and kiss we had exchanged when I arrived, this was our only intimate moment. She seemed as distant and distracted as when we had been seated on the couches nibbling at our lunch. But my blood was throbbing with desire.

—So do you like my place? she asked, swinging our hands.

—Yes.

She gave me a big kiss when the elevator doors opened.

—I'll try to have something done by the time we have dinner, I said.

I pressed *one*. The doors hadn't closed when I heard her phone ring again.

◆

—It's a plot.

—You're out of your mind.

— I'm not. It's warfare. AIDS is warfare. Born from a conspiracy.

—You are crazy! I said.

—No. I'm not. AIDS is warfare against gays and blacks and Hispanics. And it's working. Look how many of us they've killed.

—You're paranoid, I said.

—Why shouldn't I be? They're out to get us.

—Who's out to get us?

—The government.

—Roy.... That's absurd.

—Why is that absurd? There were too many of us. I don't know how we got to be too many, but we did. We have too much cultural influence. All without any real voice. For years we've been setting trends, creating art, music, fashion, literature, life-styles—all of it inherently if not overtly anti-bourgeois. And the government got its think tanks brewing as to how to counter this phenomenon and they came up with the ideal solution: a plague. The next thing you know, we have AIDS.

—You're being ridiculous. You've been reading all that fanatical left-wing or right-wing garbage.

—I haven't.

—Those people see plots in everything. They're perverted rationalists. If they can't see a first cause they invent one. That's not necessarily a bad thing, except with them it's always the government.

—Who else would do it? The government is the only group that could finance such an undertaking. I'm not saying it's some rabid anti-gay group or the John Birch Society or the KKK or anybody....

—Nobody's *doing* it. I slapped my hand on the counter. Insofar as gays don't produce anything but capital, intellectual and otherwise, they have always posed a threat to the family, and yet the family has always survived. Where's the threat?

—Not in such numbers.

—What in such numbers?

—There's more gays and less families.

—Roy....

Roy always liked to debate offbeat subjects in an offbeat manner. Usually it was challenging, and sometimes it was fun. But because he was taking this so seriously—unless the joke was on me—it was becoming tiring. When you discuss an issue with someone who is convinced something is the case and you are convinced the contrary is the case and neither of you can produce any hard evidence to back your claim, you're wasting your time.

I was almost relieved to see Kristine sashay into the store. She said hello, I said hello, Roy said hello. We were all amiable. A customer came to the cash register with a book. While I rang up the sale, Kristine marched off toward the back of the store. I could tell something was up. She removed neither her gloves nor her sunglasses. Roy whispered to me he was going upstairs to re-alphabetize books.

When the customer had gone, Kristine made her way back toward the counter. She took slow, deliberate steps. That she had come for a reason was so evident that it hung about her like a miasma.

—What did you think of Gilberte's loft? she asked.

As I said nothing immediately, she continued.

—It looked better furnished, didn't it?

—Absolutely, I said. She did a nice job, I said, emphasizing the pronoun.

Kristine smiled.

—Yes, she did, she said, also emphasizing the pronoun, to show me she had understood the thrust of my statement, as well as to contradict it without substituting a proper name for the pronoun. I was impressed with this response: there was a time when she would not have thought twice about stooping to something so crass as to state the obvious. She had come a long way. I would have to be on my toes during this discussion.

—She's happy now, she said, emphasizing the adverb in an attempt to imply that earlier—at my place—she hadn't been. She ripped off one glove. And I want her to stay happy. From her pocketbook she extracted a cigarette and lighter.

—So do I.

—I know that, Stephen. She lit her cigarette. And that's why you shouldn't disturb her. She snapped the lid shut.

—Disturb her?

I could have asked, what do you mean? But I knew what she meant, and by taking up part of her phrase and mouthing it back at her I showed my contempt.

—She's a working girl, Stephen. It's not like before, when she was staying with you.

—I'm a working boy.

I was being coy. I realized it was my visit that had perturbed Kristine.

—Then you shouldn't be taking such long lunches. She smiled malevolently. It doesn't look good for a working boy. And on a Saturday. Your busiest day. Really, Stephen.

She had me by the balls, so to speak. There was nothing I could say to defend my extended lunch: trying to justify it would make me look like the wage slave I was. In the end I would be obliged to accept her magnanimous reprieve. Moreover, the real issue here was not my absence from the store but my presence at Gilberte's so I addressed myself to this issue alone.

—She was tied up on the phone most of the time I was there, and....

—That's her business.

— I was invited for a friendly lunch.

—She doesn't have time for that just now.

—Of course, you're intimately familiar with her needs.

—Yes, I am. She snuffed out her cigarette.

—And you're here at her request to let me know my visits aren't welcome.

—I'm ... Yes, in a sense. I couldn't see through her dark glasses, but her face, like still water suddenly troubled by a gust of air, lost its composure. It would be ludicrous to straight out deny me access to Gilberte. So if this was what she desired to do, she would have to find the proper circumlocution. I was going to help her.

—In what sense? I'm curious.

—She has to concentrate on her work. She's at a critical point in her career, and she needs lots of time.

—And you've taken it upon yourself to see that she understands.

—I'm trying to tell you something, but you're not understanding, I'm afraid.

—Oh, I understand. You're playing the part of her guardian angel. You want to wave your wand and make everyone go away.

—Not precisely. She gritted her teeth.

—Only people you disapprove of.

—You know, Stephen, you are a nuisance. Has anybody ever told you that?

—I'm not in the mood to exchange confidences. Just tell me what you want to tell me.

I had perhaps gone too far. Kristine collected herself. She yanked on her glove, picked up her pocketbook, and said:

—I don't want you meddling in Gilberte's life. She needs to work. She doesn't need you.

I was getting ready to protest, when Kristine continued.

—I've done a lot for that girl, and I don't need you in there fucking it up. Do you understand?

She marched out of the store and climbed into her limousine, which, during the course of our conversation, had materialized, and was waiting, double parked, in front of the store. I stared after her, speechless. As the limousine didn't immediately pull away, I continued to stare at the tinted glass window behind which she was sitting. The phone rang. It was Kristine.

—And if you ever mention our conversation to....

—I hung up.

◆

I began work on the screenplay. I thought it was going to re-quire numerous and long discussions with Gilberte. I had been hoping for nothing less. But the words came to me. Oh, not without effort. I had to struggle. The great thing was I could work. I could write, and I knew what I was writing was good. Probably, working on the treatment had prepared me because while writing it I had imagined what the dialogue would be. I had written some of it down on the back of one of the rough drafts. This helped me organize my thoughts about the story and how to drive it from one sequence to another. Now these lines aided me in putting together the screenplay.

Gilberte called me when I had nearly finished the first half. She was in Bermuda with Kristine. She wanted to know how I was coming along.

—Splendidly, I told her.

—I trust you, she said. I have faith in you.

I drank myself sick that night. Spent more time hanging over the toilet heaving than I had sucking at the bottle. Be-cause as soon as she had said she trusted me, had faith in me, I knew that that was why I was working. She had faith in me. It was absurd. Someone trusted me, had confidence in my talent, whereas I lacked all conviction. I never believed in myself sufficiently to do something with my life. What was particularly brutal about this re-recognition of my deplorable condition was how indifferent I was to my lack of drive and self-confidence. How I could stumble through life like a sleepwalker.

That's when I doubled down on my drinking. Soon the alcohol loosened my repressive consciousness and I began regretting decisions I might or might not have made had I been more self-assured. I started pitying myself for not persisting in the face of uncertainty. That's when I began really sucking at the bottle. It was the self-loathing for pitying myself that made me sick.

What perplexed me, however, was my inability to find the turning point. I was convinced I couldn't have given up all my dreams in one fell swoop. Could I? The decision, or the failure to make one, must have been the result of a long battle between my weak and strong psychic forces. Perhaps I had never surrendered, only resigned myself to the forces I felt I couldn't fight. Or even identify. Because I wasn't strong enough to live in contradiction with myself for long. Resignation is the illogical resolution of a contradictory state of being. So presumably I had found the means to reduce the tension in my life by admitting I had no self-confidence. Gilberte's comment that night had brought back the full force of what I had written off as impossible.

My final spiteful act that night was to rip up what I had written. I would tell her I was incapable. After all, if I couldn't do it for myself, why should I do it for her?

♦

Gilberte called me when she got back from her vacation. I had just completed the sixtieth page (it had taken me hours to tape together what I had torn up), which was, at a minute a page, the halfway point in an hour-and-twenty-minute film. She promised we would get together the following week to review my progress. When I didn't hear from her, I called. Suzanne told me she had gone to California.

♦

Weeks went by before I saw Gilberte again. She breezed into the store the first day I felt it necessary to turn on the air conditioner.

—Already? she asked. It's beautiful out.

—The humidity is ninety percent.

—It's wonderful for your skin, she said. She leaned over the counter to give me a kiss on the cheek. You look good, she said.

—Thanks, I said. You look great. She was tan and appeared rested. It's been a while, I said, reaching out and taking her hand in mine. I thought we were going to have lunch or dinner. Weren't you going to call me? I scolded her.

—I know, I know. But look, your phone works too.

—And I called.

—I know....

—And that was after that little visit from your friend. I decided right there and then I was going to mention Kristine's visit. Threats never stopped me from doing anything.

—Kristine? Why?

—She didn't tell you?

—No.

—She was upset that we had lunch. I guess she felt threatened, I said.

—But how did she know about it?

—Didn't you tell her?

—We weren't alone, I pointed out.

—You mean Suzanne?

—Who pays her? The foundation?

—Yes,

—Well?

Roy came down from the mezzanine.

—Are you going out to lunch now? he asked me.

—I don't know. What are you doing for lunch? I asked Gilberte.

—I don't have any plans, she said.

—I'll take you to lunch.

—Don't be too long. I've got to eat too, Roy reminded me.

We went to Raoul's.

—How was Bermuda?

—Great. I had a fabulous time.

—And California?

—Fantastic. You can't believe what they're doing there, I mean in L.A. There are new museums everywhere. The support for the arts is incredible.

After the waiter had taken our orders, I asked:

—What's wrong?

—Nothing's wrong, she said, emphasizing the word wrong.

—What is it? I persisted. Is it Kristine?

She shrugged her shoulders. This indeterminate, nonverbal response was a sure sign I was on the right track.

—What happened? Are you fighting? Is it over? What can I do?

—Nothing.

—Is it hopeless?

—No, no, she said. Calm down. Not yet.

The use of these two adverbs was ominous.

—Well, when? Soon?

—No, no, she said.

I couldn't get anything out of her.

—What is it? Tell me.

—She's too much, she said.

—That tells me too little, I said.

—I mean, she thinks this is the nineteen seventies and she's liberated.

I surmised she took this to be a definitive description of the situation as she saw it.

—Liberated from what?

—Her life as a wife. The waiter set down our food.

—What does she want?

—*Moi.*

I laughed. I had never heard her utter a foreign word before.

—Don't, she commanded, laughing too. It's not funny. She wants a new life. With me.

—With you. Why?

Gilberte slurped up some spaghetti.

—I don't know, she said.

—What do you mean, you don't know. You know. Why?

—I don't know. I mean, we had this sort of affair for a while. We still sort of do, but not really.

—So you're having an affair and you don't know why she wants a new life? I laughed again. Are you still sleeping with her?

—No. I mean, not anymore. Or not often. She's stayed a couple of nights since we've been back.

—Kristine is in love with you.

—I think so. I was into it in the beginning. She's really sensual. But then it got to be too much.

—Being with her, or being with a woman?

—Her. I like women, just like I like men. But I'm tired of her now, and she wants this heavy commitment. She's always talking about changing life-styles and how she's been re-pressed all this time, and all that garbage. And now every time she drinks she starts kissing me and telling me how good I am for her. But it's all just her fantasy, you know. Lots of women like to fool around. Especially if they're married. It's like they can cheat without cheating, or something.

She paused.

—And ... I don't know. I mean, she is attractive and I am attracted to her. But lately she's been almost living at my place. And she's starting to drive me nuts. She never shuts up. And she says she's not kidding about beginning a new life with me. Roger calls all the time. He's suspicious of what's going on. It's pretty intense and not what I need just now.

—Do you think she'll leave Roger?

—No. And that's the thing. Because she'd like to think being with me has changed her forever. And maybe it has, but that doesn't mean your life has to change. If you turn left in-stead of right on the street, your life is changed forever too, but you still get where you're going. You know, she's like a kid.

She's just giddy because when she's with me her life is so different from when she's with Roger.

—And....

—She's not essential to my life, and for the moment she thinks I'm essential to hers. And everything's all fucked up.

—That must be why she came by to see me, I mused.

—Ooh, she hates you. Gilberte smiled wickedly.

—Do you still need her? I asked.

—To be perfectly honest, I could get along without her, but I'd have to work a lot harder. That sounds crass, and I'm not like that. I can do whatever I have to do to live. I'm not afraid of making sacrifices. But I don't want to hurt her. And I don't want her to hurt me.

—Do you think she'd be hurt if you stopped seeing her?

—Absolutely.

—How hurt?

—What do you mean?

—I mean, vindictive hurt.

—I don't know. That's the problem. That's what I can't figure out. And that's where the manipulative part comes in, and I don't want to be like that. And I don't know what to do.

This was her purpose in coming to me. She needed advice. I was at a loss. I thought about changing the subject and talking about the screenplay to distract her for a while, which would give me time to consider a possible course of action to suggest to her. But she was looking at me so intensely, waiting for me to offer the solution, that I was unable to think.

—You can always come back to my place. It was as much as I could manage.

—Thanks, she said. She reached across the table and took my hand.

—How are you? she asked.

—Fine.

—Everything all right?
—Everything's fine.
—You're not too lonely over there by yourself?
—I'm fine.
She thought for a moment.
—You're so brave.
—What do you mean?
—To go through everything alone. I don't know if I'll be able to do that.

♦

I didn't see Gilberte again for months. Aside from two or three phone conversations about the state of the screenplay, we didn't speak. I didn't know if I had said something during our lunch that had upset her. Or whether I should have said something she wanted to hear. Or whether she had been swept into the stream of business affairs and adventures she preferred not to speak to me about.

One thing was sure. She was the rising art star of the moment. I saw her name in the art journals and in the gossip magazines, her picture in the tabloids and newspapers. She created a stir when she switched galleries.

Her new gallery immediately gave her a one-woman show. I was invited to the opening but didn't go. I waited a week, in vain, for her to telephone to ask why I hadn't come, then I went to look at the show. I thought it preposterous they hung work like this and called it art. I was ashamed for Gilberte. My opinion of her work sank to an all-time low. I sent Gilberte a note saying I was sorry I had missed the opening. I told her I had gone to the show later. I penned a few acerbic comments about what I had seen. She followed up with a telephone call.

We chatted for more than an hour. About nothing. She was effusive. She thanked me for the note. Noted how much time it had taken her to prepare for the show. Said she had another project in the works that was sapping her strength, but she didn't want to talk about it over the phone. We would have to have lunch soon, she said. I couldn't get a word in. Her manic monologue silenced me. I sensed desperation in her voice. She and Kristine had resolved everything. That was what she wanted me to believe. She was patronizing me, treating me like one of the blue-haired ladies she had to humor to wheedle a commission out of them. When she had said all that she wanted to say, I wouldn't let her get off the phone. I made her talk more. When she ran out of things to tell me, I began asking questions. I attempted to break down her resistance. I provoked her. I tried to get through to her, endeavored to discover what she was feeling. I got nowhere. She was in top form. She didn't let on. After hanging up, I realized Suzanne had probably been lurking in the background, listening to Gilberte's every word.

◆

Despite my low opinion about her latest work, her show sold out. And what she told me about resolving everything with Kristine became credible, because every time I saw Gilberte's name, Kristine's name was not far off, usually only a conjunction away. They were photographed together everywhere they went. I studied the two of them assiduously. Gilberte looked fine. In fact, I had never seen her look so sexy as in the pictures I saw of her in the papers and journals during this period. I examined her eyes with a magnifying glass, peering into the grainy surface of the paper for signs of sadness, melancholy, anger, duplicity. I saw nothing. She looked as happy as she had said she was when we talked. In one photograph, taken at the opening of her costume jewelry collection, which Bendel's was going to carry, she appeared absolutely ecstatic. I kept telling myself it might merely be because she was making money. And lots of it.

In a picture of her taken at the fashion show where some clothes she had designed were unveiled, she looked a bit fatigued. Kristine, too, seemed worn out. But they had both undoubtedly been slaving long hours. Rumor had it Gilberte and Kristine had negotiated a contract with an Italian manufacturer, who was going to produce a line of ready-to-wear women's clothes for them. Gilberte was going to design the line and Kristine was going to be responsible for marketing it. They were setting up a business. Roy got the dirt for me from one of his friends who worked on Seventh Avenue. Gilberte was poised to make millions, he said. (This was confirmed in *Women's Wear Daily* shortly after Roy had told me about it.)

That she had entered into a commercial venture with Kristine seemed perfectly logical to me. Gilberte had been headed in that direction for some time. Moreover, there were plenty of precedents. Many young artists in the so-called brat pack thought nothing of selling their talent to the first manufacturer who was willing to mass-produce their marque.

Her going commercial didn't perturb me. What I found reprehensible was that Gilberte was using her emotional ties to Kristine to further her capital interests. She had done the same thing to get her start in the art world. But at the time she had genuine feelings for Kristine. Our meeting at Raoul's had left me with the definite impression she was fed up with her. I had surmised, mistakenly as it turned out, that she was associating with her only until she figured out how to break off their relationship gracefully. Now it looked as if she had just sealed another pact with her. It was so obviously a mercenary move that, obtuse though Kristine was, I was surprised she hadn't sensed it. Of course, she might have. And she might have agreed to start up a business because she realized it was the price she had to pay to keep Gilberte. Or—and this I didn't want to believe—perhaps Gilberte had beguiled her into believing everything was all right between them.

One thing was certain. Gilberte was exploiting her moment in the sun. It was sad that she would disregard the moral consequences of what she was doing to prosper, to become rich. However, I saw her decision was probably a calculation like any other entrepreneurial undertaking. It wasn't personal, it was business.

◆

Sitting at my kitchen table, I downed the last of another vodka martini. I had just finished the screenplay. Writing it had taken me much longer than I had estimated. Anxious to complete it, toward the end I had been unable to work on it because I knew finishing it would mark the end of my relationship with Gilberte. It would break the last thread that bound us together. I straightened the one hundred twenty-five sheets of paper and got up to make another drink, another one of my ultimate vodka martinis. I kept martini glasses, extra-dry vermouth, and Smirnoff vodka in the freezer. When I wanted a drink, I rinsed a glass with the vermouth and then added the vodka and an olive. The major drawback with my having perfected my technique was that a martini made by anyone else tasted insipid.

I mixed a drink. Before going over the manuscript one final time, with a bottle of Liquid Paper and a pen, I put on *Tosca*. Listening to it gave me something to do while I proofread the text one last time. The music didn't disturb me because I no longer needed to concentrate on the text, only check for typos. Just now, the second act was beginning. I strained my ears to hear:

> *Ella verrà per amor del suo Mario!*
> *Per amor del suo Mario al piacer mio*
> *s'farrenderà. Tal dei profondi amori*
> *è la profonda miseria.*

Mario. There was a *bien aimé*. I had never been loved well. Not that I had made it easy for anyone to love me. But I had expected to find someone who wanted to. I wasn't bitter about it. Long ago I realized I would never choose a lover who was capable of loving me. I employed this tactic to keep me from becoming permanently involved with one person. Which was the strategy necessitated, perhaps, by my multivalent sexual orientation. My strategy for sanity, you might say. Because after all these years, and after reading nearly every book on the subject, I still didn't understand my sexual identity. Or whether, in fact, there was such a thing. Well, there was no *coming out* for someone like me. No social validation. Nothing. And I didn't really care. Honestly, I didn't. Letting my desire guide me to whichever love object it chose seemed to me the bravest thing I would ever do. And maybe it was. I thought acknowledging the indeterminacy of my desire would simplify my life and let me live in peace. Peace—what a laugh! My current state of being was as far as I had come toward settling the issue. It was probably as far as I would ever get. The war was still raging within me. No settlement was in sight. I was, as Roy had once diplomatically put it, a half-breed. And.... No, I had to stop. I sipped my drink. I was relieved to have finished the screenplay. I wanted to celebrate. I owed it to myself. It had been such a struggle, such an undertaking. It had required enormous sacrifices. Gilberte would never properly appreciate what I had done. I lifted up my glass, and it came to me just then, as I stared at the ceiling, my head tilted back, that I had finished this *because* I had made sacrifices. I had never accomplished anything else because I hadn't been willing to sacrifice anything. That was it. I saw it in an instant. I had never made anything out of myself because I wasn't prepared to make sacrifices. Tosca was singing:

Che v'ho fatto in vita mia?
son io
che così torturate! ...Torturate
L'anima...
Sì, mi torturate l'anima!

God, that was beautiful! I finished my drink and made my way to the refrigerator to prepare another, my last. It would be my last whether I liked it or not, because I never put more than four glasses in the freezer at one time. And I couldn't possibly drink a vodka martini in a glass that hadn't been properly chilled. Not at home. Anyway, I had to remain sober enough to consider this discovery of mine, one I was eager to erase with drink. My decision to get up to make another drink just at the moment when a close analysis was called for was similar to my lighting a cigarette when I would sit at my desk and prepare to write down a story line or description that had just occurred to me. Which subsequently went up in smoke. I wasn't going to let this one go. *Sacrifice.* I had it. I saw it. This was my main fault, my undoing. Discipline, which I possessed intermittently, was nothing compared to sacrifice. Even Gilberte seemed to know that. She made sacrifices. Why, she was willing to put her self-respect, not to mention my esteem for her, on the altar. Because she wanted to reap the rewards. So what if people like me sat back smug and made snide comments about her corruption. *So what* was the attitude you had to adopt to get to the top. Gilberte would crawl out from under the calumny people like me heaped upon her. When she solidified her success and became the star she wanted to become, people would talk reverently of what she had done to get where she was. They would see her sacrifice as part of the price she had to pay, part of what achieving success had demanded. Her sacrifice would be metamorphosed into something necessary, impersonal, and therefore amoral. People would say she was totally committed. They would be in awe.

I wasn't committed. That's where we differed, Gilberte and I. Because at some point she must have decided there was nothing she wouldn't do to get what she wanted: and she knew what she wanted. I knew there were things I wouldn't do, but I never knew exactly what I wanted. Not with that kind of exactitude.

I heard Tosca singing *Vissi d'arte, vissi d'amore.*

It was beautiful.

But I had an ugly thought. I had let my ambition be sapped by my narcissistic preoccupation with myself. It was a form of selfishness and it had most likely cost me the love of others, as well.

What was I going to do now? Tosca had just delivered her kiss. I took another sip from my drink and lit another cigarette. I had unwittingly stumbled upon one more quality I lacked. It was surprising that with so much missing I could be considered human. Surprising that I could stomach myself. I was tolerant, that was why. Forgiving. I had an unyielding respect for knowing, for seeking. I was always after the truth. The Truth. My truth. It didn't matter. Moreover, I still fervently believed that regardless of my failure to create anything, my love of The Good and The True and The Beautiful prevented my standards, and possibly my life, from being dragged into the gutter.

I had crossed a threshold of some sort. But as with so many of the other times I had crossed thresholds or had epiphanies or attained self-enlightenment, I was still nowhere. I had to stop. I was collapsing on the table. I needed air. A promenade on the fire escape was called for. A blast of fresh air would fix me right up. And it did. Standing out there in the chill air, I took long drags off my cigarette and blew out billowing clouds of white smoke. I was never going to solve the mystery of my existence. Like the smoke I exhaled, it seemed to take some kind of shape for one split second before dissolving before me, flying off into space. It didn't matter. I knew what mattered. To go on. To push ahead. To keep seeking. To keep trying. To be kind and to care. To be ... I....

◆

I called Gilberte several times to tell her I had finished the screenplay. Each time I called, I reached either the answering machine or Suzanne. I left messages with both, and both promised my call would be returned as soon as possible, but neither kept the promise.

After two weeks of telephoning almost daily, I told Suzanne I was going to come by with the manuscript the following week. I wanted to rid myself of it. Suzanne tried to discourage me. She said I should just drop it in the mail. I told her I was bringing it over and I hoped to see Gilberte while I was there.

When I showed up with the manila envelope tucked under my arm, Suzanne informed me Gilberte wasn't home. She invited me upstairs but didn't let me in the loft. I passed the package to her through the half-opened door. She admonished me for not having called first. However, if I had called first I would never have believed, as I did now, that Gilberte wasn't home. Before I got back in the elevator, Suzanne suggested two or three times when I might catch Gilberte at home.

I tried to reach her during the suggested times—and many other times as well—but only reached Suzanne or the answering machine and a promise that Gilberte would call me as soon as possible.

I didn't think Gilberte was avoiding me. Therefore, I also had to believe Suzanne when she told me the reason Gilberte wasn't returning my calls was that she was extremely busy. She had entered into business negotiations. They completely absorbed her. There were thousands of little wrinkles to be ironed out, Suzanne told me. I felt, nonetheless, Gilberte could have made time for me. I was hurt by her neglect.

After another week of almost daily calling, I gave up. I didn't hear from Gilberte for another week. She called one evening just as I was about to close the store.

—Don't be mad, she whined. You can't be mad, she commanded, growing bolder. I know I've been bad, but I've been so caught up, you can't imagine. I mean, even I couldn't imagine. And it's not just you I've put off, it's everyone, she said.

I might have felt better had she told me she had made me wait because she thought I was special and would understand her predicament.

—Anyway, I read the screenplay. It's beautiful, she said. Really beautiful.

—Thank you, I said.

— I didn't think you could do that. I mean.... You know, this is what you should be doing instead of working in that store.

—Well....

—No. You should.

— I can't do it *ex nihilo*. I'm reactively creative, I found myself admitting.

—I'll give you ideas, she offered. We'll team up.

I made a consenting murmur.

—In the meantime, I've got to get this sold. And I can't concentrate on it now because of everything else.

—How is everything else? I asked.

—Good. Wait! She covered the mouthpiece.

I heard muffled noises in the background.

—Listen, I'm going to have to dash. I just wanted you to know that it's good. And I'm really happy. And we'll have to get together soon. All right?

—You say when.

—You're such a doll. OK. I'll ring you. Ciao.

I reread my photocopy of the screenplay again that night. It was good. But beautiful? I wondered if she had liked it at all.

◆

I had just finished ringing up a sale when Roger walked in the door.

—Hi, he said.

I returned his greeting and then rang up the next customer's books. It was a Saturday. Business was brisk. When I was through, Roger sidled over to the counter.

—What about lunch?

—Roy's not here yet.

—Oh. He shook his head. What time does he come?

—He should have been here.

Roger consulted his watch. He was calculating.

—I've got to do something in mid-town, he said. And frankly, if I could do it now that would give us a little more time. So how about if we meet up there?

I suppose I didn't look enthusiastic, because he then continued:

—Take the cab fare out of your petty cash, and I'll drop you off down here after we eat. Where do you want to go?

—It's your part of town.

—Four Seasons? Let's say Four Seasons. I'll call from the car. I can always get a table there. You know where it is?

—Yes.

—Say one-thirty.

—One-thirty.

—Good, he concluded. He buttoned his jacket and departed. I had no idea what he wanted to see me about. We hadn't spoken for some time. I tried to recall when exactly I had last seen him. At first I thought it was at Gilberte's opening. But then I remembered I had talked to him at her housewarming. I tried to figure out how long ago that had been. It seemed to me to have taken place months ago, but I concluded it must have been in February, because the housewarming had also been a birthday celebration for Gilberte, and her birthday was in February. It was now May. The last time I'd seen Roger was three months ago. My memory was not my strong point. There were no landmark dates in my life. Events, yes. But I never felt any compulsion to mark time. To remember a date was to delineate a space within the infinite progression of moments and appropriate it. I was never inclined that way.

When Roy came, I explained I had to rush right out. He shrugged his shoulders.

—You're lucky you have me, he said.

—I know. On West Broadway, I realized I would probably have to wear a tie, or a jacket, I forgot which, so I made a quick trip home. I caught a cab on my street and headed uptown. It was a dismal day. Warm but wet. Clouds hung low over the city. Earlier in the morning an undifferentiated gray precipitate had fallen from the sky and wet the streets. It was so humid that they hadn't yet dried.

Roger had a table abutting the pool. He couldn't wangle a table in the Grill Room on such short notice. Sipping his Scotch, he was staring off over the water, out the windows that gave onto Park Avenue.

—Sorry, I apologized. But you should have reminded me I would need a jacket.

—Oh, you don't really, he said. A quick check of the clientele revealed all the men present were wearing them, which did not, however, demonstrate they were required.

—Oh well, I said.

He smiled contentedly. A waiter came and wanted to know if I would have something from the bar. I declined. Roger then asked for the menus and the wine list.

—Have you been here before?

—Not in a long time.

—It doesn't change much. Fortunately. They have this new Spa Cuisine, if you like that.

I studied the menu until Roger asked if I was ready to order, which I interpreted to mean he was. Upon receiving my agreement, he signaled to a waiter, who indicated he would be right there.

When the waiter came, Roger ordered breast of quail with figs as an appetizer, followed by a skillet steak with onions. Having to make my mind up under pressure, I said I would like duck pâté to begin, followed by French lamb chops. Roger then insisted I order a bottle of wine. I consulted the wine list.

—See anything you like?

—How much are we spending?

—You decide.

I ordered a 1975 Chateau Figeac, which I looked forward to more than the meal.

—How was the wedding? I asked him. I had read the notice in the *Times*, and seen some pictures in a gossip magazine.

—It was marvelous, Roger said. It was the best wedding I've ever been to. I'm not just saying that. And you know it's true because I didn't pay for it. It was better than Kristine's and mine, he concluded.

I was impressed.

—Where did they go on their honeymoon?

—Rio. Roger smiled broadly. That boy knows how to live.

I shook my head in agreement. The waiter brought the wine. I inspected the label before giving my permission for it to be opened. After smelling the cork, he poured a small quantity into my glass. The color was magnificent. It had a perfect nose. One swirl revealed the legs walking around the inside of the glass. I rinsed my mouth with it. Even without being aired, it was round and robust, full of vim and vigor. Excellent. I gave my approval with a nod. The waiter filled Roger's glass and then mine. Roger stuck to his Scotch. We toasted our health. Then Roger broke into the issue I supposed he had invited me to discuss.

—Have you thought about the position?

—What position? I was a little lost.

—On the board of the foundation.

—Oh, yes ... I lied. I had completely forgotten. It had seemed like such a wild idea that I hadn't taken Roger seriously. It then came to me that the last time I saw Roger was at my loft, for lunch, and we had discussed this issue.

—And....

Roger was waiting.

I had to think. It didn't take long.

—Sure, I'd like to be on the board.

—I knew you'd say yes. He proposed another toast. To my first board member.

—What's its name again? I asked.

—I don't know. He was chagrined. I guess we'll work that out at the first meeting. Here's to the no-name foundation. We drank again.

—I was under the impression there had already been meetings, I said, thinking of the money Gilberte was receiving.

—Well, Kristine made some decisions on her own. Which is why, in fact, we're going to have a board.

I was beginning to understand.

—But tell me, does she know you asked me to be on it?

—No.

—Why not? I mean, why wouldn't you tell her?

—Because you hadn't accepted, or not until just now. Now I'll tell her.

This was a reasonable response.

—Do you think it will upset her?

—Possibly.

—Are you trying to upset her?

—Why are you suspicious? I thought it might amuse you to be on the board of a foundation, and here you won't take it at face value.

I understood this was as far as I could go in my investigation to get at his ulterior motive, but I had one more question.

—I don't know quite how to phrase this, but you must be somewhat aware of how things stand between Kristine and me, and....

—I know. Listen. I need somebody. Somebody I can rely on. All right? Just thinking about how much she spends on your friend is incredible to me. I don't understand it. And I've got to put a stop to all this.... You know, they just tried to get me to back some crazy venture with an Italian, Roger said, using the past tense. A count no less. But he's really just a rag merchant with a fancy name. Roger began drinking the wine.

—That was their big chance, I pointed out. Word had it that they were going to make millions.

—Millions my ass. If Kris weren't my wife I'd sue her for malfeasance. And that other financial wizard, he said, without indicating whom he had in mind. I just happened to read the contracts they had drawn up. I came into my office one day and they were on my desk, with a note from my lawyer. The note had one word written on it. *Kill.*

The waiter arrived and set down our appetizers. Roger began to eat. I followed suit.

—How is yours? Roger asked me, indicating the food with his fork.

—Delicious, I said.

—It's very good here, he said, looking around to take in the room, surreptitiously scanning all the tables, searching, I supposed, for people he knew.

—Anyway, where was I? he asked, taking another mouthful.

—Your lawyer told you the contract was no good?

—Right. The way the damn thing was written, this count was going to have full control. I mean, it actually called for dollars to be deposited in an account, where they would stay until the exchange rate was favorable, at which point they would be transferred to his account, in Switzerland. His account! Can you imagine?

—What did you do?

—I called him and told him no deal.

—And that was it?

—No. He telephoned Kristine. Tried to go around behind my back. Incredible. He made another proposal. Said she should hire him as a consultant and utilize his connections in Europe. Kristine was all for it. She was ready to write a retainer. I called him back again and said there was nothing to consult about, there wasn't going to be any deal, any manufacturing, and if he accepted any money from my wife I would see to it he was put someplace where money wouldn't do him any good. Kristine was furious. Said I made a fool of her. And she ran off to her friend's place.

Roger couldn't bring himself to say her name.

—Is that where she is now? I wanted to know.

Roger shook his head yes.

—She was pissed that I nixed her deal. She thinks it's because I don't like your friend, and that's not it at all. Although I do think she is a bit of an opportunist.

Our main dish arrived. Roger signaled he would like the waiter to pour me some more wine.

A sudden urge to reveal what I knew swept over me. I stopped myself. Aside from the fact I wasn't altogether sure how much I knew, it might hurt Roger so much he would never want to see Kristine again. And where would Kristine go if her marriage broke up? At this point she wouldn't have to go anywhere. She would stay with Gilberte. Which was just what I didn't want.

Roger continued to try to analyze the situation. He searched for the reasons for his wife's obsession with Gilberte, speculated on how she had let herself get dragged into such a scam, especially after more or less successfully running two businesses.

I was enjoying myself tremendously. It was just like the old days when we used to meet regularly. I felt close to him again.

—How's your life? he asked.

—Good.

—Staying healthy?

—Healthy?

—You know....

I knew.

—Don't worry, I said.

—Well, I do, I'll admit it. I hope you're taking all those precautions they're talking about and being sensible.

—I am.

— Good, good, he said.

—Dessert? he asked.

—No, thanks.

—Sure?

—Yes.

He signaled to the waiter he was ready to pay the bill. In the car on the way downtown, he said:

—I'm counting on you.

—I know.

—Thanks. He slapped me on the knee. Just remember I'm behind you. So whatever Kristine says or does, you've got me backing you up. All right?

—Agreed.

—You're a good man.

♦

Gilberte was sitting on the steps of my building, smoking, surrounded by suitcases and sacks.

—Hi, she said, jumping up.

—Hi, I said, giving her a big hug.

—I'm back, she said.

—Is that what you are? Somehow I wasn't thrilled.

—I mean, if you'll let me come back.

—Sure.

—Just until I find another place, she said.

—Looks like you're going to need some help, I said, indicating her bags. It took two trips in the elevator to get them up.

—Shit, she said when we were finished lugging her luggage across the loft. She collapsed on the couch that used to be her bed. I sat down next to her. We stared at the motley collection of gym sacks, overnight bags, camera cases, knapsacks, duffel bags, suitcases, portfolios. There wasn't a single pillowcase.

—I've accumulated a lot, she sighed.

—No furniture?

—I left it all, she said proudly.

I didn't bother to explain I was being sarcastic.

—I could have taken some of it, she continued. Because some it was a gift. But I left everything I didn't buy with my own money.

I considered using her last comment as a bridge to a discussion about what had happened, but I didn't want to appear too curious.

I wasn't prepared to deal with her sudden appearance. We had had so little contact these last few months I had no idea how her relationship with Kristine had evolved. It would take hours for her to bring me up to date. And I didn't want to listen for hours just now. Like anything you follow periodically, when there is too big a lapse between installments you lose interest. Frankly, my interest in Gilberte had reached its nadir: her position in my field of desire was no longer of any significant value. Time had anesthetized me. I couldn't respond to her needs at this moment as I would have had she left Kristine right after leaving me, or one or two months later. Or after I had finished and delivered the screenplay. Now I didn't feel anything but disinterested friendship. I wasn't overcome by the urge to pounce upon her that used to overtake me whenever I sat this close to her. Because our encounters had been infrequent and disappointing, I had gradually ceased to fantasize about her. When I thought about her at all now, it was with simple, disaffected wonder, uncomplicated curiosity.

—I'm going to have to leave you, I informed her. I had a date. An unforeseen event such as this would permit me to break it gracefully, and honestly, but I felt oppressed by Gilberte's presence and wanted to go out.

—Sure, go ahead. She shrugged her shoulders. Tried to smile.

—Really?

—Absolutely. I'd love to eat something, though. And then I think I'll just go to bed, she said, without saying where, exactly, she planned on sleeping.

—You know where everything is, I reminded her.

She shook her head, then leaned toward me, letting her head fall on my shoulder. She snuggled into my side and put her arms around me.

—I can't be like this. I've got to keep moving. I've got thousands of things to do. I've got to figure everything out again. I don't know if I'll be able to stand it.

I put my arm around her.

—I couldn't take it anymore. She was crying softly. I couldn't.

She began to shake and I began to stroke her head, and once again I was enthralled.

♦

A few days later, after Gilberte had finished an emotional phone conversation with Kristine, the story emerged.

— ... so when Roger put the kybosh on the deal with Count Orsini, Kris said she was moving in, just like that. She had been more or less threatening to do it for a long time. I think I told you. Every time she fought with Roger she said she was through, this was it, she had had it, you know. And I always talked her out of it. But this time I couldn't. She was too angry.

—She moved in bag and baggage? I asked.

—Bag and baggage. It took her chauffeur I don't know how many trips to get all her clothes and personal effects. And then she kind of took over. As if it was her place. So I didn't have a life of my own anymore. Things got tense pretty fast. We started bitching at each other. I told her I didn't think it was working. And she knew it too. But the more it seemed like it was ending, the more she tried to continue it. Like she could see it was over, that she had overreacted moving in, but she didn't want to admit it. She was just trying to teach Roger a lesson. I mean, it was really a mess.

—Didn't you say anything?

—What was I going to say?

—Didn't you hint that maybe....

—You don't hint with Kristine. Anyway, she always came up with some reason for why we weren't getting along—you know, something superficial that could be fixed. And she was smart enough to always make the problem her fault. But it wasn't that.

—Wasn't what? I was lost.

—I don't know. It was partly me, I guess. I wasn't ready for her to dominate me. That's why you and I got along so well, because you always left me alone. I mean, it was different between us, and though I always felt that you would rather have me do what you wanted me to do, you never forced it on me.

—It took a lot of effort, I admitted.

—Kristine couldn't control herself. She had to dominate. Our whole relationship was one big power play. And she
wanted to be in love too much. But I could tell that as much as
she complained about her husband, she loved him. Or needed
him, at least. She was rebelling against him and smothering me
to prove she loved me. And I told her.

I laughed.

—Anyway, it just became too overwhelming. She got this
idea that the reason I didn't want to live with her was because
I thought she wasn't serious about us. And that's what finally flipped me out. Because she said she was going to divorce
Roger. Just to prove that she was serious about us. Can you
imagine?

—Do you think she's telling the truth?

—About what?

— You! About divorcing Roger.

—No. It's just that she's never had an experience like this
before. She only wanted the experience. You know, right after
she moved in her sex drive took a nose dive. Couldn't do it
anymore unless she was really drunk. And she wouldn't let me
see anyone else.

—But does she genuinely like women?

—Yes, I think so. But....

—But....

—What do you want me to say. Is she gay? Are you gay?
Am I gay? You know better than that. We are what we are.
No one is or isn't. You are and then you do. And what you do
doesn't mean you are what you do.

—I know. But why did she come on to you?

This was a question I had been longing to ask for a long
time.

—I don't know, she said. I guess because she found some pictures of me and this girl.

—What pictures?

—Some soft-porn stuff. My old girlfriend and I would fool around and one day we took these pictures of ourselves. We were just having fun. But they were beautiful shots so I saved them. I think I had some up on my wall at the old loft that you rescued me from.

That Kristine had visited Gilberte that long ago hurt me to a degree I wouldn't have thought possible, but I didn't wince.

—Where are they? My seeing them was the only thing that would assuage the pain this revelation caused me.

—I destroyed them, she said firmly, trying to get me to believe her.

—Why?

—Because they could get me in trouble. I didn't want to take a chance on having them surface again. Not that everybody doesn't have something like that in their closet, she said defensively.

I didn't know whether to believe her or not, but this wasn't the moment for a further cross-examination.

—Anyway, she said, it's going to look bad, my leaving her now when I've finally started making money. But I've got to. It's such a mess, she signed. And I know it's my fault. I should have listened to you. What can I do?

I didn't have an answer.

—I'll have to hustle, she confided. The bottom has dropped out of the photo market. Or at least the new art photo market.

—I thought it was going great guns.

—People are still buying, but mostly old stuff. Newer photographers aren't making any money.

—What will you do?

—Well. I'm going to have to hustle the film like crazy. I haven't given it much time because of the clothing deal. She thought for a moment. I've got some money left over from some grants I received. And when Suzanne gets my new applications for grants submitted, I should know whether I'll be getting more money. I should have money coming in from some furniture I designed. I should be all right for a while.

—You're not totally dependent upon Kristine? I wanted to weigh the possibility of a reconciliation. It seemed to me the best way to do this was to determine how Gilberte was going to make ends meet.

—Not totally. No. But.... it would be a little difficult if my foundation funds were cut. She considered this possibility for a moment. I wonder if Kris would cut my money off.

—You mean you get an allowance?

—I receive a grant from the foundation, she corrected me. If that stops, I'll be in big trouble. I'd never forgive her if she did that.

I surmised from this comment that the so-called grant probably made up the bulk of her income.

—But I wonder if she can do that. There's supposed to be a board of directors or something. I remember she was all pissed off about that. Wouldn't they have to vote on cutting off funds to someone? You would think so, wouldn't you?

—I would, I said. I then volunteered to find out from Roger exactly how the foundation was set up.

—Could you do that? She was elated.

—I'd like a heads-up. You know, so I can be prepared.

—Sure, I said. She was so thrilled about the service I offered to render her she didn't bother to ask why Roger would
make me privy to such information. I hadn't told her I was on
the board because I didn't want her to ask me to do something
for her I would have done on my own. And more important,
I didn't want her to think I was able to work miracles for her
when I didn't yet know how much power I would have. Nor
did I want her to hold me responsible for acting or failing to
act in her behalf.

◆

Our life together resumed. It was and wasn't the same. Which
is to say we acted the same toward each other but didn't feel
the same toward each other. It only took two nights before she
began sleeping in my bed. Physically this posed no problems:
my bed had as much space as it had previously had. Mentally
it took some adjustment: our relationship had become prob-
lematical. The first night she climbed in I was half-asleep and
we slept side by side, hardly touching, but sleeping hardly at
all to remain sensitive to each other's moves. On the second
night, when I thought if I remained vigilant like the previous night I would collapse at the store the following day, we
pounced on each other and ravished each other until dawn.
The next morning, I was as bright and chipper as if I had slept
twelve hours.

She was starved for sex. She couldn't get enough, or I
couldn't give enough—it was never clear. And for the next few
weeks we held a nonstop orgy. I fed my desire for her by studying her intensely, clandestinely, whenever I could. The more I
studied her, the more I noticed she had changed. She had put

on weight. When I first met her, and until she left me for Kristine, she had been thin and athletic-looking. In bed with her now for the first time since her return, I realized I was no longer looking at the body of a lithesome young woman, but at a woman with a generous bosom and voluptuous curving hips. In a word, seductive. This new woman daunted me at first but finished by intriguing me. When we first met, I had thought there was something smart and sassy and provocative about her: everything had been out in the open. But a transformation had taken place: somehow she had become mysterious. She had become beautiful. Her extra pounds of padding pleased me. I told her so. She said she had been eating too much. I said she had been eating too well. There was more, too. Her whole body spoke a different language now. Her step was less agile. She no longer pranced around, she glided. Her hips swayed invitingly, instead of jerking provocatively from side to side. I found her incredibly sexy. I could barely keep my hands off her. When we were in my room, naked, basking in the light of the TV, I was constantly touching her, caressing her, fondling her, making love to her.

Then, to my dismay, the excitement wore off, and sex wasn't enjoyable anymore. I don't know how it happened.

Visually she still stimulated me. Often simply watching her undress or comb her hair in the mirror would give me an erection. If she touched any part of my body, my member would spring up, ready for action. But, the consummation of our desire was no longer always satisfying. I think it was the same for her, too. Once our superficial somatic needs had been fulfilled, our sex life was no more than the recreational exercise it had been just prior to her moving out. Sating our physical needs without a corresponding emotional bond drained our passion of its intensity.

It didn't matter. We had other pressing matters to attend to. For example, where was Gilberte going to go when she left my loft, and what was she going to do for money? Also, she was under tremendous pressure from Kristine, who didn't cease to harass her. Her constant calling was enough to sap anyone's libido. Especially since they fought all the time. One of them was always hanging up on the other. The phone would ring again. They would talk again. Fight again. Hang up again. I told Gilberte not to answer the phone. I pointed out that with the answering machine she was able to screen all incoming calls and, theoretically, never have to talk to Kristine. But Gilberte was frightened of provoking her to some rash act. Like cutting off her money.

◆

—Well, I guess it's finished now, she said one night after hanging up.

—What do you mean, finished now?

—She's going back to her husband.

—She's been in your loft all this time? I asked. I had tried not to become too involved and had never inquired as to Kristine's whereabouts.

—Yeah. She said I could move back in if I wanted.

—Will you?

—I don't know. I don't know if it's a good idea. I don't think I want to live there anymore. Anyway, I think she's going to sell it.

—Vindictive, isn't she?

—Doesn't matter to me, Gilberte said.

—What do you plan to do?

—What do you mean?

—Do you want to stay? I couldn't believe I was asking her this.

—With you?

—Who else?

—I'd love to, she said, turning toward me. But I can't. It wouldn't work. I'd be disappointing you all the time. And you'd end up hating me.

This was an astute observation. I wasn't prepared to respond to it adequately.

—I don't think I could ever hate you, was my fatuous response.

—No. And I probably couldn't hate you either. But we'd torture each other. And I'm not the type who would feel guilty enough to change, you know. I can't be different from what I am. And neither can you.

I lit a cigarette out of embarrassment.

—I like you so much. I may be in love with you. You've done so much for me. More, really, than anyone else, she said.

This sudden admission took me by surprise. I was touched.

—You've made me see a lot of things. Helped me define a lot of things I might not have been able to do alone. In a way, it was you who made me realize I could do what I wanted to do in New York. I might not have worked as hard if it wasn't for you. I may not have accomplished what you wanted me to, but I have done a lot, she said.

I understood now. I was being praised for having done a fine job, but my services were no longer required. I was being dismissed. This was the end. She would be moving out soon.

I finished my cigarette in silence. When I put it out, Gilberte shut off the television and we made love. Very satisfactorily.

♦

—Fifty-ninth and Fifth, I said to the driver, closing the door behind me. Without acknowledging me, he pushed the button on his meter. When the light changed, we lurched ahead. I leaned forward to read the name on his license: E. Gonzales. Then I leaned back. Lit a cigarette. Relaxed. He began tapping on the translucent, bulletproof partition that separated us. In broken English, he informed me there was no smoking allowed in his cab. There was a little sign, which I had not seen upon entering, that said exactly that. I told him I would either smoke or exit. Since he kept pointing at the sign and shaking his head, I told him to stop. He did and I hopped out. I heard him screaming at me in Spanish as I walked toward the cab directly behind us. I held up my cigarette so the driver could see it. He held his up for me to see. The meter was already running when I got inside.

—Fifty-ninth and Fifth, I said.

—Wouldn't let you smoke? asked H. Disimone.

—Nope.

—Those guys, idiots.

He turned around and made a broad, sweeping gesture with his hairy hand. Then he shook his head. He was just ready to say something else, when I cut him off with:

—You can go up Madison and let me off at Fifty-ninth. I then turned away immediately and stared out the window. I didn't want to become embroiled in a cab conversation. I had things to think about.

Roger had called me the previous day. He wanted to meet with me. I hadn't asked him what he wanted to talk about, because I had been busy, but I assumed it must have something to do with the foundation. Perhaps we were going to have the first board meeting. If that was indeed the case, I would be able to obtain the information I had told Gilberte I had access to. I had decided I would do everything behind the scenes. And under no circumstances would I let Gilberte know I was on the board. If I managed to help her, I didn't want her to feel she owed me anything.

The most attractive aspect of serving on the board was being able to thwart Kristine's nefarious plans. Yet, I had to admit I wasn't sure they were nefarious. In the weeks since Gilberte had moved back to my loft, Kristine had shown herself to be quite levelheaded. She had stopped calling so often, at least while I was home, and according to Gilberte she never threatened, never let drop the slightest hint she might cut off her funds. She seemed, in fact, genuinely concerned for Gilberte's welfare, eager to do whatever was necessary to minimize the trauma their separation was causing. Her mature behavior was having an effect on Gilberte, too. Kristine managed to convince her they should meet and try to talk things out. Gilberte agreed to see her. They met for lunch. And as they hadn't enough time to talk through everything during their meal, they arranged to meet again. After this second meeting, Gilberte no longer saw any reason why she and Kristine couldn't remain friends. She stopped being the recluse she had become since arriving at my loft and began going out again. She was aware that I frowned upon what she was doing, because she swore every evening she spent with Kristine had actually been arranged months before and there was no way she could possibly cancel at this late date. So once again she began attending openings and galas, dinners and benefits at BAM, The Kitchen, and Asia House. I was waiting for the day when she would announce she was moving back to White Street.

—She wants a reconciliation, doesn't she? I had confronted her.

She didn't answer.

—You know, by seeing her, you're only encouraging her to think it might be possible.

—We had a long talk.

—And...?

—I said I didn't know what I wanted.

—What? I simply couldn't believe it.

—Well, what did you want me to say? I didn't know what to say. Anyway, what difference does it make?

Gilberte could more easily justify her behavior to herself than to me, because in her calculus there were unknown variables of self-interest I could never factor into my evaluation of the situation. Nevertheless, it was plain they could not be together again that I was revolted at the mere suggestion of it.

—You don't have any feelings left for her, I had said.

—That's not true. I do. She's a friend.

—You don't really care for her, I pontificated. You're only afraid she'll undo everything she's done for you.

—No. But she has done a lot for me.

—You would only go back to her to protect your interests. It's too disgusting.

She began to cry.

—And who else is going to watch out for my interests? I just can't say go to hell, she screamed.

I was at a loss.

—You can't go back to her, I said, but with less vigor.

She began wiping her eyes.

—I'm not going to.

—You promise?

—Yes.

—And you'll make all your decisions independently of her?

—I can't. Don't you understand? Not everybody can be like you and do just what they fucking well want to all the time. I can't. I still need her. And if I just have to use her, I have to. And if that disgusts you ... that's the way it is. Shit!

She had left me and walked out.

—How do you wanna go? the cabdriver asked me.

—Go up Madison. If it gets too bad, do whatever you think is best.

—OK, boss, Disimone said.

I had failed to make her relinquish Kristine. I had pushed her as far as I could. There was nothing more I could do. All I wanted was for Gilberte go out in the world on her own. Make it on her own. Her rupture with Kristine was her second chance. It had seemed like the perfect opportunity for me to say what I wanted to say for a long time. At least now I saw that my advice wouldn't have made any difference. Not then, not now.

I realized it must be hell for her at my place. Hell to be away from the home she had made. She was probably suffering withdrawal. More than likely what had fueled our debauches during the previous weeks was the pent-up, frustrated energy resulting from her life outside the charmed circle. No place chic to go, nobody powerful to talk to, nothing to do but fuck. As I thought back on it now, I saw it was partly her melancholy vulnerability that had made her seductive. And though it had seemed to me we managed to extinguish the fires burning within us, it was perhaps only mine that had died, while hers were still consuming her, eating away at her until she couldn't take it anymore and had agreed to meet with Kristine.

I watched as people pushed and plied their way along the crowded sidewalks. We had just crossed Twenty-third Street. I couldn't figure out why there were so many people. Then I read on a clock that it was twelve-thirty and understood we were in a business district and all these people were on their lunch break. Most of them appeared harassed as they hurried along. They had only so much time and could accomplish only so much. It was a race against the clock. Any minute they would have to report back to their offices. The only place people seemed prepared to wait was in a line to buy Lotto tickets. The line at one vendor was nearly half a block long. Somehow, I was sure the length of the line could be used as a measure of misery, an index of discontent. All those people were longing to escape their condition, to acquire something more for themselves. They knew no matter how hard they worked, the only way their condition in life was going to change was if they got lucky. I wished I could change my condition, my life. I had moved to New York from the country's heartland—the Midwest—because I believed New York was the heart of the country: that it set the beat, that it pumped out the vital forces necessary to keep the rest of the country alive and growing. But New York had meant more than that to me then. I had seen it as the transcendental exemplar of what a city, and city life, should be like. Vibrant. Magical. Elegant. Civilized. I supposed at one time it had been all those things. And in some ways it still was. But it had been robbed of its charm. Attempts at civic pride aside, it was, like any major third-world metropolis, a raucous, rowdy, dangerous, dirty place to live. In fact, it often seemed like you were in a foreign city, because of the vast numbers of people who didn't speak or understand English. Half of those who could utter a word or two comprehended only the rudiments. Hardly enough to work behind a cash register, or a steering wheel, say, or to check a model number in a store, or to dish out hamburgers or bagels. It made day-to-day life unpleasant. You felt you couldn't make yourself understood. It left you feeling frustrated, isolated, angry.

There were just too damn many people in New York. The compression compromised people's dignity.

—I think go down to Park or Third and cut over later, Disimone suggested.

Traffic had stopped moving. Homs blared all around us.

—No, I instructed. Just keep going.

—This is no good. He slapped the steering wheel and glared at me in the mirror, as if it were my fault.

I shrugged my shoulders.

Everyone who came to New York was after something. Usually money. There was too much desire directed toward this one object. This craving for wealth drove people to extremes. People came in droves because they could pursue their objective twenty-four hours a day. It was common knowledge. A Korean cabdriver I had talked to (although that was putting it strongly, because he could hardly mumble English) had confirmed this sentiment for me just the other day. He had come to New York because it was the only place where he could drive a cab eighteen hours a day, seven days a week, which he did. He bought his independence from the cab company in the form of a medallion. Now he was working practically around-the-clock, seven days a week, to pay off the mortgage on the medallion, as well as to raise the money for a down payment on a vegetable stand. *Like money much wife*, he had told me. That was the extent of his desire. Money. The nucleus of his family cell. The reason why your senses were continually tormented as people went their way doing what they had to do. The reason why the city was ugly, why everyone was stressed, why encounters were often brusque, discourteous, abusive, uncaring. Too many people seeking to realize their dreams here had created a nightmare.

Of course, there were counterexamples to everything. I could be challenged at every point. But that was how I was beginning to see things. Nevertheless, I no longer had a reason to stay here. The career I had hoped for never materialized. The intellectual life I wanted to participate in had eluded me. I was beyond the age where anything I saw at a gallery or a museum would change me the way I had wanted to be changed as a youth. Vice was the only thing of any continuing interest left to me, and that would kill me if I gave in to it. If I left, I wouldn't have the same cultural opportunities, but who needed them? If I saw less of my friends it would be no great loss. We rarely saw each other as it was. More often we spoke on the phone. And wherever I went, there would be phones. My loft? Well, I would rent it. All the reasons I had traditionally used to justify my stay in New York ceased to matter. Even the opportunity to serve on the board of directors of Roger's foundation didn't appeal to me. It was ridiculous. I couldn't care less. In fact, it was a trap. If I succumbed, I might find myself still bogged down in this quagmire ten years from now. And the last place I wanted to be ten years from now was in New York. I didn't want to admit it, but my affair with Gilberte had infused me with a healthy disgust for everything. My feelings for her had changed. I still liked her. I was attracted to her, in some ways more than ever, but this was probably because of her new look and, more importantly, because my most profound feelings for her were no longer affected by what she did.

We couldn't cross Forty-Second Street. The light seemed to be always red. During the few seconds it remained green, we couldn't move because of the people blocking our advance. When the light was against us, they came surging off the sidewalks in waves, and when the light was against them they continued to flow into the street. My driver fired off a few blasts of his horn and then others joined in: a regular fusillade ensued. Finally, we began inching forward.

By the time we reached Fifty-seventh Street I was exhausted. The rocking and weaving and honking and jerking and starting and stopping had worn me out. As we seemed unable to cross, I told the driver I was going to walk.

In the lobby I met with the usual security measures, executed with élan and officiousness by a burly-looking guard. You could see the swagger and swell of his chest as he called upstairs.

Coming out of the elevator, I was met by more security people. After being checked out, I was led down the hall by Ms. Bundle, who commented upon the length of time that had passed since my last visit. She turned me over to Ms. Thorten, who treated me to her usual dour welcome.

I was surprised I was the only one in the waiting room. I asked Ms. Thorten if the others had already arrived.

—What others? was her curt response.

I didn't elaborate, and she rebuked me with a disdainful look. After she had left, I strolled around. The ventilation system was hissing noisily, as if the air were leaking out of the building. Outside, from this height, the city looked fixed, immobile, innocuous.

—Would you follow me? Ms. Thorten wanted to know.

We walked down the hall in silence. As usual, Roger's door was closed. Ms. Thorten knocked and then opened it, indicating I should enter. Roger was on the phone. He signaled I should come in and have a seat. He concluded his conversation, came around the desk and shook my hand and slapped me on the shoulder. He sat down in the chair next to mine.

—You look good, he exclaimed.

—You're doing all right yourself, I said.

—I'm trying.

—Where is everybody? I asked him.

—Everybody who? He seemed to be at as great a loss as Ms. Thorten.

—You mean this isn't a board meeting?

—Ah, no. He chuckled to himself. Not at all. That's been put on hold.

— Oh. I covered my disappointment.

—What's up, then?

—Well, I don't know how to put this without making it sound more serious than it is.

—Say it.

—I want to sell the store.

—The store? I didn't quite understand.

—Yes, the bookstore where you work. Do you want to buy it?

—The bookstore? I was incredulous.

—Yes. I want to sell it, he repeated. Do you have any money? Or maybe the first question should be, do you want to buy it?

—How much?

He named the price. It was incredibly low.

—I can make you a loan if you'd like, he said.

If I hadn't been aware the store made a profit, I would have thought he was trying to unload an albatross.

—But why?

—I'm tired of it.

It was incredible. It was exactly what I had been thinking. Sell everything (in a manner of speaking). Get out.

—Both boutiques, he emphasized.

—Any reason?

—Retail's not a place I want to be. Not that you aren't doing a wonderful job. He reached over and grabbed my arm.

—But I just don't want to be involved in it anymore. There's no money in it. My accountant says it's bad for my taxes. What do you think?

—It sounds good, I said.

—It is good. Just say the word, and I'll have the papers ready for you to sign early next week. How much cash can you put up front?

I had some money in stocks and bonds that I was saving for emergencies. As far as I could tell this didn't count as one. I named the paltry sum I had in my savings account.

—Fine, Roger said, rising and going behind his desk, where he noted down what I supposed was the figure I had named. Now there's only one more thing.

This was it, the catch I had been waiting for.

—What?

—I don't want you to mention this to anyone until it's a done deal. Understand?

It was too simple.

—Yes, I said, just to see if this was all there was to it.

—Not to your roommate or Kristine or anyone.

—Sounds easy enough.

—It is. All right. That's all the time I can give you today. Let's say we get together again next Thursday and sign all the necessary papers. How does that sound?

—Great, I said.

He got up and came around to shake my hand. He put his arm around my shoulder as we walked to the door.

—Call me Wednesday afternoon to confirm the appointment Thursday, OK?

—All right, I said. What about the board meeting for the foundation?

—There isn't going to be one. It's been, shall we say, disbanded. If I have a minute next week, maybe we'll have lunch and I'll tell you all about it, although there isn't a lot to tell.

—All right. I stuck out my hand, and we shook.

On the way home in the cab, I realized I had just concluded a deal that would keep me in New York. But the deal was such that I would have had to be a fool to turn it down. My life finally seemed to be set. I was going to be a shopkeeper forever.

◆

I was in the Village before I began to grasp the ramifications of what I had done. I had the cab stop at the first phone booth I spotted and called Roger. He had rushed to another meeting, off site, and could not be reached, I was informed by Elly the Argus.

—Reach him, was my impertinent command. When I had him on the line, I made him repeat the terms of the agreement we had just made. He let me know it was difficult for him to talk. I reiterated everything we had said, rephrasing the points I had had some doubts about in the cab, and he answered either yes or no. He was patient. None of his answers diverged from what I had understood in his office.

—Are you drunk? he whispered.

—Not yet. We agreed to discuss the matter further in the morning. I paid the cabdriver and wandered off into the depths of the West Village.

◆

By the time I arrived home, I was incoherent and barely able to swallow the requisite number of glasses of water (one eight-ounce glass for each drink) necessary to protect me from a vicious hangover. Gilberte, curious about this mid-week saturnalia, put me to bed, without getting from me the reason for my debauch.

The next morning my head was throbbing. I managed to make it to the bathroom, where I relieved myself. Every time my body came into contact with something, there was an explosion in my head. I needed more water. And aspirin. I took four and washed them down with two big glasses of water. It was eight-thirty. Gilberte had already departed. I found a note on the kitchen table, saying Roger had called and that I should call him back. Told him you're home OK, the note said. I needed more sleep. I returned to my bed. I would get up at ten and dash out to the store.

When I awoke again, Gilberte was beside me. As she appeared to be up, I asked:

—What time is it?

—Nearly twelve.

—Shit, I said, flinging off the covers.

Gilberte restrained me with her arm.

—Night, not morning, she said.

—Shit.

—You were really out of it. Roger called again.

—Oh.

—You can call him tomorrow. What's up? She was curious.

—Nothing is up.

—Oh, she said, not satisfied. Well, you were in bad shape. She moved close to me and began to rub my chest.

—I know, I said. I got up and went to the bathroom, relieved myself and drank some more water. This had been my sole occupation for the last twenty-four hours. I did feel much better, but I was woozy and my stomach felt like a sandstorm were blowing through it. What I needed was an antacid. Or maybe something to eat.

—I'm going to make something to eat, I said to Gilberte, opting for food rather than medication.

—Do you want me to make it? she asked, sitting up.

—No, that's OK. Thanks. Go to sleep. I heard the television click on as I stepped into the living room.

I realized I should have put on my robe, for it was much cooler in the kitchen than in the bedroom, and a fairly chill current of air was sweeping along the floor. But instead of returning to the bedroom to fetch my robe, I went to the closet and took out my raincoat and put it on. It was just like being under the blankets.

As I hadn't been out shopping, there was nothing much to eat. Eggs or tuna fish. I chose eggs because they would be hot. I decided to scramble them the French way, by breaking them in a double boiler full of melted butter and stirring them until they stiffened up. I nearly talked myself into having a Bloody Mary while waiting for my eggs to stiffen to just the right degree but, prudently, decided against it.

My revel had cost me a full day of work. I hadn't done such a thing before. It was disgraceful. I wondered if Roy—or, though it was highly unlikely, Gilberte—had opened up for business. I almost ran back to the bedroom to ask her what had happened, until I noticed the bedroom was dark and silent.

I wasn't in any condition to wash dishes. I ate my eggs directly from the pot. While eating, I strolled through the loft.

As I circled past the front windows I saw the twin towers looming in the distance, creating immense luminous lines of light in the sky. They gave the impression of efficiency, order, productivity, power. They were mesmerizing. Out of the back window, too, there were lights as far as I could see. I was struck by just how many there were at this hour on a weekday. But in the city, there were any number of insomniacs: swing-shift workers, artists who didn't have to wake up in the morning, lovers whose passions had to be sated, students studying, television addicts. I wouldn't see this sort of thing in the country. If that was, indeed, where I was going—despite my just having agreed to buy the bookstore. People in the country led regular lives, kept regular hours. If I moved to the country, I would have to do so too. Oh, I might stay up late one night to read, or to watch a film, or to perversely drink myself into oblivion. But

I wouldn't expect to find thousands of others like me. In fact, I would have to be more like them: a conscientious bourgeois. Not that I wasn't conscientious now, but once I became a shop-keeper I would have additional responsibilities.

Moving out of New York was too difficult to think about at this hour, given my condition. In fact, I was surprised to find myself thinking about it again. My musings in the cab on the way to see Roger must have been much more deeply rooted than I had suspected. I began to wonder if buying the store was such a good idea after all. To own and operate a business was not at all the same thing as running someone else's business. Then again, it was the same thing. The work wouldn't change. No, it wasn't that. It was that finally I was going to be respon-sible for something. Something of my own.

I finished my eggs, and on the return trip past the kitchen I placed the saucepan in the sink and filled it with water. Walk-ing by the kitchen table, I took a cigarette from the box and lit it.

En route again, I decided I was experiencing a classic case of reversal of fortune. Except my fortunes hadn't been at their nadir, or ebbing. It was my spirits that had sunk to new lows. Peculiarly, the deal Roger and I had struck hadn't done much to lift them. The immediate appeal of the deal was that it would provide me with sure work and a steady income. As long as I didn't fuck it up, the store's profits would be mine. With prac-tically no investment, and absolutely no risk. I would have been a fool to turn Roger down. I could semi-retire. Live in style. If I hired a manager, I could let him supervise the daily operations at the store. This idea had such an immediate ap-peal I was sure it was the right thing to do. I would move out of the city. I would hire a manager to oversee the day-to-day operations. I would rent my loft and buy a piece of property up by Tarrytown, or in Croton-on-Hudson. I could already see myself riding the rails into midtown. Sitting on a late-morning, half-empty train, reading the *Times* and the *Wall Street Journal*, exiting at Grand Central Terminal and taking a cab down to the store. How civilized. Once there, I would perform a cursory audit, check the displays, the reorder list, perhaps pick up a few things to read, visit some galleries, have lunch, and slip back to my villa before the rush- hour madness seized the city. I would become a country gentleman.

Taking a deep drag off my cigarette, I realized I had just come through a crisis. I had resolved a nagging problem. Of course, I had compromised. By holding on to the store, I was still tied to the city. I wasn't escaping. But maybe this was all I could do. Put distance between myself and the city but never escape from it totally. For the moment I didn't care. In the country I was sure to have quiet. It would be clean, restful, relaxing. In the dappled light of leaf-strewn paths I would find respite, rejuvenation. I might once again pursue my artistic ambitions. After all, why not? Earning my living would no longer be a problem. The issue of my sexuality was as settled as it ever could be settled. What would prevent me from sitting down and beginning, or recommencing, to write the books I had always wanted to write?

I suspected the answer to this question was that I was still myself. I racked my brain, trying to come up with something that would incline me to believe I had somehow become a different person. I came up with nothing. I hadn't changed. Sure, this was a major turning point in my life, an event that should have made me stop and think about who I was and where I was going (although I now knew the answer to the latter question). But when I thought of what I had just been through, and of how tired I was, I forgave myself. Tomorrow, I told myself, I would sit down and think about it. Right now, I decided, it was time to go to bed.

Gilberte was snoring lightly when I returned to her. Her right arm was flung over my pillow.

◆

I was trying to decide whether to rename the store or to fly a banner announcing it was under new management. Neither was necessary. But the publicity might be beneficial. How, exactly, it would benefit me I wasn't sure. Summer was the slow season, and hanging an under-new-management banner wasn't going to rustle up much business. Nor was changing the name. Of the two, however, hanging a banner would clearly be the most cost-effective, because I wouldn't have to order new stationery, checks, bags, and bookmarks. Actually, I wasn't sure I wanted to do one or the other. It had been Roger's idea. I thought I might get one estimate as to how much a banner would cost, so I could say I had investigated the idea if ever he asked. I was thumbing through the yellow pages, looking for companies that printed such things, when Kristine charged in.

—You've gone too far, she announced without bidding me hello. I thought she was going to launch into a tirade about how the store had been sold behind her back, but not at all.

—What are you talking about? I decided I was going to play stupid.

—You know, she said, raising her voice to such a pitch that some of the customers turned around. You told her not to come back to me. She glared at me. So it was Gilberte she was upset about. This put a whole different light on her anger.

—Are you out of your mind? I whispered.

She stared at me fiercely. I thought for a moment she was going to slap me.

—It's your fault. You ... you faggot, she screeched. Her voice was quivering and uncertain, but raised so that the customers who hadn't heard her the first time heard it now and turned toward us.

—I'm afraid I can neither affirm nor deny that statement, I said, smiling at her.

—But why should you care what she does? What business is it of yours? You're jealous, you bastard.

I ignored her name calling

—I'm not jealous. Do you think we could discuss this some other time? I suggested.

—No, I'm going to discuss it now. I warned you before. This is the last time. She lowered her voice. You let her make up her own mind, do you hear? You let her, or.... One way or another, we'll see. With this she stormed out of the store.

◆

The moment of truth came two weeks later just after Gilberte moved out of my loft into one of her own, one I had helped her find and secure (I had made her a small loan). Kristine arrived in a fury.

—I'm disappointed in you, Stephen, she said.

—Disappointed about what? I asked disingenuously.

—I told you I wasn't going to stand for this.

—Kristine, I have a business to run. I don't have time for this.

—You're going to have plenty of time.

—What do you mean?

—I'm going to sell the store. A malignant smile came to her lips. It took all my self-control to keep from laughing. I realized Roger hadn't told her.

—What are you smiling at?

I ignored her question.

—How are you going to do that? I asked.

—Don't be stupid. I'm going to find a buyer.

This was the moment.

—And if I don't want to sell?

—What do you mean?

—What if I don't feel like selling to your buyer?

—You've got no choice. It's not your store. I make the decisions. She said this with total conviction. I was in seventh heaven.

—You don't make any decisions here.

I couldn't restrain myself from giggling just a little.

—What? She wanted to know.

—Ask your husband. I had promised Roger I wouldn't tell her. It would have given me pleasure to do so, but I didn't want to be burdened with the memory of her expression when she learned what had taken place behind her back. Moreover, it seemed crueler to let her linger in ignorance as long as possible.

She collected herself.

—Don't think I believe there's anything that could stop me from doing what I intend to do. Roger may like you, but I'll get my way.

I smiled.

—Ask him, I said.

She was ready to go, but hesitated.

—Go talk to Roger. He'll tell you.

—I'll do just that, she spat out.

—Speak to Roger. Get the whole story.

—I will, she promised.

Then she stormed out.

We never spoke again. And except for an occasional rare social event where we found each other in the same room, I didn't see her again.

♦

My life changed radically after this. I broke off contact with almost everyone. Roger I saw now and again for lunch. But he withdrew into his own world and didn't have time for me. Now I was no more than a necessary nuisance, but as with any property in which he had invested money, he felt obliged to follow the store's progress to see how it fared. Our brief conversations never strayed far from my business or his business. Thus, I never discovered what had occurred between him and Kristine when she confronted him with her demand he sell the store. I did know, however, that he and Kristine were still together, because I saw their pictures in the magazines. Nor did he ever go into more detail about what had become of the foundation. My guess was that it had been merely a front for Kristine to funnel money into Gilberte's bank account and Roger had wanted to control it. And when Kristine and Gilberte broke up, the foundation lost its raison d'etre. I would have liked to ask, but the aura that surrounded our meetings just wasn't propitious to such probing. I was forced to conclude that when Roger had relieved himself of the store, he had, as far as possible, also relieved himself of me. He was always courteous, cordial, and correct, but the sense of camaraderie we had once had was gone.

♦

Gilberte dropped out of sight altogether. I didn't see or hear from her for months. She hadn't had a phone when she moved into her new place, and if she had gotten one she hadn't bothered to call to give me her number. I had gone by her building several times and rung her bell, but nobody answered. For a while I worried that Kristine had carried out her threat to get even with her and had cut off all her funds, and that maybe she wasn't living there anymore (her name wasn't on her mailbox). This had prompted me to ask one of her neighbors whether she was still living in the building. She was, but apparently she didn't spend much time there.

I supposed one of the reasons she might be avoiding me, if indeed she was, was because she owed me money and didn't have it. I thought about dropping her a note, but I decided I would let her live her life in peace and would wait until she was ready to contact me.

♦

I was in the final stage of moving to Croton-on-Hudson. I had come to the store to help resolve a problem, and was preparing to be on my way when Gilberte walked in. She had a man in tow.

—Hi! She greeted me enthusiastically. Then she introduced her friend. This is Richard.

We shook hands.

—I've got something for you, Gilberte announced. Richard took this as his cue to wander off to browse.

—Here, Gilberte said, pulling an envelope from her bag and handing it to me. It was full of money.

—It's all there, she said proudly. Every cent of what I borrowed.

I put it in my pocket.

—Aren't you going to count it?

—This isn't a drug deal, I pointed out. She laughed. It was an open, expansive, genuine laugh.

—It's been so long, she said, taking out a cigarette.

—It has, I concurred. She had changed.

She had lost a lot of weight and was as thin as she had been when we first met. She was aggressive, cocky, on edge, just as she had been then.

—We're getting married, she said, blowing out a cloud of smoke.

—Married?

—Why not? She was insulted.

—I don't know.

—We get along well together, she said.

—And Kristine?

—All that's finished.

—Everything?

—Everything. I work exclusively with Richard. He's from California, too.

I took a quick look. Tall, rangy, with a ruddy complexion, he could have hailed from anywhere.

—Are you happy? I asked her.

—Of course! And you?

—I'm not unhappy, I said, using the double negative to indicate a nuance I couldn't express in other words.

—You're always so complicated, she complained.

—Where will you live?

—We're moving to L. A.

—I thought you didn't want to live in California.

—That was before.

—I see. What ever happened to the screenplay? I asked.

—Didn't I tell you? I found some producers. There's no money yet. But once I close the deal we should both make something from it.

—Will you direct it?

—No. And it's all your fault. She laughed. They think it's too big for me. I'm working on another one. Something smaller. Richard is writing it with me. And he's also going to help produce it. We should finish it in the next couple of months.

At this point, her husband-to-be came up to her and put his arm around her in a proprietary way. From the manner in which she snuggled into his embrace and looked up at him, I could see she was in love. I had never known the tenderness that surely accompanied a look like that. I was jealous.

After some polite small talk, they were on their way. The last thing Gilberte said to me was that she would invite me to the wedding.

Oddly enough, she did send me an invitation. I didn't go. I sent a wedding gift. A photograph by André Kertész she had liked. I had bought it at a benefit auction for The Kitchen or Franklin Furnace or some such place years before. Gilberte sent me a thank-you note. They had started shooting her new film, she informed me. She was sure to be in New York to screen it when it was done. At which time we were certain to see each other again.

For a long time after that I waited for word of her. I checked the papers and journals and reviews for news of her. All I ever found was an unenthusiastic review of some photographs she was showing in an L.A. gallery. There was nothing in the film journals, or daily papers about her film. I checked week after week. Eventually I stopped thinking about her. One day our paths would cross again.

◆

I had nothing to complain about. I had good tenants in the loft. The store was profitable. I had a dedicated, trustworthy manager. My house was everything I had wanted. Living out of town agreed with me. I had lots of land. After browsing through some books on English country houses and landscaping, I decided I was going to thoroughly landscape my five acres. Thus I began reading everything I could get my hands on about horticulture and began studying garden design. I traveled to England to visit country houses and decided to expand my own. I had a pool put in, a hill created. I planted hedges. Cut paths. Pruned and planted trees. For the next few years I devoted myself entirely to planning and planting, potting and digging, raking and hoeing. To great effect, I might add.

When winter came that first year, I thought I might settle in at my desk and put pen to paper. Out of boredom if nothing else. But I didn't. Not then, nor the year after. I rescued a dog from the local shelter instead. We got along great. Of course, my life was still incomplete—it was that incompleteness I was trying to express when I said to Gilberte that I was not unhappy—but it was bearable. From time to time I experienced a dull ache, a yearning for companionship, but I was happier than I had ever been.